THE
ROBERT
SILVERBERG
SCIENCE
FICTION
MEGAPACK®

THE ROBERT SILVERBERG SCIENCE FICTION MEGAPACK®

WILDSIDE PRESS

The Robert Silverberg MEGAPACK® is copyright © 2016 by Agberg, Ltd. All rights reserved.

The MEGAPACK® ebook series name is a trademark of Wildside Press, LLC. All rights reserved.

Copyright © 1956, 1957, 1958, 1961, 1984, 1985, 1986, 2016 by Agberg, Ltd. First published in *The Original Science Fiction, Future Science Fiction, Amazing Stories, Saturn, Science Fiction Adventures, Galaxy, Astounding Science Fiction,* and *New Worlds.*

CONTENTS

INTRODUCTION 7
ALAREE 9
BIRDS OF A FEATHER 21
BLAZE OF GLORY 39
DELIVERY GUARANTEED 51
THE DESSICATOR 64
THE HAPPY UNFORTUNATE 70
THE HUNTED HEROES 87
THE IRON STAR 99
THE ISOLATIONISTS 119
THE LONELY ONE 128
THE MAN WHO CAME BACK 141
NEUTRAL PLANET 153
OZYMANDIAS 167
THE PAIN PEDDLERS 182
THE PLEASURE OF THEIR COMPANY 191
POINT OF FOCUS 206
POSTMARK GANYMEDE 220
PRIME COMMANDMENT 228
THE SONGS OF SUMMER 237
SPACEROGUE 251
THERE WAS AN OLD WOMAN 285

THE WOMAN YOU WANTED. 296
VALLEY BEYOND TIME 309
WE KNOW WHO WE ARE. 345

INTRODUCTION

These are stories from the dawn of my career—the earliest of them was written about sixty years ago—and they are as surprised as I am still to be alive here in the second decade of the 21st century.

I began reading science fiction when I was a boy—H.G. Wells, Jules Verne, and then such magazines as *Amazing Stories* and *Astounding Science Fiction*—and I started writing it almost at once, sending my first stories off to the magazines of the day when I was 13. The editors sent them back, of course—first with printed rejection slips, then with encouraging letters—and, by 1954, when I was in my late teens and my junior year at college, with checks. Very quickly I found myself launched as a professional writer while still an undergraduate, making three sales in 1954, more than two dozen in 1955, and more in 1956 than I want to take the time now to count. By then it was clear to me that I was going to be able to make my living by writing, and when I got my B.A. degree from Columbia in June, 1956, I set up shop immediately as a full-time writer, and remained one for the next six decades, until, in my seventies, I began to slide off into retirement.

The oldest story in this book is "The Desiccator," which I wrote some time in 1954 and sold, a year or so later, to the very capable editor Robert W. Lowndes, whose misfortune it was to love science fiction dearly but to be given a rock-bottom editorial budget by his penurious publisher. It was just a little one-punch joke of a story, but Lowndes needed it to fill a hole in the May, 1956 issue of his magazine, *The Original Science Fiction Stories*, and paid me $24 for it. That doesn't sound like very much, and in fact it wasn't, but the 1956 dollar had at least ten times the purchasing power of today's money, so my $24 fee (minus $2.40 for my agent) was enough to buy dinner for two at almost any pretty good Manhattan restaurant.

Bob Lowndes and I quickly became friends—he gave me my first cat, in December, 1956—and he bought a great many stories from me for *The Original Science Fiction Stories* (which we all referred to simply as "The Original") and its companion, *Future Science Fiction*. A number of them are reprinted here: "The Lonely One," "The Songs of Summer," "Neutral Planet," "Prime Commandment," "Delivery Guaranteed," "The

Isolationists," and "The Woman You Wanted." Because I was so prolific, some of these appeared under pseudonyms: "The Isolationist" as by "George Osborne" and several of the others as by "Calvin M. Knox."

There were plenty of other science fiction magazines in those days, and I wrote for them all. Larry Shaw edited two, the fairly sophisticated *Infinity Science Fiction* and a companion dedicated to fast-paced action stories, appropriately called *Science Fiction Adventures*. I had a story in nearly every issue of *Infinity* and wrote *Science Fiction Adventures* almost single-handed, with one or two long stories in each issue and sometimes more. (Four of them are here, "Spacerogue," "There Was an Old Woman," "Ozymandias," and "Valley Beyond Time.") About the same time I became a staff writer for Howard Browne's *Amazing Stories* and *Fantastic*, who also wanted old-fashioned slam-bang pulp adventure fiction, and I worked hard at supplying it, turning in two or three stories a month for him. That long list is represented in this collection by "Postmark Ganymede," "The Happy Unfortunate," and "The Hunted Heroes." (The titles of the last two were invented by editor Browne; I don't remember what my original ones were.) At the same time I was writing for the two top magazines of the era, John W. Campbell's *Astounding* and Horace Gold's *Galaxy*. Those two magazines paid much more per word than the lesser titles of the field, but their editors were very demanding indeed, and it was always a red-letter day when I sold something to them. "Birds of a Feather" went to *Galaxy*, and "Point of Focus" to Campbell. Both were published in 1958, which by then was my fourth year as a very active professional writer.

It was a heady time. I loved writing all those stories, some of them at breakneck speed. (Occasionally I did a story in the morning, knocked off for lunch, and did another in the afternoon.) Eventually most of the magazines that were my regular markets went out of business, and I gave up short-story writing in favor of doing books, though I never completely abandoned the shorter form even when novels were my primary source of income. The stories collected here, though, represent the furious productivity of my first years as a writer, showing not only the flaws but also the fierce energy with which all those stories came tumbling from my red-hot typewriter.

—Robert Silverberg
February, 2016

ALAREE

Originally published in *Saturn Science Fiction*, March 1958.

When our ship left its carefully planned trajectory and started to wobble through space in dizzy circles, I knew we shouldn't have passed up that opportunity for an overhauling on Spica IV. My men and I were anxious to get back to Earth, and a hasty check had assured us that the Aaron Burr was in tiptop shape, so we had turned down the offer of an overhaul, which would have meant a month's delay, and set out straight for home.

As so often happens, what seemed like the most direct route home turned out to be the longest. We had spent far too much time on this survey trip already, and we were rejoicing in the prospect of an immediate return to Earth when the ship started turning cartwheels.

Willendorf, computerman first class, came to me looking sheepish, a few minutes after I'd noticed we were off course.

"What is it, Gus?" I asked.

"The feed network's oscillating, sir," he said, tugging at his unruly reddish-brown beard. "It won't stop, sir."

"Is Ketteridge working on it?"

"I've just called him," Willendorf said. His stolid face reflected acute embarrassment. Willendorf always took it personally whenever one of the cybers went haywire, as if it were his own fault. "You know what this means, don't you, sir?"

I grinned. "Take a look at this, Willendorf," I said, shoving the trajectory graphs towards him. I sketched out with my stylus the confused circles we had been traveling in all morning. "That's what your feed network's doing to us," I said, "and we'll keep on doing it until we get it fixed."

"What are you going to do, sir?"

I sensed his impatience with me. Willendorf was a good man, but his psych charts indicated a latent desire for officerhood. Deep down inside, he was sure he was at least as competent as I was to run this ship and probably a good deal more so.

"Send me Upper Navigating Technician Haley," I snapped. "We're going to have to find a planet in the neighborhood and put down for repairs."

It turned out there was an insignificant solar system in the vicinity, consisting of a small but hot white star and a single unexplored planet, Terra-size, a few hundred million miles out. After Haley and I had decided that that was the nearest port of refuge, I called a general meeting...

Quickly and positively I outlined our situation and explained what would have to be done. I sensed the immediate disappointment, but, gratifyingly, the reaction was followed by a general feeling of resigned pitching in. If we all worked, we'd get back to Earth, sooner or later. If we didn't, we'd spend the next century flip-flopping aimlessly in space.

After the meeting we set about the business of recovering control of the ship and putting it down for repairs. The feed network, luckily, gave up the ghost about ninety minutes later; it meant we had to stoke the fuel by hand, but at least it stopped that accursed oscillating.

We got the ship going, and Haley, navigating by feel in a way I never would have dreamed possible, brought us into the nearby solar system in hardly any time at all. Finally we swung into our landing orbit and made our looping way down to the surface of the little planet.

I studied my crew's faces carefully. We had spent a great deal of time together in space—much too much, really, for comfort—and an incident like this might very well snap them all if we didn't get going again soon enough. I could foresee disagreements, bickering, declaration of opinion where no opinion was called for.

I was relieved to discover that the planet's air was breathable. A rather high nitrogen concentration, to be sure—82 percent—but that left 17 percent for oxygen, plus some miscellaneous inerts, and it wouldn't be too rough on the lungs. I decreed a one-hour free break before beginning repairs.

Remaining aboard ship, I gloomily surveyed the scrambled feed network and tried to formulate a preliminary plan of action for getting the complex cybernetic instrument to function again, while my crew went outside to relax.

Ten minutes after I had opened the lock and let them out, I heard someone clanking around in the aft supplies cabin.

"Who's there?" I yelled.

"Me," grunted a heavy voice that could only be Willendorf's. "I'm looking for the thought-converter, sir."

I ran hastily through the corridor, flipped up the latch on the supplies cabin, and confronted him. "What do you want the converter for?" I snapped.

"Found an alien, sir," he said laconically.

My eyes widened. The survey chart said nothing about intelligent extraterrestrials in this limb of the galaxy, but then again this planet hadn't been explored yet.

I gestured towards the rear cabinet. "The converter helmets are in there," I said. "I'll be out in a little while. Make sure you follow technique in making contact."

"Of course, sir." Willendorf took the converter helmet and went out, leaving me standing there. I waited a few minutes, then climbed the catwalk to the air lock and peered out.

They were all clustered around a small alien being who looked weak and inconsequential in the midst of the circle. I smiled at the sight. The alien was roughly humanoid in shape, with the usual complement of arms and legs, and a pale-green complexion that blended well with the muted violet coloring of his world. He was wearing the thought-converter somewhat lopsidedly, and I saw a small green furry ear protruding from the left side. Willendorf was talking to him.

Then someone saw me standing at the open air lock, and I heard Haley yell to me, "Come on down, Chief!"

They were ringed around the alien in a tight circle. I shouldered my way into their midst. Willendorf turned to me.

"Meet Alaree, sir," he said. "Alaree, this is our commander."

"We are pleased to meet you," the alien said gravely. The converter automatically turned his thoughts into English, but maintained the trace of his oddly inflected accent. "You have been saying that you are from the skies."

"His grammar's pretty shaky," Willendorf interposed. "He keeps referring to any of us as 'you'—even you, who just got here."

"Odd," I said. "The converter's supposed to conform to the rules of grammar." I turned to the alien, who seemed perfectly at ease among us. "My name is Bryson," I said. "This is Willendorf, over here."

The alien wrinkled his soft-skinned forehead in momentary confusion. "We are Alaree," he said again.

"We? You and who else?"

"We and we else," Alaree said blandly. I stared at him for a moment, then gave up. The complexities of an alien mind are often too much for a mere Terran to fathom.

"You are welcome to our world," Alaree said after a few moments of silence.

"Thanks," I said. "Thanks."

I turned away, leaving the alien with my men. They had twenty-six minutes left of the break I'd given them, after which we would have to get back to the serious business of repairing the ship. Making friends with floppy-eared aliens was one thing, getting back to Earth was another.

* * * *

The planet was a warm, friendly sort of place, with rolling fields and acres of pleasant-looking purple vegetation. We had landed in a clearing at the edge of a fair-sized copse. Great broad-beamed trees shot up all around us.

Alaree returned to visit us every day, until he became almost a mascot of the crew. I liked the little alien myself and spent some time with him, although I found his conversation generally incomprehensible. No doubt he had the same trouble with us. The converter had only limited efficiency, after all.

He was the only representative of his species who came. For all we knew, he was the only one of his kind on the whole planet. There was no sign of life elsewhere, and, although Willendorf led an unauthorized scouting party during some free time on the third day, he failed to find a village of any sort. Where Alaree went every night and how he had found us in the first place remained mysteries.

As for the feed network, progress was slow. Ketteridge, the technician in charge, had tracked down the foul-up and was trying to repair it without building a completely new network. Shortcuts again. He tinkered away for four days, setting up a tentative circuit, trying it out, watching it sputter and blow out, building another.

There was nothing I could do. But I sensed tension heightening among the crewmen. They were annoyed at themselves, at each other, at me, at everything.

On the fifth day, Ketteridge and Willendorf finally let their accumulated tenseness explode. They had been working together on the network, but they quarreled, and Ketteridge came storming into my cabin immediately afterward.

"Sir, I demand to be allowed to work on the network by myself. It's my speciality, and Willendorf's only snarling things up."

"Get me Willendorf," I said.

When Willendorf showed up I heard the whole story, decided quickly to let Ketteridge have his way—it was, after all, his specialty—and calmed Willendorf down. Then, reaching casually for some papers on my desk, I dismissed both of them. I knew they'd come to their senses in a day or so.

I spent most of the next day sitting placidly in the sun, while Ketteridge tinkered with the feed network some more. I watched the faces of the men. They were starting to smoulder. They wanted to get home, and they weren't getting there. Besides, this was a fairly dull planet, and even the novelty of Alaree wore off after a while. The little alien had a way of hanging around men who were busy scraping fuel deposits out of the jet tubes, or something equally unpleasant, and bothering them with all sorts of questions.

The following morning I was lying blissfully on the grass near the ship, talking to Alaree. Ketteridge came to me, and by the tightness of his lips I knew he was in trouble.

I brushed some antlike blue insects off my trousers and rose to a sitting position, leaning against the tall, tough-barked tree behind me. "What's the matter, Ketteridge? How's the feed network?"

He glanced uneasily at Alaree for a moment before speaking. "I'm stuck, sir. I'll have to admit I was wrong. I can't fix it by myself."

I stood up and put my hand on his shoulder. "That's a noble thing to say, Ketteridge. It takes a big man to admit he's been a fool. Will you work with Willendorf now?"

"If he'll work with me, sir," Ketteridge said miserably.

"I think he will," I said. Ketteridge saluted and turned away, and I felt a burst of satisfaction. I'd met the crisis in the only way possible; if I had ordered them to cooperate, I would have gotten no place. The psychological situation no longer allowed for unbending military discipline.

After Ketteridge had gone, Alaree, who had been silent all this time, looked up at me in puzzlement. "We do not understand," he said.

"Not *we*," I corrected. "*I*. You're only one person. *We* means many people."

"We are only one person?" Alaree said tentatively.

"No. *I* am only one person. Get it?"

He worried the thought around for a few moments; I could see his browless forehead contract in deep concentration.

"Look," I said. "I'm one person. Ketteridge is another person. Willendorf is another. Each one of them is an independent individual, an *I*."

"And together you make *we*?" Alaree asked brightly.

"Yes and no," I said. "*We* is composed of many *I*'s—but we still remain *I*."

Again he sank deep in concentration, and then he smiled, scratched the ear that protruded from one side of the thought-helmet, and said, "*We* do not understand. But *I* do. Each of you is—is an *I*."

"An individual," I said.

"An individual," he repeated. "A complete person. And together, to fly your ship, you must become a *we*."

"But only temporarily," I said. "There still can be conflict between the parts. That's necessary, for progress. I can always think of the rest of them as *they*."

"I...they," Alaree repeated slowly. "*They*." He nodded. "It is difficult for me to grasp all this. I...think differently. But I am coming to understand, and I am worried."

That was a new idea. Alaree worried? Could be, I reflected. I had no way of knowing. I knew so little about Alaree—where on the planet he came from, what his tribal life was like, what sort of civilization he had, were all blanks.

"What kind of worries, Alaree?"

"You would not understand," he said solemnly and would say no more.

Towards afternoon, as golden shadows started to slant through the closely packed trees, I returned to the ship. Willendorf and Ketteridge were aft, working over the feed network, and the whole crew had gathered around to watch and offer suggestions. Even Alaree was there, looking absurdly comical in his copper-alloy thought-converter helmet, standing on tiptoe and trying to see what was happening.

About an hour later, I spotted the alien sitting by himself beneath the long-limbed tree that towered over the ship. He was lost in thought. Evidently whatever his problem was, it was really eating him.

Towards evening, he made a decision. I had been watching him with a great deal of concern, wondering what was going on in that small but unfathomable mind. I saw him brighten, leap up suddenly, and cross the field, heading in my direction.

"Captain!"

"What is it, Alaree?"

He waddled up and stared gravely at me. "Your ship will be ready to leave soon. What was wrong is nearly right again."

He paused, obviously uncertain of how to phrase his next statement, and I waited patiently. Finally he blurted out, "May I come back to your world with you?"

Automatically, the regulations flashed through my mind. I pride myself on my knowledge of the rules. And I knew this one.

ARTICLE 101A

No intelligent extraterrestrial life is to be transported from its own world to any civilized world under any reason whatsoever, without explicit beforehand clearance. The penalty for doing so is...

And it listed a fine of more money than was ever dreamed of in my philosophy.

I shook my head. "Can't take you, Alaree. This is your world, and you belong here."

A ripple of agony ran over his face. Suddenly he ceased to be the cheerful, roly-poly creature it was so impossible to take seriously, and became a very worried entity indeed. "You cannot understand," he said. "I no longer belong here."

* * * *

No matter how hard he pleaded, I remained adamant. And when to no one's surprise Ketteridge and Willendorf announced, a day later, that their pooled labors had succeeded in repairing the feed network, I had to tell Alaree that we were going to leave—without him.

He nodded stiffly, accepting the fact, and without a word stalked tragically away, into the purple tangle of foliage that surrounded our clearing.

He returned a while later, or so I thought. He was not wearing the thought-converter. That surprised me. Alaree knew the helmet was a valuable item, and he had been cautioned to take good care of it.

I sent a man inside to get another helmet for him. I put it on him—this time tucking that wayward ear underneath properly—and looked at him sternly. "Where's the other helmet, Alaree?"

"We do not have it," he said.

"*We?* No more I?"

"We," Alaree said. And as he spoke, the leaves parted and another alien—Alaree's very double—stepped out into the clearing.

Then I saw the helmet on the newcomer's head, and realized that he was no double. He was Alaree, and the other alien was the stranger!

"I see you're here already," the alien I knew as Alaree said to the other. They were standing about ten feet apart, staring coldly at each other. I glanced at both of them quickly. They might have been identical twins.

"We are here," the stranger said, "We have come to get you."

I took a step backward, sensing that some incomprehensible drama was being played out here among these aliens.

"What's going on, Alaree?" I asked.

"We are having difficulties," both of them said, as one.

Both of them.

I turned to the second alien. "What's your name?"

"Alaree," he said.

"Are you all named that?" I demanded.

"We are Alaree," Alaree Two said.

"They are Alaree," Alaree One said. "And *I* am Alaree. *I*."

At that moment there was a disturbance in the shrubbery, and half a dozen more aliens stepped through and confronted Alarees One and

ALAREE | 15

Two.

"We are Alaree," Alaree Two repeated exasperatingly. He made a sweeping gesture that embraced all seven of the aliens to my left, but pointedly excluded Alaree One at my right.

"Are we—you coming with we—us?" Alaree Two demanded. I heard the six others say something in approximately the same tone of voice, but since they weren't wearing converters, their words were only scrambled nonsense to me.

Alaree One looked at me in pain, then back at his seven fellows. I saw an expression of sheer terror in the small creature's eyes. He turned to me.

"I must go with them," he said softly. He was quivering with fear.

Without a further word, the eight marched silently away. I stood there, shaking my head in bewilderment.

We were scheduled to leave the next day. I said nothing to my crew about the bizarre incident of the evening before, but noted in my log that the native life of the planet would require careful study at some future time.

Blast-off was slated for 1100. As the crew moved efficiently through the ship, securing things, packing, preparing for departure, I sensed a general feeling of jubilation. They were happy to be on their way again, and I didn't blame them.

About half an hour before blast-off, Willendorf came to me. "Sir, Alaree's down below," he said. "He wants to come up and see you. He looks very troubled, sir."

I frowned. Probably the alien still wanted to go back with us. Well, it was cruel to deny the request, but I wasn't going to risk that fine. I intended to make that clear to him.

"Send him up," I said.

A moment later Alaree came stumbling into my cabin. Before he could speak I said, "I told you before—I can't take you off this planet, Alaree. I'm sorry about it."

He looked up pitiably and said, "You mustn't leave me!" He was trembling uncontrollably.

"What's wrong, Alaree?" I asked.

He stared intensely at me for a long moment, mastering himself, trying to arrange what he wanted to tell me into a coherent argument. Finally he said, "They would not take me back. I am alone."

"Who wouldn't take you back, Alaree?"

"*They.* Last night, Alaree came for me, to take me back. They are a *we*—an entity, a oneness. You cannot understand. When they saw what I had become, they cast me out."

I shook my head dizzily. "What do you mean?"

"You taught me…to become an *I*," he said, moistening his lips. "Before, I was part of *we—they*. I learned your ways from you, and now there is no room for me here. They have cut me off. When the final break comes, I will not be able to stay on this world."

Sweat was pouring down his pale face, and he was breathing harder. "It will come any minute. They are gathering strength for it. But I am *I*," he said triumphantly. He shook violently and gasped for breath.

I understood now. They were *all* Alaree. It was one planet-wide, self-aware corporate entity, composed of any number of individual cells. He had been one of them—but he had learned independence.

Then he had returned to the group—but he carried with him the seeds of individualism, the deadly, contagious germ we Terrans spread everywhere. Individualism would be fatal to such a group mind; it was cutting him loose to save itself. Just as diseased cells must be excised for the good of the entire body, Alaree was inexorably being cut off from his fellows lest he destroy the bond that made them one.

I watched him as he sobbed weakly on my acceleration cradle. "They…are…cutting…me…loose…*now!*"

He writhed horribly for a brief moment, and then relaxed and sat up on the edge of the cradle. "It is over," he said calmly. "I am fully independent."

I saw a stark *aloneness* reflected in his eyes, and behind that a gentle indictment of me for having done this to him. This world, I realized, was no place for Earthmen. What had happened was our fault—mine more than anyone else's.

"Will you take me with you?" he asked again. "If I stay here, Alaree will kill me."

I scowled wretchedly for a moment, fighting a brief battle within myself, and then I looked up. There was only one thing to do—and I was sure, once I explained on Earth, that I would not suffer for it.

I took his hand. It was cold and limp; whatever he had just been through, it must have been hell. "Yes," I said softly. "You can come with us."

And so Alaree joined the crew of the *Aaron Burr*. I told them about it just before blast-off, and they welcomed him aboard in traditional manner.

We gave the sad-eyed little alien a cabin near the cargo hold, and he established himself quite comfortably. He had no personal possessions— "It is not *their* custom" he said—and promised that he'd keep the cabin clean.

He had brought with him a rough-edged, violet fruit that he said was his staple food. I turned it over to Kechnie for synthesizing, and we blasted off.

Alaree was right at home aboard the *Burr*. He spent much time with me—asking questions.

"Tell me about Earth," Alaree would ask. The alien wanted desperately to know what sort of a world he was going to.

He would listen gravely while I explained. I told him of cities and wars and spaceships, and he nodded sagely, trying to fit the concepts into a mind only newly liberated from the gestalt. I knew he could comprehend only a fraction of what I was saying, but I enjoyed telling him. It made me feel as if Earth were coming closer that much faster, simply to talk about it.

And he went around begging everyone, "Tell me about Earth." They enjoyed telling him, too—for a while.

Then it began to get a little tiresome. We had grown accustomed to Alaree's presence on the ship, flopping around the corridors doing whatever menial job he had been assigned to. But—although I had told the men why I had brought him with us, and though we all pitied the poor lonely creature and admired his struggle to survive as an individual entity—we were slowly coming to the realization that Alaree was something of a nuisance aboard ship.

Especially later, when he began to change.

Willendorf noticed it first, twelve days out from Alaree's planet. "Alaree's been acting pretty strange these days, sir," he told me.

"What's wrong?" I asked.

"Haven't you spotted it, sir? He's been moping around like a lost soul—very quiet and withdrawn, like."

"Is he eating well?"

Willendorf chuckled loudly. "I'll say he is! Kechnie made up some synthetics based on the piece of fruit he brought with him, and he's been stuffing himself wildly. He's gained ten pounds since he came on ship. No, it's not lack of food!"

"I guess not," I said. "Keep an eye on him, will you? I feel responsible for his being here, and I want him to come through the voyage in good health."

After that, I began to observe Alaree more closely myself, and I detected the change in his personality too. He was no longer the cheerful, childlike being who delighted in pouring out questions in endless profusion. Now he was moody, silent, always brooding, and hard to approach.

On the sixteenth day out—and by now I was worried seriously about him—a new manifestation appeared. I was in the hallway, heading from my cabin to the chartroom, when Alaree stepped out of an alcove. He reached up, grasped my uniform lapel, and, maintaining his silence, drew my head down and stared pleadingly into my eyes.

Too astonished to say anything, I returned his gaze for nearly thirty seconds. I peered into his transparent pupils, wondering what he was up to. After a good while had passed, he released me, and I saw something like a tear trickle down his cheek.

"What's the trouble, Alaree?"

He shook his head mournfully and shuffled away.

I got reports from the crewmen that day and next that he had been doing this regularly for the past eighteen hours—waylaying crewmen, staring long and deep at them as if trying to express some unspeakable sadness, and walking away. He had approached almost everyone on the ship.

I wondered now how wise it had been to allow an extraterrestrial, no matter how friendly, to enter the ship. There was no telling what this latest action meant.

I started to form a theory. I suspected what he was aiming at, and the realization chilled me. But once I reached my conclusion, there was nothing I could do but wait for confirmation.

On the nineteenth day, Alaree again met me in the corridor. This time our encounter was more brief. He plucked me by the sleeve, shook his head sadly and shrugged his shoulders, and walked away.

That night, he took to his cabin, and by morning he was dead. He had apparently died peacefully in his sleep.

* * * *

"I guess we'll never understand him, poor fellow," Willendorf said, after we had committed the body to space. "You think he had too much to eat, sir?"

"No," I said. "It wasn't that. He was lonely, that's all. He didn't belong here, among us."

"But you said he had broken away from that group-mind," Willendorf objected.

I shook my head. "Not really. That group-mind arose out of some deep psychological and physiological needs of those people. You can't just declare your independence and be able to exist as an individual from then on if you're part of that group-entity. Alaree had grasped the concept intellectually, to some extent, but he wasn't suited for life away from the corporate mind, no matter how much he wanted to be."

"He couldn't stand alone?"

"Not after his people had evolved that gestalt setup. He learned independence from us," I said. "But he couldn't live with us, really. He needed to be part of a whole. He found out his mistake after he came aboard and tried to remedy things."

I saw Willendorf pale. "What do you mean, sir?"

"You know what I mean. When he came up to us and stared soulfully into our eyes. *He was trying to form a new gestalt—out of us!* Somehow he was trying to link us together, the way his people had been linked."

"He couldn't do it, though," Willendorf said fervently.

"Of course not. Human beings don't have whatever need it is that forced those people to merge. He found that out, after a while, when he failed to get anywhere with us."

"He just couldn't do it," Willendorf repeated.

"No. And then he ran out of strength," I said somberly, feeling the heavy weight of my guilt. "He was like an organ removed from a living body. It can exist for a little while by itself, but not indefinitely. He failed to find a new source of life—and he died." I stared bitterly at my fingertips.

"What do we call it in my medical report?" asked Ship Surgeon Thomas, who had been silent up till then. "How can we explain what he died from?"

"Call it—*malnutrition*," I said.

BIRDS OF A FEATHER

Originally published in *Galaxy Magazine*, November 1958.

It was our first day of recruiting on the planet, and the alien life forms had lined up for hundreds of feet back from my rented office. As I came down the block from the hotel, I could hear and see and smell them with ease.

My three staff men, Auchinleck, Stebbins, and Ludlow, walked shieldwise in front of me. I peered between them to size up the crop. The aliens came in every shape and form, in all colors and textures—and all of them eager for a Corrigan contract. The Galaxy is full of bizarre beings, but there's barely a species anywhere that can resist the old exhibitionist urge.

"Send them in one at a time," I told Stebbins. I ducked into the office, took my place back of the desk, and waited for the procession to begin.

The name of the planet was MacTavish IV (if you went by the official Terran listing) or Ghryne (if you called it by what its people were accustomed to calling it). I thought of it privately as MacTavish IV and referred to it publicly as Ghryne. I believe in keeping the locals happy wherever I go.

Through the front window of the office, I could see our big gay tridim sign plastered to a facing wall: WANTED—EXTRATERRESTRIALS! We had saturated MacTavish IV with our promotional poop for a month preceding arrival. Stuff like this:

Want to visit Earth—see the Galaxy's most glittering and exclusive world? Want to draw good pay, work short hours, experience the thrills of show business on romantic Terra? If you are a non-terrestrial, there may be a place for you in the Corrigan Institute of Morphological Science. No freaks wanted—normal beings only. J. F. Corrigan will hold interviews in person on Ghryne from Thirdday to Fifthday of Tenmonth. His last visit to the Caledonia Cluster until 2937, so don't miss your chance! Hurry! A life of wonder and riches can be yours!

Broadsides like that, distributed wholesale in half a thousand languages, always bring them running. And the Corrigan Institute really packs in the crowds back on Earth. Why not? It's the best of its kind, the only really decent place where Earthmen can get a gander at the other species of the universe.

The office buzzer sounded. Auchinleck said unctuously, "The first applicant is ready to see you, sir."

"Send him, her, or it in."

The door opened and a timid-looking life form advanced toward me on nervous little legs. He was a globular creature about the size of a big basketball, yellowish green, with two spindly double-kneed legs and five double-elbowed arms, the latter spaced regularly around his body. There was a lidless eye at the top of his head and five lidded ones, one above each arm. Plus a big, gaping, toothless mouth.

His voice was a surprisingly resounding basso. "You are Mr. Corrigan?"

"That's right." I reached for a data blank. "Before we begin, I'll need certain information about—"

"I am a being of Regulus II," came the grave, booming reply, even before I had picked up the blank. "I need no special care and I am not a fugitive from the law of any world."

"Your name?"

"Lawrence R. Fitzgerald."

I throttled my exclamation of surprise, concealing it behind a quick cough. "Let me have that again, please?"

"Certainly. My name is Lawrence R. Fitzgerald. The R stands for Raymond."

"Of course, that's not the name you were born with."

The being closed his eyes and toddled around in a 360-degree rotation, remaining in place. On his world, that gesture is the equivalent of an apologetic smile. "My Regulan name no longer matters. I am now and shall evermore be Lawrence R. Fitzgerald. I am a Terraphile, you see."

The little Regulan was as good as hired. Only the formalities remained. "You understand our terms, Mr. Fitzgerald?"

"I'll be placed on exhibition at your institute on Earth. You'll pay for my services, transportation, and expenses. I'll be required to remain on exhibit no more than one-third of each Terran sidereal day."

"And the pay will be—ah—fifty dollars Galactic a week, plus expenses and transportation."

The spherical creature clapped his hands in joy, three hands clapping on one side, two on the other. "Wonderful! I will see Earth at last! I accept the terms!"

I buzzed for Ludlow and gave him the fast signal that meant we were signing this alien up at half the usual pay, and Ludlow took him into the other office to sign him up.

I grinned, pleased with myself. We needed a green Regulan in our show; the last one had quit four years ago. But just because we needed him didn't mean we had to be extravagant in hiring him. A Terraphile alien who goes to the extent of rechristening himself with a Terran moniker would work for nothing, or even pay us, just so long as we let him get to Earth. My conscience won't let me really exploit a being, but I don't believe in throwing money away, either.

The next applicant was a beefy ursinoid from Aldebaran IX. Our outfit has all the ursinoids it needs or is likely to need in the next few decades, and so I got rid of him in a couple of minutes. He was followed by a roly-poly blue-skinned humanoid from Donovan's Planet, four feet high and five hundred pounds heavy. We already had a couple of his species in the show, but they made good crowd-pleasers, being so plump and cheerful. I passed him along to Auchinleck to sign at anything short of top rate.

Next came a bedraggled Sirian spider who was more interested in a handout than a job. If there's any species we have a real oversupply of, it's those silver-colored spiders, but this seedy specimen gave it a try anyway. He got the gate in half a minute, and he didn't even get the handout he was angling for. I don't approve of begging.

The flow of applicants was steady. Ghryne is in the heart of the Caledonia Cluster, where the interstellar crossroads meet. We had figured to pick up plenty of new exhibits here and we were right.

It was the isolationism of the late twenty-ninth century that turned me into the successful proprietor of Corrigan's Institute, after some years as an impoverished carnival man in the Betelgeuse system. Back in 2903, the World Congress declared Terra off bounds for non-terrestrial beings, as an offshoot of the Terra for Terrans movement.

Before then, anyone could visit Earth. After the gate clanged down, a non-terrestrial could only get onto Sol III as a specimen in a scientific collection—in short, as an exhibit in a zoo.

That's what the Corrigan Institute of Morphological Science really is, of course. A zoo. But we don't go out and hunt for our specimens; we advertise and they come flocking to us. Every alien wants to see Earth once in his lifetime, and there's only one way he can do it.

We don't keep too big an inventory. At last count we had 690 specimens before this trip, representing 298 different intelligent life forms. My goal is at least one member of at least 500 different races. When I reach that, I'll sit back and let the competition catch up—if it can.

After an hour of steady work that morning, we had signed on eleven new specimens. At the same time, we had turned away a dozen ursinoids, fifty of the reptilian natives of Ghryne, seven Sirian spiders, and no less than nineteen chlorine-breathing Procyonites wearing gas masks.

It was also my sad duty to nix a Vegan who was negotiating through a Ghrynian agent. A Vegan would be a top-flight attraction, being some four hundred feet long and appropriately fearsome to the eye, but I didn't see how we could take one on. They're gentle and likable beings, but their upkeep runs into literally tons of fresh meat a day, and not just any old kind of meat either. So we had to do without the Vegan.

"One more specimen before lunch," I told Stebbins, "to make it an even dozen."

He looked at me queerly and nodded. A being entered. I took a long close look at the life form when it came in, and after that I took another one. I wondered what kind of stunt was being pulled. So far as I could tell, the being was quite plainly nothing but an Earthman.

He sat down facing me without being asked and crossed his legs. He was tall and extremely thin, with pale-blue eyes and dirty-blond hair, and though he was clean and reasonably well dressed, he had a shabby look about him. He said, in level Terran accents, "I'm looking for a job with your outfit, Corrigan."

"There's been a mistake. We're interested in non-terrestrials only."

"I'm a non-terrestrial. My name is Ildwar Gorb, of the planet Wazzenazz XIII."

I don't mind conning the public from time to time, but I draw the line at getting bilked myself. "Look, friend, I'm busy, and I'm not known for my sense of humor. Or my generosity."

"I'm not panhandling. I'm looking for a job."

"Then try elsewhere. Suppose you stop wasting my time, bud. You're as Earthborn as I am."

"I've never been within a dozen parsecs of Earth," he said smoothly. "I happen to be a representative of the only Earthlike race that exists anywhere in the Galaxy but on Earth itself. Wazzenazz XIII is a small and little-known planet in the Crab Nebula. Through an evolutionary fluke, my race is identical with yours. Now, don't you want me in your circus?"

"No. And it's not a circus. It's—"

"A scientific institute. I stand corrected."

There was something glib and appealing about this preposterous phony. I guess I recognized a kindred spirit or I would have tossed him out on his ear without another word. Instead I played along. "If you're from such a distant place, how come you speak English so well?"

"I'm not speaking. I'm a telepath—not the kind that reads minds, just the kind that projects. I communicate in symbols that you translate back to colloquial speech."

"Very clever, Mr. Gorb." I grinned at him and shook my head. "You spin a good yarn—but for my money, you're really Sam Jones or Phil Smith from Earth, stranded here and out of cash. You want a free trip back to Earth. No deal. The demand for beings from Wazzenazz XIII is pretty low these days. Zero, in fact. Good-bye, Mr. Gorb."

He pointed a finger squarely at me and said, "You're making a big mistake. I'm just what your outfit needs. A representative of a hitherto utterly unknown race identical to humanity in every respect! Look here, examine my teeth. Absolutely like human teeth! And—"

I pulled away from his yawning mouth. "Good-bye, Mr. Gorb," I repeated.

"All I ask is a contract, Corrigan. It isn't much. I'll be a big attraction. I'll—"

"Good-bye, Mr. Gorb!"

He glowered at me reproachfully for a moment, stood up, and sauntered to the door. "I thought you were a man of acumen, Corrigan. Well, think it over. Maybe you'll regret your hastiness. I'll be back to give you another chance."

He slammed the door and I let my grim expression relax into a smile. This was the best con switch yet—an Earthman posing as an alien to get a job!

But I wasn't buying it, even if I could appreciate his cleverness intellectually. There's no such place as Wazzenazz XIII and there's only one human race in the Galaxy—on Earth. I was going to need some real good reason before I gave a down-and-out grifter a free ticket home.

I didn't know it then, but before the day was out, I would have that reason. And, with it, plenty of trouble on my hands.

The first harbinger of woe turned up after lunch in the person of a Kallerian. The Kallerian was the sixth applicant that afternoon. I had turned away three more ursinoids, hired a vegetable from Miazan, and said no to a scaly pseudo-armadillo from one of the Delta Worlds. Hardly had the 'dillo scuttled dejectedly out of my office when the Kallerian came striding in, not even waiting for Stebbins to admit him officially.

He was big even for his kind—in the neighborhood of nine feet high, and getting on toward a ton. He planted himself firmly on his three stocky feet, extended his massive arms in a Kallerian greeting gesture, and growled, "I am Vallo Heraal, Freeman of Kaller IV. You will sign me immediately to a contract!"

"Sit down, Freeman Heraal. I like to make my own decisions, thanks."

"You will grant me a contract!"

"Will you please sit down?"

He said sulkily, "I will remain standing."

"As you prefer." My desk has a few concealed features which are sometimes useful in dealing with belligerent or disappointed life forms. My fingers roamed to the mesh-gun trigger, just in case of trouble.

The Kallerian stood motionless before me. They're hairy creatures, and this one had a coarse, thick mat of blue fur completely covering his body. Two fierce eyes glimmered out through the otherwise dense blanket of fur. He was wearing the kilt, girdle, and ceremonial blaster of his warlike race.

I said, "You'll have to understand, Freeman Heraal, that it's not our policy to maintain more than a few members of each species at our Institute. And we're not currently in need of any Kallerian males, because—"

"You will hire me or trouble I will make!"

I opened our inventory chart. I showed him that we were already carrying four Kallerians, and that was more than plenty.

The beady little eyes flashed like beacons in the fur. "Yes, you have four representatives—of the Clan Verdrokh! None of the Clan Gursdrinn! For three years I have waited for a chance to avenge this insult to the noble Clan Gursdrinn!"

At the key word avenge, I readied myself to ensnarl the Kallerian in a spume of tanglemesh the instant he went for his blaster, but he didn't move. He bellowed, "I have vowed a vow, Earthman. Take me to Earth, enroll a Gursdrinn, or the consequences will be terrible!"

I'm a man of principles, like all straightforward double-dealers, and one of the most important of those principles is that I never let myself be bullied by anyone. "I deeply regret having unintentionally insulted your clan, Freeman Heraal. Will you accept my apologies?"

He glared at me in silence.

I went on, "Please be assured that I'll undo the insult at the earliest possible opportunity. It's not feasible for us to hire another Kallerian now, but I'll give preference to the Clan Gursdrinn as soon as a vacancy—"

"No. You will hire me now."

"It can't be done, Freeman Heraal. We have a budget, and we stick to it."

"You will rue! I will take drastic measures!"

"Threats will get you nowhere, Freeman Heraal. I give you my word I'll get in touch with you as soon as our organization has room for another Kallerian. And now, please, there are many applicants waiting—"

You'd think it would be sort of humiliating to become a specimen in a zoo, but most of these races take it as an honor. And there's always the chance that, by picking a given member of a race, we're insulting all the others.

I nudged the trouble button on the side of my desk and Auchinleck and Ludlow appeared simultaneously from the two doors at right and left. They surrounded the towering Kallerian and sweet-talkingly led him away. He wasn't minded to quarrel physically, or he could have knocked them both into the next city with a backhand swipe of his shaggy paw, but he kept up a growling flow of invective and threats until he was out in the hall.

I mopped sweat from my forehead and began to buzz Stebbins for the next applicant. But before my finger touched the button, the door popped open and a small being came scooting in, followed by an angry Stebbins.

"Come here, you!"

"Stebbins?" I said gently.

"I'm sorry, Mr. Corrigan. I lost sight of this one for a moment, and he came running in—"

"Please, please," squeaked the little alien pitifully. "I must see you, honored sir!"

"It isn't his turn in line," Stebbins protested. "There are at least fifty ahead of him."

"All right," I said tiredly. "As long as he's in here already, I might as well see him. Be more careful next time, Stebbins."

Stebbins nodded dolefully and backed out.

The alien was a pathetic sight: a Stortulian, a squirrely-looking creature about three feet high. His fur, which should have been a lustrous black, was a dull gray, and his eyes were wet and sad. His tail drooped. His voice was little more than a faint whimper, even at full volume.

"Begging your most honored pardon most humbly, important sir. I am a being of Stortul XII, having sold my last few possessions to travel to Ghryne for the miserable purpose of obtaining an interview with yourself."

I said, "I'd better tell you right at the outset that we're already carrying our full complement of Stortulians. We have both a male and a female now and—"

"This is known to me. The female—is her name perchance Tiress?"

I glanced down at the inventory chart until I found the Stortulian entry. "Yes, that's her name."

The little being immediately emitted a soul-shaking gasp. "It is she! It is she!"

"I'm afraid we don't have room for any more—"

"You are not in full understanding of my plight. The female Tiress, she is—was—my own Fire-sent spouse, my comfort and my warmth, my life and my love."

"Funny," I said. "When we signed her three years ago, she said she was single. It's right here on the chart."

"She lied! She left my burrow because she longed to see the splendors of Earth. And I am alone, bound by our sacred customs never to remarry, languishing in sadness and pining for her return. You must take me to Earth!"

"But—"

"I must see her—her and this disgrace-bringing lover of hers. I must reason with her. Earthman, can't you see I must appeal to her inner flame? I must bring her back!"

My face was expressionless. "You don't really intend to join our organization at all—you just want free passage to Earth?"

"Yes, yes!" wailed the Stortulian. "Find some other member of my race, if you must! Let me have my wife again, Earthman! Is your heart a dead lump of stone?"

It isn't, but another of my principles is to refuse to be swayed by sentiment. I felt sorry for this being's domestic troubles, but I wasn't going to break up a good act just to make an alien squirrel happy—not to mention footing the transportation.

I said, "I don't see how we can manage it. The laws are very strict on the subject of bringing alien life to Earth. It has to be for scientific purposes only. And if I know in advance that your purpose in coming isn't scientific, I can't in all conscience lie for you, can I?"

"Well—"

"Of course not." I took advantage of his pathetic upset to steam right along. "Now if you had come in here and simply asked me to sign you up, I might conceivably have done it. But no—you had to go unburden your heart to me."

"I thought the truth would move you."

"It did. But in effect you're now asking me to conspire in a fraudulent criminal act. Friend, I can't do it. My reputation means too much to me," I said piously.

"Then you will refuse me?"

"My heart melts to nothingness for you. But I can't take you to Earth."

"Perhaps you will send my wife to me here?"

There's a clause in every contract that allows me to jettison an unwanted specimen. All I have to do is declare it no longer of scientific interest, and the World Government will deport the undesirable alien back to its home world. But I wouldn't pull a low trick like that on our female Stortulian.

I said, "I'll ask her about coming home. But I won't ship her back against her will. And maybe she's happier where she is."

The Stortulian seemed to shrivel. His eyelids closed halfway to mask his tears. He turned and shambled slowly to the door, walking like a living dishrag. In a bleak voice he said, "There is no hope then. All is lost. I will never see my soul mate again. Good day, Earthman."

He spoke in a drab monotone that almost, but not quite, had me weeping. I watched him shuffle out. I do have some conscience, and I had the uneasy feeling I had just been talking to a being who was about to commit suicide on my account.

About fifty more applicants were processed without a hitch. Then life started to get complicated again.

Nine of the fifty were okay. The rest were unacceptable for one reason or another, and they took the bad news quietly enough. The haul for the day so far was close to two dozen new life forms under contract.

I had just about begun to forget about the incidents of the Kallerian's outraged pride and the Stortulian's flighty wife when the door opened and the Earthman who called himself Ildwar Gorb of Wazzenazz XIII stepped in.

"How did you get in here?" I demanded.

"Your man happened to be looking the wrong way," he said cheerily. "Change your mind about me yet?"

"Get out before I have you thrown out."

Gorb shrugged. "I figured you hadn't changed your mind, so I've changed my pitch a bit. If you won't believe I'm from Wazzenazz XIII, suppose I tell you that I am Earthborn, and that I'm looking for a job on your staff."

"I don't care what your story is! Get out or—"

"—you'll have me thrown out. Okay, okay. Just give me half a second. Corrigan, you're no fool, and neither am I—but that fellow of yours outside is. He doesn't know how to handle alien beings. How many times today has a life form come in here unexpectedly?"

I scowled at him. "Too damn many."

"You see? He's incompetent. Suppose you fire him, take me on instead. I've been living in the outworlds half my life; I know all there is to know about alien life forms. You can use me, Corrigan."

I took a deep breath and glanced all around the paneled ceiling of the office before I spoke. "Listen, Gorb, or whatever your name is, I've had a hard day. There's been a Kallerian in here who just about threatened murder, and there's been a Stortulian in here who's about to commit suicide because of me. I have a conscience and it's troubling me. But get this: I just want to finish off my recruiting, pack up, and go home to

Earth. I don't want you hanging around here bothering me. I'm not looking to hire new staff members, and if you switch back to claiming you're an unknown life form from Wazzenazz XIII, the answer is that I'm not looking for any of those either. Now will you scram or—"

The office door crashed open at that point and Heraal, the Kallerian, came thundering in. He was dressed from head to toe in glittering metalfoil, and instead of his ceremonial blaster he was wielding a sword the length of a human being. Stebbins and Auchinleck came dragging helplessly along in his wake, hanging desperately on to his belt.

"Sorry, Chief," Stebbins gasped. "I tried to keep him out, but—"

Heraal, who had planted himself in front of my desk, drowned him out with a roar. "Earthman, you have mortally insulted the Clan Gursdrinn!"

Sitting with my hands poised near the mesh-gun trigger, I was ready to let him have it at the first sign of actual violence.

Heraal boomed, "You are responsible for what is to happen now. I have notified the authorities and you prosecuted will be for causing the death of a life form! Suffer, Earthborn ape! Suffer!"

"Watch it, Chief," Stebbins yelled. "He's going to—"

An instant before my numb fingers could tighten on the mesh-gun trigger, Heraal swung that huge sword through the air and plunged it savagely through his body. He toppled forward onto the carpet with the sword projecting a couple of feet out of his back. A few driblets of bluish-purple blood spread from beneath him.

Before I could react to the big life form's hara-kiri, the office door flew open again and three sleek reptilian beings entered, garbed in the green sashes of the local police force.

Their golden eyes goggled down at the figure on the floor, then came to rest on me.

"You are J. F. Corrigan?" the leader asked.

"Y-yes."

"We have received word of a complaint against you. Said complaint being—"

"—that your unethical actions have directly contributed to the untimely death of an intelligent life form," filled in the second of the Ghrynian policemen.

"The evidence lies before us," intoned the leader, "in the cadaver of the unfortunate Kallerian who filed the complaint with us several minutes ago."

"And therefore," said the third lizard, "it is our duty to, arrest you for this crime and declare you subject to a fine of no less than a hundred thousand dollars Galactic or two years in prison."

"Hold on!" I stormed. "You mean that any being from anywhere in the Universe can come in here and gut himself on my carpet, and I'm responsible?"

"This is the law. Do you deny that your stubborn refusal to yield to this late life form's request lies at the root of his sad demise?"

"Well, no, but—"

"Failure to deny is admission of guilt. You are guilty, Earthman."

Closing my eyes wearily, I tried to wish the whole babbling lot of them away. If I had to, I could pony up the hundred-grand fine, but it was going to put an awful dent in this year's take. And I shuddered when I remembered that any minute that scrawny little Stortulian was likely to come bursting in here to kill himself too. Was it a fine of $100,000 per suicide? At that rate, I could be out of business by nightfall.

I was spared further such morbid thoughts by yet another unannounced arrival.

The small figure of the Stortulian trudged through the open doorway and stationed itself limply near the threshold. The three Ghrynian policemen and my three assistants forgot the dead Kallerian for a moment and turned to eye the newcomer.

I had visions of unending troubles with the law here on Ghryne. I resolved never to come here on a recruiting trip again—or, if I did come, to figure out some more effective way of screening myself against crackpots.

In heartrending tones, the Stortulian declared, "Life is no longer worth living. My last hope is gone. There is only one thing left for me to do."

I was quivering at the thought of another hundred thousand smackers going down the drain. "Stop him, somebody! He's going to kill himself! He's—"

Then somebody sprinted toward me, hit me amidships, and knocked me flying out from behind my desk before I had a chance to fire the mesh-gun. My head walloped the floor, and for five or six seconds, I guess I wasn't fully aware of what was going on.

Gradually the scene took shape around me. There was a monstrous hole in the wall behind my desk; a smoking blaster lay on the floor, and I saw the three Ghrynian policemen sitting on the raving Stortulian. The man who called himself Ildwar Gorb was getting to his feet and dusting himself off.

He helped me up. "Sorry to have had to tackle you, Corrigan. But that Stortulian wasn't here to commit suicide, you see. He was out to get you."

I weaved dizzily toward my desk and dropped into my chair. A flying fragment of wall had deflated my pneumatic cushion. The smell of ashed plaster was everywhere. The police were effectively cocooning the struggling little alien in an unbreakable tanglemesh.

"Evidently you don't know as much as you think you do about Stortulian psychology, Corrigan," Gorb said lightly. "Suicide is completely abhorrent to them. When they're troubled, they kill the person who caused their trouble. In this case, you."

I began to chuckle—more of a tension-relieving snicker than a full-bodied laugh.

"Funny," I said.

"What is?" asked the self-styled Wazzenazzian.

"These aliens. Big blustery Heraal came in with murder in his eye and killed himself, and the pint-sized Stortulian who looked so meek and pathetic damn near blew my head off." I shuddered. "Thanks for the tackle job."

"Don't mention it," Gorb said.

I glared at the Ghrynian police. "Well? What are you waiting for? Take that murderous little beast out of here! Or isn't murder against the local laws?"

"The Stortulian will be duly punished," replied the leader of the Ghrynian cops calmly. "But there is the matter of the dead Kallerian and the fine of—"

"—one hundred thousand dollars. I know." I groaned and turned to Stebbins. "Get the Terran Consulate on the phone, Stebbins. Have them send down a legal adviser. Find out if there's any way we can get out of this mess with our skins intact."

"Right, Chief." Stebbins moved toward the visi-phone.

Gorb stepped forward and put a hand on his chest.

"Hold it," the Wazzenazzian said crisply. "The Consulate can't help you. I can."

"You?" I said.

"I can get you out of this cheap."

"How cheap?"

Gorb grinned rakishly. "Five thousand in cash plus a contract as a specimen with your outfit. In advance, of course. That's a heck of a lot better than forking over a hundred grand, isn't it?"

I eyed Gorb uncertainly. The Terran Consulate people probably wouldn't be much help; they tried to keep out of local squabbles unless they were really serious, and I knew from past experiences that no officials ever worried much about the state of my pocketbook. On the other hand, giving this shyster a contract might be a risky proposition.

"Tell you what," I said finally. "You've got yourself a deal—but on a contingency basis. Get me out of this and you'll have five grand and the contract. Otherwise, nothing."

Gorb shrugged. "What have I to lose?"

Before the police could interfere, Gorb trotted over to the hulking corpse of the Kallerian and fetched it a mighty kick.

"Wake up, you faker! Stop playing possum and stand up! You aren't fooling anyone!"

The Ghrynians got off the huddled little assassin and tried to stop Gorb. "Your pardon, but the dead require your respect," began one of the lizards mildly.

Gorb whirled angrily. "Maybe the dead do—but this character isn't dead!"

He knelt and said loudly in the Kallerian's dish-like ear, "You might as well quit it, Heraal. Listen to this, you shamming mountain of meat— your mother knits doilies for the Clan Verdrokh!"

The supposedly dead Kallerian emitted a twenty-cycle rumble that shook the floor, and clambered to his feet, pulling the sword out of his body and waving it in the air. Gorb leaped back nimbly, snatched up the Stortulian's fallen blaster, and trained it neatly on the big alien's throat before he could do any damage. The Kallerian grumbled and lowered his sword.

I felt groggy. I thought I knew plenty about non-terrestrial life forms, but I was learning a few things today. "I don't understand. How—"

The police were blue with chagrin. "A thousand pardons, Earthman. There seems to have been some error."

"There seems to have been a cute little con game," Gorb remarked quietly.

I recovered my balance. "Try to milk me of a hundred grand when there's been no crime?" I snapped. "I'll say there's been an error! If I weren't a forgiving man, I'd clap the bunch of you in jail for attempting to defraud an Earthman! Get out of here! And take that would-be murderer with you!"

They got, and they got fast, burbling apologies as they went. They had tried to fox an Earthman, and that's a dangerous sport. They dragged the cocooned form of the Stortulian with them. The air seemed to clear, and peace was restored. I signaled to Auchinleck and he slammed the door.

"All right." I looked at Gorb and jerked a thumb at the Kallerian. "That's a nice trick. How does it work?"

Gorb smiled pleasantly. He was enjoying this, I could see. "Kallerians of the Clan Gursdrinn specialize in a kind of mental discipline, Corrigan. It isn't too widely known in this area of the Galaxy, but men of that clan have unusual mental control over their bodies. They can cut off circulation and nervous-system response in large chunks of their bodies for hours at a stretch—an absolutely perfect imitation of death. And, of course, when Heraal put the sword through himself, it was a simple matter to avoid hitting any vital organs en route."

The Kallerian, still at gunpoint, hung his head in shame.

I turned on him. "So—try to swindle me, eh? You cooked up this whole fake suicide in collusion with those cops."

He looked quite a sight, with that gaping slash running clear through his body. But the wound had begun to heal already. "I regret the incident, Earthman. I am mortified. Be good enough to destroy this unworthy person."

It was a tempting idea, but a notion was forming in my showman's mind. "No, I won't destroy you. Tell me—how often can you do that trick?"

"The tissues will regenerate in a few hours."

"Would you mind having to kill yourself every day, Heraal? And twice on Sundays?"

Heraal looked doubtful. "Well, for the honor of my clan, perhaps—"

Stebbins said, "Boss, you mean—"

"Shut up. Heraal, you're hired—seventy-five dollars a week plus expenses. Stebbins, get me a contract form—and type in a clause requiring Heraal to perform his suicide stunt at least five but no more than eight times a week."

I felt a satisfied glow. There's nothing more pleasing than to turn a swindle into a sure-fire crowd-puller.

"Aren't you forgetting something, Corrigan?" asked Ildwar Gorb in a quietly menacing voice. "We had a little agreement, you know."

"Oh. Yes." I moistened my lips and glanced shiftily around the office. There had been too many witnesses. I couldn't back down. I had no choice but to write out a check for five grand and give Gorb a standard alien-specimen contract. Unless...

"Just a second," I said. "To enter Earth as an alien exhibit, you need proof of alien origin."

He grinned, pulled out a batch of documents. "Nothing to it. Everything's stamped and in order—and anybody who wants to prove these papers are fraudulent will have to find Wazzenazz XIII first!"

We signed and I filed the contracts away. But only then did it occur to me that the events of the past hour might have been even more complicated than they looked. Suppose, I wondered, Gorb had conspired with Heraal to stage the fake suicide, and run in the cops as well—with contracts for both of them the price of my getting off the hook?

It could very well be. And if it was, it meant I had been taken as neatly as any chump I'd ever conned.

Carefully keeping a poker face, I did a silent burn. Gorb, or whatever his real name was, was going to find himself living up to that contract he'd signed—every damn word and letter of it!

We left Ghryne later that week, having interviewed some eleven hundred alien life forms and having hired fifty-two. It brought the register of our zoo—pardon me, the Institute—to a nice pleasant 742 specimens representing 326 intelligent life forms.

Ildwar Gorb, the Wazzenazzian—who admitted that his real name was Mike Higgins, of St. Louis—turned out to be a tower of strength on the return voyage. It developed that he really did know all there was to know about alien life forms.

When he found out I had turned down the four-hundred-foot-long Vegan because the upkeep would be too big, Gorb-Higgins rushed off to the Vegan's agent and concluded a deal whereby we acquired a fertilized Vegan ovum, weighing hardly more than an ounce. Transporting that was a lot cheaper than lugging a full-grown adult Vegan. Besides which, he assured me that the infant beast could be adapted to a diet of vegetables without any difficulty.

He made life a lot easier for me during the six-week voyage to Earth in our specially constructed ship. With fifty-two alien life forms aboard, all sorts of dietary problems arose, not to mention the headaches that popped up over pride of place and the like. The Kallerian simply refused to be quartered anywhere but on the left-hand side of the ship, for example—but that was the side we had reserved for low-gravity creatures, and there was no room for him there.

"We'll be traveling in hyperspace all the way to Earth," Gorb-Higgins assured the stubborn Kallerian. "Our cosmostatic polarity will be reversed, you see."

"Hah?" asked Heraal in confusion.

"The cosmostatic polarity. If you take a bunk on the left-hand side of the ship, you'll be traveling on the right-hand side all the way there!"

"Oh," said the big Kallerian. "I didn't know that. Thank you for explaining."

He gratefully took the stateroom we assigned him.

Higgins really had a way with the creatures, all right. He made us look like fumbling amateurs, and I had been operating in this business more than fifteen years.

Somehow Higgins managed to be on the spot whenever trouble broke out. A high-strung Norvennith started a feud with a pair of Vanoinans over an alleged moral impropriety—Norvennithi can be very stuffy sometimes. But Gorb convinced the outraged being that what the Vanoinans were doing in the washroom was perfectly proper. Well, it was, but I'd never have thought of using that particular analogy.

I could list half a dozen other incidents in which Gorb-Higgins' special knowledge of outworld beings saved us from annoying hassles on that trip back. It was the first time I had ever had another man with brains in the organization, and I was getting worried.

When I first set up the Institute back in the early 2920s, it was with my own capital, scraped together while running a comparative biology show on Betelgeuse IX. I saw to it that I was the sole owner. And I took care to hire competent but unspectacular men as my staffers—men like Stebbins, Auchinleck, and Ludlow.

Only now I had a viper in my bosom, in the person of this Ildwar Gorb-Mike Higgins. He could think for himself. He knew a good racket when he saw one. We were birds of a feather, Higgins and I. I doubted if there was room for both of us in this outfit.

I sent for him just before we were about to make Earthfall, offered him a few slugs of brandy before I got to the point. "Mike, I've watched the way you handled the exhibits on the way back here."

"The other exhibits," he pointed out. "I'm one of them, not a staff man."

"Your Wazzenazzian status is just a fiction cooked up to get you past the immigration authorities, Mike. But I've got a proposition for you."

"Propose away."

"I'm getting a little too old for this starcombing routine," I said. "Up to now, I've been doing my own recruiting, but only because I couldn't trust anyone else to do the job. I think you could handle it, though." I stubbed out my cigarette and lit another. "Tell you what, Mike—I'll rip up your contract as an exhibit, and I'll give you another one as a staff-man, paying twice as much. Your job will be to roam the planets finding new material for us. How about it?"

I had the new contract all drawn up. I pushed it toward him, but he put his hand down over mine and smiled amiably as he said, "No go."

"No? Not even for twice the pay?"

"I've done my own share of roaming," he said. "Don't offer me more money. I just want to settle down on Earth, Jim. I don't care about the cash. Honest."

It was very touching, and also very phony, but there was nothing I could do. I couldn't get rid of him that way—I had to bring him to Earth.

The immigration officials argued about his papers, but he'd had the things so clearly faked that there was no way of proving he wasn't from Wazzenazz XIII. We set him up in a key spot of the building.

The Kallerian, Heraal, is one of our top attractions now. Every day at two in the afternoon, he commits ritual suicide, and soon afterward rises from death to the accompaniment of a trumpet fanfare. The four other Kallerians we had before are wildly jealous of the crowds he draws, but they're just not trained to do his act.

But the unquestioned number-one attraction here is confidence man Mike Higgins. He's billed as the only absolutely human life form from an extraterrestrial planet, and though we've had our share of debunking, it has only increased business.

Funny that the biggest draw at a zoo like ours should be a homegrown Earthman, but that's show business.

A couple of weeks after we got back, Mike added a new wrinkle to the act. He turned up with a blond showgirl named Marie, and now we have a woman from Wazzenazz too. It's more fun for Mike that way. And downright clever.

He's too clever, in fact. Like I said, I appreciate a good confidence man, the way some people appreciate fine wine. But I wish I had left Ildwar Gorb back on Ghryne instead of signing him up with us.

Yesterday he stopped by at my office after we had closed down for the day. He was wearing that pleasant smile he always wears when he's up to something.

He accepted a drink, as usual, and then he said, "Jim, I was talking to Lawrence R. Fitzgerald yesterday."

"The little Regulan? The green basketball?"

"That's the one. He tells me he's only getting fifty dollars a week. And a lot of the other boys here are drawing pretty low pay too."

My stomach gave a warning twinge. "Mike, if you're looking for a raise, I've told you time and again you're worth it to me. How about twenty a week?"

He held up one hand. "I'm not angling for a raise for me, Jim."

"What then?"

He smiled beatifically. "The boys and I held a little meeting yesterday evening, and we—ah—formed a union, with me as leader. I'd like to discuss the idea of a general wage increase for every one of the exhibits here."

"Higgins, you blackmailer, how can I afford—"

"Easy," he said. "You'd hate to lose a few weeks' gross, wouldn't you?"

"You mean you'd call a strike?"

He shrugged. "If you leave me no choice, how else can I protect my members' interests?"

After about half an hour of haggling, he sweated me into an across-the-board increase for the entire mob, with a distinct hint of further raises to come. But he also casually let me know the price he's asking to call off the hounds. He wants a partnership in the Institute; a share in the receipts.

If he gets that, it makes him a member of management, and he'll have to quit as union leader. That way I won't have him to contend with as a negotiator.

But I will have him firmly embedded in the organization, and once he gets his foot in the door, he won't be satisfied until he's on top—which means when I'm out.

But I'm not licked yet! Not after a full lifetime of conniving and swindling! I've been over and over the angles and there's one thing you can always count on—a trickster will always outsmart himself if you give him the chance. I did it with Higgins. Now he's done it with me.

He'll be back here in half an hour to find out whether he gets his partnership or not. Well, he'll get his answer. I'm going to affirm, as per the escape clause in the standard exhibit contract he signed, that he is no longer of scientific value, and the Feds will pick him up and deport him to his home world.

That leaves him two equally nasty choices.

Those fake documents of his were good enough to get him admitted to Earth as a legitimate alien. How the World Police get him back there is their headache—and his.

If he admits the papers were phony, the only way he'll get out of prison will be when it collapses of old age.

So I'll give him a third choice: He can sign an undated confession, which I will keep in my safe, as guarantee against future finagling.

I don't expect to be around forever, you see—though, with that little secret I picked up on Rimbaud II, it'll be a good long time, not even barring accidents—and I've been wondering whom to leave the Corrigan Institute of Morphological Science to. Higgins will make a fine successor.

Oh, one more thing he will have to sign. It remains the Corrigan Institute as long as the place is in business.

Try to out-con me, will he?

BLAZE OF GLORY

Originally published in *Galaxy*, August 1957.

They list John Murchison as one of the great heroes of space—a brave man and true, who willingly sacrificed himself to save his ship. He won his immortality on the way back from Shaula II.

One thing's wrong, though. He was brave, but he wasn't willing. He wasn't the self-sacrificing type. I'm inclined to think it was murder, or maybe execution. By remote control, you might say.

I guess they pick spaceship crews at random—say, by yanking a handful of cards from the big computer and throwing them up at the BuSpace roof. The ones that stick get picked. At least, that's the only way a man like Murchison could have been sent to Shaula II in the first place.

He was a spaceman of the old school, tall, bullnecked, coarse-featured, hard-swearing. He was a spaceman of a type that had never existed except in storytapes for the very young—the only kind Murchison was likely to have viewed. He was our chief signal officer.

Somewhere, he had picked up an awesome technical competence; he could handle any sort of communication device with supernatural ease. I once saw him tinker with a complex little Caphian artifact that had been buried for half a million years, and have it detecting the 21-centimeter "hydrogen song" within minutes. How he knew the little widget was a star-mapping device I will never understand.

But coupled with Murchison's extraordinary special skill was an irascibility, a self-centered inner moodiness flaring into seemingly unmotivated anger at unpredictable times, that made him a prime risk on a planet like Shaula II. There was something wrong with his circuit-breaker setup: you could never tell when he'd overload, start fizzing and sparking, and blow off a couple of megawatts of temper.

You must admit this is not the ideal sort of man to send to a world whose inhabitants are listed in the E-T Catalogue as *"wise, somewhat world-weary, exceedingly gentle, non-aggressive to an extreme degree and thus subject to exploitation. The Shaulans must be handled with great patience and forbearance, and should be given the respect due one of the galaxy's elder races."*

I had never been to Shaula II, but I had a sharp mental image of the Shaulans: melancholy old men pondering the whichness of the why and ready to fall apart at the first loud voice that caught them by surprise. So it caught me by surprise when the time came to affix my hancock to the roster of the *Felicific*, and I saw on the line above mine the scribbled words *Murchison, John F., Signalman First Class.*

I signed my name—*Loeb, Ernest T., Second Officer*—picked up my pay voucher, and walked away somewhat dizzily. I was thinking of the time I had seen Murchison, John F., giving a Denebolan frogman the beating of his life, for no particular reason at all. "All the rain here makes me sick" was all Murchison cared to say; the frogman lived and Big Jawn got an X on his psych report.

Now he was shipping out for Shaula? Well, maybe so...but my faith in the computer that makes up spaceship complements was seriously shaken.

* * * *

We were the fourth or fifth expedition to Shaula II. The planet—second of seven in orbit round the brightest star in Scorpio's tail—was small and scrubby, but of great strategic importance as a lookout spot for that sector of the galaxy. The natives hadn't minded our intrusion, and so a military base had been established there after a little preliminary haggling.

The *Felicific* was a standard warp-conversion-drive ship holding thirty-six men. It had the usual crew of eight, plus a cargo of twenty-eight of Terra's finest, being sent out as replacements for the current staff of the base.

We blasted on 3 July 2530, a warmish day, made the conversion from ion-drive to warp-drive as soon as we were clear of the local system, and popped back into normal space three weeks later and two hundred light-years away. It was a routine trip in all respects.

With the warp-conversion drive, a ship is equipped to travel both long distances and short. It handles the long hops via subspace warp, and the short ones by good old standard ion-drive seat-of-the-spacesuit navigating. It's a good system, and the extra mass the double drive requires is more than compensated for by the saving in time and maneuverability.

The warp-drive part of the trip was pre-plotted and just about pre-traveled for us; no headaches *there*. But when we blurped back into the continuum about half a light-year from Shaula the human factor entered the situation. Meaning Murchison, of course.

It was his job to check and tend the network of telemetering systems that acted as the ship's eyes, to make sure the mass-detectors were operating, to smooth the bugs out of the communications channels between navigator and captain and drive-deck. In brief, he was the man who made it possible for us to land.

Every ship carried a spare signalman, just in case. In normal circumstances the spare never got much work. When the time came for the landing, Captain Knight buzzed me and told me to start lining up the men who would take part, and I signaled Murchison first.

His voice was a slow rasping drawl. "Yeah?"

"Second Officer Loeb. Prepare for landing, double-fast. Navigator Henrichs has the chart set up for you and he's waiting for your call."

There was a pause. Then: "I don't feel like it, Loeb."

It was my turn to pause. I shut my eyes, held my breath, and counted to three by fractions. Then I said, "Would you mind repeating that, Signalman Murchison?"

"Yes, sir. No, sir, I mean. Hell, Loeb, I'm fixing something. Why do you want to land now?"

"I don't make up the schedules," I said.

"Then who in blazes does? Tell him I'm busy!"

I turned down my phones' volume. "Busy doing what?"

"Busy doing nothing. Get off the line and I'll call Henrichs."

I sighed and broke contact. He'd just been ragging me. Once again, Murchison had been ornery for the sheer sake of being ornery. One of these days he was going to refuse to handle the landing entirely.

And that day, I told myself, is the day we'll crate him up and shove him through the disposal lock.

Murchison was a little island. He had his skills, and he applied them—when he felt like it. But only when he believed that he, Murchison, would profit. He never did anything unwillingly, because if he couldn't find it in himself to do it willingly he wouldn't do it at all. It was impossible to *make* him do something.

Unwisely, we tolerated it. But someday he would get a captain who didn't understand him, and he'd be slapped with a sentence of mutiny during a fit of temperament. For his sake, I hoped not. The penalty for mutiny in space is death.

* * * *

With Murchison's cooperation gratefully accepted, we targeted on Shaula II, which was then at perihelion, and orbited it. Down in his little cubicle Murchison worked like a demon, taking charge of the ship's landing system in a tremendous way. He was a fantastic signalman when he wanted to be.

Later that day the spinning red ball that was Shaula II hung just ahead of us, close enough to let us see the three blobs of continents and the big, choppy hydrocarbon ocean that licked them smooth. The Terran base on Continent Three beamed as a landing-guide; Murchison picked it up, fed it through the computer bank to Navigator Henrichs, and we homed in for the landing.

The Terran base consisted of a couple of blockhouses, a sprawling barracks, and a good-sized radar parabola, all set in a ring out on an almost mathematically flat plain. Shaula II was a great world for plains; Columbus would have had the devil's time convincing people *this* world was round!

Murchison guided us to a glassy-looking area not far from the base, and we touched down. The *Felicific* creaked and groaned a little as the landing jacks absorbed its weight. Green lights went on all over the ship. We were free to go outside.

A welcoming committee was on hand: eight members of the base staff, clad in shorts and topees. Regulation uniforms went by the board on oven-hot Shaula II. The eight looked awfully happy to see us.

Coming over the flat sandy plain from the base were a dozen or so others, running, and behind them I could see even more. They were understandably glad we were here. Twenty-eight of them had spent a full year on Shaula II; they were eligible for their parity-program year's vacation.

There were some other—things—moving towards us. They moved slowly, with grace and dignity. I had expected to be impressed with the Shaulans, and I was.

They were erect bipeds about four feet tall, with long thin arms dangling to their knees; their grey skins were grainy and rough, and their dark eyes—they had three, arranged triangularly—were deepset and brooding. A fleshy sort of cowl or cobra-hood curled up from their necks to shield their round hairless skulls. The aliens were six in number, and the youngest-looking of them seemed ancient.

A brown-faced young man wearing shorts, topee, and tattooed stars stepped forward and said, "I'm General Gloster. I'm in charge here."

The Captain acknowledged his greeting. "Knight of the *Felicific*. We have your relief men with us."

"I sure as hell hope you do," Gloster said. "Be kind of silly to come all this way without them."

We all laughed a little over that. By now we were ringed in by at least fifty Earthmen, probably the entire base complement (we didn't rotate the entire base staff at once, of course), and the six aliens. The twenty-eight kids we had ferried here were looking around the place curiously, apprehensive about this hot, dry, flat planet that would be their home for the next sidereal year. The crew of the *Felicific* had gathered in a little knot near the ship. Most of them probably felt the way I did; they were glad we'd be on our way home in a couple of days.

Murchison was squinting at the six aliens. I wondered what he was thinking about.

* * * *

The bunch of us traipsed back the half mile or so to the settlement; Gloster walked with Knight and myself, prattling volubly about the progress the base was making, and the twenty-eight newcomers mingled with the twenty-eight who were being relieved. Murchison walked by himself, kicking up puffs of red dust and scowling in his usual manner. The six aliens accompanied us at some distance.

"We keep building all the time," Gloster explained when we were within the compound. "Branching out, setting up new equipment, shoring up the old stuff: That radar parabola out there wasn't up, last replacement-trip."

I looked around. "The place looks fine, General." It was strange calling a man half my age *General*, but the Service sometimes works that way. "When do you plan to set up your telescope?"

"Next year, maybe." He glanced out the window at the featureless landscape. "We keep building all the time. It's the best way to stay sane on this world."

"How about the natives?" the Captain asked. "You have much contact with them?"

Gloster shrugged. "As much as they'll allow. They're a proud old race—pretty near dried up and dead now, just a handful of them left. But what a race they must have been once! What minds! What culture!"

I found Gloster's boyish enthusiasm discomforting. "Do you think we could meet one of the aliens before we go?" I asked.

"I'll see about it." Gloster picked up a phone. "McHenry? There any natives in the compound now? Good. Send him up, will you?"

Moments later one of the shorts-clad men appeared, hand in hand with an alien. At close range the Shaulan looked almost frighteningly old. A maze of wrinkles gullied its noseless face, running from the triple optics down to the dots of nostrils to the sagging, heavy-lipped mouth.

"This is Azga," Gloster said. "Azga, meet Captain Knight and Second Officer Loeb, of the *Felicific*."

The creature offered a wobbly sort of curtsey and said, in a deep, resonant, almost-human croak, "I am very humble indeed in your presence, Captain Knight and Second Officer Loeb."

BLAZE OF GLORY | 43

Azga came out of the curtsey and the three eyes fixed on mine. I felt like squirming, but I stared back. It was like looking into a mirror that gave the wrong reflection.

Yet I enjoyed my proximity to the alien. There was something calm and wise and good about the grotesque creature; something relaxing, and terribly fragile. The rough grey skin looked like precious leather, and the hood over the skull appeared to shield it from worry and harm. A faint musty odor wandered through the room.

We looked at each other—Knight, and Gloster, and McHenry, and I—and we remained silent. Now that the Shaulan was here, what could we say? What new thing could we possibly tell the ancient creature?

I resisted an impulse to kneel. I was fumbling for words to express my emotion when the sharp buzz of the phone cut across the room.

Gloster nodded curtly to McHenry, who answered. The man listened for a moment. "Captain Knight, it's for you."

Puzzled, Knight took the receiver. He held it long enough to hear about three sentences and turned to me. "Loeb, get a landcar from someone in the compound and get back to the ship. Murchison's carrying on with one of the aliens."

* * * *

I hotfooted down into the compound and spotted an enlisted man tooling up his landcar. I pulled rank and requisitioned it, and minutes later I was parking it outside the *Felicific* and was clambering hand-over-hand up the catwalk.

An excited-looking recruit stood at the open airlock.

"Where's Murchison?" I asked.

"Down in the communicator cabin. He's got an alien in there with him. There's gonna be trouble."

I remembered Denebola, and Murchison kicking the stuffings out of a groaning frogman. I groaned a little myself, and dashed down the companionway.

The communications cabin was Murchison's *sanctum sanctorum*, a cubicle off the astro deck where he worked and kept control over the *Felicific*'s communications network. I yanked open the door and saw Murchison at the far end of the cabin holding a massive crescent wrench and glaring at a Shaulan facing him. The Shaulan had its back to me. It looked small and squat and helpless.

Murchison saw me as I entered. "Get out of here, Loeb. This isn't your affair."

"What's going on here?" I snapped.

"This alien snooping around. I'm gonna let him have it with the wrench."

"I meant no harm," the alien boomed sadly. "Mere philosophical interest in your strange machines, nothing more. If I have offended a folkway of yours I humbly apologize. It is not the way of my people to give offence."

I walked forward and took a position between them, making sure I wasn't within easy reach of Murchison's wrench. He was standing there with his nostrils spread, his eyes cold and hard, his breath pumping noisily. He was angry, and an angry Murchison was a frightening sight.

He took two heavy steps toward me. "I told you to get out. This is my cabin, Loeb. And neither you or any aliens got any business in it."

"Put down that wrench, Murchison. It's an order."

He laughed contemptuously. "Signalman First Class don't have to take orders from anyone but the Captain if he thinks the safety of the ship is jeopardized. And I do. There's a dangerous alien in here."

"Be reasonable," I said. "This Shaulan's not dangerous. He just wanted to look around. Just curious."

The wrench wiggled warningly. I wished I had a blaster with me, but I hadn't thought of bringing a weapon. The alien faced Murchison quite complacently, as if confident the signalman would never strike anything so old and delicate.

"You'd better leave," I said to the alien.

"No!" Murchison roared. He shoved me to one side and went after the Shaulan.

The alien stood there, waiting, as Murchison came on. I tried to drag the big man away, but there was no stopping him.

At least he didn't use the wrench. He let the big crescent slip clangingly to the floor and slapped the alien open-handed across its face. The Shaulan backed up a few feet. A trickle of bluish fluid worked its way along its mouth. Murchison raised his hand again. "Damned snooper! I'll teach you to poke in my cabin!" He hit the alien again.

This time the Shaulan folded up accordionwise and huddled on the floor. It focused those three deep solid-black eyes on Murchison reproachfully.

Murchison looked back. They stared at each other for a long, moment, until it seemed that their eyes were linked by an invisible cord. Then Murchison looked away.

"Get out of here," he muttered to the alien, and the Shaulan rose and departed, limping a little but still intact. Those aliens were more solid than they seemed.

"I guess you're going to put me in the brig," Murchison said to me. "Okay. I'll go quietly."

BLAZE OF GLORY | 45

* * * *

We didn't brig him, because there was nothing to be gained by that. I had seen the explosion coming right from the start. When you drop a lighted match into a tub of hydrazine, you don't punish the hydrazine for blowing up. And Murchison couldn't be blamed for what he did, either.

He got the silent treatment instead. The men at the base would have nothing to do with him whatsoever, because in their year on Shaula they had developed a respect for the aliens not far from worship, and any man who would actually use physical violence—well, he just wasn't worth wasting breath on.

The men of our crew gave him a wide berth too. He wandered among us, a tall, powerful figure with anger and loneliness stamped on his face, and he said nothing to any of us and no one said anything to him. Whenever he saw one of the aliens, he went far out of his way to avoid a meeting.

Murchison got another X on his psych report, and that second X meant he'd never be allowed to visit any world inhabited by intelligent life again. It was a BuSpace regulation, one of the many they have for the purpose of locking the barn door too late.

Three days went by this way on Shaula. On the fourth, we took aboard the twenty-eight departing men, said goodbye to Gloster and his staff and the twenty-eight we had ferried out to him, and—somewhat guiltily—goodbye to the Shaulans too.

The six of them showed up for our blastoff, including the somewhat battered one who had had the run-in with Murchison. They wished us well, gravely, without any sign of bitterness. For the hundredth time I was astonished by their patience, their wisdom, their understanding.

I held Azga's rough hand in mine and said goodbye. I told him for the first time what I had been wanting to say since our first meeting, how much I hoped we'd eventually reach the mental equilibrium and inner calm of the Shaulans. He smiled warmly at me, and I said goodbye again and entered the ship.

We ran the usual pre-blast checkups, and got ready for departure. Everything was working well; Murchison had none of his usual grumbles and complaints, and we were off the ground in record time.

A couple of days of ion-drive, three weeks of warp, two more of ion-drive deceleration, and we would be back on Earth.

* * * *

The three weeks passed slowly, of course; when Earth lies ahead of you, time drags. But after the interminable greyness of warp came the sudden wrenching twist and the bright slippery *sliding* feeling as our

Bohling generator threw us back into ordinary space.

I pushed down the communicator stud near my arm and heard the voice of Navigator Henrichs saying, "Murchison, give me the coordinates, will you?"

"Hold on," came Murchison's growl. "Patience, Sam. You'll get your coordinates as soon as I got 'em."

There was a pause; then Captain Knight said, "Murchison, what's holding up those coordinates? Where are we, anyway? Turn on the visiplates?"

"*Please*, Captain." Murchison's heavy voice was surprisingly polite. Then he ruined it. "Please, be good enough to shut up and let a man think."

"Murchison—" Knight sputtered, and stopped. We all knew one solid fact about our signalman: he did as he pleased. No one but no one coerced him into anything.

So we waited, spinning end-over-end somewhere in the vicinity of Earth, completely blind behind our wall of metal. Until Murchison chose to feed us some data, we had no way of bringing the ship down.

Three more minutes went by; then the private circuit Knight uses when he wants to talk to me alone lit up, and he said, "Loeb, go down to Communications and see what's holding Murchison up. We can't stay here forever."

"Yessir."

I pocketed a blaster—I hate making mistakes more than once—and left my cabin. I walked numbly to the companionway, turned to the left, hit the drophatch and found myself outside Murchison's door.

I knocked.

"Get away from here, Loeb!" Murchison bellowed from within.

I had forgotten that he had rigged a one-way vision circuit outside his door. I said, "Let me in, Murchison. Let me in or I'll come in blasting."

I heard a heavy sigh. "Come on in, then."

Nervously I pushed the door open and poked my head and the blaster snout in, half expecting Murchison to leap on me from above. But he was sitting at an equipment-jammed desk scribbling notes, which surprised me. I stood waiting for him to look up.

And finally he did. I gasped when I saw his face: drawn, harried, pale, tense. I had never seen an expression like that on Murchison's face before.

"What's going on?" I asked softly. "We're all waiting to get moving, and—"

He turned to face me squarely. "You want to know what's going on, Loeb? Well, listen: the ship's blind. None of the equipment is reading anything. No telemeter pickup, no visual, no nothing. *You* scrape up some coordinates, if you can."

We held a little meeting half an hour later, in the ship's Common Room. Murchison was there, and Knight, and myself, and Navigator Henrichs, and three representatives of the cargo.

"How did this happen?" Knight demanded.

Murchison shrugged. "It happened while we were in warp. We passed through something—magnetic field, maybe—and bollixed every instrument we have."

Knight glanced at Henrichs. "You ever hear of such a thing happening before?" He seemed to suspect Murchison of funny business.

But Henrichs shook his head. "No, Chief. And there's a good reason why, too. If this happens to a ship, the ship doesn't get back to tell about it."

He was right. With no contact at all with the outside, no information on location or orbits, there was no way to land the ship. And the radio, of course, was dead too; we couldn't even call for help.

Captain Knight looked grey-faced and very old. He asked worriedly, "What could have caused this thing?"

"No one knows what subspace conditions are like," Henrichs said. "It may have been a fluke magnetic field, as Murchison suggests. Or anything at all—an alien entity that swallowed our antennae, for all we know. The question's not what did it, Captain—it's how do we get back."

"Good point. Murchison, is there any chance you can repair the instruments?"

"No."

"Just like that—flat *no?* Hell, man, we've seen you do wonders with instruments on the blink before."

"No," Murchison repeated stolidly. "I tried. I can't do a damned thing."

"That means we're finished, doesn't it?" asked Ramirez, one of our returnees. His voice was a little wild. "We might just as well have stayed on Shaula! At least we'd still be alive!"

"It looks pretty lousy," Henrichs admitted. The thin-faced navigator was frowning blackly. "We don't dare try a blind landing. There's nothing we can do. Nothing at all."

"There's *one* thing," Murchison said.

All eyes turned to him. "What?" Knight asked.

"Put a man in a spacesuit and anchor him to the skin of the ship. Have him guide us in by verbal instructions. It's a way, anyway."

"Pretty farfetched," Henrichs commented.

"Yes, dammit, but it's our only hope!" Murchison snapped. "Stick a man up there and let him talk us in."

"He'd incinerate once we hit Earth's atmosphere," I said. "We'd lose a man and still have to land blind."

Murchison puckered his thick lower lip. "You'll be able to judge the ship's height by hull temperature once you're that close. Besides, once the ship's inside the ionosphere you can use ordinary radio for the rest of the way down. The trick is to get *that* far."

"I think it's worth a try," Captain Knight said. "I guess we'll have to draw lots. Loeb, get some straws from the galley." His voice was grim.

"Never mind," Murchison said.

"Huh?"

"I said, never mind. Skip it. Forget about drawing straws. *I'll* go."

"Murchison—"

"*Skip it!*" he barked. "It's a failure in my department, so I'm going to go out there. I volunteer, get it? If anyone else wants to volunteer, I'll match him for it." He looked around at us. No one moved. "I don't hear any takers. I'll assume the job's mine." Sweat streamed down his face.

There was a startled silence, broken when Ramirez made the lousiest remark I've ever heard mortal man utter. "You're trying to make it up for hitting that defenseless Shaulan, eh, Murchison? Now you want to be a hero to even things up!"

If Murchison had killed him on the spot, I think we'd all have applauded. But the big man only turned to Ramirez and said quietly, "You're just as blind as the others. You don't know how rotten those defenseless Shaulans are, any of you. Or what they did to me." He spat. "You all make me sick. I'm going out there."

He turned and walked away…out, to get into his spacesuit and climb into the ship's skin.

* * * *

Murchison's explicit instructions, relayed from the outside of the ship, allowed Henrichs to bring us in. It was quite a feat of teamwork.

At 50,000 feet above Earth, Murchison's voice suddenly cut out. We were able to pick up ground-to-ship radio by then and we taxied down. Later, they told us it seemed like a blazing candle was riding the ship's back. A bright, clear flame flared for a moment as we cleaved the atmosphere.

And I remember the look on Murchison's face as he left us to go out there. It was tense, bitter, strained—as if he were being *compelled* to go outside. As if he had no choice about volunteering for martyrdom.

I often wonder about that now. No one had ever made Murchison do

BLAZE OF GLORY | 49

anything he didn't want to do—until then.

We think of the Shaulans as gentle, meek, defenseless. Murchison crossed one of them, and he died. Gentle, meek, yes—but defenseless? Murchison didn't think so.

Maybe they whammied the ship and cursed Murchison with the urge to self-martyrdom, to punish him. Maybe. He never did trust them much.

It sort of tarnishes his glorious halo. But you know, sometimes I think Murchison was right about the Shaulans after all.

DELIVERY GUARANTEED

Originally published in *Science Fiction Stories*, February 1959, under the pseudonym "Calvin Knox."

There aren't many free-lance space-ferry operators who can claim that they carried a log cabin half way from Mars to Ganymede, and then had the log cabin carry them the rest of the way. I can, though you can bet your last tarnished megabuck that I didn't do it willingly. It was quite a trip. I left Mars not only with a log cabin on board, but a genuine muzzle-loading antique cannon, a goodly supply of cannonballs therefrom, and various other miscellaneous antiques—as well as the Curator of Historical Collections from the Ganymede Museum. There was also a stowaway on board, much to his surprise and mine—he wasn't listed in the cargo vouchers.

Let me make one thing clear: I wasn't keen on carrying any such cargo. But my free-lance ferry operator's charter is quite explicit that way, unfortunately. A ferry operator is required to hire his ship to any person of law-abiding character who will meet the (government-fixed) rates, and whose cargo to be transported neither exceeds the ship's weight allowance nor is considered contraband by any System law.

In short, I'm available to just about all comers. By the terms of my charter I've been compelled to ferry five hundred marmosets to Pluto, forced to haul ten tons of Venusian guano to Callisto, constrained to deliver fifty crates of fertilized frogs' eggs from Earth to a research station orbiting Neptune. In the latter case I made the trip twice for the same fee, thanks to the delivery guaranteed clause in the contract; the first time out my radiation shields slipped up for a few seconds, not causing me any particular genetic hardships but playing merry hell with those frog's eggs. When a bunch of four-headed tadpoles began to hatch, they served notice on me that they were not accepting delivery and would pay no fee—and, what's more, would sue if I didn't bring another load of potential frogs up from Earth, and be damned well careful about the shielding this time.

So I hauled another fifty crates of frogs' eggs, this time without mishap, and collected my fee. But I've never been happy about carrying livestock again.

This new offer wasn't livestock. I got the call while I was laying over on Mars after a trip up from Luna with a few colonists and their gear. I had submitted my name to the Transport Registry, informing them that I was on call and waiting for employment—but I was in no hurry. I still had a couple of hundred megabucks left from the last job, and I didn't mind a vacation.

The call came on the third day of my Martian layover. "Collect call for Mr. Sam Diamond, from the Transport Registry. Do you accept?"

"Yes," I muttered, and $30,000 more was chalked to my phone bill. A dollar doesn't last hardly any time at all in these days of system-wide hyperinflation.

"Sam?" a deep voice said. It was Mike Cooper of the Transport people.

"Who else would it be at this end of your collect call?" I growled. "And why can't you people pay for a phone call once in a while?"

"You know the law, Sam," Cooper said cheerfully. "I've got a job for you."

"That's nice. Another load of marmosets?"

"Nothing live this time, Sam, except your passenger. She's Miss Vanderweghe of the Ganymede Museum. Curator of Historical Collections. She wants someone to ferry her back to Ganymede with some historical relics she's picked up along the way."

"The Washington Monument?" I asked. "The Great Pyramid of Khufu? We could tow it alongside the ship, lashed down with twine—"

"Knock it off," Cooper said, unamused. "What she's got are souvenirs of the Venusian Insurrection. The log cabin that served as Macintyre's headquarters, the cannon used to drive back the Bluecoats, and a few smaller knickknacks along those lines."

"Hold it," I said. "You can't fit a log cabin into my ship. And if it's going to be a tow job, I want the Delivery Guaranteed clause stricken out of the contract. And how much does the damn cannon weigh? I've got a weight ceiling, you know."

"I know. Her entire cargo is less than eight tons, cannon and all. It's well within your tonnage restrictions. And as for the log cabin, it doesn't need to be towed. She's agreed to take it apart for shipping, and reassemble it when it gets to Ganymede."

The layover had been nice while it lasted. I said, "I was looking for some rest, Mike. Isn't there some angle I can use to wiggle out of this cargo?"

"None."

"But—"

"There isn't another free ferry in town tonight. She wants to leave tonight. So you're the boy, Sam. The job is yours."

I opened my mouth. I closed it again. Ferries are considered public services, under the law. The only way I could get a vacation that was sure to last was to apply for one in advance, and I hadn't done that.

"Okay," I said wearily. "When do I sign the contract?"

"Miss Vanderweghe is at my office now," Cooper said. "How soon can you get here?"

* * * *

I was in a surly mood as I rode downtown to Cooper's place. For the thousandth time I resented the casual way he could pluck me out of some relaxation and make me take a job. I wasn't looking forward to catering to the whims of some dried-up old museum curator all the way out to Ganymede. And I wasn't too pleased with the notion of carrying relics of the Venusian Insurrection.

The Insurrection had caused quite a fuss, a hundred years back. Bunch of Venusian colonists decided they didn't like Earth's rule—the taxation-without-representation bit, though their squawk was unjustified—and set up a wildcat independent government, improvising their equipment out of whatever they could grab. A chap name of Macintyre was in charge; the insurrectionists holed up in the jungle and held off the attacking loyalists for a couple of weeks. Then the Venusian local government appealed to Earth, a regiment of Bluecoats was shipped to Venus, and inside of a week Macintyre was a prisoner and the Insurrection ended. But some diehard Venusians still venerated the insurrectionists, and there had been a few murders and ambushes every year since the overthrow of Macintyre. I could have done without carrying Venusian cargo.

I was going to say as much to Cooper, too, in hopes that some clause of my charter would get me out of the assignment and back on vacation. But I didn't get a chance. I went storming into Cooper's office.

There was a girl sitting in the chair to the left of his desk. She was about twenty-five, well built in most every way possible, with glossy, short-cropped hair and an attractive face.

Cooper stood up and said, "Sam, I'd like you to meet Miss Erna Vanderweghe of Ganymede. Miss Vanderweghe, this is Sam Diamond, one of the best ferry men there is. He'll get you to Ganymede in style."

"I'm sure of that," she said, smiling.

"Hello," I said, gulping.

I didn't bother raising a fuss about the political implications of my cargo. I didn't grouse about weight limits, space problems aboard ship, accommodation difficulties, or anything else. I reached for the contract—it was the standard printed form, with the variables typed in by Cooper—and signed it.

"I'd like to leave tonight," she said.

"Sure. My ship's at the spaceport. Can you have your cargo delivered there by—oh, say, 1700 hours? That way we can blast off by 2100."

"I'll try. Will you be able to help me get my goods out of storage and down to the spaceport?"

I started to say that I'd be delighted to, but Cooper cut in sharply, as I knew he would. "I'm sorry, Miss Vanderweghe, but Sam's contract and charter prohibit him from any landside cargo-handling except within the actual bounds of the spaceport. You'll have to use a local carrier for getting your stuff to the ship, I'm afraid. If you want me to, I'll arrange for transportation—"

My mood was considerably different as I returned to the Deimos to check out. My tub would need five days for the journey between Mars and Ganymede. Now, conditions aboard my ship allow for a certain amount of passenger privacy, but not a devil of a lot. Log cabin or no log cabin, I was going to enjoy the proximity of Miss Erna Vanderweghe. I could think of worse troubles than having to spend five days in the same small ferry with her, and only a log cabin and a cannon for chaperones.

I was grinning as I walked over to the desk to let them know I was pulling out. Nat, the desk clerk, interpreted the grin logically enough, but wrongly.

"You talked them out of giving you the job, eh, Sam? How'd you work it?"

"Huh? Oh—no, I took the job. I'm checking out of here at 1800 hours."

"You *took* it? But you look *happy*!"

"I am," I said with a mysterious expression. I started to saunter away, but Nat called me back.

"You had a visitor a little while ago, Mr. Cooper. He wanted me to let him into your room to wait for you, but naturally I wouldn't do it."

"Visitor? Did he leave his name?"

"He's still here. Sitting right over there, next to the potted palm tree."

Frowning, I walked toward him. He was a thin, hunched-up little man with the sallow look of a Venusian colonist. He was busily reading some cheap dime-novel sort of magazine as I approached.

"Hello," I said affably. "I'm Sam Diamond. You wanted to see me?"

"You're ferrying Erna Vanderweghe to Ganymede tonight, aren't you?" His voice was thinly whining, nasty sounding, mean.

"I make a practice of keeping my business to myself," I told him. "If you're interested in hiring a ferry, you'd better go to the Transport Registry. I'm booked."

"I know you are. And I know who you're carrying. And I know *what* you're carrying."

"Look here, friend, I—"

"You're carrying General Macintyre's cabin, and other priceless relics of the Venusian Republic—and all stolen goods!" His eyes had a fanatic gleam about them. I realized who he was as soon as he used the expression "Venusian Republic." Only an insurrectionist-sympathizer would refer to the rebel group that way.

"I'm not going to discuss business affairs with you," I said. "My cargo has been officially cleared."

"It was stolen by that woman! Purchased with filthy dollars and taken from Venus by stealth!"

I started to walk away. I hate having some loudmouthed fanatic rant at me. But he followed, clutching at my elbows, and said in his best conspiratorial tone, "I warn you, Diamond—cancel that contract or you'll suffer! Those relics must return to Venus!"

Whirling around, I disengaged his hands from my arm and snapped, "I couldn't cancel a contract if I wanted to—and I don't want to. Get out of here or I'll have you jugged, whoever you are."

"Remember the warning—"

"Go on! Shoo! Scat!"

He slinked out of the lobby. Shaking my head, I went upstairs to pack. Damned idiotic cloak-and-dagger morons, I thought. Creeping around hissing warnings and leaving threatening notes, and in general trying to keep alive an underground movement that never had any real reason for existing from the start. It wasn't as if Earth had oppressed the Venusian colonists. The benefits flowed all in one direction, from Earth to Venus, and everyone on Venus knew it except for Macintyre's little bunch of ultranationalistic glory-hounds. Nobody on Venus wanted independence less than the colonists themselves, who had dandy tax exemptions and benefits from the mother world.

I forgot all about the threats by the time I was through packing my meager belongings and had grabbed a meal at the hotel restaurant. Around 1800 hours I went down to the spaceport to see what was happening there. The mechanics had already wheeled my ferry out of the storage hangars; she was out on the field getting checked over for blastoff. Erna Vanderweghe and her cargo had arrived, too. She was standing at the edge of the field, supervising the unloading of her stuff from the van of a local carrier.

The log cabin had been taken apart. It consisted of a stack of stout logs, the longest of them some sixteen feet long and the rest tapering down.

"You think you're going to be able to put that cabin back the way it was?" I asked.

"Oh, certainly. I've got each log numbered to correspond with a diagram I've made. The reassembling shouldn't be any trouble at all," she said, smiling sweetly.

I eyed the other stuff—several crates, a few smaller packages, and a cannon, not very big. "Where'd you get all these things?" I asked.

She shrugged prettily. "I bought them on Venus. Most of them were the property of descendants of the insurrectionists; they were quite happy to sell. There weren't any ferries available on Venus, so I took a commercial liner on the shuttle from Venus to Mars. They said I'd be able to get a ferry here."

"And you did," I said. "In five days we'll be landing on Ganymede."

"I can't wait to get there—to set up my exhibit!"

I frowned. "Tell me something, Miss Vanderweghe. Just how did you manage to—ah—make such an early start in the museum business?"

She grinned. "My father and grandfather were museum curators. I just come by it naturally, I suppose. And I was just about the only colonist on Ganymede who was halfway interested in having the job!"

I chuckled softly and said, "When Cooper told me I was ferrying a museum curator, I pictured a dried-up old spinster who'd nag me all the way to Ganymede. I couldn't have been wronger."

"Disappointed?"

"Not very much," I said.

* * * *

We had the ship loaded inside of an hour, everything stowed neatly away in the hold and Miss Vanderweghe's personal luggage strapped down in the passenger compartment. Since there wasn't any reason for hanging around longer, I recomputed my takeoff orbit and called the control center for authorization to blast off at 2000 hours, an hour ahead of schedule.

They were agreeable, and at 1955 hours the field sirens started to scream, warning people of an impending blast. Miss Vanderweghe—Erna—was aft, in her acceleration cradle, as I jabbed the keys that would activate the autopilot and take us up.

I started to punch the keys. The computer board started to click. There was nothing left for me to do but strap myself in and wait for brennschluss. A blastoff from Mars is no great problem in astronautics.

As the automatic took over, I flipped my seat back, converting it into an acceleration cradle, and relaxed. It seemed to me that the takeoff was a little on the bumpy side, as if I'd figured the ship's mass wrong by one or two hundred pounds. But I didn't worry about the discrepancy. I just shut my eyes and waited while the extra gees bore down on me. The sanest thing for a man to do during blastoff is to go to sleep, and that's what I did.

I woke up half an hour or so later to discover that the engines had cut out, the ship was safely in flight, and that a bloody and battered figure was bent over my controls, energetically ruining them with crowbar and shears.

I blinked. Then the fog in my head cleared and I got out of my cradle. The stowaway turned around. He was quite a mess. The capillaries of his face had popped during the brief moments of top acceleration, and fine purplish lines now wriggled over his cheeks and nose, giving him a grade-A rum blossom, and bloodshot eyes to go with it. He had some choice bruises that he must have acquired while rattling around during blastoff, and his nose had been bleeding all over his shirt. It was the little Venusian fanatic who had threatened me at the hotel.

"How the hell did you get aboard?" I demanded.

"Slipped through the security checkers...but the ship took off ahead of schedule. I did not expect to be on board when blastoff came."

"Sorry to have fouled up your plans," I told him.

"But I regained consciousness in time. Your ship is ruined! You refused to heed my warning, and now you will never reach Ganymede alive. So perish all enemies of the Venusian Republic! So perish those who have desecrated our noble shrines!"

He was practically foaming at the mouth. I started toward him. He swung the crowbar and might have bashed my head in if he had known how to handle himself under nograv conditions, but he didn't, and the only result of his exertion was to send himself drifting toward the roof of the cabin. I yanked on his leg as it went past me and dragged him down. The crowbar dropped from his numb hand. I caught it and poked him across the head with it.

There isn't any hesitation in a spaceman's mind when he finds a stowaway. Fuel is a precious thing, and so is air and food; stowaways simply aren't allowed to live. I didn't feel any qualms about what I did next, but all the same I was glad that Erna Vanderweghe wasn't awake and watching me while I went about it.

I slipped into my breathing-helmet and sealed off the cabin. Opening the airlock, I carried the unconscious Venusian out the hatch and gave him a good push, imparting enough momentum to send him out on an orbit of his own. The compensating reaction pushed me back into the airlock. I closed the hatch. The Venusian must have died instantly, without ever knowing what was happening to him.

Then I had a look-see to determine just how much damage the stowaway had been able to do before I woke up and caught him.

It was plenty.

All our communication equipment was gone, but permanently. The radio was a gutted ruin. The computer was smashed. Two auxiliary fuel tanks had been jettisoned. We were hopelessly off course in asteroid country, and the odds on reaching Ganymede looked mighty slim. By the time I finished making course corrections, we'd be down to our reserve fuel supply. Ganymede was about 350 million miles ahead of us. I didn't see how we were going to travel more than a tenth that distance before air and food troubles set in, and we weren't carrying enough fuel now for a safe landing even if we lived to reach Ganymede.

It was time to wake Miss Vanderweghe and tell her the news, I figured.

* * * *

She was lying curled up tight in her acceleration cradle, asleep, with a childlike, trusting expression on her face. I watched her for perhaps five minutes before I woke her. She sat up immediately.

"What—oh. Is everything all right? Did we make a good blastoff?"

"Fine blastoff," I said quietly. "But everything isn't all right." I told her about the stowaway and how thoroughly he had wrecked us.

"Oh—that horrible little man from Venus! I knew he had followed me to Mars—that's why I wanted to leave for Ganymede so soon. He made all sorts of absurd threats, as if the things I had bought were holy relics—"

"They are, in a way. If you worship Macintyre and his fellow rebels, then the stuff you carried away is equivalent to the True Cross, I suppose."

"I'm so sorry I got you into this, Sam."

I shrugged. "It's my own fault all the way. Your Venusian friend approached me at the hotel this afternoon and warned me off, but I didn't listen to him. I had my chance to pull out."

"Where's the stowaway now? Unconscious?"

I shook my head, jerking my thumb toward the single port in her cabin. "He's out there. Without a suit. Stowaways aren't entitled to charity under the space laws."

"Oh," she said quietly, turning pale. "I—see. You—ejected him."

I nodded. Then, to get off what promised to be an unpleasant topic, I said, "We're in real trouble. We're off course and we don't have enough fuel for making corrections—not without jettisoning everything on board, ourselves included."

"I don't mind if the cargo goes. I mean, I'd hate to lose it, but if you have to dump it—"

"Uh-uh. The ship itself is the bulk of our mass. The problem isn't the cargo. If there were only some way of jettisoning the *ship*—"

My mouth sagged open. No, I thought. It wouldn't ever work. It's too fantastic to consider.

"I have an idea," I said. "We *will* jettison the ship. And we'll get to Ganymede."

Luckily our saboteur friend hadn't bothered to rip up my charts. I spent half an hour feverishly thumbing through the volume devoted to asteroid orbits, while Erna hovered over my shoulder, not daring to ask questions but probably wondering just what in blazes I was figuring out.

Pretty soon I had a list of a dozen likely asteroids. I narrowed it down to five, then to three, then to one. I missed the convenience of my computer, but regulations require a pilot to be able to get along without one in a pinch, and I got along.

I computed a course toward the asteroid known as (719)-Albert. Luck was riding with us. (719)-Albert was on the outward swing of his orbit. On the basis of some extremely rough computations I worked out an orbit for our crippled ship that would match Albert's in a couple of hours.

Finally, I looked up at Erna and grinned. "This is known as making a virtue out of necessity," I said. "Want to know what's going on?"

"You bet I do."

I leaned back. "We're on our way to a chunk of rock known as (719)-Albert, which is chugging along not far from here on its way through the asteroid belt. (719)-Albert is a rock about three miles in diameter. Figure that it's half the size of Deimos—and Deimos is about as small as a place can get."

"But why are we going there?" she said, puzzled.

"(7I9)-Albert has an exceedingly eccentric orbit—and I mean eccentric in its astronomical sense: not a peculiar orbit, just one that's very highly elongated. At perihelion (719)-Albert passes around 20 million miles from the orbit of Earth. At aphelion, which is where he's heading now, he comes within 90 million miles of the orbit of Jupiter. Unless my figures are completely cockeyed, Jupiter is going to be about 150 million miles from Albert about a week from now."

I saw I had lost her completely. She said dimly, "But you said a little while ago that we hardly had enough fuel to take us 50 million miles."

"In the ship," I said. "Yes. But I've got other ideas. We'll land on Albert and abandon the ship. Then we ride pickaback on the asteroid until its closest approach to Jupiter—and blast off without the ship."

"Blast off—*how?*"

I smiled triumphantly. "We'll make a raft out of your blessed logs," I said. "Attach one of the ship's rocket engines at the rear, and shove off. Escape velocity from Albert is so low it hardly matters. And since the mass of our raft will only be six or seven hundred pounds—Earthside weight, of course—instead of the thirty tons or so that this ship weighs, we'll be able to coast to Ganymede with plenty of fuel left to burn."

She was looking at me as if I'd just delivered a lecture in the General Theory of Relativity. Apparently the niceties of space travel just weren't in her line at all. But she smiled and tried to look understanding. "It sounds very clever," she said with an uncertain grin.

* * * *

I felt pretty clever about everything myself, three hours later, when we landed on the surface of an asteroid that could only be (719)-Albert. It had taken only one minor course correction to get us here. Which meant that my rule-of-thumb astrogation had been pretty good.

We donned breathing-suits and clambered out of the ship to inspect our landfall. (719)-Albert wasn't very impressive. The landscape was mostly jagged upthrusts of a dark basalt-like rock. But the view was tremendous—a great backdrop of darkness, speckled with stars, and, much closer, the orbiting fragments of other lumps of rock. Albert's horizon was on the foreshortened side, dipping away almost before it began. Gravitational attraction was so meager it hardly counted. A healthy jump was likely to continue indefinitely upward, as I made clear to Erna right at the start. I didn't want her indulging in the usual hijinks that greenhorns are fond of when on a low-gravity planetoid such as this. I could visualize only too well the scene as she vanished into the void as the result of an overenthusiastic leap.

We surveyed our holdings and found that there was enough food for two people for sixteen days—so we would make it with some to spare. The air supply was less abundant, but there was enough so we didn't need to begin worrying just yet.

We set about building the raft.

Erna dragged the logs out of the cargo hold—their weight didn't amount to anything, here, though I had to caution her about throwing them around carelessly; mass and weight aren't synonymous, and those logs were sturdy enough to knock me for a loop regardless of how little they seemed to weigh. She fetched, and I assembled. We used the thirteen longest logs for the body of the raft, and trussed a couple across the bottom, and a couple more at the top. To make blastoff a little easier, we built the raft propped up against a rock outcropping, at a 45° angle.

I unshipped the smallest rocket engine and fastened it securely to the rear of the raft. I strapped down as many fuel tanks as the raft would hold.

Then—chuckling to myself—I asked Erna to help me haul the cannon out.

"The cannon? Whatever for?"

"To mount at the front of the raft."

"Are you figuring on meeting space pirates?"

"I'm figuring on using the cannon as a brake," I told her. We fastened it at the front of the raft, strapped down the supply of cannonballs and powder nearby it. The cannon would make an ideal brake. All we needed was something that would eject mass in a forwardly direction, pushing us back by courtesy of Newton's Third Law. Why waste fuel when cannonballs would achieve the same purpose?

It took us forty-eight standard Earthtime hours to build the raft. I don't know how many thousands of (719)-Albert days that was, but the little asteroid spun on its axis like a yo-yo, and it seemed that the sun was rising or setting every time we took a breath.

After I had bound the last thong around the rocket engine, Erna grinned and dashed into the ship. She returned, a few moments later, waving a red flag with some sort of blue-and-white design on it.

"What's that?"

"The flag that flew over Macintyre's cabin," she explained. "It's a rebel flag, and we're not strictly insurrectionists, but we ought to have some kind of flag on our ship."

I was agreeable, so she mounted the flag just fore of the rocket engine. Then we returned to the ship to wait.

We waited for three days, Earthtime—maybe several centuries by (719)-Albert reckoning. And in case you're wondering how we passed the time on the barren asteroid for three days, just one reasonably virile ferry pilot and one nubile museum curator, the answer is no. We didn't. I have an inflexible rule about making passes at passengers, even when we're stranded on places like (719)-Albert and when the passengers are as pretty as this one is.

That isn't to say I didn't feel temptation. Erna's breathing-suit was of the plastic kind that looked as though it was force-molded to her body. I didn't have to do much imagining. But I staunchly told Satan to get behind me, and—to my own amazement—he did. I resisted temptation and resisted it manfully.

Meanwhile Jupiter swelled bigger and bigger as (719)-Albert plunged madly along its track toward its rendezvous with Jove. If luck rode with us—translated, if my math had been right—we would find Ganymede midway in her seven-plus day orbit round the big planet.

Time came when the mass detectors in my ship informed me that Jupiter had stopped getting closer and was now getting farther away. That meant that (719)-Albert had passed its point of aphelion and was heading back toward Earth. It was time to get moving.

"All aboard," I told Erna. "Make sure everything we're taking is strapped down tight—food, fuel, air tanks, cannonballs, flags."

She checked off as if we were running down meters and gauges at a spaceport. "Food. Fuel. Air tanks. Cannonballs. Flag. All set to blast, Captain."

"Okay. Get yourself flattened out and hang onto the raft while we blast."

Blastoff was a joke. I had computed the escape velocity of (719)-Albert at approximately .0015 miles/sec. We could have shoved off with a good rearward kick.

But we had fuel to burn. *"Allons!"* I cried, slamming the rocket engine into action. A burst of flame hurled us upward into the night. *"A la belle Ètoile!"* I shouted. "To the stars!"

The raft soared off into space. Erna laughed with delight. As (719)-Albert slowly sank into the sunset, we plunged forward toward giant Jupiter. The only thing missing was soft music in the background.

* * * *

We rode the raft for three days at constant acceleration. Jupiter grew, and grew, and grew, and gleaming Ganymede became visible peeking around the edge of the great planet. Erna became worried when she saw it.

"Shouldn't we head the raft over toward Ganymede?" she asked. "We're pointed much too far forward."

I sighed. "We aren't going to reach Ganymede for another couple of days," I said. "We want to head for where Ganymede's going to be *then*, not where it happens to be right now. Isn't that obvious?"

"I suppose so," she said, pouting.

We were right on course. Two days later we were heading downward toward the surface of Ganymede. It was like riding a magic carpet. I controlled our landing with the rockets, while Erna gleefully fired ball after ball to provide the needed deceleration. If Ganymede had had an atmosphere, of course, we'd have been whiffed to cinders in a moment—but there was no atmosphere to contend with. We made a perfect no-point landing, flat on the glistening blue-white ice. Lord knows what we must have looked like approaching from space.

We had landed a hundred miles or so from the nearest entrance to the Ganymede Dome. I was dourly considering the prospect of trekking on foot, but Erna was certain we had been seen, and, sure enough, a snowcrawler manned by three incredulous colonists came out to fetch us. I never saw human eyes bulge the way those six eyes bulged at the sight of our raft.

Part of the service I offer is guaranteed delivery, and so, a couple of weeks later, I rented a ship and made a return journey to (7I9)-Albert to pick up the remaining historical relics we had been forced to leave behind—some tattered uniforms and a few boxes of pamphlets. A week after that, a repair ship was despatched to pick up my ferry, and she was hauled to the dockyard on Ganymede and put back in operating condition at a trifling cost of a few thousand megabucks.

These days I run a ferry service between the colonized moons of Jupiter and Saturn, and Erna is head curator of the Ganymede Museum. But I don't take kindly toward getting employment, because it means I have to spend time away from home—and Erna. We were married a while back, you see.

It's a funny thing about General Macintyre's log cabin. Despite Erna's careful diagram, the cabin never got put back together. It seems that the people of Ganymede decided it was of no great value to display the cabin of some Venusian rebel when they could be showing an item of much more immediate associations for Ganymedeans.

So they wouldn't let Erna take the raft apart, and I had to buy myself a new rocket engine. You can see the raft in the museum on Ganymede, any time you happen to be in the neighborhood. If the curator's around, she won't mind answering questions. But don't try to get playful with her. I'm awfully touchy about guys who make passes at my wife.

THE DESSICATOR

Originally published in *Science Fiction Stories*, May 1956.

Mirnish brought the machine into the other room, where Scrodlee was busily bent over the ledgers, and sadly put it down. "I've finished it," he said. "You can start Promoting."

Scrodlee leaped to his feet. "Antigravity! You have it! A marvelous feat, Mirnish, marvelous! This redeems all of your old blunders."

The inventor sat down heavily and caressed the small green box with his tentacles, looking at it with rue. "No. Not so, Scrodlee; I'm sorry, but I didn't quite invent antigravity this time."

Scrodlee contemplated his partner with a cosmic patience born of long experience. "You finished it, you say, and you were working on antigravity. But you didn't invent antigravity?"

"No."

The Promoter spoke slowly, choosing his words with care. "Then—what—did—you—invent?" He looked expectantly at the other, remembering a long history of Mirnish's inventions.

Mirnish assumed a humble countenance. "I seem," he said, "to have invented a Desiccator." He waited for Scrodlee's reaction, and it was not long in coming.

"A Desiccator?" the Promoter repeated, standing up and beginning to pace up and down the little room. "That is just in line with some of your other things. You mean a machine that dries things out, don't you? Just what we've all been waiting for—here on Mars, the dryest planet in the Galaxy, if not the Universe, what does Mirnish the inventor invent but a—a *Desiccator!*"

"I'm sorry, Scrodlee," Mirnish said; "I was trying to—"

"I know. Forget about it. We're in a pretty bad way and I can't afford to let this go to waste." He picked up the green box. "We've got an invention here, of a sort; there must be some use for it somewhere." He pointed to the ledger. "We'll have to make the most of it. And I'm not Scrodlee the Promoter for nothing; if we work it right, we can make millions on this thing yet! How does it work?"

"I don't know," Mirnish said. "I just put it together, using standard coordinates and all, and it—it desiccates. Say, look: perhaps we could go—"

"Some inventor," Scrodlee interrupted. "First he invents something completely useless, and then he tells me he doesn't know what it is. There are times I doubt my sanity, Mirnish; with all the inventors on this planet, whom do I promote? Mirnish."

"I'm sorry, Scrodlee. But maybe we could take the Desiccator to—"

"Quiet, I'm thinking. How could we find some use for this thing of yours? Perhaps the Grangs could use it; let me check." He stretched a tentacle up for a reference book, pulled it down from the shelf, and thumbed rapidly through it. "Umm. Guess not; they prefer to dry their victims themselves. Just as well; I hate dealing with them."

"Scrodlee."

"Yes, Mirnish?"

"Shut up. I have an idea I've been trying to slip in here sideways."

"You have an idea!" Scrodlee laughed. *"You* have an idea? Well, genius, let's hear it."

"Look. The Desiccator is worthless on Mars—everything is desiccated enough as it is. But on Earth—why, they're flooded down there. Two thirds of the planet is water! The humidity, the rain, everything—it makes me shudder. It's a miracle they don't drown in their own atmosphere. *There's* a natural market for the Desiccator; they'll snap it up, and we'll be doing a service to Civilization as well."

Scrodlee's eyes lit up with a familiar gleam. "You're right. Get your things together, Mirnish; you and I and the Desiccator are going to go to Earth. I'm not Scrodlee the Promoter for nothing!"

They arrived on Earth in due course, having booked third-class passage on the fourth-class liner *Edworm*. They put down outside the New York spaceport and Scrodlee procured a hotel room in the heart of the sprawling metropolis, grumbling about the outrageous rates.

Some judicious string-pulling, combined with the fact that they were Martians, got them an audience with the President a few days later. Scrodlee had insisted to Mimish that they should start at the top in their campaign to market the Desiccator.

Scrodlee led the way into the big room, and Mimish followed, carefully cradling the Desiccator under his end tentacle.

"You have seven minutes," said an officious-looking secretary.

"You're a busy man, Mr. President," Scrodlee said rapidly to the tired-looking chief of state, "but I think we've hit on a device that will turn your country into a Mar—pardon me, into a Paradise on Earth."

Briefly he explained the purpose and function of the Desiccator. The

President examined the green box, turned it upside-down, shook it, covertly photographed it with his wristcam just in case it might prove valuable, and handed it back to Mimish.

He leaned back in his chair. "Martian science is indeed a wonderful thing," he pronounced. "Our brothers of the elder planet are skilled in the ways of the universe."

"We realized the importance of the Desiccator immediately," Scrodlee said, "and took it straight to you; we knew you could use it."

"Sorry," said the President. "We can't; we don't have any use for it. If we removed humidity we'd offend a big chunk of farming people. We'd end up having to balance it by seeding clouds to produce rain. Take away one, give the other, where's the percentage?"

Scrodlee frowned. "But Earth is such a *humid* place," he protested; "the Desiccator would remove that excess humidity and make it a livable planet."

"We find it quite livable," the President said curtly. He stood up. "You'd be wise to keep such opinions to yourself, Mr. Scroggly. I'm afraid I don't have any use for your machine—but as a friendly tip, why not try some other country? Look in on one of the South American countries. It's pretty sticky down there, and maybe you could dry things out a little for them."

A few days later found the Martians in a white marble palace which housed the dictator of a small republic whose name Scrodlee never did manage to catch. He explained the Desiccator to the tall, much-decorated dictator, whose name Scrodlee likewise could not make out. He sat in silence, listening to Scrodlee's sales pitch, his fingers folded daintily as if in prayer.

"No," he said when Scrodlee finished; "never. Take your machine out of my country immediately."

"You can't use it?" Mirnish asked meekly.

"Certainly not! It would mean my life. Follow this picture, please: humidity goes down, banana crop fails. Banana crop fails, the Norteamericanos do not buy. They do not buy, we have no money. So we raise taxes to support the government. We raise taxes and we have a revolution and I am hung from lamppost. So I must say no. You would overthrow our entire economy and we cannot allow comfort to come first. It would be nice to have cooler country, but I am much too important to my nation to allow myself to be overthrown so."

Mirnish looked at Scrodlee, who looked back.

"Not at all?"

The dictator mopped some sweat away with an elegant handkerchief. "No; not at all. I suggest you take your invention back to your native planet."

"I guess we'll have to," Mirnish said.

"Maybe one of the neighboring countries—?" Scrodlee suggested.

"I doubt it," the dictator said. "But you may try." Scrodlee made a farewell gesture and exited, pushing Mirnish in front, wondering where to turn next.

They returned to New York after a fruitless visit to the east coast of Africa, where the tribal chieftain regarded them somewhat less than favorably. Disillusioned, they returned to their hotel suite and, tentacles drooping, waited despondently for something to happen.

They stared at the green box of the Desiccator sitting on the table.

"Let's go back home," Mirnish said. "Why not admit it: I failed; I invented something completely useless. So let's throw it away and I'll get to work on antigravity again."

Scrodlee stiffened with pride. "I'm not giving up so easily. I'm not Scrodlee the Promoter if I'm going to throw away a valuable invention like this; we'll stay here till we sell it."

Scrodlee contacted a few other buyers without success; most people just laughed at the thought of Martians inventing a Desiccator. They never left their apartment, and found it necessary to use the Desiccator at all times in order to maintain a livable atmosphere. A week passed, with Mirnish complaining bitterly about the soup that the atmosphere was—even with the Desiccator in action—and Scrodlee was becoming more and more convinced that he had finally come up with something that defeated his promoting skills.

He was about ready to give in when, one morning, a young man knocked at the door, and, when Mirnish opened it to see who was there, he entered.

"I'm Dennan. Reporter, *New York Cosmos*. Been some strange stories coming from this place and I want to check. Lord, it's dry in here!"

"It's the action of the Desiccator," Mirnish said. "It keeps us able to breathe." He explained the function of his invention.

Dennan looked hard at the Martian. "So *that's* it! You guys have been causing it after all. People drying up, groceries crumbling, grass turning brown on the penthouse. Excuse me, please." And he dashed out, exiting even more abruptly than he had entered.

"What was all that about?" asked Scrodlee, coming in from the other room. Mirnish told him. "Wonder what it means?"

They found out the next morning when the New York Cosmos dropped through the telechute and into their living room. Mirnish, who followed the newspapers with considerable interest, unfolded the front strip and began to scan it. Suddenly he gave the equivalent of a whistle and shouted for Scrodlee to come in.

"Look at this!" He held out the paper. The big red headline said:
MARTIANS PLOT MY DOOM

Underneath it was a story which began:

A daring *Cosmos* reporter yesterday uncovered a Martian plot to turn New York City into a desert.

Two Martian agents have established themselves in New York armed with a machine called a Desiccator which is responsible for the present drought and also for the curious reports of "dried-out" people in midtown New York, earlier believed to be a mysterious new epidemic.

The story continued on in that vein for almost two columns.

"Why, they're crazy!" Scrodlee exclaimed.

"They may be right, though," said Mirnish. "I never did test the field of the Desiccator. We may be Desiccating all of Manhattan by leaving the machine on."

Suddenly a rock came crashing through their window. Scrodlee ran to the broken window, coughing a little at the thick Terran air pouring through, and looked out.

There was a mob milling around the street, shouting imprecations and waving fists.

"Some inventor," Scrodlee said; "the people of Earth are yelling for our scalps."

"We don't have scalps," Mirnish said.

"Shut up; they want blood. We have to find some way of getting off this crazy planet without touching off another interplanetary war. You and your useless inventions!" Another rock came hurtling up from below and bounded off the side of the building.

"What are we going to do?" asked Mirnish.

"Sweat it out, I guess; shut off your damned Desiccator, anyway."

The visiphone chimed. Mirnish ignored it, but Scrodlee ran toward it and snatched it up. Mirnish walked to the window and stared glumly out at the milling mass of people in the street below.

Scrodlee began talking excitedly into the phone, and Mirnish watched almost with interest, unable to hear what he was saying because of the noise from the street.

When he hung up he returned to Mirnish with a triumphant look on his face. "What now?" Mirnish asked.

"When you deal with Scrodlee, you deal with a *Promotor,*" he said. "Everything's all right; one of my contacts came through and I sold the Desiccator."

"What? To whom?"

"You'll see. He was the last man on my list, but he wants it. I explained our predicament, and he's going to evacuate us by helicopter and take us to where the Desiccator's going to be installed. We'll be whisked right out from under the nose of that mob down there."

"Let's go up there and get them," a stentorian voice from below roared.

"When's he coming?" Mirnish asked anxiously.

"Any minute now; get your machine packed up, and get ready to leave."

They waited tensely as the yelling of the mob increased. Finally there came a rapping at the window, and they saw a helicopter hovering outside. It drew close and they cautiously opened a window.

"Suppose it's a trap," Mirnish whispered.

"Shut up."

A well-dressed, dignified gentleman came through the window.

"Mr. Henceford?" Scrodlee asked.

"That's right," he said in a deep, rich voice. "Owner of the Universal Vineyards. Your machine is what I've been looking for years. Looks like I just made it in the proverbial nick, I guess. Get into the copter before this mob breaks loose and we'll fly out to my place and arrange terms."

Mirnish and Scrodlee returned to Mars the following day, considerably wealthier; Mirnish again set out to conquer gravity, while Scrodlee spurred him on and kept careful watch to see that nothing went wrong this time.

As for the Desiccator, it's now busily employed in the heart of a deserted part of lower Nevada, pouring forth its desiccating rays day and night without end.

Turning grapes into raisins.

THE HAPPY UNFORTUNATE

Originally published in *Amazing Stories*, December 1957.

Rolf Dekker stared incredulously at the slim, handsome young Earther who was approaching the steps of Rolf's tumbling-down Spacertown shack. *He's got no ears*, Rolf noted in unbelief. After five years in space, Rolf had come home to a strangely-altered world, and he found it hard to accept.

Another Earther appeared. This one was about the same size, and gave the same impression of fragility. This one had ears, all right—and a pair of gleaming, two-inch horns on his forehead as well. *I'll be eternally roasted*, Rolf thought. *Now I've seen everything.*

Both Earthers were dressed in neat, gold-inlaid green tunics, costumes which looked terribly out of place amid the filth of Spacertown, and their hair was dyed a light green to match.

He had been scrutinizing them for several moments before they became aware of him. They both spotted him at once and the one with no ears turned to his companion and whispered something. Rolf, leaning forward, strained to hear.

"…beautiful, isn't he? That's the biggest one I've seen!"

"Come over here, won't you?" the horned one called, in a soft, gentle voice which contrasted oddly with the raucous bellowing Rolf had been accustomed to hearing in space. "We'd like to talk to you."

Just then Kanaday emerged from the door of the shack and limped down to the staircase.

"Hey, Rolf!" he called. "Leave those things alone!"

"Let me find out what they want first, huh?"

"Can't be any good, whatever it is," Kanaday growled. "Tell them to get out of here before I throw them back to wherever they came from. And make it fast."

* * * *

The two Earthers looked at each other uneasily. Rolf walked toward them.

"He doesn't like Earthers, that's all," Rolf explained. "But he won't do anything but yell."

Kanaday spat in disgust, turned, and limped back inside the shack.

"I didn't know you were wearing horns," Rolf said.

The Earther flushed. "New style," he said. "Very expensive."

"Oh," Rolf said. "I'm new here; I just got back. Five years in space. When I left you people looked all alike. Now you wear horns."

"It's the new trend," said the earless one. "We're Individs. When you left the Conforms were in power, style-wise. But the new surgeons can do almost anything, you see."

The shadow of a frown crossed Rolf's face. "Anything?"

"Almost. They can't transform an Earther into a Spacer, and they don't think they ever will."

"Or vice versa?" Rolf asked.

They sniggered. "What Spacer would want to become an Earther? Who would give up that life, out in the stars?"

Rolf said nothing. He kicked at the heap of litter in the filthy street. *What spacer indeed?* he thought. He suddenly realized that the two little Earthers were staring up at him as if he were some sort of beast. He probably weighed as much as both of them, he knew, and at six-four he was better than a foot taller. They looked like children next to him, like toys. The savage blast of acceleration would snap their flimsy bodies like toothpicks.

"What places have you been to?" the earless one asked.

"Two years on Mars, one on Venus, one in the Belt, one on Neptune," Rolf recited. "I didn't like Neptune. It was best in the Belt; just our one ship, prospecting. We made a pile on Ceres—enough to buy out. I shot half of it on Neptune. Still have plenty left, but I don't know what I can do with it." He didn't add that he had come home puzzled, wondering why he was a Spacer instead of an Earther, condemned to live in filthy Spacertown when Yawk was just across the river.

They were looking at his shabby clothes, at the dirty brownstone hovel he lived in—an antique of a house four or five centuries old.

"You mean you're rich?" the Earther said.

"Sure," Rolf said. "Every Spacer is. So what? What can I spend it on? My money's banked on Mars and Venus. Thanks to the law I can't legally get it to Earth. So I live in Spacertown."

"Have you ever seen an Earther city?" the earless one asked, looking around at the quiet streets of Spacertown with big powerful men sitting idly in front of every house.

"I used to live in Yawk," Rolf said. "My grandmother was an Earther; she brought me up there. I haven't been back there since I left for space."

They forced me out of Yawk, he thought. *I'm not part of their species. Not one of them.*

* * * *

The two Earthers exchanged glances.

"Can we interest you in a suggestion?" They drew in their breath as if they expected to be knocked sprawling.

Kanaday appeared at the door of the shack again.

"Rolf. Hey! You turning into an Earther? Get rid of them two cuties before there's trouble."

Rolf turned and saw a little knot of Spacers standing on the other side of the street, watching him with curiosity. He glared at them.

"I'll do whatever I damn well please," he shouted across.

He turned back to the two Earthers. "Now, what is it you want?"

"I'm giving a party next week," the earless one said. "I'd like you to come. We'd like to get the Spacer slant on life."

"Party?" Rolf repeated. "You mean, dancing, and games, and stuff like that?"

"You'll enjoy it," the Earther said coaxingly. "And we'd all love to have a real Spacer there."

"When is it?"

"A week."

"I have ten days left of my leave. All right," he said. "I'll come."

He accepted the Earther's card, looked at it mechanically, saw the name—Kal Quinton—and pocketed it. "Sure," he said. "I'll be there."

The Earthers moved toward their little jetcar, smiling gratefully. As Rolf crossed the street, the other Spacers greeted him with cold, puzzled stares.

* * * *

Kanaday was almost as tall as Rolf, and even uglier. Rolf's eyebrows were bold and heavy; Kanaday's, thick, contorted, bushy clumps of hair. Kanaday's nose had been broken long before in some barroom brawl; his cheekbones bulged; his face was strong and hard. More important, his left foot was twisted and gnarled beyond hope of redemption by the most skillful surgeon. He had been crippled in a jet explosion three years before, and was of no use to the Spacelines any more. They had pensioned him off. Part of the deal was the dilapidated old house in Spacertown which he operated as a boarding-house for transient Spacers.

"What do you want to do that for?" Kanaday asked. "Haven't those Earthers pushed you around enough, so you have to go dance at one of their wild parties?"

"Leave me alone," Rolf muttered.

"You like this filth you live in? Spacertown is just a ghetto, that's all. The Earthers have pushed you right into the muck. You're not even a human being to them—just some sort of trained ape. And now you're going to go and entertain them. I thought you had brains, Rolf!"

"Shut up!" He dashed his glass against the table; it bounced off and dropped to the floor, where it shattered.

Kanaday's girl Laney entered the room at the sound of the crash. She was tall and powerful-looking, with straight black hair and the strong cheekbones that characterized the Spacers. Immediately she stooped and began shoveling up the broken glass.

"That wasn't smart, Rolf," she said. "That'll cost you half a credit. Wasn't worth it, was it?"

Rolf laid the coin on the edge of the table. "Tell your pal to shut up, then. If he doesn't stop icing me I'll fix his other foot for him and you can buy him a dolly."

She looked from one to the other. "What's bothering you two now?"

"A couple of Earthers were here this morning," Kanaday said. "Slumming. They took a fancy to our young friend here and invited him to one of their parties. He accepted."

"He *what*? Don't go, Rolf. You're crazy to go."

"Why am I crazy?" He tried to control his voice. "Why should we keep ourselves apart from the Earthers? Why shouldn't the two races get together?"

* * * *

She put down her tray and sat next to him. "They're more than two races," she said patiently. "Earther and Spacer are two different species, Rolf. Carefully, genetically separated. They're small and weak, we're big and powerful. You've been bred for going to space; they're the castoffs, the ones who were too weak to go. The line between the two groups is too strong to break."

"And they treat us like dirt—like animals," Kanaday said. "But *they're* the dirt. They were the ones who couldn't make it."

"Don't go to the party," Laney said. "They just want to make fun of you. Look at the big ape, they'll say."

Rolf stood up. "You don't understand. Neither of you does. I'm part Earther," Rolf said. "My grandmother on my mother's side. She raised me as an Earther. She wanted me to be an Earther. But I kept getting bigger and uglier all the time. She took me to a plastic surgeon once, figuring he could make me look like an Earther. He was a little man; I don't know what he looked like to start with but some other surgeon had

THE HAPPY UNFORTUNATE | 73

made him clean-cut and straight-nosed and thin-lipped like all the other Earthers. I was bigger than he was—twice as big, and I was only fifteen. He looked at me and felt my bones and measured me. 'Healthy little ape'—those were the words he used. He told my grandmother I'd get bigger and bigger, that no amount of surgery could make me small and handsome, that I was fit only for space and didn't belong in Yawk. So I left for space the next morning."

"I see," Laney said quietly.

"I didn't say good-bye. I just left. There was no place for me in Yawk; I couldn't pass myself off as an Earther any more. But I'd like to go back and see what the old life was like, now that I know what it's like to be on the other side for a while."

"It'll hurt when you find out, Rolf."

"I'll take that chance. But I want to go. Maybe my grandmother'll be there. The surgeons made her young and pretty again every few years; she looked like my sister when I left."

Laney nodded her head. "There's no point arguing with him, Kanaday. He has to go back there and find out, so let him alone."

Rolf smiled. "Thanks for understanding." He took out Quinton's card and turned it over and over in his hand.

* * * *

Rolf went to Yawk on foot, dressed in his best clothes, with his face as clean as it had been in some years. Spacertown was just across the river from Yawk, and the bridges spanning the river were bright and gleaming in the mid-afternoon sun.

The bombs had landed on Yawk during the long-forgotten war, but somehow they had spared the sprawling borough across the river. And so Yawk had been completely rebuilt, once the radioactivity had been purged from the land, while what was now Spacertown consisted mostly of buildings that dated back to the Twentieth Century.

Yawk had been the world's greatest seaport; now it was the world's greatest spaceport. The sky was thick with incoming and outgoing liners. The passengers on the ship usually stayed at Yawk, which had become an even greater metropolis than it had been before the Bomb. The crew crossed the river to Spacertown, where they could find their own kind.

Yawk and Spacertown were like two separate planets. There were three bridges spanning the river, but most of the time they went unused, except by spacemen going back home or by spacemen going to the spaceport for embarkation. There was no regular transportation between the two cities; to get from Spacertown to Yawk, you could borrow a jet-car or you could walk. Rolf walked.

He enjoyed the trip. *I'm going back home*, he thought as he paced along the gleaming arc of the bridge, dressed in his Sunday best. He remembered the days of his own childhood, his parentless childhood. His earliest memory was of a fight at the age of six or so. He had stood off what seemed like half the neighborhood, ending the battle by picking up an older bully, much feared by everyone, and heaving him over a fence. When he told his grandmother about the way he had won the fight she cried for an hour, and never told him why. But they had never picked on him again, though he knew the other boys had jeered at him behind his back as he grew bigger and bigger over the years. "Ape," they called him. "Ape."

But never to his face.

He approached the Yawk end of the bridge. A guard was waiting there—an Earther guard, small and frail, but with a sturdy-looking blaster at his hip.

"Going back, Spacer?"

Rolf started. How did the guard know? And then he realized that all the guard meant was, are you going back to your ship?

"No. No, I'm going to a party. Kal Quinton's house."

"Tell me another, Spacer." The guard's voice was light and derisive. A swift poke in the ribs would break him in half, Rolf thought.

"I'm serious. Quinton invited me. Here's his card."

"If this is a joke it'll mean trouble. But go ahead; I'll take your word for it."

Rolf marched on past the guard, almost nonchalantly. He looked at the address on the card. *12406 Kenman Road.* He rooted around in his fading memory of Yawk, but he found the details had blurred under the impact of five years of Mars and Venus and the Belt and Neptune. He did not know where Kenman Road was.

The glowing street signs were not much help either. One said 287th Street and the other said 72nd Avenue. Kenman Road might be anywhere.

He walked on a block or two. The streets were antiseptically clean, and he had the feeling that his boots, which had lately trod in Spacertown, were leaving dirtmarks along the street. He did not look back to see.

* * * *

He looked at his wristchron. It was getting late, and Kenman Road might be anywhere. He turned into a busy thoroughfare, conscious that he was attracting attention. The streets here were crowded with little people who barely reached his chest; they were all about the same height, and most of them looked alike. A few had had radical surgical alterations, and every one of these was different. One had a unicorn-like horn; another, an extra eye which cunningly resembled his real ones. The Earthers were looking at him furtively, as they would at a tiger or an elephant strolling down a main street.

"Where are you going, Spacer?" said a voice from the middle of the street.

Rolf's first impulse was to snarl out a curse and keep moving, but he realized that the question was a good one and one whose answer he was trying to find out for himself. He turned.

Another policeman stood on the edge of the walkway. "Are you lost?" The policeman was short and delicate-looking.

Rolf produced his card.

The policeman studied it. "What business do you have with Quinton?"

"Just tell me how to get there," Rolf said. "I'm in a hurry."

The policeman backed up a step. "All right, take it easy." He pointed to a kiosk. "Take the subcar here. There's a stop at Kenman Road. You can find your way from there."

"I'd rather walk it," Rolf said. He did not want to have to stand the strain of riding in a subcar with a bunch of curious staring Earthers.

"Fine with me," the policeman said. "It's about two hundred blocks to the north. Got a good pair of legs?"

"Never mind," Rolf said. "I'll take the subcar."

* * * *

Kenman Road was a quiet little street in an expensive-looking end of Yawk. 12406 was a towering building which completely overshadowed everything else on the street. As Rolf entered the door, a perfumed little Earther with a flashing diamond where his left eye should have been and a skin stained bright purple appeared from nowhere.

"We've been waiting for you. Come on; Kal will be delighted that you're here."

The elevator zoomed up so quickly that Rolf thought for a moment that he was back in space. But it stopped suddenly at the 62nd floor, and, as the door swung open, the sounds of wild revelry drifted down the hall. Rolf had a brief moment of doubt when he pictured Laney and Kanaday at this very moment, playing cards in their mouldering hovel while he walked down this plastiline corridor back into a world he had left behind.

Quinton came out into the hall to greet him. Rolf recognized him by the missing ears; his skin was now a subdued blue to go with his orange robe.

"I'm so glad you came," the little Earther bubbled. "Come on in and I'll introduce you to everyone."

The door opened photoelectrically as they approached. Quinton seized him by the hand and dragged him in. There was the sound of laughter and of shouting. As he entered it all stopped, suddenly, as if it had been shut off. Rolf stared at them quizzically from under his lowering brows, and they looked at him with ill-concealed curiosity.

They seemed divided into two groups. Clustered at one end of the long hall was a group of Earthers who seemed completely identical, all with the same features, looking like so many dolls in a row. These were the Earthers he remembered, the ones whom the plastic surgeons had hacked at and hewn until they all conformed to the prevailing concept of beauty.

Then at the other end was a different group. They were all different. Some had glittering jewels set in their foreheads, others had no lips, no hair, extra eyes, three nostrils. They were a weird and frightening group, highest product of the plastic surgeon's art.

Both groups were staring silently at Rolf.

"Friends, this is Rolf—Rolf—"

"Dekker," Rolf said after a pause. He had almost forgotten his own last name.

"Rolf Dekker, just back from outer space. I've invited him to join us tonight. I think you'll enjoy meeting him."

The stony silence slowly dissolved into murmurs of polite conversation as the party-goers adjusted to the presence of the newcomer. They seemed to be discussing the matter earnestly among themselves, as if Quinton had done something unheard-of by bringing a Spacer into an Earther party.

A tall girl with blonde hair drifted up to him.

"Ah. Jonne," Quinton said. He turned to Rolf. "This is Jonne. She asked to be your companion at the party. She's very interested in space and things connected with it."

Things connected with it, Rolf thought. Meaning me. He looked at her. She was as tall an Earther as he had yet seen, and probably suffered for it when there were no Spacers around. Furthermore, he suspected, her height was accentuated for the evening by special shoes. She was not of the Individ persuasion, because her face was well-shaped, with smooth, even features, with no individualist distortion. Her skin was unstained. She wore a clinging off-the-breast tunic. Quite a dish, Rolf decided. He began to see that he might enjoy this party.

* * * *

The other guests began to approach timidly, now that the initial shock of his presence had worn off. They asked silly little questions about space—questions which showed that they had only a superficial interest in him and were treating him as a sort of talking dog. He answered as many as he could, looking down at their little painted faces with concealed contempt.

They think as little of me as I do of them. The thought hit him suddenly and his broad face creased in a smile at the irony. Then the music started.

* * * *

The knot of Earthers slowly broke up and drifted away to dance. He looked at Jonne, who had stood patiently at his side through all this.

"I don't dance," he said. "I never learned how." He watched the other couples moving gracefully around the floor, looking for all the world like an assemblage of puppets. He stared in the dim light, watching the couples clinging to each other as they rocked through the motions of the dance. He stood against the wall, wearing his ugliness like a shield. He saw the great gulf which separated him from the Earthers spreading before him, as he watched the dancers and the gay chatter and the empty badinage and the furtive hand-holding, and everything else from which he was cut off. The bizarre Individs were dancing together—he noticed one man putting an extra arm to full advantage—and the almost identical Conforms had formed their own group again. Rolf wondered how they told each other apart when they all looked alike.

"Come on," Jonne said. "I'll show you how to dance." He turned to look at her, with her glossy blonde hair and even features. She smiled prettily, revealing white teeth. *Probably newly purchased?* Rolf wondered.

"Actually I do know how to dance," Rolf said. "But I do it so badly—"

"That doesn't matter," she said gaily. "Come on."

She took his arm. Maybe she doesn't think I look like an ape, he thought. She doesn't treat me the way the others do. But why am I so ugly, and why is she so pretty?

He looked at her and she looked at him, and he felt her glance on his stubbly face with its ferocious teeth and burning yellowish eyes. He didn't want her to see him at all; he wished he had no face.

He folded her in his arms, feeling her warmth radiate through him. She was very tall, he realized, almost as tall as a Spacer woman—but with none of the harsh ruggedness of the women of Spacertown. They danced, she well, he clumsily. When the music stopped she guided him to the entrance of a veranda.

They walked outside into the cool night air. The lights of the city obscured most of the stars, but a few still showed, and the moon hung high above Yawk. He could dimly make out the lights of Spacertown across the river, and he thought again of Laney and Kanaday and wished Kanaday could see him now with this beautiful Earther next to him.

"You must get lonely in space," she said after a while.

"I do," he said, trying to keep his voice gentle. "But it's where I belong. I'm bred for it."

She nodded. "Yes. And any of those so-called men inside would give ten years of his life to be able to go to space. But yet you say it's lonely."

* * * *

"Those long rides through the night," he said. "They get you down. You want to be back among people. So you come back. You come back. And what do you come back to?"

"I know," she said softly. "I've seen Spacertown."

"Why must it be that way?" he demanded. "Why are Spacers so lucky and so wretched all at once?"

"Let's not talk about it now," she said.

I'd like to kiss her, he thought. But my face is rough, and I'm rough and ugly, and she'd push me away. I remember the pretty little Earther girls who ran laughing away from me when I was thirteen and fourteen, before I went to space.

"You don't have to be lonely," she said. One of her perfect eyebrows lifted just a little. "Maybe someday you'll find someone who cares, Rolf. Someday, maybe."

"Yeah," he said. "Someday, maybe." But he knew it was all wrong. Could he bring this girl to Spacertown with him? No; she must be merely playing a game, looking for an evening's diversion. Something new: make love to a Spacer.

They fell silent and he watched her again, and she watched him. He heard her breath rising and falling evenly, not at all like his own thick gasps. After a while he stepped close to her, put his arm around her, tilted her head into the crook of his elbow, bent, and kissed her.

As he did it, he saw he was botching it just like everything else. He had come too close, and his heavy boot was pressing on the tip of her shoe; and he had not quite landed square on her lips. But still, he was close to her. He was reluctant to break it up, but he felt she was only half-responding, not giving anything of herself while he had given all. He drew back a step.

She did not have time to hide the expression of distaste that involuntarily crossed her face. He watched the expression on her face as she realized the kiss was over. He watched her silently.

"Someday, maybe," he said. She stared at him, not hiding the fear that was starting to grow on her face.

He felt a cold chill deep in his stomach, and it grew until it passed through his throat and into his head.

"Yeah," he said. "Someday, maybe. But not you. Not anyone who's just playing games. That's all—you want something to tell your friends about, that's why you volunteered for tonight's assignment. It's all you can do to keep from laughing at me, but you're sticking to it. I don't want any of it, hear me? Get away."

She stepped back a pace. "You ugly, clumsy clown. You ape!" Tears began to spoil the flawless mask of her face. Blinded with anger, he grabbed roughly for her arm, but she broke away and dashed back inside.

She was trying to collect me, he thought. Her hobby: interesting dates. She wanted to add me to her collection. An Experience. Calmly he walked to the end of the veranda and stared off into the night, choking his rage. He watched the moon making its dead ride across the sky, and stared at the sprinkling of stars. The night was empty and cold, he thought, finally. But not more so than I.

* * * *

He turned and looked back through the half-opened window. He saw a girl who looked almost like her, but was not tall enough and wore a different dress. Then he spotted her. She was dancing with one of the Conforms, a frail-looking man a few inches shorter than she, with regular, handsome features. She laughed at some sly joke, and he laughed with her.

Rolf watched the moon for a moment more, thinking of Laney's warning. *They just want to make fun of you. Look at the big ape, they'll say.*

He knew he had to get out of there immediately. He was a Spacer, and they were Earthers, and he scorned them for being contemptuous little dolls, and they laughed at him for being a hulking ape. He was not a member of their species; he was not part of their world.

He went inside. Kal Quinton came rushing up to him.

"I'm going," Rolf said.

"What? You don't mean that," the little man said. "Why, the party's scarcely gotten under way, and there are dozens of people who want to meet you. And you'll miss the big show if you don't stay."

"I've already seen the big show," Rolf told him. "I want out. Now."

"You can't leave now," Quinton said. Rolf thought he saw tears in the corners of the little man's eyes. "Please don't leave. I've told everyone you'd be here—you'll disgrace me."

"What do I care? Let me out of here." Rolf started to move toward the door. Quinton attempted to push him back.

"Just a minute, Rolf. Please!"

"I have to get out," he said. He knocked Quinton out of his way with a backhand swipe of his arm and dashed down the hall frantically, looking for the elevator.

* * * *

Laney and Kanaday were sitting up waiting for him when he got back, early in the morning. He slung himself into a pneumochair and unsealed his boots, releasing his cramped, tired feet.

"Well," Laney asked. "How was the party?"

"You have fun among the Earthers, Rolf?"

He said nothing.

"It couldn't have been that bad," Laney said.

Rolf looked up at her. "I'm leaving space. I'm going to go to a surgeon and have him turn me into an Earther. I hate this filthy life!"

"He's drunk," Kanaday said.

"No, I'm not drunk," Rolf retorted. "I don't want to be an ape any more."

"Is that what you are? If you're an ape, what are they to you? Monkeys?" Kanaday laughed harshly.

"Are they really so wonderful?" Laney asked. "Does the life appeal to you so much that you'll give up space for it? Do you admire the Earthers so much?"

* * * *

She's got me, Rolf thought. I hate Spacertown, but will I like Yawk any better? Do I really want to become one of those little puppets? But there's nothing left in space for me. At least the Earthers are happy.

I wish she wouldn't look at me that way. "Leave me alone," he snarled. "I'll do whatever I want to do." Laney was staring at him, trying to poke behind his mask of anger. He looked at her wide shoulders, her muscular frame, her unbeautiful hair and rugged face, and compared it with Jonne's clinging grace, her flowing gold hair.

He picked up his boots and stumped up to bed.

* * * *

The surgeon's name was Goldring, and he was a wiry, intense man who had prevailed on one of his colleagues to give him a tiny slit of a mouth. He sat behind a shining plastiline desk, waiting patiently until Rolf finished talking.

"It can't be done," he said at last. "Plastic surgeons can do almost anything, but I can't turn you into an Earther. It's not just a matter of chopping eight or ten inches out of your legs; I'd have to alter your entire bone structure or you'd be a hideous misproportioned monstrosity. And it can't be done. I can't build you a whole new body from scratch, and if I could do it you wouldn't be able to afford it."

Rolf stamped his foot impatiently. "You're the third surgeon who's given me the same line. What is this—a conspiracy? I see what you can do. If you can graft a third arm onto somebody, you can turn me into an Earther."

"Please, Mr. Dekker. I've told you I can't. But I don't understand why you want such a change. Hardly a week goes by without some Yawk boy coming to me and asking to be turned into a Spacer, and I have to refuse him for the same reasons I'm refusing you! That's the usual course of events—the romantic Earther boy wanting to go to space, and not being able to."

An idea hit Rolf. "Was one of them Kal Quinton?"

"I'm sorry, Mr. Dekker. I just can't divulge any such information."

Rolf shot his arm across the desk and grasped the surgeon by the throat. "Answer me!"

"Yes," the surgeon gasped. "Quinton asked me for such an operation. Almost everyone wants one."

"And you can't do it?" Rolf asked.

"Of course not. I've told you: the amount of work needed to turn Earther into Spacer or Spacer into Earther is inconceivable. It'll never be done."

"I guess that's definite, then," Rolf said, slumping a little in disappointment. "But there's nothing to prevent you from giving me a new face—from taking away this face and replacing it with something people can look at without shuddering."

"I don't understand you, Mr. Dekker," the surgeon said.

"I know that! Can't you see it—I'm *ugly*! Why? Why should I look this way?"

"Please calm down, Mr. Dekker. You don't seem to realize that you're a perfectly normal-looking Spacer. *You were bred to look this way.* It's your genetic heritage. Space is not a thing for everyone; only men with extraordinary bone structure can withstand acceleration. The first men were carefully selected and bred. You see the result of five centuries of this sort of breeding. The sturdy, heavy-boned Spacers—you, Mr. Dekker, and your friends—are the only ones who are fit to travel in space. The others, the weaklings like myself, the little people, resort to plastic surgery to compensate for their deficiency. For a while the trend was to have everyone conform to a certain standard of beauty; if we couldn't be strong, we could at least be handsome. Lately a new theory of individualism has sprung up, and now we strive for original forms in our bodies. This is all because size and strength has been bred out of us and given to you."

"I know all this," Rolf said. "Why can't you—"

"Why can't I peel away your natural face and make you look like an Earther? There's no reason why; it would be a simple operation. But who would you fool? Why can't you be grateful for what you are? You can go to Mars, while we can merely look at it. If I gave you a new face, it would cut you off from both sides. The Earthers would still know you were a Spacer, and I'm sure the other Spacers would immediately cease to associate with you."

* * * *

"Who are you to say? You're not supposed to pass judgment on whether an operation should be performed, or you wouldn't pull out people's eyes and stick diamonds in!"

"It's not that, Mr. Dekker." The surgeon folded and unfolded his hands in impatience. "You must realize that you are what you are. Your appearance is a social norm, and for acceptance in your social environment you must continue to appear, well, perhaps, shall I say apelike?"

It was as bad a word as the surgeon could have chosen.

"Ape! Ape, am I! I'll show you who's an ape!" Rolf yelled, all the accumulated frustration of the last two days suddenly bursting loose. He leaped up and overturned the desk. Dr. Goldring hastily jumped backwards as the heavy desk crashed to the floor. A startled nurse dashed into the office, saw the situation, and immediately ran out.

"Give me your instruments! I'll operate on myself!" He knocked Goldring against the wall, pulled down a costly solidograph from the wall and kicked it at him, and crashed through into the operating room, where he began overturning tables and heaving chairs through glass shelves.

"I'll show you," he said. He cracked an instrument case and took out a delicate knife with a near-microscopic edge. He bent it in half and threw the crumpled wreckage away. Wildly he destroyed everything he could, raging from one end of the room to the other, ripping down furnishings, smashing, destroying, while Dr. Goldring stood at the door and yelled for help.

It was not long in coming. An army of Earther policemen erupted into the room and confronted him as he stood panting amid the wreckage. They were all short men, but there must have been twenty of them.

"Don't shoot him," someone called. And then they advanced in a body.

He picked up the operating table and hurled it at them. Three policemen crumpled under it, but the rest kept coming. He batted them away like insects, but they surrounded him and piled on. For a few moments he struggled under the load of fifteen small men, punching and kicking and yelling. He burst loose for an instant, but two of them were clinging to his legs and he hit the floor with a crash. They were on him immediately, and he stopped struggling after a while.

* * * *

The next thing he knew he was lying sprawled on the floor of his room in Spacertown, breathing dust out of the tattered carpet. He was a mass of cuts and bruises, and he knew they must have given him quite a going-over. He was sore from head to foot.

So they hadn't arrested him. No, of course not; no more than they would arrest any wild animal who went berserk. They had just dumped him back in the jungle. He tried to get up, but couldn't make it. Quite a going-over it must have been. Nothing seemed broken, but everything was slightly bent.

"Satisfied now?" said a voice from somewhere. It was a pleasant sound to hear, a voice, and he let the mere noise of it soak into his mind. "Now that you've proved to everyone that you really are just an ape?"

He twisted his neck around—slowly, because his neck was stiff and sore. Laney was sitting on the edge of his bed with two suitcases next to her.

"It really wasn't necessary to run wild there," she said. "The Earthers all knew you were just an animal anyway. You didn't have to prove it so violently."

"Okay, Laney. Quit it."

"If you want me to. I just wanted to make sure you knew what had happened. A gang of Earther cops brought you back a while ago and dumped you here. They told me the story."

"Leave me alone."

"You've been telling everyone that all along, Rolf. Look where it got you. A royal beating at the hands of a bunch of Earthers. Now that they've thrown you out for the last time, has it filtered into your mind that this is where you belong?"

"In Spacertown?"

"Only between trips. You belong in space, Rolf. No surgeon can make you an Earther. The Earthers are dead, but they don't know it yet. All their parties, their fancy clothes, their extra arms and missing ears—that means they're decadent. They're finished. You're the one who's alive; the whole universe is waiting for you to go out and step on its neck. And instead you want to turn yourself into a green-skinned little monkey! Why?"

* * * *

He pulled himself to a sitting position. "I don't know," he said. "I've been all mixed up, I think." He felt his powerful arm. "I'm a Spacer." Suddenly he glanced at her. "What are the suitcases for?" he said.

"I'm moving in," Laney said. "I need a place to sleep."

"What's the matter with Kanaday? Did he get tired of listening to you preaching? He's my friend, Laney; I'm not going to do him dirt."

"He's dead, Rolf. When the Earther cops came here to bring you back, and he saw what they did to you, his hatred overflowed. He always hated Earthers, and he hated them even more for the way you were being tricked into thinking they were worth anything. He got hold of one of those cops and just about twisted him into two pieces. They blasted him."

Rolf was silent. He let his head sink down on his knees.

"So I moved down here. It's lonely upstairs now. Come on; I'll help you get up."

She walked toward him, hooked her hand under his arm, and half-dragged, half-pushed him to his feet. Her touch was firm, and there was no denying the strength behind her.

"I have to get fixed up," he said abruptly. "My leave's up in two days. I have to get out of here. We're shipping for Pluto."

* * * *

He rocked unsteadily on his feet. "It'll really get lonely here then," he said.

"Are you really going to go? Or are you going to find some jack-surgeon who'll make your face pretty for a few dirty credits?"

"Stop it. I mean it. I'm going. I'll be gone a year on this signup. By then I'll have enough cash piled up on various planets to be a rich man. I'll get it all together and get a mansion on Venus, and have Greenie slaves."

It was getting toward noon. The sun, high in the sky, burst through the shutters and lit up the dingy room.

"I'll stay here," Laney said. "You're going to Pluto?"

He nodded.

"Kanaday was supposed to be going to Pluto. He was heading there when that explosion finished his foot. He never got there after that."

"Poor old Kanaday," Rolf said.

"I'll miss him too. I guess I'll have to run the boarding-house now. For a while. Will you come back here when your year's up?"

"I suppose so," Rolf said without looking up. "This town is no worse than any of the other Spacertowns. No better, but no worse." He slowly lifted his head and looked at her as she stood there facing him.

"I hope you come back," she said.

The sun was coming in from behind her, now, and lighting her up. She was rugged, all right, and strong: a good hard worker. And she was well built. Suddenly his aches became less painful, as he looked at her and realized that she was infinitely more beautiful than the slick, glossy-looking girl he had kissed on the veranda, who had bought her teeth at a store and had gotten her figure from a surgeon. Laney, at least, was real.

"You know," he said at last, "I think I have an idea. You wait here and I'll come get you when my year's up. I'll have enough to pay passage to Venus for two. We can get a slightly smaller mansion than I planned on getting. But we can get it. Some parts of Venus are beautiful. And the closest those monkeys from Yawk can get to it is to look at it in the night sky. You think it's a good idea?"

"I think it's a great idea," she said, moving toward him. Her head was nearly as high as his own.

"I'll go back to space. I have to, to keep my rating. But you'll wait for me, won't you?"

"I'll wait."

And as he drew her close, he knew she meant it.

THE HUNTED HEROES

Originally published in *Amazing Stories*, September 1956.

"Let's keep moving," I told Val. "The surest way to die out here on Mars is to give up." I reached over and turned up the pressure on her oxymask to make things a little easier for her. Through the glassite of the mask, I could see her face contorted in an agony of fatigue.

And she probably thought the failure of the sandcat was all my fault, too. Val's usually about the best wife a guy could ask for, but when she wants to be she can be a real flying bother.

It was beyond her to see that some grease monkey back at the Dome was at fault—whoever it was who had failed to fasten down the engine hood. Nothing but what had stopped us *could* stop a sandcat: sand in the delicate mechanism of the atomic engine.

But no; she blamed it all on me somehow: So we were out walking on the spongy sand of the Martian desert. We'd been walking a good eight hours.

"Can't we turn back now, Ron?" Val pleaded. "Maybe there isn't any uranium in this sector at all. I think we're crazy to keep on searching out here!"

I started to tell her that the UranCo chief had assured me we'd hit something out this way, but changed my mind. When Val's tired and overwrought there's no sense in arguing with her.

I stared ahead at the bleak, desolate wastes of the Martian landscape. Behind us somewhere was the comfort of the Dome, ahead nothing but the mazes and gullies of this dead world.

"Try to keep going, Val." My gloved hand reached out and clumsily enfolded hers. "Come on, kid. Remember—we're doing this for Earth. We're heroes."

She glared at me. "Heroes, hell!" she muttered. "That's the way it looked back home, but, out there it doesn't seem so glorious. And UranCo's pay is stinking."

"We didn't come out here for the pay, Val."

"I know, I know, but just the same—"

It must have been hell for her. We had wandered fruitlessly over the red sands all day, both of us listening for the clicks of the counter. And the geigers had been obstinately hushed all day, except for their constant undercurrent of meaningless noises.

Even though the Martian gravity was only a fraction of Earth's, I was starting to tire, and I knew it must have been really rough on Val with her lovely but unrugged legs.

"Heroes," she said bitterly. "We're not heroes—we're suckers! Why did I ever let you volunteer for the Geig Corps and drag me along?"

Which wasn't anywhere close to the truth. Now I knew she was at the breaking point, because Val didn't lie unless she was so exhausted she didn't know what she was doing. She had been just as much inflamed by the idea of coming to Mars to help in the search for uranium as I was. We knew the pay was poor, but we had felt it a sort of obligation, something we could do as individuals to keep the industries of radioactives-starved Earth going. And we'd always had a roving foot, both of us.

No, we had decided together to come to Mars—the way we decided together on everything. Now she was turning against me.

I tried to jolly her. "Buck up, kid," I said. I didn't dare turn up her oxy pressure any higher, but it was obvious she couldn't keep going. She was almost sleep-walking now.

We pressed on over the barren terrain. The geiger kept up a fairly steady click-pattern, but never broke into that sudden explosive tumult that meant we had found pay-dirt. I started to feel tired myself, terribly tired. I longed to lie down on the soft, spongy Martian sand and bury myself.

I looked at Val. She was dragging along with her eyes half-shut. I felt almost guilty for having dragged her out to Mars, until I recalled that I hadn't. In fact, she had come up with the idea before I did. I wished there was some way of turning the weary, bedraggled girl at my side back into the Val who had so enthusiastically suggested we join the Geigs.

Twelve steps later, I decided this was about as far as we could go.

I stopped, slipped out of the geiger harness, and lowered myself ponderously to the ground. "What'samatter, Ron?" Val asked sleepily. "Something wrong?"

"No, baby," I said, putting out a hand and taking hers. "I think we ought to rest a little before we go any further. It's been a long, hard day."

It didn't take much to persuade her. She slid down beside me, curled up, and in a moment she was fast asleep, sprawled out on the sands.

Poor kid, I thought. Maybe we shouldn't have come to Mars after all. But, I reminded myself, *someone* had to do the job.

A second thought appeared, but I squelched it:

Why the hell me?

I looked down at Valerie's sleeping form, and thought of our warm, comfortable little home on Earth. It wasn't much, but people in love don't need very fancy surroundings.

I watched her, sleeping peacefully, a wayward lock of her soft blonde hair trailing down over one eyebrow, and it seemed hard to believe that we'd exchanged Earth and all it held for us for the raw, untamed struggle that was Mars. But I knew I'd do it again, if I had the chance. It's because we wanted to keep what we had. Heroes? Hell, no. We just liked our comforts, and wanted to keep them. Which took a little work.

* * * *

Time to get moving. But then Val stirred and rolled over in her sleep, and I didn't have the heart to wake her. I sat there, holding her, staring out over the desert, watching the wind whip the sand up into weird shapes.

The Geig Corps preferred married couples, working in teams. That's what had finally decided it for us—we were a good team. We had no ties on Earth that couldn't be broken without much difficulty. So we volunteered.

And here we are. Heroes. The wind blasted a mass of sand into my face, and I felt it tinkle against the oxymask.

I glanced at the suit-chronometer. Getting late. I decided once again to wake Val. But she was tired. And I was tired too, tired from our wearying journey across the empty desert.

I started to shake Val. But I never finished. It would be *so* nice just to lean back and nuzzle up to her, down in the sand. So nice. I yawned, and stretched back.

* * * *

I awoke with a sudden startled shiver, and realized angrily I had let myself doze off. "Come on, Val," I said savagely, and started to rise to my feet.

I couldn't.

I looked down. I was neatly bound in thin, tough, plastic tanglecord, swathed from chin to boot-bottoms, my arms imprisoned, my feet caught. And tangle-cord is about as easy to get out of as a spider's web is for a trapped fly.

It wasn't Martians that had done it. There weren't any Martians, hadn't been for a million years. It was some Earthman who had bound us.

I rolled my eyes toward Val, and saw that she was similarly trussed in the sticky stuff. The tangle-cord was still fresh, giving off a faint, repugnant odor like that of drying fish. It had been spun on us only a short time ago, I realized.

"Ron—"

"Don't try to move, baby. This stuff can break your neck if you twist it wrong." She continued for a moment to struggle futilely, and I had to snap, "Lie still, Val!"

"A very wise statement," said a brittle, harsh voice from above me. I looked up and saw a helmeted figure above us. He wasn't wearing the customary skin-tight pliable oxysuits we had. He wore an outmoded, bulky spacesuit and a fishbowl helmet, all but the face area opaque. The oxygen cannisters weren't attached to his back as expected, though. They were strapped to the back of the wheelchair in which he sat.

Through the fishbowl I could see hard little eyes, a yellowed, parchment-like face, a grim-set jaw. I didn't recognize him, and this struck me odd. I thought I knew everyone on sparsely-settled Mars. Somehow I'd missed him.

What shocked me most was that he had no legs. The spacesuit ended neatly at the thighs.

He was holding in his left hand the tanglegun with which he had entrapped us, and a very efficient-looking blaster was in his right.

"I didn't want to disturb your sleep," he said coldly. "So I've been waiting here for you to wake up."

I could just see it. He might have been sitting there for hours, complacently waiting to see how we'd wake up. That was when I realized he must be totally insane. I could feel my stomach-muscles tighten, my throat constrict painfully.

Then anger ripped through me, washing away the terror. "What's going on?" I demanded, staring at the half of a man who confronted us from the wheelchair. "Who are you?"

"You'll find out soon enough," he said. "Suppose now you come with me." He reached for the tanglegun, flipped the little switch on its side to MELT, and shot a stream of watery fluid over our legs, keeping the blaster trained on us all the while. Our legs were free.

"You may get up now," he said. "Slowly, without trying to make trouble." Val and I helped each other to our feet as best we could, considering our arms were still tightly bound against the sides of our oxysuits.

"Walk," the stranger said, waving the tanglegun to indicate the direction. "I'll be right behind you." He holstered the tanglegun.

I glimpsed the bulk of an outboard atomic rigging behind him, strapped to the back of the wheelchair. He fingered a knob on the arm of the chair and the two exhaust ducts behind the wheel-housings flamed for a moment, and the chair began to roll.

Obediently, we started walking. You don't argue with a blaster, even if the man pointing it is in a wheelchair.

* * * *

"What's going on, Ron?" Val asked in a low voice as we walked. Behind us the wheelchair hissed steadily.

"I don't quite know, Val. I've never seen this guy before, and I thought I knew everyone at the Dome."

"Quiet up there!" our captor called, and we stopped talking. We trudged along together, with him following behind; I could hear the *crunch-crunch* of the wheelchair as its wheels chewed into the sand. I wondered where we were going, and why. I wondered why we had ever left Earth.

The answer to that came to me quick enough: we had to. Earth needed radioactives, and the only way to get them was to get out and look. The great atomic wars of the late 20th Century had used up much of the supply, but the amount used to blow up half the great cities of the world hardly compared with the amount we needed to put them back together again.

In three centuries the shattered world had been completely rebuilt. The wreckage of New York and Shanghai and London and all the other ruined cities had been hidden by a shining new world of gleaming towers and flying roadways. We had profited by our grandparents' mistakes. They had used their atomics to make bombs. We used ours for fuel.

It was an atomic world. Everything: power drills, printing presses, typewriters, can openers, ocean liners, powered by the inexhaustible energy of the dividing atom.

But though the energy is inexhaustible, the supply of nuclei isn't. After three centuries of heavy consumption, the supply failed. The mighty machine that was Earth's industry had started to slow down.

And that started the chain of events that led Val and me to end up as a madman's prisoners, on Mars. With every source of uranium mined dry on Earth, we had tried other possibilities. All sorts of schemes came forth. Project Sea-Dredge was trying to get uranium from the oceans. In forty or fifty years, they'd get some results, we hoped. But there wasn't forty or fifty years' worth of raw stuff to tide us over until then. In a decade or so, our power would be just about gone. I could picture the sort of dog-eat-dog world we'd revert back to. Millions of starving, freezing humans tooth-and-clawing in it in the useless shell of a great atomic civilization.

So, Mars. There's not much uranium on Mars, and it's not easy to find or any cinch to mine. But what little is there, helps. It's a stopgap effort, just to keep things moving until Project Sea-Dredge starts functioning.

Enter the Geig Corps: volunteers out on the face of Mars, combing for its uranium deposits.

And here we are, I thought.

* * * *

After we walked on a while, a Dome became visible up ahead. It slid up over the crest of a hill, set back between two hummocks on the desert. Just out of the way enough to escape observation.

For a puzzled moment I thought it was our Dome, the settlement where all of UranCo's Geig Corps were located, but another look told me that this was actually quite near us and fairly small. A one-man Dome, of all things!

"Welcome to my home," he said. "The name is Gregory Ledman." He herded us off to one side of the airlock, uttered a few words keyed to his voice, and motioned us inside when the door slid up. When we were inside he reached up, clumsily holding the blaster, and unscrewed the ancient spacesuit fishbowl.

His face was a bitter, dried-up mask. He was a man who hated.

The place was spartanly furnished. No chairs, no tape-player, no decoration of any sort. Hard bulkhead walls, rivet-studded, glared back at us. He had an automatic chef, a bed, and a writing-desk, and no other furniture.

Suddenly he drew the tanglegun and sprayed our legs again. We toppled heavily to the floor. I looked up angrily.

"I imagine you want to know the whole story," he said. "The others did, too."

Valerie looked at me anxiously. Her pretty face was a dead white behind her oxymask. "What others?"

"I never bothered to find out their names," Ledman said casually. "They were other Geigs I caught unawares, like you, out on the desert. That's the only sport I have left—Geig-hunting. Look out there."

He gestured through the translucent skin of the Dome, and I felt sick. There was a little heap of bones lying there, looking oddly bright against the redness of the sands. They were the dried, parched skeletons of Earthmen. Bits of cloth and plastic, once oxymasks and suits, still clung to them.

Suddenly I remembered. There had been a pattern there all the time. We didn't much talk about it; we chalked it off as occupational hazards. There had been a pattern of disappearances on the desert. I could think of six, eight names now. None of them had been particularly close friends.

You don't get time to make close friends out here. But we'd vowed it wouldn't happen to us.

It had.

"You've been hunting Geigs?" I asked. "*Why?* What've they ever done to you?"

He smiled, as calmly as if I'd just praised his house-keeping. "Because I hate you," he said blandly. "I intend to wipe every last one of you out, one by one."

I stared at him. I'd never seen a man like this before; I thought all his kind had died at the time of the atomic wars.

I heard Val sob, "He's a madman!"

"No," Ledman said evenly. "I'm quite sane, believe me. But I'm determined to drive the Geigs—and UranCo—off Mars. Eventually I'll scare you all away."

"Just pick us off in the desert?"

"Exactly," replied Ledman. "And I have no fears of an armed attack. This place is well fortified. I've devoted years to building it. And I'm back against those hills. They couldn't pry me out." He let his pale hand run up into his gnarled hair. "I've devoted years to this. Ever since—ever since I landed here on Mars."

* * * *

"What are you going to do with us?" Val finally asked, after a long silence.

He didn't smile this time. "Kill you," he told her. "Not your husband. I want him as an envoy, to go back and tell the others to clear off." He rocked back and forth in his wheelchair, toying with the gleaming, deadly blaster in his hand.

We stared in horror. It was a nightmare—sitting there, placidly rocking back and forth, a nightmare.

I found myself fervently wishing I was back out there on the infinitely safer desert.

"Do I shock you?" he asked. "I shouldn't—not when you see my motives."

"We don't see them," I snapped.

"Well, let me show you. You're on Mars hunting uranium, right? To mine and ship the radioactives back to Earth to keep the atomic engines going. Right?"

I nodded over at our geiger counters.

"We volunteered to come to Mars," Val said irrelevantly.

"Ah—two young heroes," Ledman said acidly. "How sad. I could almost feel sorry for you. Almost."

"Just what is it you're after?" I said, stalling, stalling.

"Atomics cost me my legs," he said. "You remember the Sadlerville Blast?" he asked.

"Of course." And I did, too. I'd never forget it. No one would. How could I forget that great accident—killing hundreds, injuring thousands more, sterilizing forty miles of Mississippi land—when the Sadlerville pile went up?

"I was there on business at the time," Ledman said. "I represented Ledman Atomics. I was there to sign a new contract for my company. You know who I am, now?"

I nodded.

"I was fairly well shielded when it happened. I never got the contract, but I got a good dose of radiation instead. Not enough to kill me," he said. "Just enough to necessitate the removal of—" he indicated the empty space at his thighs. "So I got off lightly." He gestured at the wheelchair blanket.

I still didn't understand. "But why kill us Geigs? *We* had nothing to do with it."

"You're just in this by accident," he said. "You see, after the explosion and the amputation, my fellow-members on the board of Ledman Atomics decided that a semi-basket case like myself was a poor risk as Head of the Board, and they took my company away. All quite legal, I assure you. They left me almost a pauper!" Then he snapped the punchline at me.

"They renamed Ledman Atomics. Who did you say you worked for?"

I began, "Uran—"

"Don't bother. A more inventive title than Ledman Atomics, but not quite as much heart, wouldn't you say?" He grinned. "I saved for years; then I came to Mars, lost myself, built this Dome, and swore to get even. There's not a great deal of uranium on this planet, but enough to keep me in a style to which, unfortunately, I'm no longer accustomed."

* * * *

He consulted his wrist watch. "Time for my injection." He pulled out the tanglegun and sprayed us again, just to make doubly certain. "That's another little souvenir of Sadlerville. I'm short on red blood corpuscles."

He rolled over to a wall table and fumbled in a container among a pile of hypodermics. "There are other injections, too. Adrenalin, insulin. Others. The Blast turned me into a walking pin-cushion. But I'll pay it all back," he said. He plunged the needle into his arm.

My eyes widened. It was too nightmarish to be real. I wasn't seriously worried about his threat to wipe out the entire Geig Corps, since it was unlikely that one man in a wheelchair could pick us all off. No, it wasn't the threat that disturbed me, so much as the whole concept, so strange to me, that the human mind could be as warped and twisted as Ledman's.

I saw the horror on Val's face, and I knew she felt the same way I did.

"Do you really think you can succeed?" I taunted him. "Really think you can kill every Earthman on Mars? Of all the insane, cockeyed—"

Val's quick, worried head-shake cut me off. But Ledman had felt my words, all right.

"Yes! I'll get even with every one of you for taking away my legs! If we hadn't meddled with the atom in the first place, I'd be as tall and powerful as you, today—instead of a useless cripple in a wheelchair."

"You're sick, Gregory Ledman," Val said quietly. "You've conceived an impossible scheme of revenge and now you're taking it out on innocent people who've done nothing, nothing at all to you. That's not sane!"

His eyes blazed. "Who are you to talk of sanity?"

Uneasily I caught Val's glance from a corner of my eye. Sweat was rolling down her smooth forehead faster than the auto-wiper could swab it away.

"Why don't you do something? What are you waiting for, Ron?"

"Easy, baby," I said. I knew what our ace in the hole was. But I had to get Ledman within reach of me first.

"Enough," he said. "I'm going to turn you loose outside, right after—"

"*Get sick!*" I hissed to Val, low. She began immediately to cough violently, emitting harsh, choking sobs. "Can't breathe!" She began to yell, writhing in her bonds.

That did it. Ledman hadn't much humanity left in him, but there was a little. He lowered the blaster a bit and wheeled one-hand over to see what was wrong with Val. She continued to retch and moan most horribly. It almost convinced me. I saw Val's pale, frightened face turn to me.

He approached and peered down at her. He opened his mouth to say something, and at that moment I snapped my leg up hard, tearing the tangle-cord with a snicking rasp, and kicked his wheelchair over.

The blaster went off, burning a hole through the Dome roof. The automatic sealers glued-in instantly. Ledman went sprawling helplessly out into the middle of the floor, the wheelchair upended next to him, its wheels slowly revolving in the air. The blaster flew from his hands at the impact of landing and spun out near me. In one quick motion I rolled over and covered it with my body.

Ledman clawed his way to me with tremendous effort and tried wildly to pry the blaster out from under me, but without success. I twisted a bit, reached out with my free leg, and booted him across the floor. He fetched up against the wall of the Dome and lay there.

Val rolled over to me.

"Now if I could get free of this stuff," I said, "I could get him covered before he comes to. But how?"

"Teamwork," Val said. She swivelled around on the floor until her head was near my boot. "Push my oxymask off with your foot, if you can."

I searched for the clamp and tried to flip it. No luck, with my heavy, clumsy boot. I tried again, and this time it snapped open. I got the tip of my boot in and pried upward. The oxymask came off, slowly, scraping a jagged red scratch up the side of Val's neck as it came.

"There," she breathed. "That's that."

I looked uneasily at Ledman. He was groaning and beginning to stir.

Val rolled on the floor and her face lay near my right arm. I saw what she had in mind. She began to nibble the vile-tasting tangle-cord, running her teeth up and down it until it started to give. She continued unfailingly.

Finally one strand snapped. Then another. At last I had enough use of my hand to reach out and grasp the blaster. Then I pulled myself across the floor to Ledman, removed the tanglegun, and melted the remaining tangle-cord off.

My muscles were stiff and bunched, and rising made me wince. I turned and freed Val. Then I turned and faced Ledman.

"I suppose you'll kill me now," he said.

"No. That's the difference between sane people and insane," I told him. "I'm not going to kill you at all. I'm going to see to it that you're sent back to Earth."

"*No!*" he shouted. "No! Anything but back there. I don't want to face them again—not after what they did to me—"

"Not so loud," I broke in. "They'll help you on Earth. They'll take all the hatred and sickness out of you, and turn you into a useful member of society again."

"I hate Earthmen," he spat out. "I hate all of them."

"I know," I said sarcastically. "You're just all full of hate. You hated us so much that you couldn't bear to hang around on Earth for as much as a year after the Sadlerville Blast. You had to take right off for Mars without a moment's delay, didn't you? You hated Earth so much you *had* to leave."

"Why are you telling all this to me?"

"Because if you'd stayed long enough, you'd have used some of your pension money to buy yourself a pair of prosthetic legs, and then you wouldn't need this wheelchair."

Ledman scowled, and then his face went belligerent again. "They told me I was paralyzed below the waist. That I'd never walk again, even with prosthetic legs, because I had no muscles to fit them to."

"You left Earth too quickly," Val said.

"It was the only way," he protested. "I had to get off—"

"She's right," I told him. "The atom can take away, but it can give as well. Soon after you left they developed *atomic-powered* prosthetics—amazing things, virtually robot legs. All the survivors of the Sadlerville Blast were given the necessary replacement limbs free of charge. All except you. You were so sick you had to get away from the world you despised and come here."

"You're lying," he said. "It's not true!"

"Oh, but it is," Val smiled.

I saw him wilt visibly, and for a moment I almost felt sorry for him, a pathetic legless figure propped up against the wall of the Dome at blaster-point. But then I remembered he'd killed twelve Geigs—or more—and would have added Val to the number had he had the chance.

* * * *

"You're a very sick man, Ledman," I said. "All this time you could have been happy, useful on Earth, instead of being holed up here nursing your hatred. You might have been useful, on Earth. But you decided to channel everything out as revenge."

"I still don't believe it—those legs. I might have walked again. No—no, it's all a lie. They told me I'd never walk," he said, weakly but stubbornly still.

I could see his whole structure of hate starting to topple, and I decided to give it the final push.

"Haven't you wondered how I managed to break the tangle-cord when I kicked you over?"

"Yes—human legs aren't strong enough to break tangle-cord that way."

"Of course not," I said. I gave Val the blaster and slipped out of my oxysuit. "Look," I said. I pointed to my smooth, gleaming metal legs. The almost soundless purr of their motors was the only noise in the room. "I was in the Sadlerville Blast, too," I said. "But I didn't go crazy with hate when I lost *my* legs."

Ledman was sobbing.

"Okay, Ledman," I said. Val got him into his suit, and brought him the fishbowl helmet. "Get your helmet on and let's go. Between the psychs and the prosthetics men, you'll be a new man inside of a year."

"But I'm a murderer!"

"That's right. And you'll be sentenced to psych adjustment. When they're finished, Gregory Ledman the killer will be as dead as if they'd electrocuted you, but there'll be a new—and sane—Gregory Ledman."

I turned to Val.

"Got the geigers, honey?"

For the first time since Ledman had caught us, I remembered how tired Val had been out on the desert. I realized now that I had been driving her mercilessly—me, with my chromium legs and atomic-powered muscles. No wonder she was ready to fold! And I'd been too dense to see how unfair I had been.

She lifted the geiger harnesses, and I put Ledman back in his wheelchair.

Val slipped her oxymask back on and fastened it shut.

"Let's get back to the Dome in a hurry," I said. "We'll turn Ledman over to the authorities. Then we can catch the next ship for Earth."

"Go back? *Go back?* If you think I'm backing down now and quitting you can find yourself another wife! After we dump this guy I'm sacking in for twenty hours, and then we're going back out there to finish that search-pattern. Earth needs uranium, honey, and I know you'd never be happy quitting in the middle like that." She smiled. "I can't wait to get out there and start listening for those tell-tale clicks."

I gave a joyful whoop and swung her around. When I put her down, she squeezed my hand, hard.

"Let's get moving, fellow hero," she said.

I pressed the stud for the airlock, smiling.

THE IRON STAR

Originally published in *Amazing Stories*, January 1988.

The alien ship came drifting up from behind the far side of the neutron star just as I was going on watch. It looked a little like a miniature neutron star itself: a perfect sphere, metallic, dark. But neutron stars don't have six perky little out-thrust legs and the alien craft did.

While I paused in front of the screen the alien floated diagonally upward, cutting a swathe of darkness across the brilliantly starry sky like a fast-moving black hole. It even occulted the real black hole that lay thirty light-minutes away.

I stared at the strange vessel, fascinated and annoyed, wishing I had never seen it, wishing it would softly and suddenly vanish away. This mission was sufficiently complicated already. We hadn't needed an alien ship to appear on the scene. For five days now we had circled the neutron star in seesaw orbit with the aliens, a hundred eighty degrees apart. They hadn't said anything to us and we didn't know how to say anything to them. I didn't feel good about that. I like things direct, succinct, known.

Lina Sorabji, busy enhancing sonar transparencies over at our improvised archaeology station, looked up from her work and caught me scowling. Lina is a slender, dark woman from Madras whose ancestors were priests and scholars when mine were hunting bison on the Great Plains. She said, "You shouldn't let it get to you like that, Tom."

"You know what it feels like, every time I see it cross the screen? It's like having a little speck wandering around on the visual field of your eye. Irritating, frustrating, maddening—and absolutely impossible to get rid of."

"You want to get rid of it?"

I shrugged. "Isn't this job tough enough? Attempting to scoop a sample from the core of a neutron star? Do we really have to have an alien spaceship looking over our shoulders while we work?"

"Maybe it's not a spaceship at all," Lina said cheerily. "Maybe it's just some kind of giant spacebug."

I suppose she was trying to amuse me. I wasn't amused. This was going to win me a place in the history of space exploration, sure: Chief Executive Officer of the first expedition from Earth ever to encounter intelligent extraterrestrial life. Terrific. But that wasn't what IBM/Toshiba had hired me to do. And I'm more interested in completing assignments than in making history. You don't get paid for making history.

Basically the aliens were a distraction from our real work, just as last month's discovery of a dead civilization on a nearby solar system had been, the one whose photographs Lina Sorabji now was studying. This was supposed to be a business venture involving the experimental use of new technology, not an archaeological mission or an exercise in interspecies diplomacy. And I knew that there was a ship from the Exxon/Hyundai combine loose somewhere in hyperspace right now working on the same task we'd been sent out to handle. If they brought it off first, IBM/Toshiba would suffer a very severe loss of face, which is considered very bad on the corporate level. What's bad for IBM/Toshiba would be exceedingly bad for me. For all of us.

I glowered at the screen. Then the orbit of the *Ben-wah Maru* carried us down and away and the alien disappeared from my line of sight. But not for long, I knew.

As I keyed up the log reports from my sleep period I said to Lina, "You have anything new today?" She had spent the past three weeks analysing the dead-world data. You never know what the parent companies will see as potentially profitable.

"I'm down to hundred-meter penetration now. There's a system of broad tunnels wormholing the entire planet. Some kind of pneumatic transportation network, is my guess. Here, have a look."

A holoprint sprang into vivid life in the air between us. It was a sonar scan that we had taken from ten thousand kilometers out, reaching a short distance below the surface of the dead world. I saw odd-angled tunnels lined with gleaming luminescent tiles that still pulsed with dazzling colors, centuries after the cataclysm that had destroyed all life there. Amazing decorative patterns of bright lines were plainly visible along the tunnel walls, lines that swirled and overlapped and entwined and beckoned my eye into some adjoining dimension.

Trains of sleek snub-nosed vehicles were scattered like caterpillars everywhere in the tunnels. In them and around them lay skeletons, thousands of them, millions, a whole continent full of commuters slaughtered as they waited at the station for the morning express. Lina touched the fine scan and gave me a close look: biped creatures, broad skulls tapering sharply at the sides, long apelike arms, seven-fingered hands with what seemed like an opposable thumb at each end, pelvises enlarged into peculiar bony crests jutting far out from their hips. It wasn't the first time a hyperspace exploring vessel had come across relics of extinct extraterrestrial races, even a fossil or two. But these weren't fossils. These beings had died only a few hundred years ago. And they had all died at the same time.

I shook my head somberly. "Those are some tunnels. They might have been able to convert them into pretty fair radiation shelters, is my guess. If only they'd had a little warning of what was coming."

"They never knew what hit them."

"No," I said. "They never knew a thing. A supernova brewing right next door and they must not have been able to tell what was getting ready to happen."

Lina called up another print, and another, then another. During our brief fly-by last month our sensors had captured an amazing panoramic view of this magnificent lost civilization: wide streets, spacious parks, splendid public buildings, imposing private houses, the works. Bizarre architecture, all unlikely angles and jutting crests like its creators, but unquestionably grand, noble, impressive. There had been keen intelligence at work here, and high artistry. Everything was intact and in a remarkable state of preservation, if you make allowances for the natural inroads that time and weather and I suppose the occasional earthquake will bring over three or four hundred years. Obviously this had been a wealthy, powerful society, stable and confident.

And between one instant and the next it had all been stopped dead in its tracks, wiped out, extinguished, annihilated. Perhaps they had had a fraction of a second to realize that the end of the world had come, but no more than that. I saw what surely were family groups huddling together, skeletons clumped in threes or fours or fives. I saw what I took to be couples with their seven-fingered hands still clasped in a final exchange of love. I saw some kneeling in a weird elbows-down position that might have been one of—who can say? Prayer? Despair? Acceptance?

A sun had exploded and this great world had died. I shuddered, not for the first time, thinking of it.

It hadn't even been their own sun. What had blown up was this one, forty light-years away from them, the one that was now the neutron star about which we orbited and which once had been a main-sequence sun maybe three or four times as big as Earth's. Or else it had been the other one in this binary system, thirty light-minutes from the first, the blazing young giant companion star of which nothing remained except the black hole nearby. At the moment we had no way of knowing which of these two stars had gone supernova first. Whichever one it was, though, had sent a furious burst of radiation heading outward, a lethal flux of cosmic rays capable of destroying most or perhaps all life-forms within a sphere a hundred light-years in diameter.

The planet of the underground tunnels and the noble temples had simply been in the way. One of these two suns had come to the moment when all the fuel in its core had been consumed: hydrogen had been fused into helium, helium into carbon, carbon into neon, oxygen, sulphur, silicon, until at last a core of pure iron lay at its heart. There is no atomic nucleus more strongly bound than iron. The star had reached the point where its release of energy through fusion had to cease; and with the end of energy production the star no longer could withstand the gravitational pressure of its own vast mass. In a moment, in the twinkling of an eye, the core underwent a catastrophic collapse. Its matter was compressed—beyond the point of equilibrium. And rebounded. And sent forth an intense shock wave that went rushing through the star's outer layers at a speed of 15,000 kilometers a second.

Which ripped the fabric of the star apart, generating an explosion releasing more energy than a billion suns.

The shock wave would have continued outward and outward across space, carrying debris from the exploded star with it, and interstellar gas that the debris had swept up. A fierce sleet of radiation would have been riding on that wave, too: cosmic rays, X-rays, radio waves, gamma rays, everything, all up and down the spectrum. If the sun that had gone supernova had had planets close by, they would have been vaporized immediately. Outlying worlds of that system might merely have been fried.

The people of the world of the tunnels, forty light-years distant, must have known nothing of the great explosion for a full generation after it had happened. But, all that while, the light of that shattered star was traveling towards them at a speed of 300,000 kilometers per second, and one night its frightful baleful unexpected glare must have burst suddenly into their sky in the most terrifying way. And almost in that same moment—for the deadly cosmic rays thrown off by the explosion move nearly at the speed of light—the killing blast of hard radiation would have arrived. And so these people and all else that lived on their world perished in terror and light.

All this took place a thousand light-years from Earth: that surging burst of radiation will need another six centuries to complete its journey towards our home world. At that distance, the cosmic rays will do us little or no harm. But for a time that long-dead star will shine in our skies so brilliantly that it will be visible by day, and by night it will cast deep shadows, longer than those of the Moon.

That's still in Earth's future. Here the fatal supernova, and the second one that must have happened not long afterwards, were some four hundred years in the past. What we had here now was a neutron star left over from one cataclysm and a black hole left over from the other. Plus the pathetic remains of a great civilization on a scorched planet orbiting a neighboring star. And now a ship from some alien culture. A busy corner of the galaxy, this one. A busy time for the crew of the IBM/Toshiba hyperspace ship *Ben-wah Maru*.

* * * *

I was still going over the reports that had piled up at my station during my sleep period—mass-and-output readings on the neutron star, progress bulletins on the setup procedures for the neutronium scoop, and other routine stuff of that nature—when the communicator cone in front of me started to glow. I flipped it on. Cal Bjornsen, our communications guru, was calling from Brain Central downstairs.

Bjornsen is mostly black African with some Viking genes salted in. The whole left side of his face is cyborg, the result of some extreme bit of teenage carelessness. The story is that he was gravity-vaulting and lost polarity at sixty meters. The mix of ebony skin, blue eyes, blond hair, and sculpted titanium is an odd one, but I've seen a lot of faces less friendly than Cal's. He's a good man with anything electronic.

He said, "I think they're finally trying to send us messages, Tom."

I sat up fast. "What's that?"

"We've been pulling in signals of some sort for the past ninety minutes that didn't look random, but we weren't sure about it. A dozen or so different frequencies all up and down the line, mostly in the radio band, but we're also getting what seem to be infra-red pulses, and something flashing in the ultraviolet range. A kind of scattershot noise effect, only it isn't noise."

"Are you sure of that?"

"The computer's still chewing on it," Bjornsen said. The fingers of his right hand glided nervously up and down his smooth metal cheek. "But we can see already that there are clumps of repetitive patterns."

"Coming from them? How do you know?"

"We didn't, at first. But the transmissions conked out when we lost line-of-sight with them, and started up again when they came back into view."

"I'll be right down," I said.

Bjornsen is normally a calm man, but he was running in frantic circles when I reached Brain Central three or four minutes later. There was stuff dancing on all the walls: sine waves, mainly, but plenty of other patterns jumping around on the monitors. He had already pulled in specialists from practically every department—the whole astronomy staff, two of the math guys, a couple from the external maintenance team, and somebody from engines. I felt preempted. Who was CEO on this ship, anyway? They were all babbling at once. "Fourier series," someone said, and someone yelled back, "Dirichlet factor," and someone else said, "Gibbs phenomenon!" I heard Angie Seraphin insisting vehemently, "—continuous except possibly for a finite number of finite discontinuities in the interval—pi to pi—"

"Hold it," I said, "What's going on?"

More babble, more gibberish. I got them quiet again and repeated my question, aiming it this time at Bjornsen.

"We have the analysis now," he said.

"So?"

"You understand that it's only guesswork, but Brain Central gives good guess. The way it looks, they seem to want us to broadcast a carrier wave they can tune in on, and just talk to them while they lock in with some sort of word-to-word translating device of theirs."

"That's what Brain Central thinks they're saying?"

"It's the most plausible semantic content of the patterns they're transmitting," Bjornsen answered.

I felt a chill. The aliens had word-to-word translating devices? That was a lot more than we could claim. Brain Central is one very smart computer, and if it thought that it had correctly deciphered the message coming in, them in all likelihood it had. An astonishing accomplishment, taking a bunch of ones and zeros put together by an alien mind and culling some sense out of them.

But even Brain Central wasn't capable of word-to-word translation out of some unknown language. Nothing in our technology is. The alien message had been *designed* to be easy: put together, most likely, in a careful high-redundancy manner, the computer equivalent of picture-writing. Any race able to undertake interstellar travel ought to have a computer powerful enough to sweat the essential meaning out of a message like that, and we did. We couldn't go farther than that though. Let the entropy of that message—that is, the unexpectedness of it, the unpredictability of its semantic content—rise just a little beyond the picture-writing level, and Brain Central would be lost. A computer that knows French should be able to puzzle out Spanish, and maybe even Greek. But Chinese? A tough proposition. And an *alien* language? Languages may start out logical, but they don't stay that way. And when its underlying grammatical assumptions were put together in the first place by beings with nervous systems that were wired up in ways entirely different from our own, well, the notion of instantaneous decoding becomes hopeless.

Yet our computer said that their computer could do word-to-word. That was scary.

On the other hand, if we couldn't talk to them, we wouldn't begin to find out what they were doing here and what threat, if any, they might pose to us. By revealing our language to them we might be handing them some sort of advantage, but I couldn't be sure of that, and it seemed to me we had to take the risk.

It struck me as a good idea to get some backing for that decision, though. After a dozen years as CEO aboard various corporate ships I knew the protocols. You did what you thought was right, but you didn't go all the way out on the limb by yourself if you could help it.

"Request a call for a meeting of the corporate staff," I told Bjornsen.

It wasn't so much a scientific matter now as a political one. The scientists would probably be gung-ho to go blasting straight ahead with making contact. But I wanted to hear what the Toshiba people would say, and the IBM people, and the military people. So we got everyone together and I laid the situation out and asked for a Consensus Process. And let them go at it, hammer and tongs.

Instant polarization. The Toshiba people were scared silly of the aliens. We must be cautious, Nakamura said. Caution, yes, said her cohort Nagy-Szabo. There may be danger to Earth. We have no knowledge of the aims and motivations of these beings. Avoid all contact with them, Nagy-Szabo said. Nakamura went even further. We should withdraw from the area immediately, she said, and return to Earth for additional instructions. That drew hot opposition from Jorgensen and Kalliotis, the IBM people. We had work to do here, they said. We should do it. They grudgingly conceded the need to be wary, but strongly urged continuation of the mission and advocated a circumspect opening of contact with the other ship. I think they were already starting to think about alien marketing demographics. Maybe I do them an injustice. Maybe.

The military people were about evenly divided between the two factions. A couple of them, the hair-splitting career-minded ones, wanted to play it absolutely safe and clear out of here fast, and the others, the up-and-away hero types, spoke out in favor of forging ahead with contact and to hell with the risks.

I could see there wasn't going to be any consensus. It was going to come down to me to decide.

By nature I am cautious. I might have voted with Nakamura in favor of immediate withdrawal; however that would have made my ancient cold-eyed Sioux forebears howl. Yet in the end what swayed me was an argument that came from Bryce-Williamson, one of the fiercest of the military sorts. He said that we didn't dare turn tail and run for home without making contact, because the aliens would take that either as a hostile act or a stupid one, and either way they might just slap some kind

THE IRON STAR | 105

of tracer on us that ultimately would enable them to discover the location of our home world. True caution, he said, required us to try to find out what these people were all about before we made any move to leave the scene. We couldn't just run and we couldn't simply ignore them.

I sat quietly for a long time, weighing everything.

"Well?" Bjornsen asked. "What do you want to do, Tom?"

"Send them a broadcast," I said. "Give them greetings in the name of Earth and all its peoples. Extend to them the benevolent warm wishes of the board of directors of IBM/Toshiba. And then we'll wait and see."

* * * *

We waited. But for a long while we didn't see.

Two days, and then some. We went round and round the neutron star, and they went round and round the neutron star, and no further communication came from them. We beamed them all sorts of messages at all sorts of frequencies along the spectrum, both in the radio band and via infra-red and ultraviolet as well, so that they'd have plenty of material to work with. Perhaps their translator gadget wasn't all that good, I told myself hopefully. Perhaps it was stripping its gears trying to fathom the pleasant little packets of semantic data that we had sent them.

On the third day of silence I began feeling restless. There was no way we could begin the work we had been sent here to do, not with aliens watching. The Toshiba people—the Ultra Cautious faction—got more and more nervous. Even the IBM representatives began to act a little twitchy. I started to question the wisdom of having overruled the advocates of a no-contact policy. Although the parent companies hadn't seriously expected us to run into aliens, they had covered that eventuality in our instructions, and we were under orders to do minimum tipping of our hands if we found ourselves observed by strangers. But it was too late to call back our messages and I was still eager to find out what would happen next. So we watched and waited, and then we waited and watched. Round and round the neutron star.

We had been parked in orbit for ten days now around the neutron star, an orbit calculated to bring us no closer to its surface than 9000 kilometers at the closest skim. That was close enough for us to carry out our work, but not so close that we would be subjected to troublesome and dangerous tidal effects.

The neutron star had been formed in the supernova explosion that had destroyed the smaller of the two suns in what had once been a binary star system here. At the moment of the cataclysmic collapse of the stellar sphere, all its matter had come rushing inward with such force that electrons and protons were driven into each other to become a soup of pure neutrons. Which then were squeezed so tightly that they were forced virtually into contact with one another, creating a smooth globe of the strange stuff that we call neutronium, a billion billion times denser than steel and a hundred billion billion times more incompressible.

That tiny ball of neutronium glowing dimly in our screens was the neutron star. It was just eighteen kilometers in diameter but its mass was greater than that of Earth's sun. That gave it a gravitational field a quarter of a billion billion times as strong as that of the surface of Earth. If we could somehow set foot on it, we wouldn't just be squashed flat, we'd be instantly reduced to fine powder by the colossal tidal effects—the difference in gravitational pull between the soles of our feet and the tops of our heads, stretching us towards and away from the neutron star's center with a kick of eighteen billion kilograms.

A ghostly halo of electromagnetic energy surrounded the neutron star: X-rays, radio waves, gammas, and an oily, crackling flicker of violet light. The neutron star was rotating on its axis some 550 times a second, and powerful jets of electrons were spouting from its magnetic poles at each sweep, sending forth a beacon-like pulsar broadcast of the familiar type that we have been able to detect since the middle of the twentieth century.

Behind that zone of fiercely outflung radiation lay the neutron star's atmosphere: an envelope of gaseous iron a few centimeters thick. Below that, our scan had told us, was a two-kilometers-thick crust of normal matter, heavy elements only, ranging from molybdenum on up to transuranics with atomic numbers as high as 140. And within that was the neutronium zone, the stripped nuclei of iron packed unimaginably close together, an ocean of strangeness nine kilometers deep. What lay at the heart of *that*, we could only guess.

We had come here to plunge a probe into the neutronium zone and carry off a spoonful of star-stuff that weighed 100 billion tons per cubic centimeter.

No sort of conventional landing on the neutron star was possible or even conceivable. Not only was the gravitational pull beyond our comprehension—anything that was capable of withstanding the tidal effects would still have to cope with an escape velocity requirement of 200,000 kilometers per second when it tried to take off, two thirds the speed of light—but the neutron star's surface temperature was something like 3.5 million degrees. The surface temperature of our own sun is six thousand degrees and we don't try to make landings there. Even at this distance, our heat and radiation shields were straining to the limits to keep us from being cooked. We didn't intend to go any closer.

What IBM/Toshiba wanted us to do was to put a miniature hyperspace ship into orbit around the neutron star: an astonishing little vessel no bigger than your clenched fist, powered by a fantastically scaled-down version of the drive that had carried us through the space-time manifold across a span of a thousand light-years in a dozen weeks. The little ship was a slave-drone; we would operate it from the *Ben-wah Maru*. Or, rather, Brain Central would. In a maneuver that had taken fifty computer-years to program, we would send the miniature into hyperspace and bring it out again *right inside the neutron star*. And keep it there a billionth of a second, long enough for it to gulp the spoonful of neutronium we had been sent here to collect. Then we'd head for home, with the miniature ship following us along the same hyperpath.

We'd head for home, that is, unless the slave-drone's brief intrusion into the neutron star released disruptive forces that splattered us all over this end of the galaxy. IBM/Toshiba didn't really think that was going to happen. In theory a neutron star is one of the most stable things there is in the universe, and the math didn't indicate that taking a nip from its interior would cause real problems. This neighborhood had already had its full quota of giant explosions, anyway.

Still, the possibility existed. Especially since there was a black hole just thirty light-minutes away, a souvenir of the second and much larger supernova bang that had happened here in the recent past. Having a black hole nearby is a little like playing with an extra wild card whose existence isn't made known to the players until some randomly chosen moment midway through the game. If we destabilized the neutron star in some way not anticipated by the scientists back on Earth, we might just find ourselves going for a visit to the event horizon instead of getting to go home. Or we might not. There was only one way of finding out.

I didn't know, by the way, what use the parent companies planned to make of the neutronium we had been hired to bring them. I hoped it was a good one.

But obviously we weren't going to tackle any of this while there was an alien ship in the vicinity. So all we could do was wait. And see. Right now we were doing a lot of waiting, and no seeing at all.

* * * *

Two days later Cal Bjornsen said, "We're getting a message back from them now. Audio only. In English."

We had wanted that, we had even hoped for that. And yet it shook me to learn that it was happening.

"Let's hear it," I said.

"The relay's coming over ship channel seven."

I tuned in. What I heard was an obviously synthetic voice, no undertones or overtones, not much inflection. They were trying to mimic the speech rhythms of what we had sent them, and I suppose they were actually doing a fair job of it, but the result was still unmistakably mechanical-sounding. Of course there might be nothing on board that ship but a computer, I thought, or maybe robots. I wish now that they had been robots.

It had the absolute and utter familiarity of a recurring dream. In stiff, halting, but weirdly comprehensible English came the first greetings of an alien race to the people of the planet of Earth. "This who speak be First of Nine Sparg," the voice said. Nine Sparg, we soon realized from context, was the name of their planet. First might have been the speaker's name, or his—hers, its?—title; that was unclear, and stayed that way. In an awkward pidgin-English that we nevertheless had little trouble understanding, First expressed gratitude for our transmission and asked us to send more words. To send a dictionary, in fact: now that they had the algorithm for our speech they needed more content to jam in behind it, so that we could go on to exchange more complex statements than Hello and How are you.

Bjornsen queried me on the override. "We've got an English program that we could start feeding them," he said. "Thirty thousand words: that should give them plenty. You want me to put it on for them?"

"Not so fast," I said. "We need to edit it first."

"For what?"

"Anything that might help them find the location of Earth. That's in our orders, under Eventuality of Contact with Extraterrestrials. Remember, I have Nakamura and Nagy-Szabo breathing down my neck, telling me that there's a ship full of boogiemen out there and we mustn't have anything to do with them. I don't believe that myself. But right now we don't know how friendly these Spargs are and we aren't supposed to bring strangers home with us."

"But how could a dictionary entry—"

"Suppose the sun—*our* sun—is defined as a yellow G2 type star," I said. "That gives them a pretty good beginning. Or something about the constellations as seen from Earth. I don't know, Cal. I just want to make sure we don't accidentally hand these beings a road-map to our home planet before we find out what sort of critters they are."

Three of us spent half a day screening the dictionary, and we put Brain Central to work on it too. In the end we pulled seven words—you'd laugh if you knew which they were, but we wanted to be careful—and sent the rest across to the Spargs. They were silent for nine or ten hours. When they came back on the air their command of English was immensely more fluent. Frighteningly more fluent. Yesterday First had sounded like a tourist using a Fifty Handy Phrases program. A day later, First's command of English was as good as that of an intelligent Japanese who has been living in the United States for ten or fifteen years.

It was a tense, wary conversation. Or so it seemed to me, the way it began to seem that First was male and that his way of speaking was brusque and bluntly probing. I may have been wrong on every count.

First wanted to know who we were and why we were here. Jumping right in, getting down to the heart of the matter. I felt a little like a butterfly collector who has wandered onto the grounds of a fusion plant and is being interrogated by a security guard. But I kept my tone and phrasing as neutral as I could, and told him that our planet was called Earth and that we had come on a mission of exploration and investigation.

So had they, he told me. Where is Earth?

Pretty straightforward of him, I thought. I answered that I lacked at this point a means of explaining galactic positions to him in terms that he would understand. I did volunteer the information that Earth was not anywhere close at hand.

He was willing to drop that line of inquiry for the time being. He shifted to the other obvious one:

What were we investigating?

Certain properties of collapsed stars, I said, after a bit of hesitation.

And which properties were those?

I told him that we didn't have enough vocabulary in common for me to try to explain that either.

The Nine Sparg captain seemed to accept that evasion too. And provided me with a pause that indicated that it was my turn. Fair enough.

When I asked him what *he* was doing here, he replied without any apparent trace of evasiveness that he had come on a mission of historical inquiry. I pressed for details. It has to do with the ancestry of our race, he said. We used to live in this part of the galaxy, before the great explosion. No hesitation at all about telling me that. It struck me that First was being less reticent about dealing with my queries than I was with his; but of course I had no way of judging whether I was hearing the truth from him.

"I'd like to know more," I said, as much as a test as anything else. "How long ago did your people flee this great explosion? And how far from here is your present home world?"

A long silence: several minutes. I wondered uncomfortably if I had overplayed my hand. If they were as edgy about our finding their home world as I was about their finding ours, I had to be careful not to push them into an overreaction. They might just think that the safest thing to do would be to blow us out of the sky as soon as they had learned all they could from us.

But when First spoke again it was only to say, "Are you willing to establish contact in the visual band?"

"Is such a thing possible?"

"We think so," he said.

I thought about it. Would letting them see what we looked like give them any sort of clue to the location of Earth? Perhaps, but it seemed far-fetched. Maybe they'd be able to guess that we were carbon-based oxygen-breathers, but the risk of allowing them to know that seemed relatively small. And in any case we'd find out what *they* looked like. An even trade, right?

I had my doubts that their video transmission system could be made compatible with our receiving equipment. But I gave First the go-ahead and turned the microphone over to the communications staff. Who struggled with the problem for a day and a half. Sending the signal back and forth was no big deal, but breaking it down into information that would paint a picture on a cathode-ray tube was a different matter. The communications people at both ends talked and talked and talked, while I fretted about how much technical information about us we were revealing to the Spargs. The tinkering went on and on and nothing appeared on screen except occasional strings of horizontal lines. We sent them more data about how our television system worked. They made further adjustments in their transmission devices. This time we got spots instead of lines. We sent even more data. Were they leading us on? And were we telling them too much? I came finally to the position that trying to make the video link work had been a bad idea, and started to tell Communications that. But then the haze of drifting spots on my screen abruptly cleared and I found myself looking into the face of an alien being.

An alien face, yes. Extremely alien. Suddenly this whole interchange was kicked up to a new level of reality.

A hairless wedge-shaped head, flat and broad on top, tapering to a sharp point below. Corrugated skin that looked as thick as heavy rubber. Two chilly eyes in the center of that wide forehead and two more at its extreme edges. Three mouths, vertical slits, side by side: one for speaking and the other two, maybe for separate intake of fluids and solids. The whole business supported by three long columnar necks as thick as a man's wrist, separated by open spaces two or three centimeters wide. What was below the neck we never got to see. But the head alone was plenty.

They probably thought we were just as strange.

* * * *

With video established, First and I picked up our conversation right where we had broken it off the day before. Once more he was not in the least shy about telling me things.

He had been able to calculate in our units of time the date of the great explosion that had driven his people far from home world: it had taken place 387 years ago. He didn't use the word "supernova," because it hadn't been included in the 30,000-word vocabulary we had sent them, but that was obviously what he meant by "the great explosion." The 387-year figure squared pretty well with our own calculations, which were based on an analysis of the surface temperature and rate of rotation of the neutron star.

The Nine Sparg people had had plenty of warning that their sun was behaving oddly—the first signs of instability had become apparent more than a century before the blow-up—and they had devoted all their energy for several generations to the job of packing up and clearing out. It had taken many years, it seemed, for them to accomplish their migration to the distant new world they had chosen for their new home. Did that mean, I asked myself, that their method of interstellar travel was much slower than ours, and that they had needed decades or even a century to cover fifty or a hundred light-years? Earth had less to worry about, then. Even if they wanted to make trouble for us, they wouldn't be able easily to reach us, a thousand light-years from here. Or was First saying that their new world was really distant—all the way across the galaxy, perhaps, seventy or eighty thousand light-years away, or even in some other galaxy altogether? If that was the case, we were up against truly superior beings. But there was no easy way for me to question him about such things without telling him things about our own hyperdrive and our distance from this system that I didn't care to have him know.

After a long and evidently difficult period of settling in on the new world, First went on, the Nine Sparg folk finally were well enough established to launch an inquiry into the condition of their former home planet. Thus his mission to the supernova site.

"But we are in great mystery," First admitted, and it seemed to me that a note of sadness and bewilderment had crept into his mechanical-sounding voice. "We have come to what certainly is the right location. Yet nothing seems to be correct here. We find only this little iron star. And of our former planet there is no trace."

I stared at that peculiar and unfathomable four-eyed face, that three-columned neck, those tight vertical mouths, and to my surprise something close to compassion awoke in me. I had been dealing with this creature as though he were a potential enemy capable of leading armadas of war to my world and conquering it. But in fact he might be merely a scholarly explorer who was making a nostalgic pilgrimage, and running into problems with it. I decided to relax my guard just a little.

"Have you considered," I said, "that you might not be in the right location after all?"

"What do you mean?"

"As we were completing our journey towards what you call the iron star," I said, "we discovered a planet forty light-years from here that beyond much doubt had had a great civilization, and which evidently was close enough to the exploding star system here to have been devastated by it. We have pictures of it that we could show you. Perhaps *that* was your home world."

Even as I was saying it the idea started to seem foolish to me. The skeletons we had photographed on the dead world had had broad tapering heads that might perhaps have been similar to those of First, but they hadn't shown any evidence of this unique triple-neck arrangement. Besides, First had said that his people had had several generations to prepare for evacuation. Would they have left so many millions of their people behind to die? It looked obvious from the way those skeletons were scattered around that the inhabitants of that planet hadn't had the slightest clue that doom was due to overtake them that day. And finally, I realized that First had plainly said that it was his own world's sun that had exploded, not some neighboring star. The supernova had happened here. The dead world's sun was still intact.

"Can you show me your pictures?" he said.

It seemed pointless. But I felt odd about retracting my offer. And in the new rapport that had sprung up between us I could see no harm in it.

I told Lina Sorabji to feed her sonar transparencies into the relay pickup. It was easy enough for Cal Bjornsen to shunt them into our video transmission to the alien ship.

The Nine Sparg captain withheld his comment until we had shown him the batch.

Then he said, "Oh, that was not our world. That was the world of the Garvalekkinon people."

"The Garvalekkinon?"

"We knew them. A neighboring race, not related to us. Sometimes, on rare occasions, we traded with them. Yes, they must all have died when the star exploded. It is too bad."

"They look as though they had no warning," I said. "Look: can you see them there, waiting in the train stations?"

The triple mouths fluttered in what might have been the Nine Sparg equivalent of a nod.

"I suppose they did not know the explosion was coming."

"You suppose? You mean you didn't tell them?"

All four eyes blinked at once. Expression of puzzlement.

"Tell them? Why should we have told them? We were busy with our preparations. We had no time for them. Of course the radiation would have been harmful to them, but why was that our concern? They were not related to us. They were nothing to us."

I had trouble believing I had heard him correctly. A neighboring people. Occasional trading partners. Your sun is about to blow up, and it's reasonable to assume that nearby solar systems will be affected. You have fifty or a hundred years of advance notice yourselves, and you can't even take the trouble to let these other people know what's going to happen?

I said, "You felt no need at all to warn them? That isn't easy for me to understand."

Again the four-eyed shrug.

"I have explained it to you already," said First. "They were not of our kind. They were nothing to us."

* * * *

I excused myself on some flimsy excuse and broke contact. And sat and thought a long long while. Listening to the words of the Nine Sparg captain echoing in my mind. And thinking of the millions of skeletons scattered like straws in the tunnels of that dead world that the supernova had baked. A whole people left to die because it was inconvenient to take five minutes to send them a message. Or perhaps because it simply never had occurred to anybody to bother.

The families, huddling together. The children reaching out. The husbands and wives with hands interlocked.

A world of busy, happy, intelligent, people. Boulevards and temples. Parks and gardens. Paintings, sculpture, poetry, music. History, philosophy, science. And a sudden star in the sky, and everything gone in a moment.

Why should we have told them? They were nothing to us.

I knew something of the history of my own people. We had experienced casual extermination too. But at least when the white settlers had done it to us it was because they had wanted our land.

For the first time I understood the meaning of alien.

I turned on the external screen and stared out at the unfamiliar sky of this place. The neutron star was barely visible, a dull red dot, far down in the lower left quadrant; and the black hole was high.

Once they had both been stars. What havoc must have attended their destruction! It must have been the Sparg sun that blew first, the one that had become the neutron star. And then, fifty or a hundred years later, perhaps, the other, larger star had gone the same route. Another titanic supernova, a great flare of killing light. But of course everything for hundreds of light-years around had perished already in the first blast.

The second sun had been too big to leave a neutron star behind. So great was its mass that the process of collapse had continued on beyond the neutron-star stage, matter crushing in upon itself until it broke through the normal barriers of space and took on a bizarre and almost unthinkable form, creating an object of infinitely small volume that was nevertheless of infinite density: a black hole, a pocket of incomprehensibility where once a star had been.

I stared now at the black hole before me.

I couldn't see it, of course. So powerful was the surface gravity of that grotesque thing that nothing could escape from it, not even electromagnetic radiation, not the merest particle of light. The ultimate in invisibility cloaked that infinitely deep hole in space.

But though the black hole itself was invisible, the effects that its presence caused were not. That terrible gravitational pull would rip apart and swallow any solid object that came too close; and so the hole was surrounded by a bright ring of dust and gas several hundred kilometers across. These shimmering particles constantly tumbled towards that insatiable mouth, colliding as they spiraled in, releasing flaring fountains of radiation, red-shifted into the visual spectrum by the enormous gravity: the bright green of helium, the majestic purple of hydrogen, the crimson of oxygen. That outpouring of energy was the death-cry of doomed matter. That rainbow whirlpool of blazing light was the beacon marking the maw of the black hole.

I found it oddly comforting to stare at that thing. To contemplate that zone of eternal quietude from which there was no escape. Pondering so inexorable and unanswerable an infinity was more soothing than thinking of a world of busy people destroyed by the indifference of their neighbors. Black holes offer no choices, no complexities, no shades of disagreement. They are absolute.

Why should we have told them? They were nothing to us.

After a time I restored contact with the Nine Sparg ship. First came to the screen at once, ready to continue our conversation.

"There is no question that our world once was located here," he said at once. "We have checked and rechecked the coordinates. But the changes have been extraordinary."

"Have they?"

"Once there were two stars here, our own and the brilliant blue one that was nearby. Our history is very specific on that point: a brilliant blue star that lit the entire sky. Now we have only the iron star. Apparently it has taken the place of our sun. But where has the blue one gone? Could the explosion have destroyed it too?"

I frowned. Did they really not know? Could a race be capable of attaining an interstellar spacedrive and an interspecies translating device, and nevertheless not have arrived at any understanding of the neutron star/black hole cosmogony?

Why not? They were aliens. They had come by all their understanding of the universe via a route different from ours. They might well have overlooked this feature or that of the universe about them.

"The blue star—" I began.

But First spoke right over me, saying, "It is a mystery that we must devote all our energies to solving, or our mission will be fruitless. But let us talk of other things. You have said little of your own mission. And of your home world. I am filled with great curiosity, Captain, about those subjects."

I'm sure you are, I thought.

"We have only begun our return to space travel," said First. "Thus far we have encountered no other intelligent races. And so we regard this meeting as fortunate. It is our wish to initiate contact with you. Quite likely some aspects of your technology would be valuable to us. And there will be much that you wish to purchase from us. Therefore we would be glad to establish trade relations with you."

As you did with the Garvalekkinon people, I said to myself.

I said, "We can speak of that tomorrow, Captain. I grow tired now. But before we break contact for the day, allow me to offer you the beginning of a solution to the mystery of the disappearance of the blue sun."

The four eyes widened. The slitted mouths parted in what seemed surely to be excitement.

"Can you do that?"

I took a deep breath.

"We have some preliminary knowledge. Do you see the place opposite the iron star, where energies boil and circle in the sky? As we entered this system, we found certain evidence there that may explain the fate of your former blue sun. You would do well to center your investigations on that spot."

"We are most grateful," said First.

"And now, Captain, I must bid you good night. Until tomorrow, Captain."

"Until tomorrow," said the alien.

* * * *

I was awakened in the middle of my sleep period by Lina Sorabji and Bryce-Williamson, both of them looking flushed and sweaty. I sat up, blinking and shaking my head.

"It's the alien ship," Bryce-Williamson blurted, "It's approaching the black hole."

"Is it, now?"

"Dangerously close," said Lina. "What do they think they're doing? Don't they know?"

"I don't think so," I said. "I suggested that they go exploring there. Evidently they don't regard it as a bad idea."

"You sent them there?" she said incredulously.

With a shrug I said, "I told them that if they went over there they might find the answer to the question of where one of their missing suns went. I guess they've decided to see if I was right."

"We have to warn them," said Bryce-Williamson. "Before it's too late. Especially if we're responsible for sending them there. They'll be furious with us once they realize that we failed to warn them of the danger."

"By the time they realize it," I replied calmly, "it *will* be too late. And then their fury won't matter, will it? They won't be able to tell us how annoyed they are with us. Or to report to their home world, for that matter, that they had an encounter with intelligent aliens who might be worth exploiting."

He gave me an odd look. The truth was starting to sink in.

I turned on the external screens and punched up a close look at the black hole region. Yes, there was the alien ship, the little metallic sphere, the six odd outthrust legs. It was in the zone of criticality now. It seemed hardly to be moving at all. And it was growing dimmer and dimmer as it slowed. The gravitational field had it, and it was being drawn in. Blacking out, becoming motionless. Soon it would have gone beyond the point where outside observers could perceive it. Already it was beyond the point of turning back.

I heard Lina sobbing behind me. Bryce-Williamson was muttering to himself: praying, perhaps.

I said, "Who can say what they would have done to us—in their casual, indifferent way—once they came to Earth? We know now that Spargs worry only about Spargs. Anybody else is just so much furniture." I shook my head. "To hell with them. They're gone, and in a universe this big we'll probably never come across any of them again, or they us. Which is just fine. We'll be a lot better off having nothing at all to do with them."

"But to die that way—" Lina murmured. "To sail blindly into a black hole—"

"It is a great tragedy," said Bryce-Williamson.

"A tragedy for them," I said. "For us, a reprieve, I think. And tomorrow we can get moving on the neutronium-scoop project." I tuned up the screen to the next level. The boiling cloud of matter around the mouth of the black hole blazed fiercely. But of the alien ship there was nothing to be seen.

Yes, a great tragedy, I thought. The valiant exploratory mission that had sought the remains of the Nine Sparg home world has been lost with all hands. No hope of rescue. A pity that they hadn't known how unpleasant black holes can be.

But why should we have told them? They were nothing to us.

THE ISOLATIONISTS

Originally published in *Science Fiction Stories*, November 1958.

As the small planet took shape in his screens, Andersen felt the usual twitch of anticipation. Once, as a boy on Earth twenty years before, he had contemplated a boulder by the side of a swift-flowing stream for a long moment, then tipped it over. Revealed in the moist soil beneath the boulder were wonders: white grubs three inches long, with sparkling green eyes and furious little mandibles. Anderson had never forgotten that incident. It was written large on his mind every time he prepared to make a first landing on an unexplored planet; one never knew what gaudy surprises might lie hidden and waiting.

Andersen checked his charts. The planet was the fourth of a fourteen-planet system, but it was the only one of the fourteen that looked habitable. The Mapping Corps had ticketed it for future survey. The calibrating computer keyed into his ship's mass-detector told Andersen that the planet was of 0.75 Earthmass; a 7000-mile diameter, but therefore lower in density and short of heavy elements. Andersen set up landing coordinates at once. His instructions were to visit every reasonably Earth-type planet along the sine-wave curve of his tracking course; he was to file a report on the status of the planet's inhabitants, if intelligent, and on the feasibility of Terran colonization thereof.

The planet was inhabited. The little red star on his master chart told him that much. Andersen wondered what particular grubs would lie hidden underneath this stone. Inhabited planets were always full of surprises. First contact came as a different sort of shock to different kinds of beings.

His ship dropped lower. It swung into a landing orbit. It roared through the thickening atmosphere toward the tawny land below. Perhaps, he thought, the alien beings of this world were gathering to mark his blazing path through their skies.

On his tenth orbital pass he selected a continent. He activated the braking jets. The small ship's tail dropped into landing position.

A stretch of clear flat land beckoned. Andersen jabbed the landing buttons. Flames sprouted beneath his ship. He dropped down on a fiery cushion. The ship gentled itself to a square upright landing.

He had arrived. The stone had been tipped. Now to see what was beneath!

* * * *

The aliens did not arrive on the scene for nearly two minutes, which allowed Andersen something of a breather in which to look around. He did not roam far from his ship. The samplers had shown him that the planet's atmosphere was a chlorine-hydrogen one, with lesser quantities of nitrogen and the inerts. He wore a breathing-helmet strapped over his uniform, since no more than two good whiffs of that atmosphere would be enough to scald his throat and rot his lungs.

The sky was a light yellow—due partly, Andersen decided, to the murky wisps of chlorine drifting above, and partly to some refractive trick of the atmosphere. It was an oddly pleasing effect, at any rate. The landscape was strangely rugged, with bare rock scooped into shell-like depressions by erosive action. Strange, almost surrealistic trees sprang up high, jointed and involute, twisted grotesquely, crested with bizarre and disturbing-looking flowers. In the distance, Andersen saw buildings, sleek and colorful, fashioned, evidently, from some form of pink coral. A few birds drifted in the sky. Andersen watched one come to light in an angular tree; the bird landed on a spatulate limb in an inverted position, as if it had sucker-pads instead of claws, and began to nibble on the pendulous fruits.

After his first detailed glance at the landscape, Andersen unshipped the portable Translator and set it up. He busied himself over the installation, jacking the input to his instrument belt and rigging up a booster in case the aliens refused to approach near enough for the Translator's amplifier to reach them.

But his precautions were unnecessary. A voice said in crisp and unaccented Terran, "There will be no need of that machine, Earthman. We will be able to understand you fully."

The nine-year-old Andersen had gasped in awed delight at the sight of the writhing grubs beneath the stone. The twenty-nine-year-old Andersen whirled like a startled cat when the firm voice spoke.

"Who said that?"

"We did."

Andersen turned and saw the aliens. There were seven of them in a tight group about a hundred yards to his left. Andersen had not seen them approach. And, he thought, at this distance and in this sort of atmosphere, it was odd that he had heard them so clearly.

They were beings as angular as the trees—six and a half or seven feet tall, Andersen estimated, with rich purple skins. He doubted if any of them would weigh as much as a hundred pounds under Terran gravity; here, they were even lighter.

They did not seem to have any flesh; they were merely skin stretched over bone, and light bone at that. Their heads were diamond-shaped and hairless, with long solemn chins and tapering pointed skulls; their nostrils were but slits, their mouths dark slashes, their eyes cold and hooded, their ears nonexistent. Andersen guessed that they were a cold-blooded race. There was something reptilian about them. Their legs were like sticks, terminating in splayed claws.

They walked toward Andersen in a group.

The Earthman looked uncertainly at the advancing aliens, then at his Translator.

He said, "You speak my language?"

"We speak all languages." It was impossible to tell which member of the group had spoken. Perhaps none of them had; perhaps all.

"You must be telepaths, then."

"Yes."

Can you understand what I'm saying? Andersen thought. There was no response.

"I've just thought a message at you," said the Earthman. "Didn't you get it?"

"We can only respond to subliminal projection from you, Earthman. We reach the deep layer of your mind but cannot detect surface thoughts."

Andersen frowned. He didn't care for that sort of arrangement. But he had dealt with telepathic races before. In a way, it made things a good deal easier, for if they could see the deep layers of his mind they would not have to worry about his sincerity. They could tell whenever he was lying, and Andersen did not intend to lie.

He said, "I'm not a telepath myself."

"Of course. But we can communicate with you."

"Good. Since you've looked deep into my mind, you know I've come here for peaceful purposes." There was no reply, and Andersen went on with somewhat less assurance: "You *do* know that I'm here for peaceful purposes. I'm a representative of the Terran Confederation, a group of one hundred ninety worlds of the galaxy, offering mutual benefits and harmonious fellowship. Now, since this is the first landing an Earthman has made on your planet, you undoubtedly want time to think matters over, and—"

Andersen was on the verge of launching into the standard *take-me-*

to-your-leader pitch when the calm voice of the aliens—he saw now that the voice was collectively emanating from the group—interrupted him.

"You are not the first Earthman to land here."

The statement, taken at its face value, made no sense. According to the charts, the planet was unexplored. Had the Mapping Corps outfit made a planetary landing? Unlikely. Had a previous Surveyor visited the planet and neglected to report the fact? Implausible. Had an unauthorized Earthman made an independent landing on an unexplored world? Impossible.

"I don't understand," Andersen said. "How could other Earthmen have landed here? I mean—"

"You are the third one. The other two came in ships just like yours."

"When?"

"The first was eleven years ago. The second was five years after that."

"Local years?"

"Terran years."

Andersen frowned, deeply troubled. Unreported visits by Survey men? What possible reason could a Survey man have for not reporting a planetfall? And why would it happen twice, years apart?

He took a deep breath. "At any rate, the Terran Confederation offers you—"

"We are not interested."

"At least let me tell you—"

The implacable mental voice cut him off once again. "We will join no Confederations. We do not want Earthmen landing on our planet."

Andersen took a deep breath. He had run up across this sort of insularity and intransigence before, and he had special persuasive techniques to overcome it. Earth was geared to an infinitely expanding economy; it needed an infinitely expanding market as well, and with such conditions prevailing it was imperative that all possible avenues of trade be opened.

He said, "Please don't be hasty. At least let me explain the value of entering into friendly relationship with our Confederation. For instance, it would be possible to carry on trade without the necessity of a single spaceship landing on your soil. If—"

"We are not interested."

"Give me a few minutes. In my ship I have solido slides that will be helpful in—"

"No."

Andersen began to feel exasperated. "Why won't you listen to me?" he demanded.

"We have maintained our independence for many thousands of

years. Our economy and ecology are balanced with equal precision. We are self-sufficient. We have no need of Earth and its Confederation."

"What would you do if we *forced* you to trade with us?" Andersen said rashly. He doubted that Earth would go along with him on the use of force, but he wanted to see the alien reaction.

It was a mild one. "You would not do such a thing."

"Suppose we did?"

"You would not succeed."

"Why not?"

"You *could* not succeed."

Andersen scowled. The seven aliens had not changed expression once during the colloquy, indeed had hardly as much as moved. Yet the door was slamming firmly in his face. These people wanted to remain in isolation. That much was abundantly clear. But Andersen did not give up easily.

"You owe a debt to the universe," he began, taking an abstract approach. "Your planet, your solar system, are all part of the great celestial machine. Do you think you can withdraw yourself totally from that machine? No planet is an island, friends. There has to be an intermeshing of gears. Otherwise you'll pay the price of cultural decadence. You'll go the way of all—"

"We have survived successfully for many thousands of years. Our society is stable. We are not interested in the meddling ways of Earthmen. We made this clear to the other Earthmen who visited us."

"I don't know anything about them."

"They were like you. Stubborn, self-willed, convinced they were in possession of eternal truth. Spouting generalizations about the universe, fuzzy analogies, crude and pathetic syllogisms. Leave us, Earthman."

"Hold on a second," Andersen burst out. "I'm a duly accredited ambassador from the Terran Confederation. I don't intend to be brushed off this way. I demand to be taken to someone in authority on this planet!"

"We are all equals here," said the alien voice. It sounded tired; impatient, perhaps. "Return to your ship. Depart. Do not return."

"I won't leave until I've spoken to someone who—"

"You will leave immediately."

"What if I don't?"

Andersen felt the equivalent of a mental shrug. "We are peaceful and passive people. We would not take direct steps to harm you. But if you fail to leave you will cause harm to come to yourself."

"Please," Andersen wheedled. "Don't fly off the handle. Let me try to tell you—"

"You have been warned," came the weary reply.

"But—"

Andersen heard two gentle plopping sounds above him. For an instant he did not understand; then he swiveled his head upward and he understood.

A chill quivered through him. He realized in that single panicky instant that he was about to die.

"You will not be harmed if you return to your ship at once!" came the alien voice.

Andersen stared. One of the birds he had seen in the strange trees had plummeted down and landed atop his breathing-helmet. Its sucker-equipped feet were firmly attached to the plastic dome. The bird was the size of a small hen, blue, with a bright red crest and glittering beady eyes. A conspicuous feature of the bird was its sharp and imposing beak.

At the moment that beak was clamped around Andersen's left-hand breathing-tube. One twitch of the creature's jaws and the rubber tube would be severed; his air would rush out, and the deadly alien atmosphere come filtering in.

Andersen tentatively reached his left arm up to pluck the bird away.

The alien voice said quietly, "The bird will sever your breathing-tube before you are able to remove him. You will die almost immediately."

The bird had made no attempt to bite into the tube yet; it simply sat there on his helmet, grasping the tube in its beak and remaining motionless.

Andersen froze. Any motion, he felt, might disturb the bird.

"Get him off me," he whispered harshly.

"The tube of your helmet closely resembles the large green worm of the flatlands which is this bird's chief food," the alien remarked. "The bird is anxious to feed. Only our control is preventing him from doing so."

Sweat trickled down Andersen's forehead faster than his air-conditioners could pump his helmet dry. "What do you want me to do?"

"Walk slowly toward your ship."

"And if I don't?"

"We will order the bird to sever the tube. You see, the choice is entirely in your hands. Refusal to enter your ship would be tantamount to suicide."

"You'll—*order*—the bird?"

"All life on this planet is in harmony, Earthman. This is why we have no need of your Confederation. The bird understands our orders. But the bird is hungry, Earthman."

Andersen did not need further hints. He began to edge across the flat terrain, slowly, cautiously, as if the creature perched on his helmet were highly explosive. He was twenty feet from his ship. Crossing those twenty feet seemed to take forever.

At length he reached the open hatch of the ship. His alien tormentors were eyeing him gravely from where they stood.

"All right," Andersen growled. "I'm back at my ship. Call off your bird!"

"Enter the ship."

"With the bird?"

"The bird will leave you."

Bitterly, Andersen grabbed the handhold and pulled himself up into the hatchway. Just before he drew himself back into the ship, he heard two loud popping sounds, and saw the blue bird fluttering up into the air.

He exhaled feelingly. Having those pincers on his air-tube had been like having a hand round his throat.

The bird hovered ominously in the air a few feet above the ship, flying in a tight little circle, obviously ready to pounce again if Andersen should attempt to emerge. But he knew that this time the beak would close, and he remained where he was. "Is your answer final?" he said to the aliens.

"Our ecology is a closed cycle and our economy is stable. We value our stability. We have no desire for contact, Earthman."

Andersen nodded. The door had slammed shut. Short of coercion, there was no way to make these beings see reason.

He glowered at the hovering bird. He scowled at the motionless knot of aliens. He frowned at the whole weird landscape and yellow sky.

Failure.

Andersen's hand grasped the actuating lever of the airlock control. He yanked. The metal sheath rolled smoothly into place, blotting out bird and aliens and landscape and sky.

Minutes later, his ship was streaking out of the chlorinated atmosphere and heading for space.

* * * *

Andersen knew why the two previous Survey men had neglected to mention the fact of their visits to the small world. Obviously they had been too humiliated to care to record their encounter in the official record. The planet was an ecological whole; apparently the lean purple humanoids were merely first among equals. And the planet's inhabitants wanted to remain what they were—isolated.

They would have cooperated to repulse any invasion. They had driven him away with a bird the size of a hen—and no doubt they had been equally imaginative in driving away the two previous Survey men. Andersen amused himself by trying to picture the scene. A cloud of gnats? A horde of small lizards? It didn't matter. Humanity could not hope to win a conflict waged against the total inhabitants of a world. Defeating humanoids can be done; but when the birds and insects and perhaps even the filterable viruses join the fray, victory for the Confederation becomes impossible.

Andersen brooded long and hard before he tapped out his report on the planet. The easiest thing to do would be simply to neglect to mention the stop, as his predecessors had done; but he was too conscientious for that. He had to file a report.

He filed it.

* * * *

Report of Survey Scout J. F. Andersen on World Four of System 107b332.

Planet is inhabited by intelligent life. Contact was made but dominant life-forms show little interest in galactic affairs.

Hostile non-intelligent life-forms make the planet highly undesirable. This operative nearly lost his life in an encounter with a dangerous native life-form. Probability of other hostile life-forms is high.

Recommendation: This planet's inhabitants are not promising members of the Confederation nor is the planet itself suitable for Terran habitation. Therefore it seems unwise to attempt further contact with this world.

* * * *

Andersen typed the report out on the black-bordered paper used for negative reports, and dropped the completed report in the polar facsimilizer. An electronic impulse flickered out along the subspace channels, and an instant later a reproduction of his report had arrived at the main headquarters of the Survey Corps, on Earth.

He knew the procedure. The report would be filed in the *negative* bank, and all references to World Four of System 107b332 would be altered to show the planet as not suitable for contact. In the course of events, his negative report would come up for review, as regulations provided. He would be called upon to explain his reasons for filing such a report.

But, at last word, the Central Board was fifty years behind on reviewing. Andersen shrugged and set up the coordinates for his next stop.

By the time they got around to calling him up for an explanation, he would be pensioned off and no longer concerned with matters of pride. But, just for now, he thought, it was better that no one found out that on World Four of System 107b332 the mighty Terran Confederation had been repulsed by a bright-colored bird the size of a small hen.

THE LONELY ONE

Originally published in *Science Fiction Stories*, July 1956.

Jannes very carefully guided the two-man cruiser out through the *Haughtsmith's* lock, while Norb Kendon paced up and down in the tiny confines of the little ship, watching the red dot of light that was Sol.

"I feel kind of funny about this, Harl." Norb stared at the small hard point of red light. "I feel like a kid going where the grownups belong."

Jannes said nothing till the cruiser was in free fall; then he wheeled around to face the other. "So what if it's Earth? Those wild men down there can't be anything to get sentimental about. That's your trouble, Norb—sentiment. You haven't learned, have you?"

Norb repressed a tiny beat of anger that rose suddenly within him. "You know I'm not being sentimental. It's just that—just that here's the planet that gave birth to life. The source of all mankind; and here it is dead or almost dead."

"And that's not being sentimental, eh? What do you call it, then?"

Norb frowned. "You win you long-nosed devil; I'm being sentimental. So what? Is it a crime? I just can't help feeling reverential right now."

"I'll lay off," Jannes said. A smile creased his face, and pulled his long, twisting snake of a nose into an even more grotesque shape.

The cruiser began to spiral down into its landing orbit. Jannes skillfully cut the orbit to minimum and sat the ship gently on its tail. He deactivated the pile, while Norb tested the atmosphere. "How is it, Norb?"

"What do you expect? Cold as hell, but breathable."

"How cold?"

"Plenty; five below, I hope the natives have some warm igloos for us."

"If we find natives, that is," Jannes rejoined. "We haven't heard a peep out of Earth for twenty years, and there were only a few hundred left then."

"We'll find them," Norb said. "Life doesn't give up so easily on this planet, methinks. Man'll stick pretty closely to his home world."

"Sentiment again," Jannes snorted, as they snapped open the lock and headed out.

The snow was soft and unbroken, and the two spacemen sank in to their hips. They floundered around in the drifts for a few moments.

"Hey," Jannes called shouting to make himself heard over the whistling wind. "We'd better clear a path in front of us, or we'll never get anywhere."

They fumbled out their blasters and began to melt a path through the snow. The warmth fanned out around them.

"Which way is that colony?" Norb asked.

"Mukennik said due east which is thataway. If it's a colony, that is; how anything could survive in this kind of territory is beyond me."

They pushed on through the snow, leaving a little river of warmth behind them. The day was dark with the perpetual gloom of a dying world, and the dwarfed sun afforded little illumination and less heat. For as far as they could see, there was nothing but the shiny glint of the snow, broken occasionally by the few twisted, leafless trees which pierced the white blanket and stood out sharp against the grey skies.

"Are we headed east, Harl?"

"Don't you trust the compass?" Jannes asked. "It says we're going east. Not that it matters much."

"It's just that I don't see any sign of that colony. If Mukennik could see signs of life from the *Haughtsmith* we ought to be able to find them from down here. And there's nothing in sight in any direction."

Jannes stared hard at the compass. "It says east is out that way; and we'll go that way. If we don't find anything, we'll turn back. Let Mukennik come down here and freeze for a while; I don't see why that green-faced clown couldn't come looking for his own colonies, instead of sending us."

Norb looked quizzically at his companion. "Quit it, Harl. You know a Sirian couldn't stand this kind of climate, or else Mukennik would be down here without any coaxing. Besides, we volunteered."

"Yeah. I almost forgot that, didn't I?" Jannes wiped a speck of snow from the end of his nose. "Let's look real hard, yes? Maybe bring back a live Earthman or two for Mukennik's collection."

Norb said nothing. He squinted out toward the horizon, hoping to catch the slow rising of smoke or some other token of life. Suddenly he stretched up on tiptoe. "You see that out there Harl? That look like a living thing to you?"

"Where? You mean that tree all the way out there?" Jannes pointed.

"Right direction, but it's not a tree; looks like a moving figure to me."

"I'll take your word for it. Say, is Mukennik serious about that offer?"

"I'm sure he is," said Norb, straining hard to see the distant figure.

"He'll feel pretty foolish if we do find them. He'll have one hell of a time trying to fit them all aboard the *Haughtsmith.*" Mentioning the ship reminded Jannes that he had descended from space in a ship, and he hastily turned to look for the cruiser. He was somewhat surprised to see that the trail they had blazed extended only a few hundred meters back to the ship.

"Look at that, Kendon; I was sure we'd gone farther than that."

"Must be your mind snapping," Norb retorted. "Say, that *is* a figure out there!"

Jannes stared and agreed. They began to shout and run as fast as they could—which was not—very fast—through the snow toward the far-off shape.

The old man had caught sight of them as they ran, and was standing in the snow, arms akimbo, waiting for them to approach. He was waiting by one of the gnarled trees, and, Norb observed, he was as gnarled himself as the twisted tree he leaned against. He was very old and terribly dried-out looking; Norb hoped he wasn't deaf.

"Greetings, Earthman," Norb said slowly and carefully once they were within speaking range. "We have come from the skies in silver bird." Norb illustrated this with his hands, and Jannes followed Norb's lead.

"Do you understand us, old one?" Jannes asked, rolling each syllable out with care.

The wrinkled oldster smiled. "Of course I do, son. Why do you star people insist on treating us like savages, anyway?" The old man's voice was husky and impossibly deep. "I've been speaking this language for as long as both of you've been alive."

The two spacemen looked at each other in surprise. "Sorry," Norb said, smiling. "It's just that Earth's been out of touch with the System for so many years that we didn't know exactly what to expect."

"Quite all right, believe me. Welcome to Earth. Where'd you say you were from, anyway?"

"Starship *Haughtsmith,* out of Vega II."

"Is Vega II a beautiful planet, young man?"

"That it is," Norb said. "Our winters are only a few degrees cooler than our summers, and the Climate Constant is one of the best in the galaxy."

"Interesting," the old man said.

"We'll be glad to get back there," Jannes replied. "No snow."

Norb heard a low rumbling coming from the Earth. It grew steadily in intensity. "What's that?"

"Earthquake," the old man said. "Means Earth's annoyed at what you said about going back. She likes to keep her visitors around for a while."

"We'll be here a while," Jannes said; "and then we'll clear out as fast as we can—if we're not frozen solid first." The ground began to quiver and the two Vegans fell forward in the snow. The old Earthman remained upright calmly ripping up the bark of the tree with horny fingers and stuffing the pieces of bark into a sack as they came off.

"Guess you got her angry, all right. Come; I've got all the bark I need now, so let me take you to see the king before you get into some real trouble. My name's Kalvin, by the way; I'm just about the oldest man on Earth, I guess. McNeil's been expecting you for years—ever since the transmitter broke down." Kalvin gestured and led them off in a path through the snow.

Suddenly, the old man disappeared from sight. His voice boomed up from the ground below. "Keep moving; the entrance is right in front of you."

The two spacemen moved cautiously forward, Norb in the lead, and felt the ground beginning to slope. Abruptly the snow fell away and Norb saw there was a slanting hole in the ground. He entered.

Kalvin was standing there with a knot of people around him. Most of them were old, Norb noted, all thin and knotty-looking. There were a few children, not many.

"Welcome to the capital city of Earth," Kalvin said, "the last survivors of the glory that was Terra salute you."

"Do you all live here?" Jannes asked.

"All hundred and two of us," replied Kalvin, waving. "You see before you the guardians of man's immortal heritage. That's what they told us when they left us behind." He laughed raucously.

A tall man appeared from somewhere in the back of the cavern. Like the others, he was warmly dressed in animal furs, and in his flowing white hair was a crown made of shining metal. As he approached the spacemen saw that he was very tall indeed.

"I'm McNeil," the tall man said. Norb looked him up and down and decided he was almost three meters tall from shining crown to fur-swathed feet—the tallest man he had ever seen. "Welcome to Earth," McNeil said. "I'm the king."

Jannes and Norb exchanged uncertain glances. The space manual didn't say anything about proper behavior in front of kings. "We're honored, Your Majesty," Norb began uncertainly. "We represent the Starship *Haughtsmith* out of Vega II."

"Just call me McNeil," the big man said. "Pleasure is all mine; I've been expecting visitors from space for twenty years—ever since our transmitter went off. Sorry we had to hide from you, but when I saw your ship up there I figured the best thing to do was to cover up all traces of our city until we knew whether it was safe or not. I think you saw us from up there before we had a chance to cover up, because you seemed to know where to land." McNeil turned to Kalvin, who was standing nearby. "Hey, oldster, you've earned another."

The king took a strip of fur from his collar and put it around Kalvin's neck, where, Norb observed, there already were a number of similar strips. Kalvin smiled, bowed, and fingered the new fur strip pleasedly.

"Kalvin's our most honored knight," McNeil explained. "The old dog's lived so long he's been knighted ten times over. I was hoping the spacemen would eat you when you went out to get them, leatherface." He gave the old man a playful shove and Kalvin backed slowly away.

"He said there were just a hundred and two of you," Norb said.

"That's right. There used to be more, but we're slowly dying out. This life isn't an easy one, and Earth seems to get colder every year. I won't give us more than another century, and then this'll be a dead planet. Come on, I'll show you a room you can have while you're here."

Norb and Jannes followed the tall king down a winding corridor. Jannes was still too amazed to say very much, and followed along in silence.

"That's why we came," Norb said; "we weren't sure anyone was left on Earth or not. But now you won't have to fight the cold anymore; we're going to take you back to Vega with us—all of you—and you can spend the rest of your lives in warmth."

"I'm afraid it's too late for that," said McNeil; "better forget the idea. Here's your room. The people will be putting on a dance for you tonight, and we'll come get you when it's time." The king showed them a small room carved out of the side of the cavern, bowed, and vanished into the corridor.

"I guess you were right," Jannes said, as soon as they were alone.

Norb smiled at the smaller man. "I guess so, Longnose. It's wonderful to find the home of civilization again, isn't it? When we get them back to Vega, we can give them a whole village and make it into a living museum to preserve the ways of dead Earth. Mukennik'll really be delighted by this."

"Somehow I don't like it though," said Jannes. "First, Kalvin telling us to watch out, and now McNeil saying it's too late for them to leave. I smell trouble cooking."

"My father warned me to watch out for people with long noses,"

Norb said. "They find trouble where there's none to be found."

"Have it your own way, Kendon. You're so thrilled to be on Earth that you can't see beyond the end of your nose—which isn't so small itself."

Norb settled back on his bed of straw and did not answer. It had been an exhausting walk through the snow and now was the time for some sleep.

It seemed to be an instant later that there was a timid rap on the wall of their room. A girl tiptoed in and stood there. She was bundled in furs except for her pretty, somewhat dirty, high-cheekboned face. About eighteen, Norb judged, as he waited for her to master her fear.

"The dance is about to start, sirs," she whispered. "McNeil thinks you'll be interested." Having delivered her message, she turned quickly and dashed away into the corridor.

"We'd better go," Jannes said; "they're expecting us."

"Right." They wandered down the corridor toward where they heard the sound of drums.

All hundred and two inhabitants of Earth were gathered in the largest room of the underground village. They were massed in a compact group—except for McNeil, who stood in front, and two drummers pounding drums made of animal-skin.

"We're about ready to start," said McNeil. "We hold these dances regularly, but this is the first time we've had outsiders to watch. They're all very excited about it."

McNeil sat down at the side of the room, beckoning to the two Vegans to follow suit. "It's our only remaining art form to speak of. We had to discourage other forms of art because they weren't useful; but at least the people get some exercise out of this."

"What sort of a dance is it?"

"It's really an historical pageant. It dramatizes the history of Earth from its time of greatest strength to its old age. Which reminds me—are you still thinking of taking the Earthfolk off to Vega with you?"

"Yes," Norb said.

"Forget about it; we can't come. And don't try to get any of my younger men to come back with you. You'll be in for a surprise or two, I think."

"But why, McNeil? Here we offer you free transportation, and all the comforts of the universe on a warm planet, and you refuse. Do you really enjoy living in this frozen hole?"

"Whisper, please," said the king; "I don't want to alarm my subjects. No, of course we don't enjoy living here. But it isn't as bad as it seems; Earth's been freezing for thousands of years, and we're used to cold weather and nothing else; we've never known any other. But that's not the reason why we can't leave. You'll find out during the dance. I think they're ready to start."

The drummers began to beat in a tricky syncopation, and the massed Earthmen in the center of the room slowly began to move. They were interweaving in intricate patterns, moving faster and faster, winding around one another in snakelike rhythms.

"That represents Earth as it used to be," said McNeil; "the crowded home of mankind."

Norb and Jannes watched as the motion became more and more rapid, the Earthmen entangling themselves in complex patterns and then patterns still more complex.

Suddenly there was a terrible pounding on the drums, and one of the dancers burst from the twisting multitude and ran toward an empty corner of the room.

"First interplanetary voyage," McNeil whispered.

The rest of the dancers continued to move in a close-packed mass. Then, another drumroll and a second dancer detached himself and headed for another corner of the room. "The second," McNeil said.

Now the dancers ran in more dizzy patterns than before, and a third and fourth ran off to corners. The drumbeats grew more frenzied.

"Here comes the exodus," said McNeil. "The big push outward that left Earth almost deserted."

The drummers practically went wild, as one after another of the dancers pranced out from the center and headed for one corner or another, until there were more dancers in the clusters in the corners of the room than in the center. Those in the center began to move more slowly now, as their numbers diminished.

Only about ten Earthmen were still in the center of the room, out of the original ninety-nine. They continued to weave through their patterns, but more and more slowly. One dancer finally pulled himself free and ran to the most distant corner. Another followed. Then another.

Finally, there were just three left in the center, revolving slowly around each other. Their movements grew more and more tortured, and they writhed as if their feet were glued to the floor. Slowly they sank to the cold floor and stayed there, their bodies still wriggling. They stretched out flat on the ground, moving now a finger, now a toe, but seemingly unable to rise. One by one they stopped moving completely, until the last one let his head drop.

That was the signal for a wild demonstration by all the dancers. They began shouting and singing, and the three in the middle leaped up and joined them. The dance was over.

Norb and Jannes sat transfixed. "That's our last art form," said McNeil. "What do you think of it?"

"It's wonderful," Norb said, suddenly jarred back to reality. "But I didn't quite catch the symbolism at the end. Why didn't the last three run off to join the others on the other planets?"

"I thought it would be obvious," McNeil said; "but perhaps it's just that I've seen the dance so many times. Look: they would have left but they couldn't; the planet wouldn't let them."

"What's that?" said Jannes in surprise.

"Earth is a very lonely world, Vegans. She's not getting much heat from her sun any more, and she knows she's dying. And she doesn't want to die alone. Just about all of her people have left her, but she's clinging with all her might to her last hundred-and-two. It's been centuries since any Earthman's been allowed to get off-planet. Earth doesn't want us to leave, and she's holding us in a tight grip."

"Don't give us that, McNeil," said Jannes angrily. "I know you think that we regard you as savages, but that doesn't mean you have to play along. There's some other reason why you don't want to leave. Don't start spouting mythology at me. We know—"

Jannes suddenly spilled to the floor. The ground gave a convulsive shudder.

"Earthquake," McNeil said calmly. "It's pretty common now. Every time the Earth gets angry—and I suppose you made her angry. I think you'd better get back to your ship before there's worse trouble. Kalvin, you'd better guide them to their ship."

"Wait. Before you let us go, we want to speak to our commander and find out what he thinks."

"What he thinks can't possibly concern us," McNeil said; "but go ahead if it'll please you."

Jannes began to set up the radio equipment. It was fairly simple work for an experienced pilot like Jannes; but for some reason, his hands shook and it took longer than usual. He dialed the *Haughtsmith,* and Mukennik's familiar voice crackled down to them.

"How's it going?" the commander asked. "We watched you go into that hole with the Earthman; what's been happening?"

"You'd better do the talking," Jannes whispered to Norb. Norb replaced him at the controls of the set.

"Trouble, chief," Norb said. "We found the Earthmen all right—a hundred and two of them—and they say they're the whole population of the planet."

"Healthy?"

"Healthier than we are. It's about five below down here and I guess

THE LONELY ONE | 135

that keeps them in shape."

"Are they savages?"

Norb looked around. A knot of curious Earthmen had gathered around the transmitter and were watching closely. "No, Mukennik. But they're—well, not quite civilized either." Norb heard a snort of protest from McNeil.

"What do you mean? Have you asked them to leave Earth?"

"Yes," Norb said. "I told them all about Vega; but they're not going to come."

"Not coming? Why?"

"We spoke to the king here, and he tells us there's an Earth-spirit which is lonely and dying, and won't let them leave. He seems to say they'd like to get to a warmer planet, but they're stuck here for good."

"Oh," Mukennik said. He was obviously disappointed. "So they won't come at all."

"No."

There was silence from the *Haughtsmith* for a moment. "Well, don't try to force them," Mukennik said, finally. "It doesn't pay to meddle with tribal customs. Might as well give it up as a bad job and come back; we'll do up a report on it and let it go at that. At least we've found the legendary Earthmen."

"Yes," Norb said. "At least we've found them. Well, we're going to head for our ship now; get the airlock ready to receive us."

The trek across the snow to where the gleaming two-man ship stood upright was a long and slow one. Kalvin accompanied them—the old man was seemingly tireless—and stared with apparent amazement at the ship.

Norb and Jannes began to climb the catwalk to the entrance of the cruiser. Kalvin stood below, watching.

"So long, old man," Norb said.

"So long," Jannes echoed; "we'll remember you on Vega. It's nice and warm there, you know. An old chap like you could live forever in that warm climate."

"I know," boomed Kalvin. "But I belong here. Farewell, Longnose. Farewell, Squarehead."

"Farewell, Kalvin," Norb said, a little miffed at the nickname.

"Don't rush about blasting off," said Kalvin. "I want to be clear of the ship before you do... *If* you do, that is." The old man emitted a series of deep chuckles from the back of his throat and wandered off in the snow, heading toward his people.

Norb watched him retreat. "Well, that's that. They're funny people, these Earthmen; the cold has made them strong and—and sort of noble."

"You're still sentimental," Jannes said. "Take a last look before we blast off."

Norb stared out the port at the flickering red sun which so soon would be dark. Jannes reached for the firing stud.

"Hey!"

Norb turned and saw Jannes straining to touch the firing stud; his arm was not fully unbent at the elbow. "Something's wrong; I can't straighten my arm. You better come over here and push the stud for me."

Norb hurried over to the control board. "I'm not too sure how it works."

"Nothing to it," said Jannes, grimacing from the sharp pain in his arm. "Just reach out and push the stud."

Norb extended his arm. It did not reach the stud. "I can't do it."

He looked at Jannes with growing horror. "I can't touch the stud."

"Go ahead," Jannes urged. "Just push it." The pilot continued to rub his bent arm trying to straighten it out.

Beads of perspiration broke out on Norb's forehead. He tried to push his hand forward to meet the stud. "It's as if there's a wall around it," Norb said. "I can't get to it." He tried again and then sat down in a rage of frustration.

Jannes reached out with his good arm. "I can't do it either." He looked at Norb; Norb looked at him.

"You know what I think?" Jannes demanded, quietly.

Norb nodded. "I think so too." He made another attempt to push the stud, and failed.

Norb stared out at the reflection of the red sun along the snow. Jannes watched him silently.

"But it's crazy," he finally burst out. "You don't believe that story about the Earth-spirit, do you?"

"I'm the sentimental one, remember, Jannes?"

"This is no time for bickering. Why can't we touch that stud?"

Norb said slowly, "They believe in the Earth-spirit. Maybe the Earth-folk hypnotized us during that dance, and left a post-hypnotic command not to go near the firing stud. There's no physical reason why we can't touch it."

"Can we un-hypnotize ourselves?" Jannes joined Norb at the port and looked out over the snow.

"I'm just guessing that that's what they did. That whatever happened, they did it. But for all I *know,* it's the Earth herself that won't let us go."

"But that's crazy!" Jannes shouted. He leaped to the board and tried to press the stud. He made no contact. "It must be hypnotism," he said. "I can put my arm out, but when I reach the stud I draw back; I just can't

THE LONELY ONE | 137

bring myself to touch it."

"Maybe if you keep your hand there, and I back up into you, and accidently nudge your hand into the stud—"

"It's worth a try," Jannes said. He put his finger as close to the gleaming stud as he could, and waited. Norb casually sauntered up behind him, whistling, and suddenly pushed.

Jannes screamed and held up his finger. "It's no use; there might just as well be a wall around that stud."

Norb frowned. "Look out the port," he said pointing. "Under that tree."

Kalvin was sitting cross-legged in the snow, about a hundred meters from the ship, watching and waiting.

"They know exactly what's going on in here," Jannes said. "I'll bet he's roaring with laughter."

Savagely he grabbed a length of pipe from the tool-cabinet and brought it down on the firing stud.

The ship stayed on the ground.

The stud broke off.

"Now you've done it," Norb said. "How do you plan to get up now? Do you know anything about repairing the starting mechanism?"

"Not much, but we don't have to bother; I'm going to call Mukennik and have them come down and pick us up."

"Suppose *they* get stuck here, too?"

"At least we're no worse off, and we'll have company."

"That's not a very good attitude, Harl; but I suppose I'm being sentimental again."

"Shut up." Jannes was dialing in the *Haughtsmith*.

"I thought you were coming back up," said Mukennik immediately. "We're waiting for you."

"We're stuck. We can't get the ship up."

"What's the trouble? Mechanical difficulties?" Mukennik sighed. "Or won't the Earth-spirit let *you* go?"

"We've broken the firing stud."

"Use the auxiliary; it's under the rear cover."

They looked. It was. They failed to make contact.

"We can't touch it," Norb said. "I think the Earthmen left us with a posthypnotic command against blasting off."

Jannes looked out the port. "Kalvin's still there. Why don't we get him in here and get him to push the stud for us?"

"That's out," said Mukennik; "we'd only have to return him afterward."

"What do we do?" Jannes demanded.

"Hold on a while. I'm going to send down the other ship to get you out of this, you idiots."

In a short while, the second cruiser stood on its tail in the snow not far from the first. Norb saw that Kalvin was watching with evident interest as the rescue-cruiser came down.

Two well-clad spacemen came dashing down the cat-walk and hurried toward Norb and Jannes. "Hurry up," one of them said. "Mukennik doesn't want to waste any more time than necessary. Kinnear's going to take you two up in our ship, and I'll bring yours in alone."

Norb and Jannes headed back to the second ship with Kinnear. Kalvin stood up under his tree and yawned loudly.

Kinnear tried to push the stud; he failed.

"Are we *all* crazy?" he demanded.

"It looks as if it's contagious," Norb said. He glanced through the port. "Doesn't seem as if Bartle's gotten very far with our ship, either."

Kalvin was wandering in slow circles in the snow.

"Is there any way out of this?" Kinnear asked. "Let's call Mukennik and ask him to bring the *Haughtsmith* down for us."

"You don't think *he's* going to risk getting stranded here himself, do you?"

"He can't leave four men here."

"You don't know Mukennik, then." Norb waved to Kalvin, who was still outside. The old man approached and stood outside the ship.

"What's the trouble spacemen? I thought you'd be gone long before."

"We can't blast off," Norb said.

"Oh? Motor trouble?"

"No. You know what it is?"

Kalvin smiled. "We'll welcome you at our little village; it isn't often that we get new blood."

"Isn't there any way out?"

"The earth is a lonely planet," Kalvin said. "It wants all the company it can get."

Norb looked back toward the control room. Jannes was talking into the transmitter and Mukennik's voice crackled faintly through the air.

"What's happening?"

"They won't come," Jannes said. "He's awarding us all medals and leaving us behind."

"Leaving us behind? Why?"

"He wants to get out of the atmosphere fast. He's afraid this Earth-spirit will get him to bring the *Haughtsmith* down here, and that would never do. You know how Mukennik hates cold weather."

Norb felt an icy chill growing inside him.

"That's too bad," Kalvin said. "It would have been nice to have the big ship down here, too. We all could have lived in that instead of our cave."

"Yeah, too bad. I'm really sorry for you," Jannes said.

Bartle came trotting over from the other ship. They explained what had happened.

They looked up. The giant silvery form of the *Haughtsmith* was still circling in its orbit around the Earth. Norb turned and went back into the ship.

"They're starting to move," Jannes called from outside.

"Come on back in," Norb yelled. "One last try." They all crowded into the little ship except Kalvin. The old Earthman stood by the side of the ship.

Norb reached for the stud and made no contact.

"That's it," he said. "Let's go. Hope you like cold weather, fellow Earthmen."

They climbed silently down the catwalk and Kalvin led them through the path in the snow toward the little village of Earthmen. There would be all the time in the world to find the answers. But right now, the air seemed warmer and softer, as if Earth was happy, now that there were a hundred and six to comfort her dying days.

THE MAN WHO CAME BACK

Originally published in *New Worlds Science Fiction,* February 1961.

Naturally, there was a tremendous fuss made over him, since he was the first man actually to buy his indenture up and return from a colony-world. He'd been away eighteen years, farming on bleak Novotny IX, and who knew how many of those years he'd been slaving and saving to win his passage home?

Besides, the rumor had it that there was a girl involved—that it was the big romance of the century, perhaps. Even before the ship carrying him had docked at Long Island Spaceport, John Burkhardt was a system-famed celebrity. Word of his return had preceded him—word, and all manner of rumor, legend, and myth.

He was on board the starship *Lincoln,* which was returning from a colony-seeding trip in the outer reaches of the galaxy. For the first time in its career, the *Lincoln* was carrying an Earthward-bound passenger. A small army of newsmen impatiently awaited the *Lincoln's* landing, and the nine worlds waited with them.

When he stepped out onto the unloading elevator and made his descent, a hum of comment rippled through the waiting crowd. Burkhardt looked his part perfectly. He was a tall man, so lean that he hardly seemed to have an ounce of extra flesh. His face was solemn, his lips thin and pale, his hair going grey though he was only in his forties. And his eyes—deep-set, glowering, commanding. Everything fitted the myth—the face, the eyes, the figure. They were the eyes and figure and face of a man who could renounce Earth for unrequited love, and then toil for eighteen years out of the sheer strength of that love.

Cameras ground. Bulbs flashed. Five hundred reporters felt their tongues going dry with anticipation of the big story.

* * * *

Burkhardt smiled coldly and waved at the horde of newsmen. He did not blink, shield his eyes, or turn away. He seemed almost unnaturally in control of himself. They had expected him to weep, perhaps, or maybe to kneel and kiss the soil of Mother Earth. He did none of those things. He merely smiled and waved.

The Global Wire man stepped forward. He had won the lottery. It was his privilege to conduct the first interview.

"Welcome back to Earth, Mr. Burkhardt! How does it feel to be back?"

"I'm very glad to be here." Burkhardt's voice was slow, deep, measured, controlled like every other aspect of him.

"This army of pressmen doesn't upset you, does it?"

"I haven't seen this many people all at once in eighteen years. But no—they don't upset me."

"You know, Mr. Burkhardt, you've done something special. You're the only man ever to return to Earth after signing out on an indenture."

"Am I the only one?" Burkhardt asked easily. "I wasn't aware of that."

"You are indeed, sir. And I'd like to know, if I may—for the benefit of billions of viewers—if you care to tell us a little of the story behind your story? Why did you leave Earth in the first place, Mr. Burkhardt? And why did you decide to return?"

Burkhardt smiled gravely. "There was a woman," he said. "A lovely woman, a very famous woman now. We loved each other, once and when she stopped loving me I left Earth. I have reason to believe I can regain her love now, so I have returned. And now, if you'll pardon me—"

"Couldn't you give us any details?"

"I've had a long trip, and I prefer to rest now. I'll be glad to answer your questions at a formal press conference tomorrow afternoon."

And he cut through the crowd toward a waiting cab, supplied by the Colonization Bureau, and was gone.

* * * *

Nearly everyone in the system had seen the brief interview or had heard reports of it. It had certainly been a masterly job. If people had been curious about Burkhardt before, they were obsessed with him now. To give up Earth out of unrequited love, to labor eighteen years for a second chance—why, he was like some figure out of Dumas, brought to life in the middle of the 24th Century.

It was no mean feat to buy one's self back out of a colonization indenture, either. The Colonization Bureau of the Solar Federation undertook to transport potential colonists to distant worlds and set them up as homesteaders. In return for one-way transportation, tools, and land, the colonists merely had to promise to remain settled, to marry, and to raise the maximum practical number of children. This program, a hundred years old now had resulted in the seeding of Terran colonies over a galactic radius of better than five hundred light-years.

It was theoretically possible for a colonist to return to Earth, of course. But few of them seemed to want to, and none before Burkhardt ever had. To return, you had first to pay off your debt to the government—which was figured theoretically at $20,000 for round-trip passage, $5000 for land, $5000 for tools—plus 6% interest per year. Since nobody with any assets would ever become a colonist, and since it was next to impossible for a colonist, farming an unworked world, to accumulate any capital, no case of an attempted buy-out had ever arisen.

Until Burkhardt. He had done it, working round the clock, outproducing his neighbors on Novotny IX and selling them his surplus, cabling his extra pennies back to Earth to be invested in blue-chip securities and finally—after eighteen years—amassing the $30,000-plus-accrued-interest that would spring him from indenture.

Twenty billion people on nine worlds wanted to know why.

* * * *

The day after his return, he held a press conference in the hotel suite provided for him by the Colonization Bureau.

Admission was strictly limited—one man from each of the twenty leading news services, no more.

Wearing a faded purplish tunic and battered sandals, Burkhardt came out to greet the reporters. He looked tremendously dignified—an overbearing figure of a man thin but solid, with enormous gnarled hands and powerful forearms. The grey in his hair gave him a patriarchic look on a world dedicated to cosmetic rejuvenation. And his eyes, shining like twin beacons, roved round the room, transfixing everyone once, causing discomfort and uneasiness. No one had seen eyes like that on a human being before. But no one had ever seen a returned colonist before, either.

He smiled without warmth. "Very well, gentlemen. I'm at your disposal."

They started with peripheral questions first.

"What sort of planet is Novotny IX, Mr. Burkhardt?"

"Cold. The temperature never gets above sixty. The soil is marginally fertile. A man has to work ceaselessly if he wants to stay alive there."

"Did you know that when you signed up to go there?"

Burkhardt nodded. "I asked for the least desirable of the available colony worlds."

"Are there many colonists there?"

"About twenty thousand, I think. It isn't a popular planet, you understand."

"Mr. Burkhardt, part of the terms of the colonist's indenture specify that he must marry. Did you fulfill this part of the contract?"

Burkhardt smiled sadly. "I married less than a week after my arrival there in 2319. My wife died the first winter of our marriage. There were no children. I didn't remarry."

"And when did you get the idea of buying up your indenture and returning to Earth?"

"In my third year on Novotny IX."

"In other words, you devoted fifteen years to getting back to Earth?"

"That's correct."

It was a young reporter from Tran universe News who took the plunge toward the real meat of the universe. "Could you tell us why you changed your mind about remaining a colonist? At the spaceport you said something about there being a woman—"

"Yes." Burkhardt chuckled mirthlessly. "I was very young when I threw myself into the colonization plan—twenty-five, in point of fact. There was a woman; I loved her; she married someone else. I did the romantic thing and signed up for Novotny IX. Three years later, the news tape from Earth told me that she had been divorced. This was in 2322. I resolved to return to Earth and try to persuade her to marry me."

"So for fifteen years you struggled to get back so you could patch up your old romance," another newsman said. "But how did you know she hadn't remarried in all that time?"

"She did remarry," Burkhardt said stunningly.

"But—"

"I received word of her remarriage in 2324, and of her subsequent divorce in 2325. Of her remarriage in 2327, and of her subsequent divorce in 2329. Of her remarriage in the same year, and her subsequent divorce in 2334. Of her remarriage in 2335, and of her divorce four months ago. Unless I have missed the announcement, she has not remarried this last time."

"Did you abandon your project every time you heard of one of these marriages?"

Burkhardt shook his head. "I kept on saving. I was confident that none of her marriages would last. All these years, you see, she's been trying to find a substitute for *me*. But human beings are unique. There are no substitutes. I weathered five of her marriages. Her sixth husband will be myself."

"Could you tell us—could you tell us the name of this woman, Mr. Burkhardt?"

The returned colonist's smile was frigid. "I'm not ready to reveal her name, just yet," he said. "Are there any further questions?"

* * * *

Along toward mid-afternoon, Burkhardt ended the conference. He had told them in detail of his efforts to pile up the money; he had talked about life as a colonist; he had done everything but tell them the name of the woman for whose sake he had done all this.

Alone in the suite after they had gone, Burkhardt stared out at the other glittering towers of New York. Jet liners droned overhead; a billion lights shattered the darkness. New York, he thought, was as chaotic and as repugnant to him as ever. He missed Novotny IX.

But he had had to come back. Smiling gently, he opaque the windows of his suite. It was winter, now, on Novotny Ax's colonized continent. A time for burrowing away, for digging in against the mountain-high drifts of blue-white snow. Winter was eight standard months long, on Novotny IX; only four out of the sixteen standard months of the planet's year were really livable. Yet a man could see the results of his own labor, out there. He could use his hands and measure his gains.

And there were friends there. Not the other settlers, though they were good people and hard workers. But the natives, the Aurania.

The survey charts said nothing about them. There were only about five hundred of them left, anyway, or so Donnie had claimed. Burkhardt had never seen more than a dozen of the Aurania at any one time, and he had never been able to tell one from another. They looked like slim elves, half the height of a man, grey-skinned, chinless, sad-eyed. They went naked against their planet's bitter cold. They lived in caves, somewhere below the surface. And Donnie had become Burckhardt's friend.

* * * *

Burkhardt smiled, remembering. He had found the little alien in a snowdrift, so close to dead it was hard to be certain one way or the other. Donnie had lived, and had recovered, and had spent the winter in Burckhardt's cabin, talking a little, but mostly listening.

Burkhardt had done the talking. He had talked it all out, telling the little being of his foolishness, of his delusion that Lily loved him, of his wild maniac desire to get back to Earth.

And Donnie had said, when he understood the situation, *"You will get back to Earth. And she will be yours."*

That had been between the first divorce and the second marriage. The day the new stapes had brought word of Lily's remarriage had nearly finished Burkhardt, but Donnie was there, comforting, consoling, and from that day on Burkhardt never worried again. Lily's marriages were made, weakened, broke up, and Burkhardt worked unfalteringly knowing that when he returned to Earth he could have Lily at last.

Donnie had told him solemnly, *"It is all a matter of channeling your desires. Look: I lay dying in a snowdrift, and I willed you to find me. You came; I lived."*

"But I'm not Aurania," Burkhardt had protested. "My will isn't strong enough to influence another person."

"Any creature that thinks can assert its will. Give me your hand, and I will show you."

Burkhardt smiled back across fifteen years, remembering the feel of Donnie's limp, almost boneless hand in his own, remembering the stiff jolt of power that had flowed from the alien. His hand had tingled for days afterward. But he knew, from that moment, that he would succeed.

* * * *

Burkhardt had a visitor the next morning. A press conference was scheduled again for the afternoon and Burkhardt had said he would grant no interviews before then, but the visitor had been insistent. Finally, the desk had phoned up to tell Burkhardt that a Mr. Richardson Elliott was here, and demanded to see him.

The name rang a bell. "Send him up," Burkhardt said.

A few minutes later, the elevator disgorged Mr. Richardson Elliott. He was shorter than Burkhardt, plump, pink-skinned, clean-shaven. A ring glistened on his finger, and there was a gem of some alien origin mounted on a stickpin near his throat. He extended his hand. Burkhardt took it. The hand was carefully manicured, pudgy, somehow oily.

"You're not at all as I pictured you," Burkhardt said.

"You are. Exactly."

"Why did you come here?"

Elliott tapped the newsfax crumpled under his arm. He unfolded it, showing Burkhardt the front-page spread. "I read the story, Burkhardt. I knew at once who the girl—the woman—was. I came to warn you not to get involved with her."

Burckhardt's eyes twinkled. "And why not?"

"She's a witch," Elliott muttered. "She'll drain a man dry and throw the husk away. Believe me, I know. You only loved her. I married her."

"Yes," Burkhardt said. "You took her away from me eighteen years ago."

"You know that isn't true. She walked out on you because she thought I could further her career, which was so. I didn't even know another man had been in the picture until she got that letter from you, postmarked the day your ship took off. She showed it to me—laughing. I can't repeat the things she said about you, Burkhardt. But I was shocked. My marriage to her started to come apart right then and there, even though it was another

146 | ROBERT SILVERBERG

three years before we called it quits. She threw herself at me. I didn't steal her from anybody. Believe me, Burkhardt."

"I believe you."

Elliott mopped his pink forehead. "It was the same way with all the other husbands. I've followed her career all along. She exists only for Lily Leigh, and nobody else. When she left me, it was to marry Alderson. Well, she killed him as good as if she'd shot him, when she told him she was pulling out. Man his age had no business marrying her. And then it was Michaels, and after him Dan Cartwright, and then Jim Thorne. Right up the ladder to fame and fortune, leaving a trail of used-up husbands behind her."

Burkhardt shrugged. "The past is of no concern to me."

"You actually think Lily will marry you?"

"I do," Burkhardt said. "She'll jump at it. The publicity values will be irresistible. The sollie star with five broken marriages to millionaires now stooping to wed her youthful love, who is now a penniless ex-colonist."

Elliott moistened his lips unhappily. "Perhaps you've got something there," he admitted. "Lily might just do a thing like that. But how long would it last? Six months, a year—until the publicity dies down. And then she'll dump you. She doesn't want a penniless husband."

"She won't dump me."

"You sound pretty confident, Burkhardt."

"I am."

For a moment there was silence. Then Elliott said, "You seem determined to stick your head in the lion's mouth. What is it—an obsession to marry her?"

"Call it that."

"It's crazy. I tell you, she's a witch. You're in love with an imaginary goddess. The real Lily Leigh is the most loathsome female ever spawned. As the first of her five husbands, I can take oath to that."

"Did you come here just to tell me that?"

"Not exactly," Elliott said. "I've got a proposition for you. I want you to come into my firm as a Vice-President. You're system-famous, and we can use the publicity. I'll start you at sixty thousand. You'll be the most eligible bachelor in the universe. We'll get you a rejuvenation and you'll look twenty-five again. Only none of this Lily Leigh nonsense. I'll set you up, you'll marry some good-looking kid, and all your years on Whatsit Nine will be just so much nightmare."

"The answer is no."

"I'm not doing this out of charity, you understand. I think you'll be an asset to me. But I also think you ought to be protected against Lily. I feel I owe you something, for what I did to you unknowingly eighteen years ago."

"You don't owe me a thing. Thanks for the warning, Mr. Elliott, but I don't need it. And the answer to the proposition is No. I'm not for sale."

"I beg you—"

"No."

Color flared in Elliott's cheeks for a moment. He rose, started to say something, stopped. "All right," he said heavily. "Go to Lily. Like a moth drawn to a flame. The offer remains, Mr. Burkhardt. And you have my deepest sympathy."

* * * *

At his press conference that afternoon, Burkhardt revealed her name. The system's interest was at peak, now; another day without the revelation and the peak would pass, frustration would cause interest to subside. Burkhardt told them. Within an hour it was all over the system.

Glamorous Lily Leigh, for a decade and a half queen of the solidofilms, was named today as the woman for whom John Burkhardt bought himself out of indenture. Burkhardt explained that Miss Leigh, then an unknown starlet, terminated their engagement in 2319 to marry California industrialist Richardson Elliott. The marriage, like Miss Leigh's four later ones, ended in divorce.

"I hope now to make her my wife," the mystery man from Novotny IX declared. "After eighteen years I still love her as strongly as ever."

Miss Leigh, in seclusion at her Scottsdale, Arizona home following her recent divorce from sollie-distributing magnate James Thorne, refused to comment on the statement.

For three days, Lily Leigh remained in seclusion, seeing no one, issuing no statements to the press. Burkhardt was patient. Eighteen years of waiting teaches patience. And Donnie had told him, as they trudged through the grey slush of rising spring, *"The man who rushes ahead foolishly forfeits all advantage in a contest of wills."*

Donnie carried the wisdom of a race at the end of its span. Burkhardt remained in his hotel suite, mulling over the advice of the little alien. Donnie had never passed judgment on the merits and drawbacks of Burckhardt's goal; he had simply advised, and suggested, and taught.

* * * *

The press had run out of things to say about Burkhardt, and he declined to supply them with anything new to print. So, inevitably, they lost interest in him. By the third day, it was no longer necessary to hold a press conference. He had come back; he had revealed his love for the sollie queen, Lily Leigh; now he was sitting tight. There was nothing to do but wait for further developments, if any. And neither Burkhardt nor Lily Leigh seemed to be creating further developments.

It was hard to remain calm, Burkhardt thought. It was queer to be here on Earth, in the quiet autumn, while winter fury raged on Novotny IX. Fury of a different kind raged here, the fury of a world of five billion eager, active human beings, but Burkhardt kept himself aloof from all that. Eighteen years of near-solitude had left him unfit for that sort of world.

It was hard to sit quietly, though, with Lily just a visicall away. Burkhardt compelled himself to be patient. She would call, sooner or later.

She called on the fourth day. Burckhardt's skin crawled as he heard the hotel operator say—in tones regulated only with enormous effort—"Miss Leigh is calling from Arizona, Mr. Burkhardt."

"Put the call on."

She had not used the visi-circuit. Burkhardt kept his screen blank too.

She said, without preliminaries, "Why have you come back after all these years, John?"

"Because I love you."

"Still?"

"Yes."

She laughed—the famous LL laugh, for his benefit alone. "You're a bigger fool now than you were then, John."

"Perhaps," he admitted.

"I suppose I ought to thank you, though. This is the best publicity I've had all year. And at my age I need all the publicity I can get."

"I'm glad for you," he said.

"You aren't serious, though, about wanting to marry me, are you? Not after all these years. Nobody stays in love that long."

"I did."

"Damn you, what do you want from me?" The voice, suddenly shrill, betrayed a whisper of age.

"Yourself," Burkhardt said calmly.

"What makes you think I'll marry you? Sure, you're a hero today, The Man Who Came Back From The Stars. But you're nothing, John. All you have to show for eighteen years is calluses. At least back then you had your youth. You don't even have that any more."

"Let me come to see you, Lily."

THE MAN WHO CAME BACK | 149

"I don't want to see you."

"Please. It's a small thing—let me have half an hour alone with you."

She was silent.

"I've given you half a lifetime of love, Lily. Let me have half an hour."

After a long moment she said, simply, hoarsely, "All right. You can come. But I won't marry you."

* * * *

He left New York shortly before midnight. The Colonization Bureau had hired a private plane for him, and he slipped out unnoticed, in the dark. Publicity now would be fatal. The plane was a jet, somewhat out of date; they were using photon-rockets for the really fast travel. But, obsolete or no, it crossed the continent in three hours. It was just midnight, local time, when the plane landed in Phoenix. As they had arranged it, Lily had her chauffeur waiting, with a long, sleek limousine. Burkhardt climbed in. Turbines throbbed; the car glided out toward Lily's desert home.

It was a mansion, a sprawled-out villa moated off—a *moat,* in water-hungry Arizona!—and topped with a spiring pink stucco tower. Burkhardt was ushered through open fern-lined courtyards to an inner maze of hallways, and through them into a small room where Lily Leigh sat waiting.

He repressed a gasp. She wore a gown worth a planet's ransom, but the girl within the gown had not changed in eighteen years. Her face was the same, impish, the eyes dancing and gay. Her hair had lost none of its glossy sheen. Her skin was the skin of a girl of nineteen.

"It's like stepping back in time," he murmured.

"I have good doctors. You wouldn't believe I'm forty, would you? But everyone knows it, of course." She laughed. "You look like an old man, John."

"Forty-three isn't old."

"It is when you let your age show. I'll give you some money, John, and you can get fixed up. Better still, I'll send my doctors to you."

Burkhardt shook his head. "I'm honest about the passing of time. I look this way because of what I've done these past eighteen years. I wouldn't want a doctor's skill to wipe out the traces of those years."

She shrugged lightly. "It was only an offer, not a slur. What do you want with me, John?"

"I want you to marry me."

Her laughter was a silvery tinkle, ultimately striking a false note. "That made sense in 2319. It doesn't now. People would say you married me for my money. I've got lots of money, John, you know."

"I'm not interested in your money. I want *you.*"

"You think you love me, but how can you? I'm not the sweet little girl you once loved. I never was that sweet little girl. I was a grasping, greedy little girl—and now I'm a grasping, greedy old woman who still looks like a little girl. Go away, John. I'm not for you."

"Marry me, Lily. We'll be happy. I know we will."

"You're a stupid monomaniac."

Burkhardt only smiled. "It'll be good publicity. After five marriages for profit, you're marrying for love. All the worlds love a lover, Lily. You'll be everyone's sweetheart again. Give me your hand, Lily."

Like a sleepwalker, she extended it. Burkhardt took the hand, frowning at its coldness, its limpness.

"But I don't love you, John."

"Let the world think you do. That's all that matters."

"I don't understand you. You—"

She stopped. Burckhardt's grip tightened on her thin hand. He thought of Donnie, a grey shadow against the snow, holding his hand, letting the power flow from body to body, from slim alien to tall Earthman. *It is all a matter of channeling your desires,* he had said. *Any creature that thinks can learn how to assert its will. The technique is simple.*

Lily lowered her head. After a moment, she raised it. She was smiling.

* * * *

"It won't last a month," Richardson Elliott grunted, at the sight of the announcement in the paper.

"The poor dumb idiot," Jim Thorne said, reading the news at his Martian ranch. "Falling in love with a dream-Lily that never existed, and actually marrying her. She'll suck him dry. But at least it gets me off the alimony hook. I ought to be grateful."

On nine worlds, people read the story and talked about it. Many of them were pleased; it was the proper finish for the storybook courtship. But those who knew Lily Leigh were less happy about it. "She's got some angle," they said. "It's all a publicity stunt. She'll drop him as soon as the fanfare dies down. And she'll drop him so hard he won't ever get up."

Burkhardt and Lily were married on the tenth day after his return from space. It was a civil ceremony, held secretly. Their honeymoon trip was shrouded in mystery. While they were gone, gossip columnists speculated. How could the brittle, sophisticated, much-married Lily be happy with a simple farmer from a colony-world?

Two days after their return to Earth from the honeymoon Burkhardt and his wife held a joint press conference. It lasted only five minutes. Burkhardt, holding his wife's hand tightly, said, "I'm happy to announce that Miss Leigh is distributing all of her possessions to charity. We've both signed up as indentured colonists and we're leaving for Novotny IX tomorrow."

"Really, Miss Leigh?"

"Yes," Lily said. "I belong at John's side. We'll work his old farm together. It'll be the first useful thing I've ever done in my life."

The newsmen, thunderstruck, scattered to shout their story to the waiting worlds. Mr. and Mrs. John Burkhardt closed the door behind them.

"Happy?" Burkhardt asked.

Lily nodded. She was still smiling. Burkhardt, watching her closely, saw the momentary flicker of her eyes, the brief clearing-away of the cloud that shrouded them—as though someone were trapped behind those lovely eyes, struggling to get out. But Burckhardt's control never lapsed. Bending, he kissed her soft lips lightly.

"Bedtime," he said.

"Yes. Bedtime."

Burkhardt kissed her again. Donnie had been right, he thought. Control was possible. He had channeled desire eighteen years, and now Lily was his. Perhaps she was no longer Lily as men had known her, but what did that matter? She was the Lily of his lonely dreams. He had created her in the tingling moment of a handshake, from the raw material of her old self.

He turned off the light and began to undress. He thought with cozy pleasure that in only a few weeks he would be setting foot once again on the bleak tundra of Novotny IX—this time, with his loving bride.

NEUTRAL PLANET

Originally published in *Science Fiction Stories*, July 1957.

From the fore viewing bay of the Terran starship *Peccable,* the twin planets Fasolt and Fafnir had become visible—uninhabited Fasolt a violet ball the size of a quarter-credit piece dead ahead, and Fafnir, home of the gnorphs, a bright-red dot far to the right, beyond the mighty curve of the big ship's outsweeping wing.

The nameless, tiny blue sun about which both worlds orbited rode high above them, at a sharp 36 degrees off the ecliptic. And, majestic in its vastness, great Antares served as a huge bright-red backdrop for the entire scene.

"Fasolt dead ahead," came the word from Navigation. "Prepare for decelerating orbit."

The eighteen men who comprised the Terran mission to the gnorphs of Fafnir moved rapidly and smoothly toward their landing stations. This was a functioning team; they had a big job, and they were ready for it.

In Control Cabin, Shipmaster Deev Harskin was strapping himself into the acceleration cradle when the voice of Observer First Rank Snollgren broke in.

"Chief? Snollgren. Read me?"

"Go ahead, boy. What's up?"

"That Rigelian ship—the one we saw yesterday? I just found it again. Ten light-seconds off starboard, and credits to crawfish it's orbiting in on Fasolt!"

Harskin gripped the side of the cradle anxiously. "You sure it's not Fafnir they're heading for? How's your depth-perception out there?"

"A-one. That boat's going the same place we are, chief!"

Sighing, Harskin said, "It could have been worse, I guess." He snapped on the all-ship communicator and said, "Gentlemen, our job has been complicated somewhat. Observer Snollgren reports a Rigelian ship orbiting in on Fasolt, and it looks likely they have the same idea we have. Well, this'll be a test of our mettle. We'll have a chance to snatch Fafnir right out from under their alleged noses!"

A voice said, "Why not blast the Rigelians first? They're our enemies, aren't they?"

Harskin recognized the voice as belonging to Leefman—a first-rate linguist, rather innocent of the niceties of interstellar protocol. No reply from Harskin was needed. The hoarse voice of Military Attaché Ramos broke in.

"This is a neutral system, Leefman. Rigelian-Terran hostilities are suspended pending contact with the gnorphs. Someday you'll understand that war has its code too."

Alone in Control Cabin, Shipmaster Harskin smiled. It was a good crew; a little overspecialized, perhaps, but more than adequate for the purpose. Having Rigelians on hand would be just so much additional challenge. Shipmaster Harskin enjoyed challenges.

Beneath him, the engines of the *Peccable* throbbed magnificently. He was proud of his ship, proud of his crew. The *Peccable* swept into the deadly atmosphere of Fasolt, swung downward in big looping spirals, and headed for land.

Not too far behind came the Rigelians. Harskin leaned back and let the crash of deceleration eddy up over him, and waited.

* * * *

Fasolt was mostly rock, except for the hydrogen-fluoride oceans and the hydrogenous air. It was not an appealing planet.

The spacesuited men of the *Peccable* were quick to debouch and extrude their dome. Atmosphere issued into it. "A little home away from home," Harskin remarked.

Biochemist Carver squinted balefully at the choppy hydrofluoric-acid sea. "Nice world. Good thing these goldfish bowls aren't made out of glass, yes? And better caution your men about using the dome airlock. A little of our oxygen gets out into that atmosphere and we'll have the loveliest rainstorm you ever want to see—with us a thousand feet up, looking down."

Harskin nodded. "It's not a pleasant place at all. But it's not a pleasant war we're fighting."

He glanced up at the murky sky. Fafnir was full, a broad red globe barely a million miles away. And, completing the group, there was the feint blue sun about which both worlds revolved, the entire system forming a neat Trojan equilateral with vast Antares.

Snollgren appeared. The keen-eyed observer had been in the ship, and apparently had made it from the *Peccable* to the endomed temporary camp on a dead run, no little feat in Fasolt's 1.5-g field.

"Well?" Harskin asked.

The observer opened his face plate and sucked in some of the dome's high-oxygen atmosphere. "The Rigelians," he gasped. "They've landed. I saw them in orbit."

"Where?"

"I'd estimate five hundred miles westward. They're definitely on this continent."

Harskin glanced at the chronometer set in the wrist of Snollgren's spacesuit. "We'll give them an hour to set up their camp. Then we'll contact them and find out what goes."

* * * *

The Rigelian captain's name was Fourteen Deathless. He spoke Galactic with a sharp, crisp accent that Harskin attributed to his ursine ancestry.

"Coincidence we're both here at the same time, eh, Shipmaster Harskin? Strange are the ways of the Guiding Forces."

"They certainly are," Harskin said. He stared at the hand-mike, wishing it were a screen so he could see the sly, smug expression on the Rigelian's furry face. Obviously, someone had intercepted Harskin's allegedly secret orders and studied them carefully before forwarding them to their recipient.

Coincidences didn't happen in interstellar war. The Rigelians were here because they knew the Earthmen were.

"We have arrived at a knotty problem in ethics," remarked Captain Fourteen Deathless. "Both of us are here for the same purpose, that of negotiating trading rights with the gnorphs. Now—ah—which of us is to make the first attempt to deal with these people?"

"Obviously," said Harskin, "the ship which landed on Fasolt first has prior claim."

"This is suitable," said the Rigelian.

"We'll set out at once, then. Since the *Peccable* landed at least half an hour before your ship, we have clear priority."

"Interesting," Captain Fourteen Deathless said. "But just how do you compute you arrived before we did? By our instruments we were down long before you."

Harskin started to sputter, then checked himself. "Impossible!"

"Oh? Cite your landing time, please, with reference to Galactic Absolute."

"We put down at..." Harskin paused. "No. Suppose you tell me what time you landed, and then I'll give you our figures."

"That's hardly fair," said the Rigelian. "How do we know you won't alter your figures once we've given ours?"

"And how do *we* know, on the other hand...?"

"It won't work," said the alien. "Neither of us will allow the other priority."

Shrugging, Harskin saw the truth of that. Regardless of the fact that the *Peccable* actually *had* landed first, the Rigelians would never admit it. It was a problem in simple relativity; without an external observer to supply impartial data, it was Fourteen Deathless' word against Harskin's.

"All right," Harskin said wearily. "Call it a stalemate. Suppose we *both* go to Fafnir now, and have them choose between us."

There was silence at the other end for a while. Then the Rigelian said, "This is acceptable. The rights of the neutral parties must be respected, of course."

"Of course. Until this system is settled, we're *all* neutrals, remember?"

"Naturally," said the Rigelian.

* * * *

It was not, thought Harskin, a totally satisfactory arrangement. Still, it could hardly be helped.

By the very strict rules with which the Terran-Rigelian "war" was being fought, a system was considered neutral until a majority of its intelligently inhabited worlds had declared a preference for one power or the other.

In the Antares system, a majority vote would have to be a unanimous one. Of the eleven highly variegated worlds that circled the giant red star, only Fafnir bore life. The gnorphs were an intelligent race of biped humanoids—the classic shape of intelligent life. The Terrans were simianoid; the Rigelians, ursinoid. But the gnorphs owed their appearance neither to apes nor bears; they were reptilians, erect and tailless. Fafnir was not hospitable to mammalian life.

Harskin stared broodingly out the viewing bay as the blood-red seas of Fafnir grew larger. The Rigelian ship could not be seen, but he knew it was on its way. He made a mental note to inform Terran Intelligence that the secrecy of the high command's secret orders was open to some question.

It was a strange war—a war fought with documents rather than energy cannons. The shooting stage of the war between the galaxy's two leading races had long since ended in sheer futility; the development of the Martineau Negascreen, which happily drank up every megawatt of a bombardment and fired it back at triple intensity, had quickly put an end to active hostility.

Now, the war was carried on at a subtler level—the economic one.

Rigel and Terra strove to outdo each other in extracting exclusive trading rights from systems, hoping to choke each other's lifelines. The universe was infinite, or close enough to infinite to keep both systems busy for quite a few millennia to come.

Harskin shrugged. Terran scouts had visited Fafnir and had reported little anxiety on the part of the gnorphs to take part in the Galactic stream of things. Presumably, Rigel IV had not yet visited the world; it was simpler to pirate the Terran scout reports.

Well, this would really be a test.

"Preparing to land, sir," said Navigator Dominic. "Any instructions?"

"Yes," Harskin said. "Bring us down where it's dry."

The landing was a good one, on the centermost of the island group that made up Fafnir's main land mass. Harskin and his twelve men—he had left five behind in the dome on Fasolt to hedge his bet—left the ship.

It would not be necessary to erect a dome here; Fafnir's air was breathable, more or less. It was 11 percent oxygen, 86 percent nitrogen, and a whopping 3 percent of inerts, but a decent filter system easily strained the excess nitro and argon out and pumped in oxygen.

Wearing breathing-masks and converters, the thirteen Terrans advanced inland. At their backs was the ocean, red and glimmering in Antares' light.

"Here come the Rigelians," Observer Snollgren cried.

"As usual, they're hanging back and waiting to see what we do." Harskin frowned. "This time, we won't wait for them. Let's take advantage of our head start."

The gnorph village was five miles inland, but the party had not gone more than two miles when they were greeted by a group of aliens.

There were about a hundred of them, advancing in a wedge-shaped phalanx. They were moving slowly, without any overt belligerent ideas, but Harskin felt uneasy. A hundred aroused savages could make quick work of thirteen Terrans armed with handguns.

He glanced at Mawley, Contact Technician First Class. "Go ahead. Get up there and tell 'em we're friends."

Mawley was a tall redhead with knobby cheekbones and, at the moment, an expression of grave self-concern. He nodded, checked his lingual converter to make sure it was operating, and stepped forward, one hand upraised.

"Greetings," he said loudly. "We come in peace."

The gnorphs spread out into a loose formation and stared stolidly ahead. Harskin, waiting tensely for Mawley to achieve his rapport with the aliens, peered curiously at them.

They were short—five-six or so—and correspondingly broad-beamed. Their chocolate-brown skin was glossy and scaled; it hung loosely, in corrugated folds. Thick antennae twined upward from either side of their bald heads, and equally thick fleshy processes dangled comb-like from their jaws. As for their eyes, Harskin was unable to see them; they were hidden in deep shadow, set back two inches in their skull and protected by projecting, brooding rims of bone that circled completely around each eye.

Three of the gnorphs stepped out of the ranks, and the middle alien stepped forward, flanked slightly to the rear by his companions. He spoke in a harsh, guttural voice.

The converter rendered it as "What do you want here?"

Mawley was prepared for the question. "Friendship. Peace. Mutual happiness of our worlds."

"Where are you from?"

Mawley gestured to the sky. "Far away, beyond the sky. Beyond the stars. Much distance."

The gnorph looked skeptical. "How many days' sailing from here?"

"Many days. Many, *many* days."

"Then why come to us?"

"To establish friendship," said Mawley. "To build a bond between your world and ours."

At that, the alien did an abrupt about-face and conferred with his two companions. Harskin kept an eye on the spears twitching in the alien hands.

The conference seemed to be prolonging itself indefinitely. Mawley glanced back at Harskin as if to ask what he should do next, but the shipmaster merely smiled in approval and encouragement.

Finally the aliens broke up their huddle and the lead man turned back to the Terrans. "We think you should leave us," he grunted. "Go. At once."

There was nothing in Mawley's instructions to cover this. The contact technician opened and closed his mouth a few times without speaking. Gravely, the aliens turned and marched away, leaving the Terrans alone.

First Contact had been achieved.

"This has to be done in a very careful way," Harskin said. "Any news from the Rigelians?"

"They're situated about eight miles from here," Snollgren said.

"Hmmm. That means they're as far from the village as we are." Harskin put his hands to his head. "The gnorphs are certainly not leaping all over the place to sign a treaty with us, that's for sure. We'll have to handle them gently or we may make them angry enough to sign up with the Rigelians."

"I doubt that," offered Sociologist Yang. "They probably won't be any more anxious to deal with the Rigelians than they are with us. They're neutrals, and they want to stay that way."

Harskin leaned back. "This is a problem we haven't hit before. None of the worlds in either sphere of influence ever had any isolationist ideas. What do we do? Just pull up and leave?"

The blue sun was setting. Antares still hovered on the horizon, a shapeless blob of pale red eating up half the sky. "We'll have to send a man to spy on the Rigelians. Archer, you're elected."

The man in question rose. "Yes, sir."

"Keep an eye on them, watch their dealings with the gnorphs, and above all don't let the Rigelians see you." Another idea occurred to the shipmaster. "Lloyd?"

"Yes, sir?"

"In all probability the Rigelians have slapped a spy on *us*. You're our counterespionage man, effective now. Scout around and see if you can turn up their spy."

Archer and Lloyd departed. Harskin turned to the sociologist. "Yang, there has to be some way of pushing these gnorphs to one side or the other."

"Agreed. I'll have to see more of a pattern, though, before I can help you."

Harskin nodded. "We'll make contact with the gnorphs again after Archer returns with the word of what the Rigelians are up to. We'll profit by their mistakes."

* * * *

Antares had set as far as it was going to set, which was about three quarters of the way below the horizon, and the blue sun was spiraling its way into the heavens again, when the quiet air of Fafnir was split by an earth-shaking explosion.

The men of the *Peccable* were awake in an instant—those eight who had been sleeping, at any rate. A two-man skeleton team had been guarding the ship. Harskin had been meditating in Control Cabin, and Archer and Lloyd had not yet returned from their scouting missions.

Almost simultaneously with the explosion came the clangor of the alarm bell at the main airlock, signifying someone wanted in. A moment later, Observer First Class Snollgren was on the wire, excitedly jabbering something incoherent.

Harskin switched on the all-ship communicator and yelled, *"Stop!*

Whoa! Halt!"

There was silence. He said, "Clyde, see what's going on at the airlock. Snollgren, slow down and tell me what you just saw."

"It was the Rigelian ship, sir!" the observer said. "It just left. That was the noise we heard."

"You sure of that?"

"Double positive. It took off in one hell of a hurry and I caught it on a tangent bound out of here."

"Okay. Clyde, what's at the airlock?"

"It's Lloyd, sir. He's back, and he's got a Rigelian prisoner with him."

"Prisoner? What the—all right, have them both come up here."

Radioman Klaristenfeld was next on the line. He said, "Sir, report coming in from the base on Fasolt. They confirm blast-off of a ship from Fafnir. They thought it might be us."

"Tell the idiots it isn't," Harskin snapped. "And tell them to watch out for the Rigelian ship. It's probably on its way back to Fasolt."

The door-annunciator chimed. Harskin pressed *admit* and Lloyd entered, preceded at blaster-point by a very angry-looking Rigelian.

"Where'd you find him?" Harskin asked.

"Mousing around near the ship," Lloyd said. The thin spaceman was pale and tense-looking. "I was patrolling the area as you suggested when I heard the explosion. I looked up and saw the Rigelian ship overhead and heading outward. And then this guy came crashing out of the underbrush and started cursing a blue streak in Rigelian. He didn't even see me until I had the blaster pointing in his face."

Harskin glanced at the Rigelian. "What's your name and rank, Rigelian?"

"Three Ninety-Seven Indomitable," the alien said. He was a formidably burly seven-footer, covered with stiff, coarse black hair and wearing a light-yellow leather harness. His eyes glinted coldly. He looked angry. "Espionage man first order," he said.

"That explains what you were doing near our ship, then, Three Ninety-Seven Indomitable," Harskin said. "What can you tell me about this quick blast-off?"

"Not a thing. The first I knew of it was when it happened. They marooned me! They left me here!" The alien slipped from Galactic into a Rigelian tongue and growled what must have been some highly picturesque profanity.

"They just *left* you?" Harskin repeated in amazement. "Something must have made them decide to clear out of here in an awful hurry, then." He turned to Lloyd. "Convey the prisoner to the brig and see that he's put there to stay. Then pick two men and start combing the countryside for Archer. I want to know what made the Rigelians get out of here so fast they didn't have time to pick up their own spy."

* * * *

As it developed, very little countryside combing was necessary to locate Archer. Harskin's spy returned to the *Peccable* about three quarters of an hour later, extremely winded after his long cross-country trot.

It took him five minutes to catch his breath enough to deliver his report.

"I tracked the Rigelians back to their ship," he said. "They were all gathered around it, and I waited in the underbrush. After a while they proceeded to the gnorph village, and I followed them."

"Any attempt at counterespionage?" Harskin asked.

"Yes, sir." Archer grinned uncomfortably. "I killed him."

Harskin nodded. "Go on."

"They reached the village. I stayed about thirty yards behind them and switched on my converter so I could hear what they were saying."

"Bad, but unavoidable," Harskin said. "They might have had a man at the ship tracing the energy flow. I guess they didn't, though. What happened to the village?"

"They introduced themselves, and gave the usual line—the same thing we said, about peace and friendship and stuff. Then they started handing out gifts. Captain Fourteen Deathless said this was to cement Rigel's friendship with Fafnir—only he didn't call it Fafnir, naturally.

"They handed mirrors all around, and little forcewave generators, and all sorts of trinkets and gadgets. The gnorphs took each one and stacked it in a heap off to one side. The Rigelians kept handing out more and more, and the stack kept growing. Then, finally, Fourteen Deathless said he felt the gifts had been sufficient. He started to explain the nature of the treaty. And one of the gnorphs stepped out and pointed to the stack of gifts. 'Are you quite finished delivering things?' he asked, in a very stuffy tone. The Rigelian looked flustered and said more gifts would be forthcoming after the treaty was signed. And that blew the roof off."

"How do you mean?"

"It happened so fast I'm not sure. But suddenly all the gnorphs started waving their spears and looking menacing, and then someone threw a spear at a Rigelian. That started it. The Rigelians had some handguns with them, but they were so close they hardly had a chance to use them. It was a real massacre. About half the Rigelians escaped, including Captain Deathless. I hid in the underbrush till it was all over. Then I came back here."

Harskin looked at Sociologist Yang. "Well? What do you make of it?"

"Obviously a greedy sort of culture," the sociologist remarked. "The Rigelians made the mistake of being too stingy. I suggest we wait till morning and go to that village ourselves, and shoot the works. With the Rigelians gone we've got a clear field, and if we're liberal enough the planet will be ours."

"Don't be too sure of that," Harskin said broodingly. "That Rigelian was no bigger a fool than I am. When we go to that village, we'll go well armed."

* * * *

The gnorph village was a cluster of thatched huts set in a wide semicircle over some extremely marshy swampland. Both Antares and the blue companion were in the sky when the Earthmen arrived; Fasolt was making its daily occultation of the giant sun.

Harskin had taken six of his men with him: Yang, Leefman, Archer, Mawley, Ramos, and Carver. Six more remained at the ship, seeing to it that the *Peccable* was primed for a quick getaway, if necessary.

The gifts of the Rigelians lay in a scattered heap in the center of the village, smashed and battered. Nearby lay half a dozen mutilated Rigelian bodies. Harskin shuddered despite himself; these gnorphs were cold-blooded in more than the literal biological sense!

A group of them filtered out of their huts and confronted the approaching Earthmen. In the mingled blue-and-red light of the two suns—one huge and dim, the other small and dim—the blank, scaly faces looked strange and menacing, the bone-hooded sockets cold and ugly.

"What do you want here, strangers?"

"We have come to thank you," Mawley said, "for killing our enemies, the fur-men." He had been instructed to stress the distinction between the group of Rigelians and the Earthmen. "The fur-men were here last night, bearing niggling gifts. They are our enemies. We of Earth offer you peace and goodwill."

The gnorphs stared squarely at the tense little party of Earthmen. Each of the seven Terrans carried a powerful blaster set for wide-beam stunning, highly efficient if not particularly deadly as a close-range weapon. In the event of a battle, the Earthmen would at least be ready.

"What is it you want here?" the gnorph leader asked with thinly concealed impatience.

"We wish to sign a treaty between your world and ours," said Mawley. "A bond of eternal friendship, of loyalty and fellowship between worlds."

Somewhere in the distance an unseen beast emitted a mumbling reptilian honk—quite spoiling the effect, Harskin thought.

"Friendship? Fellowship?" the gnorph repeated, indicating by a quivering shake of his wattles that these were difficult concepts for him to grasp.

"Yes," said Mawley. "And as signs of our friendship we bring you gifts—not piddling trinkets such as our enemies foisted on you last night, but gifts of incomparable richness, gifts which will be just part of the bounty to fall upon you if you will sign with us."

At a signal from Harskin, they began unloading the gifts they had brought with them: miniaturized cameras, game-detectors, dozens of other treasures calculated to impress the gnorphs.

And then it began.

Harskin had been on the lookout for the explosion ever since they had arrived, and when he saw the spears beginning to bristle in the gnorph ranks, he yanked his blaster out and fired.

The stunning beam swept the front rank of gnorphs; they fell. The others growled menacingly and advanced.

The seven Earthmen jammed together in a unit and fired constantly; gnorphs lay unconscious all over, and still more came pouring from the huts. The Terrans started to run. Spears sailed past their heads.

It was a long, grim retreat to the ship.

* * * *

They were still a quarter of a million miles from Fasolt when Radioman Klaristenfeld reported that Captain Fourteen Deathless of the Rigelian ship was calling.

"We see you have left also," the Rigelian said when Harskin took the phone. "You were evidently as unsuccessful as we."

"Not quite," Harskin said. "At least we got out of there without any casualties. I counted six dead Rigelians outside that village—plus the man you left behind to watch over us. He's in our brig."

"Ah. I had wondered what became of him. Well, Harskin, do we declare Fafnir a neutral planet and leave it at that? It's a rather unsatisfactory finish to our little encounter."

"Agreed. But what can we do? We dumped nearly fifty thousand credits' worth of trinkets when we escaped."

"You Terrans are lavish," the Rigelian observed. "Our goods were worth but half that."

"That's the way it goes," Harskin said. "Well, best wishes, Fourteen Deathless."

"One moment! Is the decision a dual withdrawal?"

"I'm not so sure," Harskin said, and broke the contact.

When they reached Fasolt and rejoined the men in the dome, Harskin ordered a general meeting. He had an idea.

"The aliens," he said, "offered the gnorphs twenty-five thousand credits of goods, and were repulsed angrily. We offered twice as much—and, if Archer's account of the Rigelian incident was accurate, we were repulsed about twice as fast. Yang, does that suggest anything to you?"

The little sociologist wrinkled his head. "The pattern still is not clear," he said.

"I didn't think so." Harskin knotted his fingers in concentration. "Let me put it this way: the degree of insult the gnorphs felt was in direct variance with the degree of wealth offered. That sound plausible?"

Yang nodded.

"Tell me: what happens when an isolated, biologically glum race is visited by warm-blooded aliens from the skies? Suppose those warm-blooded aliens want a treaty of friendship—and offer to *pay* for it? How will the natives react, Yang?"

"I see. They'll get highly insulted. We're treating them in a cavalier fashion."

"More than that. We're obliging them to us. We're *purchasing* that treaty with our gifts. But obviously gifts are worth more than a treaty of friendship, so they feel they'll still owe us something if they accept. They don't want to owe us anything. So they chase us away.

"Now," continued Harskin, "if we reverse the situation—if we make ourselves beholden to them, and *beg* for the signing of the treaty instead of trying to *buy* a treaty—why, that gives them a chance to seem lordly." He turned to Ramos, the military attaché. "Ramos, do you think a solar system is worth a spaceship?"

"Eh?"

"I mean, if it becomes necessary to sacrifice our ship in order to win the Antares system, will that be a strategically sound move?"

"I imagine so," Ramos said cautiously.

Harskin flicked a bead of sweat from his forehead. "Very well, then. Mawley, you and I and Navigator Dominic are going to take the *Peccable* on her final cruise. Klaristenfeld, I want you to get a subradio sending set inside my spacesuit, and make damned sure you don't put it where it'll bother me. Snollgren, you monitor the area and keep me posted on what the Rigelians are doing, if anything."

He pointed to the Navigator. "Come up to Control Cabin, Dominic. We're going to work out the most precise orbit you'll ever need to compute."

* * * *

Antares was sinking in the sky and the blue sun was in partial eclipse. Suddenly, the *Peccable* flashed across the sky of Fafnir, trailing smoke at both jets, roaring like a wounded giant as it circled in wildly for its crash landing.

The three men aboard were huddled in their acceleration cradles, groaning in pain as the increasing grav buffeted and bruised them. Below, Fafnir sprang up to meet the ship.

Harskin was bathed in his own sweat. So many things could go wrong...

They might have computed one tenth-place decimal awry—and would land square in the heart of the swampland.

The stabilizer jets might be consumed by the blaze they had set too soon, and the impact of their landing would kill them.

The airlock might refuse to open.

The gnorphs might fail to act as expected...

It was, he thought, an insane venture.

The ship throbbed suddenly as the stabilizer jets went into action. The *Peccable* froze for a fraction of a second, then began to glide.

It struck the blood-red ocean nose first. Furiously, Harskin climbed from his cradle and into his spacesuit. *Now, if we only figured the buoyancy factor right...*

Two spacesuited figures waited for him at the airlock. He grinned at them, threw open the hatch, and stepped into the outer chamber. The door opened; a wall of water rushed at him. He squirted out of the sinking ship and popped to the surface like a cork. A moment later he saw Mawley and Dominic come bobbing above the water nearby.

He turned. All that was visible of the *Peccable* was the rear jet assembly and the tips of the once-proud wings. An oily slick was starting to cover the bright-red water. The ship was sinking rapidly as water poured into the lock.

"Look over there!" Mawley exclaimed.

Harskin looked. Something that looked like a small island with a neck was approaching him: a monstrous turtle-like thing with a thick, saurian neck and a crested unintelligent head, from which dangled seven or eight fleshy barbels.

And riding in a sort of howdah erected on the broad carapace were three gnorphs, peering curiously at the three spacesuited men bobbing in the water.

The rescue party was on time.

"Help!" cried Harskin. "Rescue us! Oh, I beg of you, rescue us, and we'll be eternally obliged to you! Rescue us!"

He hoped the converter was translating the words with a suitable inflection of piteous despair.

DOUBLEPLUS PRIORITY 03-16-2952 ABS XPF32 EXP FORCE ANTARES SYSTEM TO HIGH COMMAND TERRA:

BE ADVISED ANTARES SYSTEM IN TERRAN FOLD. RIGELIANS ON HAND HAVE VALIDATED OUR TREATY WITH INHABITANTS OF FAFNIR, ANTARES' ONE WORLD. ALL IS WELL AND NO CASUALTIES EXCEPT SHIP PECCABLE ACCIDENTALLY DESTROYED. FIFTEEN MEMBERS OF CREW LIVING IN DOME ON COMPANION WORLD FASOLT, THREE OF US LIVING ON FAFNIR. PLEASE SEND PICKUP SHIP DOUBLE FAST AS WE ARE CURRENTLY IN MENIAL SERVITUDE.

ALL THE BEST, LOVE AND KISSES, ETC.

HARSKIN

OZYMANDIAS

Originally published in *Infinity Science Fiction*, November 1958.

The planet had been dead about a million years. That was our first impression, as our ship orbited down to its sere brown surface, and as it happened our first impression turned out to be right. There had been a civilization here once—but Earth had swung around Sol ten-to-the-sixth times since the last living being of this world had drawn breath.

"A dead planet," Colonel Mattern exclaimed bitterly. "Nothing here that's of any use. We might as well pack up and move on."

It was hardly surprising that Mattern would feel that way. In urging a quick departure and an immediate removal to some world of greater utilitarian value, Mattern was, after all, only serving the best interests of his employers. His employers were the General Staff of the Armed Forces of the United States of America. They expected Mattern and his half of the crew to produce results, and by way of results they meant new weapons and military alliances. They hadn't tossed in 70 percent of the budget for this trip just to sponsor a lot of archaeological putterings.

But lucky for *our* half of the outfit—the archaeological putterers' half—Mattern did not have an absolute voice in the affairs of the outfit. Perhaps the General Staff had kicked in for 70 percent of our budget, but the cautious men of the military's Public Liaison branch had seen to it that we had at least some rights.

Dr. Leopold, head of the non-military segment of the expedition, said brusquely, "Sorry, Mattern, but I'll have to apply the limiting clause here."

Mattern started to sputter. "But—"

"But nothing, Mattern. We're here. We've spent a good chunk of American cash in getting here. I insist that we spend the minimum time allotted for scientific research, as long as we *are* here."

Mattern scowled, looking down at the table, supporting his chin on his thumbs and digging the rest of his fingers in hard back of his jawbone. He was annoyed, but he was smart enough to know he didn't have much of a case to make against Leopold.

The rest of us—four archaeologists and seven military men; they outnumbered us a trifle—watched eagerly as our superiors battled. My eyes strayed through the porthole and I looked at the dry windblown plain, marked here and there with the stumps of what might have been massive monuments millennia ago.

Mattern said bleakly, "The world is of utterly no strategic consequence. Why, it's so old that even the vestiges of civilization have turned to dust!"

"Nevertheless, I reserve the right granted to me to explore any world we land on, for a period of at least one hundred sixty-eight hours," Leopold returned implacably.

Exasperated, Mattern burst out, "Dammit, *why?* Just to spite me? Just to prove the innate intellectual superiority of the scientist to the man of war?"

"Mattern, I'm not injecting personalities into this."

"I'd like to know what you *are* doing, then? Here we are on a world that's obviously useless to me and probably just as useless to you. Yet you stick me on a technicality and force me to waste a week here. Why, if not out of spite?"

"We've made only the most superficial reconnaissance so far," Leopold, said. "For all we know this place may be the answer to many questions of galactic history. It may even be a treasure-trove of superbombs, for all—"

"Pretty damned likely!" Mattern exploded. He glared around the conference room, fixing each of the scientific members of the committee with a baleful stare. He was making it quite clear that he was trapped into a wasteful expense of time by our foggy-eyed desire for Knowledge.

Useless knowledge. Not good hard practical knowledge of the kind *he* valued.

"All right," he said finally. "I've protested and I've lost, Leopold. You're within your rights in insisting on remaining here one week. But you'd damned well better be ready to blast off when your time's up!"

It had been foregone all along, of course. The charter of our expedition was explicit on the matter. We had been sent out to comb a stretch of worlds near the Galactic Rim that had already been brushed over hastily by a survey mission.

The surveyors had been looking simply for signs of life, and, finding none, they had moved on. We were entrusted with the task of investigating in detail. Some of the planets in the group had been inhabited once, the surveyors had reported. None bore present life.

Our job was to comb through the assigned worlds with diligence. Leopold, leading our group, had the task of doing pure archaeological research on the dead civilizations; Mattern and his men had the more immediately practical job of looking for fissionable material, leftover alien weapons, possible sources of lithium or tritium for fusion, and other such militarily useful things. You could argue that in a strictly pragmatic sense our segment of the group was just dead weight, carted along for the ride at great expense, and you would be right.

But the public temper over the last few hundred years in America had frowned on purely military expeditions. And so, as a sop to the nation's conscience, five archaeologists, of little empirical consequence so far as national security mattered, were tacked onto the expedition.

Us.

Mattern made it quite clear at the outset that *his* boys were the Really Important members of the expedition, and that we were simply ballast. In a way, we had to agree. Tension was mounting once again on our sadly disunited planet; there was no telling when the Other Hemisphere would rouse from its quiescence of a hundred years and decide to plunge once more into space. If anything of military value lay out here, we knew we had to find it before They did.

The good old armaments race. Hi-ho! The old space stories used to talk about expeditions from Earth. Well, we **were** from Earth, abstractly speaking—but in actuality we were from America, period. Global unity was as much of a pipedream as it had been three hundred years earlier, in the remote and primitive chemical-rocket era of space travel. Amen. End of sermon. We got to work.

* * * *

The planet had no name, and we didn't give it one; a special commission of what was laughably termed the United Nations Organization was working on the problem of assigning names to the hundreds of worlds of the galaxy, using the old idea of borrowing from ancient Terran mythologies in analogy to the Mercury-Venus-Mars nomenclature of our own system.

Probably they would end up saddling this world with something like Thoth or Bel-Marduk or perhaps Avalokitesvara. We knew it simply as Planet Four of the system belonging to a yellow-white FS IV Procyonoid sun, Revised HD Catalogue # 170861.

It was roughly Earthtype, with a diameter of 6100 miles, a gravity index of .93, a mean temperature of 45 degrees F. with a daily fluctuation range of about ten degrees, and a thin, nasty atmosphere composed mostly of carbon dioxide with wisps of helium and hydrogen and the barest smidgeon of oxygen. Quite possibly the air had been breathable by humanoid life millions of years ago—but that was millions of years ago. We took good care to practice our breathing-mask drills before we ventured out of the ship.

The sun, as noted, was an FS IV and fairly hot, but Planet Four was a hundred eighty-five million miles away from it at perihelion, and a good deal further when it was at the other swing of its rather eccentric orbit; the good old Keplerian ellipse took quite a bit of punishment in this system. Planet Four reminded me in many ways of Mars—except that Mars, of course, had never known intelligent life of any kind, at least none that had troubled to leave a hint of its existence, while this planet had obviously had a flourishing civilization at a time when Pithecanthropus was Earth's noblest being.

In any event, once we had thrashed out the matter of whether or not we were going to stay here or pull up and head for the next planet on our schedule, the five of us set to work. We knew we had only a week—Mattern would never grant us an extension unless we came up with something good enough to change his mind, which was improbable—and we wanted to get as much done in that week as possible. With the sky as full of worlds as it is, this planet might never be visited by Earth scientists again.

Mattern and his men served notice right away that they were going to help us, but reluctantly and minimally. We unlimbered the three small halftracks carried aboard ship and got them into functioning order. We stowed our gear—cameras, picks and shovels, camel's-hair brushes—and donned our breathing-masks, and Mattern's men helped us get the halftracks out of the ship and pointed in the right direction.

Then they stood back and waited for us to shove off.

"Don't any of you plan to accompany us?" Leopold asked. The halftracks each held up to four men.

Mattern shook his head. "You fellows go out by yourselves today and let us know what you find. We can make better use of the time filing and catching up on back log entries."

I saw Leopold start to scowl. Mattern was being openly contemptuous; the least he could do was have his men make a token search for fissionable or fusionable matter! But Leopold swallowed down his anger.

"Okay," he said. "You do that. If we come across any raw veins of plutonium I'll radio back."

"Sure," Mattern said. "Thanks for the favor. Let me know if you find a brass mine, too." He laughed harshly. "Raw plutonium! I half believe you're serious!"

* * * *

We had worked out a rough sketch of the area, and we split up into three units. Leopold, alone, headed straight due west, towards the dry riverbed we had spotted from the air. He intended to check alluvial deposits, I guess.

Marshall and Webster, sharing one halftrack, struck out to the hilly country southeast of our landing point. A substantial city appeared to be buried under the sand there. Gerhardt and I, in the other vehicle, made off to the north, where we hoped to find remnants of yet another city. It was a bleak, windy day; the endless sand that covered this world mounted into little dunes before us, and the wind picked up handfuls and tossed it against the plastic dome that covered our truck. Underneath the steel cleats of our tractor-belt, there was a steady crunch-crunch of metal coming down on sand that hadn't been disturbed in millennia.

Neither of us spoke for a while. Then Gerhardt said, "I hope the ship's still there when we get back to the base."

Frowning, I turned to look at him as I drove. Gerhardt had always been an enigma: a small scrunchy guy with untidy brown hair flapping in his eyes, eyes that were set a little too close together. He had a degree from the University of Kansas and had put in some time on their field staff with distinction, or so his references said.

I said, "What the hell do you mean?"

"I don't trust Mattern. He hates us."

"He doesn't. Mattern's no villain—just a fellow who wants to do his job and go home. But what do you mean, the ship not being there?"

"He'll blast off without us. You see the way he sent us all out into the desert and kept his own men back. I tell you, he'll strand us here!"

I snorted. "Don't be a paranoid. Mattern won't do anything of the sort."

"He thinks we're dead weight on the expedition," Gerhardt insisted. "What better way to get rid of us?"

The halftrack breasted a hump in the desert. I kept wishing a vulture would squeal somewhere, but there was not even that. Life had left this world ages ago. I said, "Mattern doesn't have much use for us, sure. But would he blast off and leave three perfectly good halftracks behind? Would he?"

It was a good point. Gerhardt grunted agreement after a while. Mattern would never toss equipment away, though he might not have such scruples about five surplus archaeologists.

We rode along silently for a while longer. By now we had covered twenty miles through this utterly barren land. As far as I could see, we might just as well have stayed at the ship. At least there we had a surface lie of building foundations.

But another ten miles and we came across our city. It seemed to be of linear form, no more than half a mile wide and stretching out as far as we could see—maybe six or seven hundred miles; if we had time, we would check the dimensions from the air.

Of course it wasn't much of a city. The sand had pretty well covered everything, but we could see foundations jutting up here and there, weathered lumps of structural concrete and reinforced metal. We got out and unpacked the power-shovel.

An hour later, we were sticky with sweat under our thin spacesuits and we had succeeded in transferring a few thousand cubic yards of soil from the ground to an area a dozen yards away. We had dug one devil of a big hole in the ground.

And we had nothing.

Nothing. Not an artifact, not a skull, not a yellowed tooth. No spoons, no knives, no baby-rattles.

Nothing.

The foundations of some of the buildings had endured, though whittled down to stumps by a million years of sand and wind and rain. But nothing else of this civilization had survived. Mattern, in his scorn, had been right, I admitted ruefully: this planet was as useless to us as it was to them. Weathered foundations could tell us little except that there had once been a civilization here. An imaginative palaeontologist can reconstruct a dinosaur from a fragment of a thighbone, can sketch out a presentable saurian with only a fossilized ischium to guide him. But could we extrapolate a culture, a code of laws, a technology, a philosophy, from bare weathered building foundations?

Not very likely.

We moved on and dug somewhere else half a mile away, hoping at least to unearth one tangible remnant of the civilization that had been. But time had done its work; we were lucky to have the building foundations. All else was gone.

"*Boundless and bare, the lone and level sands stretch far away,*" I muttered.

Gerhardt looked up from his digging. "Eh? What's that?" he demanded.

"Shelley," I told him.

"Oh. Him."

He went back to digging.

* * * *

Late in the afternoon we finally decided to call it quits and head back to the base. We had been in the field for seven hours and had nothing to show for it except a few hundred feet of tridim films of building foundations.

The sun was beginning to set; Planet Four had a thirty-five hour day, and it was coming to its end. The sky, always somber, was darkening now. There was no moon. Planet Four had no satellites. It seemed a bit unfair; Three and Five of the system each had four moons, while around the massive gas giant that was Eight a cluster of thirteen moonlets whirled.

We wheeled round and headed back, taking an alternate route three miles east of the one we had used on the way out, in case we might spot something. It was a forlorn hope, though.

Six miles along our journey, the truck radio came to life. The dry, testy voice of Dr. Leopold reached us:

"Calling Trucks Two and Three. Two and Three, do you read me? Come in, Two and Three."

Gerhardt was driving. I reached across his knee to key in the response channel and said, "Anderson and Gerhardt in Number Three, sir. We read you."

A moment later, somewhat more faintly, came the sound of Number Two keying into the three-way channel, and I heard Marshall saying, "Marshall and Webster in Two, Dr. Leopold. Is something wrong?"

"I've found something," Leopold said.

From the way Marshall exclaimed *"Really!"* I knew that Truck Number Two had had no better luck than we. I said, "That makes one of us, then."

"You've had no luck, Anderson?"

"Not a scrap. Not a potsherd."

"How about you, Marshall?"

"Check. Scattered signs of a city, but nothing of archaeological value, sir."

I heard Leopold chuckle before he said, "Well, I've found something. It's a little too heavy for me to manage by myself. I want both outfits to come out here and take a look at it."

"What is it, sir?" Marshall and I asked simultaneously, in just about the same words.

But Leopold was fond of playing the Man of Mystery. He said, "You'll see when you get here. Take down my coordinates and get a move on. I want to be back at the base by nightfall."

Shrugging, we changed course to head for Leopold's location. He was about seventeen miles southwest of us, it seemed. Marshall and Webster had an equally long trip to make; they were sharply southeast of Leopold's position.

The sky was fairly dark when we arrived at what Leopold had computed as his coordinates. The headlamps of the halftrack lit up the desert for nearly a mile, and at first there was no sign of anyone or anything. Then I spotted Leopold's halftrack parked off to the east, and from the south Gerhardt saw the lights of the third truck rolling towards us.

We reached Leopold at about the same time. He was not alone. There was an—object—with him.

"Greetings, gentlemen." He had a smug grin on his whiskery face. "I seem to have made a find."

He stepped back and, as if drawing an imaginary curtain, let us take a peek at his find. I frowned in surprise and puzzlement. Standing in the sand behind Leopold's halftrack was something that looked very much like a robot.

It was tall, seven feet or more, and vaguely humanoid; that is, it had arms extending from its shoulders, a head on those shoulders, and legs. The head was furnished with receptor plates where eyes, ears, and mouth would be on humans. There were no other openings. The robot's body was massive and squarish, with sloping shoulders, and its dark metal skin was pitted and corroded as by the workings of the elements over uncountable centuries.

It was buried up to its knees in sand. Leopold, still grinning smugly (and understandably proud of his find) said, "Say something to us, robot."

From the mouth-receptors came a clanking sound, the gnashing of—what? Gears?—and a voice came forth, oddly high-pitched but audible. The words were alien and were spoken in a slippery singsong kind of inflection. I felt a chill go quivering down my back.

"It understands what you say?" Gerhardt questioned.

"I don't think so," Leopold said. "Not yet, anyway. But when I address it directly, it starts spouting. I think it's a kind of—well, guide to the ruins, so to speak. Built by the ancients to provide information to passersby; only it seems to have survived the ancients and their monuments as well."

I studied the thing. It *did* look incredibly old—and sturdy; it was so massively solid that it might indeed have outlasted every other vestige of civilization on this planet. It had stopped talking, now, and was simply staring ahead. Suddenly it wheeled ponderously on its base, swung an arm up to take in the landscape nearby, and started speaking again.

I could almost put the words in its mouth: *"—and over here we have the ruins of the Parthenon, chief temple of Athena on the Acropolis. Completed in the year 438 B.C., it was partially destroyed by an explosion in 1687 while in use as a powder magazine by the Turks—"*

"It *does* seem to be a sort of a guide," Webster remarked. "I get the definite feeling that we're being given an historical narration now, all about the wondrous monuments that must have been on this site once."

"If only we could understand what it's saying!" Marshall exclaimed.

"We can try to decipher the language somehow," Leopold said. "Anyway, it's a magnificent find, isn't it? And—"

I began to laugh suddenly. Leopold, offended, glared at me and said, "May I ask what's so funny, Dr. Anderson?"

"Ozymandias!" I said, when I had subsided a bit. "It's a natural! Ozymandias!"

"I'm afraid I don't—"

"Listen to him," I said. "It's as if he was built and put here for those who follow after, to explain to us the glories of the race that built the cities. Only the cities are gone, and the robot is still here! Doesn't he seem to be saying, *'Look on my works, ye Mighty, and despair'?*"

"*'Nothing beside remains,'*" Webster quoted. "It's apt. Builders and cities all gone, but the poor robot doesn't know it, and delivers his spiel nonetheless. Yes. We ought to call him Ozymandias!"

Gerhardt said, "What shall we do with it?"

"You say you couldn't budge it?" Webster asked Leopold.

"It weighs five or six hundred pounds. It can move of its own volition, but I couldn't move it myself."

"Maybe the five of us—" Webster suggested.

"No," Leopold said. An odd smile crossed his face. "We will leave it here."

"What?"

"Only temporarily," he added. "We'll save it—as a sort, of surprise for Mattern. We'll spring it on him the final day, letting him think all along that this planet was worthless. He can rib us all he wants—but when it's time to go, we'll produce our prize!"

"You think it's safe to leave it out here?" Gerhardt asked.

"Nobody's going to steal it," Marshall said.

"And it won't melt in the rain," Webster added.

"But—suppose it walks away?" Gerhardt demanded. "It can do that, can't it?"

Leopold said, "Of course. But where would it go? It will remain where it is, I think. If it moves, we can always trace it with the radar. Back to the base, now; it grows late."

We climbed back into our halftracks. The robot, silent once again, planted knee-deep in the sand, outlined against the darkening sky, swivelled to face us and lifted one thick arm in a kind of salute.

"Remember," Leopold warned us as we left. "Not one word about this to Mattern!"

* * * *

At the base that night, Colonel Mattern and his seven aides were remarkably curious about our day's activities. They tried to make it seem as if they were taking a sincere interest in our work, but it was perfectly obvious to us that they were simply goading us into telling them what they had anticipated—that we had found absolutely nothing. This was the response they got, since Leopold forbade mentioning Ozymandias. Aside from the robot, the truth was that we had found nothing, and when they learned of this they smiled knowingly, as if saying that had we listened to them in the first place we would all be back on Earth seven days earlier, with no loss.

The following morning after breakfast Mattern announced that he was sending out a squad to look for fissionable materials, unless we objected.

"We'll only need one of the halftracks," he said. "That leaves two for you. You don't mind, do you?"

"We can get along with two," Leopold replied a little sourly. "Just so you keep out of our territory."

"Which is?"

Instead of telling him, Leopold merely said, "We've adequately examined the area to the southeast of here, and found nothing of note. It won't matter to us if your geological equipment chews the place up."

Mattern nodded, eyeing Leopold curiously as if the obvious concealment of our place of operations had aroused suspicions. I wondered whether it was wise to conceal information from Mattern. Well, Leopold wanted to play his little game, I thought; and one way to keep Mattern from seeing Ozymandias was not to tell him where we would be working.

"I thought you said this planet was useless from your viewpoint, Colonel," I remarked.

Mattern stared at me. "I'm sure of it. But it would be idiotic of me not to have a look, wouldn't it—as long as we're spending the time here anyway?"

I had to admit that he was right. "Do you expect to find anything, though?"

He shrugged. "No fissionables, certainly. It's a safe bet that everything radioactive on *this* planet has long since decomposed. But there's always the possibility of lithium, you know."

"Or pure tritium," Leopold said acidly. Mattern merely laughed, and made no reply.

Half an hour later we were bound westward again to the point where we had left Ozymandias. Gerhardt, Webster, and I rode together in one halftrack, and Leopold and Marshall occupied the other. The third, with two of Mattern's men and the prospecting equipment, ventured off to the southeast towards the area Marshall and Webster had fruitlessly combed the day before.

Ozymandias was where we had left him, with the sun coming up behind him and glowing round his sides. I wondered how many sunrises he had seen. Billions, perhaps.

We parked the halftracks not far from the robot and approached, Webster filming him in the bright light of morning. A wind was whistling down from the north, kicking up eddies in the sand.

"Ozymandias have remain here," the robot said as we drew near.

In English.

For a moment we didn't realize what had happened, but what followed afterwards was a five-man quadruple-take. While we gabbled in confusion the robot said, "Ozymandias decipher the language somehow. Seem to be a sort of guide."

"Why—he's parroting fragments from our conversation yesterday," Marshall said.

"I don't think he's parroting," I said. "The words form coherent concepts. He's *talking* to us!"

"Built by the ancients to provide information to passersby," Ozymandias said.

"Ozymandias!" Leopold said. "Do you speak English?"

The response was a clicking noise, followed moments later by, "Ozymandias understand. Not have words enough. Talk more."

The five of us trembled with common excitement. It was apparent now what had happened, and the happening was nothing short of incredible. Ozymandias had listened patiently to everything we had said the night before; then, after we had gone, he had applied his million-year-old mind to the problem of organizing our sounds into sense, and somehow had succeeded. Now it was merely a matter of feeding vocabulary to the creature and letting him assimilate the new words. We had a walking and talking Rosetta Stone!

Two hours flew by so rapidly we hardly noticed their passing. We tossed words at Ozymandias as fast as we could, defining them when possible to aid him in relating them to the others already engraved on his mind.

By the end of that time he could hold a passable conversation with us. He ripped his legs free of the sand that had bound them for centuries—and, serving the function for which he had been built millennia ago, he took us on a guided tour of the civilization that had been and had built him.

Ozymandias was a fabulous storehouse of archaeological data. We could mine him for years.

His people, he told us, had called themselves the Thaiquens (or so it sounded)—had lived and thrived for three hundred thousand local years, and in the declining days of their history had built him, as indestructible guide to their indestructible cities. But the cities had crumbled, and Ozymandias alone remained—bearing with him memories of what had been.

"This was the city of Durab. In its day it held eight million people. Where I stand now was the temple of Decamon, sixteen hundred feet of your measurement high. It faced the Street of the Winds—"

"The Eleventh Dynasty was begun by the accession to the Presidium of Chonnigar IV, in the eighteen thousandth year of the city. It was in the reign of this dynasty that the neighboring planets first were reached—"

"The Library of Durab was on this spot. It boasted fourteen million volumes. None exist today. Long after the builders had gone, I spent time reading the books of the Library and they are memorized within me—"

"The Plague struck down nine thousand a day for more than a year, in that time—"

It went on and on, a cyclopean newsreel, growing in detail as Ozymandias absorbed our comments and added new words to his vocabulary. We followed the robot as he wheeled his way through the desert, our recorders gobbling in each word, our minds numbed and dazed by the magnitude of our find. In this single robot lay waiting to be tapped the totality of a culture that had lasted three hundred thousand years! We could mine Ozymandias the rest of our lives, and still not exhaust the fund of data implanted in his all-encompassing mind.

When, finally, we ripped ourselves away and, leaving Ozymandias in the desert, returned to the base, we were full to bursting. Never in the history of our science had such a find been vouchsafed: a complete record, accessible and translated for us.

We agreed to conceal our find from Mattern once again. But, like small boys newly given a toy of great value, we found it hard to hide our feelings. Although we said nothing explicit, our overexcited manner certainly must have hinted to Mattern that we had not had as fruitless a day as we had claimed.

That, and Leopold's refusal to tell him exactly where we had been working during the day, must have aroused Mattern's suspicions. In any event, during the night as we lay in bed I heard the sound of halftracks rumbling off into the desert; and the following morning, when we entered the messhall for breakfast, Mattern and his men, unshaven and untidy, turned to look at us with peculiar vindictive gleams in their eyes.

Mattern said, "Good morning, gentlemen. We've been waiting for some time for you to arise."

"It's no later than usual, is it?" Leopold asked.

"Not at all. But my men and I have been up all night. We—ah—did a bit of archaeological prospecting while you slept." The Colonel leaned forward, fingering his rumpled lapels, and said, "Dr. Leopold, for what reason did you choose to conceal from me the fact that you had discovered an object of extreme strategic importance?"

"What do you mean?" Leopold demanded—with a quiver taking the authority out of his voice.

"I mean," said Mattern quietly, "the robot you named Ozymandias. Just why did you decide not to tell me about it?"

"I had every intention of doing so before our departure," Leopold said.

Mattern shrugged. "Be that as it may. You concealed the existence of your find. But your manner last night led us to investigate the area—and since the detectors showed a metal object some twenty miles to the west, we headed that way. Ozymandias was quite surprised to learn that there were other Earthmen here."

There was a moment of crackling silence. Then Leopold said, "I'll have to ask you not to meddle with that robot, Colonel Mattern. I apologize for having neglected to tell you of it—I didn't think you were quite so interested in our work—but now I must insist you and your men keep away from it."

"Oh?" Mattern said crisply. "Why?"

"Because it's an archaeological treasure-trove, Colonel. I can't begin to stress its value to us. Your men might perform some casual experiment with it and short circuit its memory channels, or something like that. And so I'll have to assert the rights of the archaeological group of this expedition. I'll have to declare Ozymandias part of our preserve, and off bounds for you."

Mattern's voice suddenly hardened. "Sorry, Dr. Leopold. You can't invoke that now."

"Why not?"

"Because Ozymandias is part of *our* preserve. And off bounds for you, Doctor."

I thought Leopold would have an apoplectic fit right there in the messhall. He stiffened and went white and strode awkwardly across the room towards Mattern. He choked out a question, inaudible to me.

Mattern replied, "Security, Doctor. Ozymandias is of military use. Accordingly we've brought him to the ship and placed him in sealed quarters, under top-level wraps. With the power entrusted to me for such emergencies, I'm declaring this expedition ended. We return to Earth at once with Ozymandias."

Leopold's eyes bugged. He looked at us for support, but we said nothing. Finally, incredulously, he said, "He's—of military use?"

"Of course. He's a storehouse of data on the ancient Thaiquen weapons. We've already learned things from him that are unbelievable in their scope. Why do you think this planet is bare of life, Dr. Leopold? Not even a blade of grass? A million years won't do that. But a superweapon *will*. The Thaiquens developed that weapon. And others, too. Weapons that can make your hair curl. And Ozymandias knows every detail of them. Do you think we can waste time letting you people fool with that robot, when he's loaded with military information that can make America totally impregnable? Sorry, Doctor. Ozymandias is your find, but he belongs to us. And we're taking him back to Earth."

Again the room was silent. Leopold looked at me, at Webster, at Marshall, at Gerhardt. There was nothing that could be said.

This was basically a militaristic mission. Sure, a few archaeologists had been tacked onto the crew, but fundamentally it was Mattern's men and not Leopold's who were important. We weren't out here so much to increase the fund of general knowledge as to find new weapons and new sources of strategic materials for possible use against the Other Hemisphere.

And new weapons had been found. New, undreamed-of weapons, product of a science that had endured for three hundred thousand years. All locked up in Ozymandias' imperishable skull.

In a harsh voice Leopold said, "Very well, Colonel. I can't stop you, I suppose."

He turned and shuffled out without touching his food, a broken, beaten, suddenly very old man.

I felt sick.

Mattern had insisted the planet was useless and that stopping here was a waste of time; Leopold had disagreed, and Leopold had turned out to be right. We had found something of great value.

We had found a machine that could spew forth new and awesome recipes for death. We held in our hands the sum and essence of the Thaiquen science—the science that had culminated in magnificent weapons, weapons so superb they had succeeded in destroying all life on this world. And now we had access to those weapons. Dead by their own hand, the Thaiquens had thoughtfully left us a heritage of death.

Grey-faced, I rose from the table and went to my cabin. I wasn't hungry now.

"We'll be blasting off in an hour," Mattern said behind me as I left. "Get your things in order."

I hardly heard him. I was thinking of the deadly cargo we carried, the robot so eager to disgorge its fund of data. I was thinking what would happen when our scientists back on Earth began learning from Ozymandias.

The works of the Thaiquens now were ours. I thought of the poet's lines: *"Look on my works, ye Mighty—and despair."*

THE PAIN PEDDLERS

Originally published in *Galaxy*, August 1963.

Pain is Gain.
—Greek proverb

The phone bleeped. Northrop nudged the cut-in switch and heard Maurillo say, "We got a gangrene, chief. They're amputating tonight."

Northrop's pulse quickened at the thought of action. "What's the tab?" he asked.

"Five thousand, all rights."

"Anesthetic?"

"Natch," Maurillo said. "I tried it the other way."

"What did you offer?"

"Ten. It was no go."

Northrop sighed. "I'll have to handle it myself, I guess. Where's the patient?"

"Clinton General. In the wards."

Northrop raised a heavy eyebrow and glowered into the screen. "In the *wards*?" he bellowed. "And you couldn't get them to agree?"

Maurillo seemed to shrink. "It was the relatives, chief. They were stubborn. The old man, he didn't seem to give a damn, but the relatives—"

"Okay. You stay there. I'm coming over to close the deal," Northrop snapped. He cut the phone out and pulled a couple of blank waiver forms out of his desk, just in case the relatives backed down. Gangrene was gangrene, but ten grand was ten grand. And business was business. The networks were yelling. He had to supply the goods or get out.

He thumbed the autosecretary. "I want my car ready in thirty seconds. South Street exit."

"Yes, Mr. Northrop."

"If anyone calls for me in the next half hour, record it. I'm going to Clinton General Hospital, but I don't want to be called there."

"Yes, Mr. Northrop."

"If Rayfield calls from the network office, tell him I'm getting him a dandy. Tell him—oh, hell, tell him I'll call him back in an hour. That's all."

"Yes, Mr. Northrop."

Northrop scowled at the machine and left his office. The gravshaft took him down forty stories in almost literally no time flat. His car was waiting, as ordered, a long, sleek '08 Frontenac with bubble top. Bulletproof, of course. Network producers were vulnerable to crack- pot attacks.

He sat back, nestling into the plush upholstery. The car asked him where he was going, and he answered.

"Let's have a pep pill," he said.

A pill rolled out of the dispenser in front of him. He gulped it down. *Maurillo, you make me sick,* he thought. *Why can't you close a deal without me? Just once?*

He made a mental note. Maurillo had to go. The organization couldn't tolerate inefficiency.

* * * *

The hospital was an old one. It was housed in one of the vulgar green-glass architectural monstrosities so popular sixty years before, a tasteless slab-sided thing without character or grace. The main door irised and Northrop stepped through, and the familiar hospital smell hit his nostrils. Most people found it unpleasant, but not Northrop. It was the smell of dollars, for him.

The hospital was so old that it still had nurses and orderlies. Oh, plenty of mechanicals skittered up and down the corridors, but here and there a middle-aged nurse, smugly clinging to her tenure, pushed a tray of mush along, or a doddering orderly propelled a broom. In his early days on video, Northrop had done a documentary on these people, these living fossils in the hospital corridors. He had won an award for the film, with its crosscuts from baggy-faced nurses to gleaming mechanicals, its vivid presentation of the inhumanity of the new hospitals. It was a long time since Northrop had done a documentary of that sort. A different kind of show was the order of the day now, ever since the intensifiers had come in.

A mechanical took him to Ward Seven. Maurillo was waiting there, a short, bouncy little man who wasn't bouncing much now, because he knew he had fumbled. Maurillo grinned up at Northrop, a hollow grin, and said, "You sure made it fast, chief!"

"How long would it take for the competition to cut in?" Northrop countered. "Where's the patient?"

"Down by the end. You see where the curtain is? I had the curtain put

THE PAIN PEDDLERS | 183

up. To get in good with the heirs. The relatives, I mean."

"Fill me in," Northrop said. "Who's in charge?"

"The oldest son. Harry. Watch out for him. Greedy."

"Who isn't?" Northrop sighed. They were at the curtain, now. Maurillo parted it. All through the long ward, patients were stirring. Potential subjects for taping, all of them, Northrop thought. The world was so full of different kinds of sickness—and one sickness fed on another.

He stepped through the curtain. There was a man in the bed, drawn and gaunt, his hollow face greenish, stubbly. A mechanical stood next to the bed, with an intravenous tube running across and under the covers. The patient looked at least ninety. Knocking off ten years for the effects of illness still made him pretty old, Northrop thought.

He confronted the relatives.

There were eight of them. Five women, ranging from middle age down to teens. Three men, the oldest about fifty, the other two in their forties. Sons and daughters and nieces and granddaughters, Northrop figured.

He said gravely, "I know what a terrible tragedy this must be for all of you. A man in the prime of his life—head of a happy family…" Northrop stared at the patient. "But I know he'll pull through. I can see the strength in him."

The oldest relative said, "I'm Harry Gardner. I'm his son. You're from the network?"

"I'm the producer," Northrop said. "I don't ordinarily come in person, but my assistant told me what a great human situation there was here, what a brave person your father is…"

The man in the bed slept on. He looked bad.

Harry Gardner said, "We made an arrangement. Five thousand bucks. We wouldn't do it, except for the hospital bills. They can really wreck you."

"I understand perfectly," Northrop said in his most unctuous tones. "That's why we're prepared to raise our offer. We're well aware of the disastrous effects of hospitalization on a small family, even today, in these times of protection. And so we can offer—"

"No! There's got to be anesthetic!" It was one of the daughters, a round, drab woman with colorless thin lips. "We ain't going to let you make him suffer!"

Northrop smiled. "It would only be a moment of pain for him. Believe me. We'd begin the anesthesia immediately after the amputation. Just let us capture that single instant of—"

"It ain't right! He's old, he's got to be given the best treatment! The pain could kill him!"

"On the contrary," Northrop said blandly. "Scientific research has shown that pain is often beneficial in amputation cases. It creates a nerve block, you see, that causes a kind of anesthesia of its own, without the harmful side effects of chemotherapy. And once the danger vectors are controlled, the normal anesthetic procedures can be invoked, and—" He took a deep breath, and went rolling glibly on to the crusher, "with the extra fee we'll provide, you can give your dear one the absolute finest in medical care. There'll be no reason to stint."

Wary glances were exchanged. Harry Gardner said, "How much are you offering?"

"May I see the leg?" Northrop countered.

The coverlet was peeled back. Northrop stared.

It was a nasty case. Northrop was no doctor, but he had been in this line of work for five years, and that was long enough to give him an amateur acquaintance with disease. He knew the old man was in bad shape. It looked as though there had been a severe burn, high up along the calf, which had probably been treated only with first aid. Then, in happy proletarian ignorance, the family had let the old man rot until he was gangrenous. Now the leg was blackened, glossy, and swollen from midcalf to the ends of the toes. Everything looked soft and decayed. Northrop had the feeling that he could reach out and break the puffy toes off, one at a time.

The patient wasn't going to survive. Amputation or not, he was probably rotten to the core by this time, and if the shock of amputation didn't do him in, general debilitation would. It was a good prospect for the show. It was the kind of stomach-turning vicarious suffering that millions of viewers gobbled up avidly.

Northrop looked up and said, "Fifteen thousand if you'll allow a network-approved surgeon to amputate under our conditions. And we'll pay the surgeon's fee besides."

"Well..."

"And we'll also underwrite the entire cost of postoperative care for your father," Northrop added smoothly. "Even if he stays in the hospital for six months, we'll pay every nickel, over and above the telecast fee."

He had them. He could see the greed shining in their eyes. They were faced with bankruptcy, and he had come to rescue them, and did it matter all that much if the old man didn't have anesthetic when they sawed his leg off? He was hardly conscious even now. He wouldn't really feel a thing, not really.

Northrop produced the documents, the waivers, the contracts covering residuals and Latin-American reruns, the payment vouchers, all the paraphernalia. He sent Maurillo scuttling off for a secretary, and a few moments later a glistening mechanical was taking it all down.

"If you'll put your name here, Mr. Gardner…"

Northrop handed the pen to the eldest son. Signed, sealed, delivered.

"We'll operate tonight," Northrop said. "I'll send our surgeon over immediately. One of our best men. We'll give your father the care he deserves."

He pocketed the documents. It was done. Maybe it was barbaric to operate on an old man that way, Northrop thought, but he didn't bear the responsibility, after all. He was just giving the public what it wanted, and the public wanted spouting blood and tortured nerves. And what did it matter to the old man, really? Any experienced medic could tell you he was as good as dead. The operation wouldn't save him. Anesthesia wouldn't save him. If the gangrene didn't get him, postoperative shock would do him in. At worst, he would suffer only a few minutes under the knife, but at least his family would be free from the fear of financial ruin.

On the way out, Maurillo said, "Don't you think it's a little risky, chief? Offering to pay the hospitalization expenses, I mean?"

"You've got to gamble a little sometimes to get what you want," Northrop said.

"Yeah, but that could run to fifty, sixty thousand! What'll that do to the budget?"

Northrop shrugged. "We'll survive. Which is more than the old man will. He can't make it through the night. We haven't risked a penny, Maurillo. Not a stinking cent."

* * * *

Returning to the office, Northrop turned the papers on the Gardner amputation over to his assistants, set the wheels in motion for the show, and prepared to call it a day. There was only one bit of dirty work left to do. He had to fire Maurillo.

It wasn't called firing, of course. Maurillo had tenure, just like the hospital orderlies and everyone else below executive rank. It was more a demotion than anything else. Northrop had been increasingly dissatisfied with the little man's work for months, now, and today had been the clincher. Maurillo had no imagination. He didn't know how to close a deal. Why hadn't he thought of underwriting the hospitalization? *If I can't delegate responsibility to him,* Northrop told himself, *I can't use him at all.* There were plenty of other assistant producers in the outfit who'd be glad to step in.

Northrop spoke to a couple of them. He made his choice. A young fellow named Barton, who had been working on documentaries all year. Barton had done the plane-crash deal in London in the spring. He had a fine touch for the gruesome. He had been on hand at the World's Fair fire last year in Juneau. Yes, Barton was the man.

The next part was the sticky one. Northrop phoned Maurillo, even though Maurillo was only two rooms away—these things were never done in person—and said, "I've got some good news for you, Ted. We're shifting you to a new program."

"Shifting…?"

"That's right. We had a talk in here this afternoon, and we decided you were being wasted on the blood and guts show. You need more scope for your talents. So we're moving you over to Kiddie Time. We think you'll really blossom there. You and Sam Kline and Ed Bragan ought to make a terrific team."

Northrop saw Maurillo's pudgy face crumble. The arithmetic was getting home; over here, Maurillo was Number Two, and on the new show, a much less important one, he'd be Number Three. It was a thumping boot downstairs, and Maurillo knew it.

The *mores* of the situation called for Maurillo to pretend he was receiving a rare honor. He didn't play the game. He squinted and said, "Just because I didn't sign up that old man's amputation?"

"What makes you think…?"

"Three years I've been with you! Three years, and you kick me out just like that!"

"I told you, Ted, we thought this would be a big opportunity for you. It's a step up the ladder. It's—"

Maurillo's fleshy face puffed up with rage. "It's getting junked," he said bitterly. "Well, never mind, huh? It so happens I've got another offer. I'm quitting before you can can me. You can take your tenure and—"

Northrop blanked the screen.

The idiot, he thought. *The fat little idiot. Well, to hell with him!*

He cleared his desk, and cleared his mind of Ted Maurillo and his problems. Life was real, life was earnest. Maurillo just couldn't take the pace, that was all.

Northrop prepared to go home. It had been a long day.

* * * *

At eight that evening came word that old Gardner was about to undergo the amputation. At ten, Northrop was phoned by the network's own head surgeon, Dr. Steele, with the news that the operation had failed.

"We lost him," Steele said in a flat, unconcerned voice. "We did our best, but he was a mess. Fibrillation set in, and his heart just ran away. Not a damned thing we could do."

"Did the leg come off?"

"Oh, sure. All this was *after* the operation."

"Did it get taped?"

"They're processing it now. I'm on my way out."

"Okay," Northrop said. "Thanks for calling."

"Sorry about the patient."

"Don't worry yourself," Northrop said. "It happens to the best of us."

The next morning, Northrop had a look at the rushes. The screening was in the twenty-third floor studio, and a select audience was on hand—Northrop, his new assistant producer Barton, a handful of network executives, a couple of men from the cutting room. Slick, bosomy girls handed out intensifier helmets—no mechanicals doing the work here!

Northrop slipped the helmet on over his head. He felt the familiar surge of excitement as the electrodes descended, as contact was made. He closed his eyes. There was a thrum of power somewhere in the room as the EEG-amplifier went into action. The screen brightened.

There was the old man. There was the gangrenous leg. There was Dr. Steele, crisp and rugged and dimple-chinned, the network's star surgeon, $250,000-a-year's worth of talent. There was the scalpel, gleaming in Steele's hand.

Northrop began to sweat. The amplified brain waves were coming through the intensifier, and he felt the throbbing in the old man's leg, felt the dull haze of pain behind the old man's forehead, felt the weakness of being eighty years old and half dead.

Steele was checking out the electronic scalpel, now, while the nurses fussed around, preparing the man for the amputation. In the finished tape, there would be music, narration, all the trimmings, but now there was just a soundless series of images, and, of course, the tapped brainwaves of the sick man.

The leg was bare.

The scalpel descended.

Northrop winced as vicarious agony shot through him. He could feel the blazing pain, the brief searing hellishness as the scalpel slashed through diseased flesh and rotting bone. His whole body trembled, and he bit down hard on his lips and clenched his fists and then it was over.

There was a cessation of pain. A catharsis. The leg no longer sent its pulsating messages to the weary brain. Now there was shock, the anesthesia of hyped-up pain, and with the shock came calmness. Steele went about the mop-up operation. He tidied the stump, bound it.

The rushes flickered out in anticlimax. Later, the production crew would tie up the program with interviews of the family, perhaps a shot of the funeral, a few observations on the problem of gangrene in the aged. Those things were the extras. What counted, what the viewers wanted, was the sheer nastiness of vicarious pain, and that they got in full measure. It was a gladiatorial contest without the gladiators, masochism concealed as medicine. It worked. It pulled in the viewers by the millions.

Northrop patted sweat from his forehead.

"Looks like we got ourselves quite a little show here, boys," he said in satisfaction.

* * * *

The mood of satisfaction was still on him as he left the building that day. All day he had worked hard, getting the show into its final shape, cutting and polishing. He enjoyed the element of craftsmanship. It helped him to forget some of the sordidness of the program.

Night had fallen when he left. He stepped out of the main entrance and a figure strode forward, a bulky figure, medium height, tired face. A hand reached out, thrusting him roughly back into the lobby of the building.

At first Northrop didn't recognize the face of the man. It was a blank face, a nothing face, a middle-aged empty face. Then he placed it.

Harry Gardner. The son of the dead man.

"Murderer!" Gardner shrilled. "You killed him! He would have lived if you'd used anesthetics! You phony, you murdered him so people would have thrills on television!"

Northrop glanced up the lobby. Someone was coming around the bend. Northrop felt calm. He could stare this nobody down until he fled in fear.

"Listen," Northrop said, "we did the best medical science can do for your father. We gave him the ultimate in scientific care. We—"

"You murdered him!"

"No," Northrop said, and then he said no more, because he saw the sudden flicker of a slice-gun in the blank-faced man's fat hand. He backed away, but it didn't help, because Gardner punched the trigger and an incandescent bolt flared out and sliced across Northrop's belly just as efficiently as the surgeon's scalpel had cut through the gangrenous leg.

Gardner raced away, feet clattering on the marble floor. Northrop dropped, clutching himself. His suit was seared, and there was a slash through his abdomen, a burn an eighth of an inch wide and perhaps four inches deep, cutting through intestines, through organs, through flesh. The pain hadn't begun yet. His nerves weren't getting the message through to his stunned brain. But then they were, and Northrop coiled and twisted in agony that was anything but vicarious now.

Footsteps approached.

"Jeez," a voice said.

Northrop forced an eye open. Maurillo. Of all people, Maurillo.

"A doctor," Northrop wheezed. "Fast! Christ, the pain! Help me, Ted!"

Maurillo looked down, and smiled. Without a word, he stepped to the telephone booth six feet away, dropped in a token, punched out a call.

"Get a van over here, fast. I've got a subject, chief."

Northrop writhed in torment. Maurillo crouched next to him. "A doctor," Northrop murmured. "A needle, at least. Gimme a needle! The pain—"

"You want me to kill the pain?" Maurillo laughed. "Nothing doing, chief. You just hang on. You stay alive till we get that hat on your head and tape the whole thing."

"But you don't work for me—you're off the program—"

"Sure," Maurillo said. "I'm with Transcontinental now. They're starting a blood-and-guts show too. Only they don't need waivers."

Northrop gaped. Transcontinental? That bootleg outfit that peddled tapes in Afghanistan and Mexico and Ghana and God knew where else? Not even a network show, he thought. No fee. Dying in agony for the benefit of a bunch of lousy tapeleggers. That was the worst part, Northrop thought. Only Maurillo would pull a deal like that.

"A needle! For God's sake, Maurillo, a needle!"

"Nothing doing, chief. The van'll be here any minute. They'll sew you up, and we'll tape it nice."

Northrop closed his eyes. He felt the coiling intestines blazing within him. He willed himself to die, to cheat Maurillo and his bunch of ghouls. But it was no use. He remained alive and suffering.

He lived for an hour. That was plenty of time to tape his dying agonies. The last thought he had was that it was a damned shame he couldn't star on his own show.

THE PLEASURE OF THEIR COMPANY

Originally published in *Infinity* (1970).

He was the only man aboard the ship, one man inside a sleek shining cylinder heading away from Bradley's World at ten thousand miles a second, and yet he was far from alone. He had wife, father, daughter, son for company, and plenty of others, Ovid and Hemingway and Plato, and Shakespeare and Goethe, Attila the Hun and Alexander the Great, a stack of fancy cubes to go with the family ones. And his old friend Juan was along, too, the man who had shared his dream, his utopian fantasy, Juan who had been with him at the beginning and almost until the end. He had a dozen fellow voyagers in all. He wouldn't be lonely, though he had three years of solitary travel ahead of him before he reached his landfall, his place of exile.

It was the third hour of his voyage. He was growing calm, now, after the frenzy of his escape. Aboard ship he had showered, changed, rested. The sweat and grime of that wild dash through the safety tunnel were gone, now, though he wouldn't quickly shake from his mind the smell of that passageway, like rotting teeth, nor the memory of his terrifying fumbling with the security gate's copper arms as the junta's storm-troopers trotted toward him. But the gate had opened, and the ship had been there, and he had escaped, and he was safe. And he was safe.

I'll try some cubes, he thought.

The receptor slots in the control room held six cubes at once. He picked six at random, slipped them into place, actuated the evoker. Then he went into the ship's garden. There were screens and speakers all over the ship.

The air was moist and sweet in the garden. A plump, toga-clad man, clean-shaven, big-nosed, blossomed on one screen and said, "What a lovely garden! How I adore plants! You must have a gift for making things grow."

"Everything grows by itself. You're—"

"Publius Ovidius Naso."

"Thomas Voigtland. Former President of the Citizens' Council on Bradley's World. Now president-in-exile, I guess. A coup d'etat by the military."

"My sympathies. Tragic, tragic!"

"I was lucky to escape alive. I may never be able to return. They've probably got a price on my head."

"I know how terrible it is to be sundered from your homeland. Were you able to bring your wife?"

"I'm over here," Lydia said. "Tom? Tom, introduce me to Mr. Naso."

"I didn't have time to bring her," Voigtland said. "But at least I took a cube of her with me."

Lydia was three screens down from Ovid, just above a clump of glistening ferns. She looked glorious, her auburn hair a little too deep in tone but otherwise quite a convincing replica. He had cubed her two years before; her face showed none of the lines that the recent troubles had engraved on it. Voigtland said to her, "Not Mr. Naso, dear. Ovid. The poet Ovid."

"Of course. I'm sorry. How did you happen to choose him?"

"Because he's charming and civilized. And he understands what exile is like."

Ovid said softly, "Ten years by the Black Sea. Smelly barbarians my only companions. Yet one learns to adapt. My wife remained in Rome to manage my property and to intercede for me—"

"And mine remains on Bradley's World," said Voigtland. "Along with—along with—"

Lydia said, "What's this about exile, Tom? What happened?"

He began to explain about McAllister and the junta. He hadn't told her, back when he was having her cubed, why he wanted a cube of her. He had seen the coup coming. She hadn't.

As he spoke, a screen brightened between Ovid and Lydia and the seamed, leathery face of old Juan appeared. They had redrafted the constitution of Bradley's World together, twenty years earlier.

"It happened, then," Juan said instantly. "Well, we both knew it would. Did they kill very many?"

"I don't know. I got out fast once they started to—" He faltered. "It was a perfectly executed coup. You're still there. I suppose you're organizing the underground resistance by now. And I—And I—"

Needles of fire sprouted in his brain.

And I ran away, he said silently.

The other screens were alive now. On the fourth, someone with white robes, gentle eyes, dark curling hair. Voigtland guessed him to be Plato. On the fifth, Shakespeare, instantly recognizable, for the cube-makers had modeled him after the First Folio portrait: high forehead, long hair, pursed quizzical lips. On the sixth, a fierce, demonic-looking little man. Attila the Hun? They were all talking, activating themselves at random, introducing themselves to one another and to him. Their voices danced along the top of his skull. He could not follow their words. Restless, he moved among the plants, touching their leaves, inhaling the perfume of their flowers.

Out of the chaos came Lydia's voice.

"Where are you heading now, Tom?"

"Rigel XIX. I'll wait out the revolution there. It was my only option once hell broke loose. Get in the ship and—"

"It's so far," she said. "You're traveling alone?"

"I have you, don't I? And Mark and Lynx, and Juan, and Dad, and all these others."

"Cubes, that's all."

"Cubes will have to do," Voigtland said. Suddenly the fragrance of the garden seemed to be choking him. He went out, into the viewing salon next door, where the black splendor of space glistened through a wide port. Screens were mounted opposite the window. Juan and Attila seemed to be getting along marvelously well; Plato and Ovid were bickering; Shakespeare brooded silently; Lydia, looking worried, stared out of her screen at him. He studied the sweep of the stars.

"Which is our world?" Lydia asked.

"This," he said.

"So small. So far away."

"I've only been traveling a few hours. It'll get smaller."

* * * *

He hadn't had time to take anyone with him. The members of his family had been scattered all over the planet when the alarm came, not one of them within five hours of home—Lydia and Lynx holidaying in the South Polar Sea, Mark archaeologizing on the Westerland Plateau. The integrator net told him it was a Contingency C situation: get off-planet within ninety minutes, or get ready to die. The forces of the junta had reached the capital and were on their way to pick him up. The escape ship had been ready, gathering dust in its buried vault. He hadn't been able to reach Juan. He hadn't been able to reach anybody. He used up sixty of his ninety minutes trying to get in touch with people, and then, with stunner shells already hissing overhead, he had gone into the ship and taken off. Alone.

But he had the cubes.

Cunning things. A whole personality encapsulated in a shimmering plastic box a couple of centimeters high. Over the past few years, as the likelihood of Contingency C had grown steadily greater, Voigtland had cubed everyone who was really close to him and stored the cubes aboard the escape ship, just in case.

It took an hour to get yourself cubed; and at the end of it, they had your soul in the box, your motion habits, your speech patterns, your way of thinking, your entire package of standard reactions. Plug your cube into a receptor slot and you came to life on the screen, smiling as you would smile, moving as you would move, sounding as you would sound, saying things you would say. Of course, the thing on the screen was unreal, a computer-actuated mockup, but it was programmed to respond to conversation, to absorb new data and change its outlook in the light of what it learned, to generate questions without the need of previous inputs; in short, to behave as a real person would.

The cube-makers also could supply a cube of anyone who had ever lived, or, for that matter, any character of fiction. Why not? It wasn't necessary to draw a cube's program from a living subject. How hard was it to tabulate and synthesize a collection of responses, typical phrases, and attitudes, feed them into a cube, and call what came out Plato or Shakespeare or Attila? Naturally a custom-made synthesized cube of some historical figure ran high, because of the man-hours of research and programming involved, and a cube of someone's own departed great-aunt was even more costly, since there wasn't much chance that it could be used as a manufacturer's prototype for further sales. But there was a wide array of standard-model historicals in the catalog when he was stocking his getaway ship; Voigtland had chosen eight of them.

Fellow voyagers. Companions on the long solitary journey into exile that he knew that he might someday have to take. Great thinkers. Heroes and villains. He flattered himself that he was worthy of their company. He had picked a mix of personality types, to keep him from losing his mind on his trip. There wasn't another habitable planet within a light-year of Bradley's World. If he ever had to flee, he would have to flee *far*.

He walked from the viewing salon to the sleeping cabin, and from there to the galley, and on into the control room. The voices of his companions followed him from room to room. He paid little attention to what they were saying, but they didn't seem to mind. They were talking to each other. Lydia and Shakespeare, Ovid and Plato, Juan and Attila, like old friends at a cosmic cocktail party.

"—not for its own sake, no but I'd say it's necessary to encourage mass killing and looting in order to keep your people from losing momentum, I guess, when—"

"—such a sad moment, when Prince Hal says he doesn't know Falstaff. I cry every time—"

"—when I said what I did about poets and musicians in an ideal Republic, it was not, I assure you, with the intent that I should have to live in such a Republic myself—"

"—the short sword, such as the Romans use, that's best, but—"

"—a throng of men and women in the brain, and one must let them find their freedom on the page—"

"—a slender young lad is fine, but yet I always had a leaning toward the ladies, you understand—"

"—massacre as a technique of political manipulation—"

"—Tom and I read your plays aloud to one another—"

"—good thick red wine, hardly watered—"

"—I loved Hamlet the dearest, my true son he was—"

"—the axe, ah, the axe!—"

Voigtland closed his throbbing eyes. He realized that it was soon in his voyage for company, too soon, too soon. Only the first day of his escape, it was. He had lost his world in an instant, in the twinkling of an eye. He needed time to come to terms with that, time and solitude, while he examined his soul. Later he could talk to his fellow voyagers. Later he could play with his cubed playmates.

He began pulling the cubes from the slots, Attila first, then Plato, Ovid, Shakespeare. One by one the screens went dark. Juan winked at him as he vanished, Lydia dabbed at her eyes. Voigtland pulled her cube too.

When they were all gone, he felt as if he had killed them.

* * * *

For three days he roamed the ship in silence. There was nothing for him to do except read, think, watch, eat, sleep, and try to relax. The ship was self-programmed and entirely homeostatic; it ran without need of him, and indeed he had no notion of how to operate it. He knew how to program a takeoff, a landing, and a change of course, and the ship did all the rest. Sometimes he spent hours in front of his viewing port, watching Bradley's World disappear into the maze of the heavens. Sometimes he took his cubes out and arranged them in little stacks, four stacks of three, then three stacks of four, then six of two. But he did not play any of them. Goethe and Plato and Lydia and Lynx and Mark remained silent. They were his opiates against loneliness; very well, he would wait until the loneliness became intolerable.

He considered starting to write his memoirs. He decided to let them wait a while, too, until time had given him a clearer perspective on his downfall.

He thought a great deal about what might be taking place on Bradley's World just now. The jailings, the kangaroo trials, the purges. Lydia in prison? His son and daughter? Juan? Were those whom he had left behind cursing him for a coward, running off to Rigel this way in his plush little escape vessel? Did you desert your planet, Voigtland. Did you run out?

No. No. No. No.

Better to live in exile than to join the glorious company of martyrs. This way you can send inspiring messages to the underground, you can serve as a symbol of resistance, you can go back someday and guide the oppressed fatherland toward freedom, you can lead the counterrevolution and return to the capital with everybody cheering…Can a martyr do any of that?

So he had saved himself. So he had stayed alive to fight another day. It sounded good. He was almost convinced.

He wanted desperately to know what was going on back there on Bradley's World, though.

The trouble with fleeing to another star system was that it wasn't the same thing as fleeing to a mountain-top hideout or some remote island on your own world. It would take so long to get to the other system, so long to make the triumphant return. His ship was a pleasure cruiser, not really meant for big interstellar hops. It wasn't capable of heavy acceleration, and its top velocity, which it reached only after a buildup of many weeks, was less than .50 lights. If he went all the way to the Rigel system and headed right back home, six years would have elapsed on Bradley's World between his departure and his return. What would happen in those six years?

What was happening there now?

His ship had a tachyon-beam ultrawave communicator. He could reach with it any world within a sphere ten light-years in radius, in a matter of minutes. If he chose, he could call clear across the galaxy, right to the limits of man's expansion, and get an answer in less than an hour.

He could call Bradley's World and find out how all those he loved had fared in the first hours of the dictatorship.

If he did, though, he'd paint a tachyon trail like a blazing line across the cosmos. And they could track him and come after him in their ramjet fighters at .75 lights, and there was about one chance in three that they could locate him with only a single point-source coordinate, and overtake him, and pick him up. He didn't want to risk it, not yet, not while he was still this close to home.

But what if the junta had been crushed at the outset? What if the coup had failed? What if he spent the next three years foolishly fleeing toward

Rigel, when all was well at home, and a single call could tell him that?

He stared at the ultrawave set. He nearly turned it on.

A thousand times during those three days he reached toward it, hesitated, halted.

Don't. Don't. They'll detect you and come after you.

But what if I don't need to keep running?

It was Contingency C. The cause was lost.

That's what our integrator net said. But machines can be wrong. Suppose our side managed to stay on top? I want to talk to Juan. I want to talk to Mark. I want to talk to Lydia.

That's why you brought the cubes along. Keep away from the ultrawave.

On the fourth day, he picked out six cubes and put them in the receptor slots.

* * * *

Screens glowed. He saw his father, his son, his oldest friend. He also saw Hemingway, Goethe, Alexander the Great.

"I have to know what's happening at home," Voigtland said. "I want to call them."

"I'll tell you." It was Juan who spoke, the man who was closer to him than any brother. The old revolutionary, the student of conspiracies. "The junta is rounding up everyone who might have dangerous ideas and locking them away. It's telling everybody else not to worry, stability is here at last. McAllister is in full control; calling himself provisional president or something similar."

"Maybe not. Maybe it's safe for me to turn and go back."

"What happened?" Voigtland's son asked. His cube hadn't been activated before. He knew nothing of events since he had been cubed, ten months earlier. "Were you overthrown?"

Juan started to explain about the coup to Mark. Voigtland turned to his father. At least the old man was safe from the rebellious colonels; he had died two years ago, in his eighties, just after making the cube. The cube was all that was left of him. "I'm glad this didn't happen in your time," Voigtland said. "Do you remember, when I was a boy, and you were President of the Council, how you told me about the uprisings on other colonies? And I said, No, Bradley's World is different, we all work together here."

The old man smiled. He looked pale and waxy, an echo of the man he had been. "No world is different, Tom. Political entities go through similar cycles everywhere, and part of the cycle involves an impatience with democracy. I'm sorry that the impatience had to strike while you were in charge, son."

"Homer tells us that men would rather have their fill of sleep, love, singing, and dancing than of war," Goethe offered, smooth-voiced, courtly, civilized. "But there will always be some who love war above all else. Who can say why the gods gave us Achilles?"

"I can," Hemingway growled. "You define man by looking at the opposites inside him. Love and hate. War and peace. Kissing and killing. That's where his borders are. What's wrong with that? Every man's a bundle of opposites. So is every society. And sometimes the killers get the upper hand on the kissers. Besides, how do you know the fellows who overthrew you were so wrong?"

"Let me speak of Achilles," said Alexander, tossing his ringlets, holding his hands high. "I know him better than any of you, for I carry his spirit within me. And I tell you that warriors are best fit to rule, so long as they have wisdom as well as strength, for they have given their lives as pledges in return for the power they hold. Achilles—"

Voigtland was not interested in Achilles. To Juan he said, "I have to call. It's four days, now. I can't just sit in this ship and remain cut off."

"If you call, they're likely to catch you."

"I know that. But what if the coup failed?" Voigtland was trembling. He moved closer to the ultrawave set.

Mark said, "Dad, if the coup failed, Juan will be sending a ship to intercept you. They won't let you just ride all the way to Rigel for nothing."

Yes, Voigtland thought, dazed with relief. Yes, yes, of course. How simple. Why hadn't I thought of that?

"You hear that?" Juan asked. "You won't call?"

"I won't call," Voigtland promised.

* * * *

The days passed. He played all twelve cubes, chatted with Mark and Lynx, Lydia, Juan. Idle chatter, talk of old holidays, friends, growing up. He loved the sight of his cool elegant daughter and his rugged long-limbed son, and wondered how he could have sired them, he who was short and thick-bodied, with blunt features and massive bones. He talked with his father about government, with Juan about revolution. He talked with Ovid about exile, and with Plato about the nature of injustice, and with Hemingway about the definition of courage. They helped him through some of the difficult moments. Each day had its difficult moments.

The nights were much worse.

He ran screaming and ablaze down the tunnels of his own soul. He saw faces looming like huge white lamps above him. Men in black uniforms and mirror-bright boots paraded in somber phalanxes over his fallen body. Citizens lined up to jeer him. ENEMY OF THE STATE. ENEMY OF THE STATE. ENEMY OF THE STATE. They brought Juan to him in his dreams. COWARD. COWARD. COWARD. Juan's lean bony body was ridged and gouged; he had been put through the tortures, the wires in the skull, the lights in the eyes, the truncheons in the ribs. I STAYED. YOU FLED. I STAYED. YOU FLED. I STAYED. YOU FLED. They showed him his own face in a mirror, a jackal's face, with long yellow teeth and little twitching eyes. ARE YOU PROUD OF YOURSELF? ARE YOU PLEASED? ARE YOU HAPPY TO BE ALIVE?

He asked the ship for help. The ship wrapped him in a cradle of silvery fibers and slid snouts against his skin that filled his veins with cold droplets of unknown drugs. He slipped into a deeper sleep, and underneath the sleep, burrowing up, came dragons and gorgons and serpents and basilisks, whispering mockery as he slept. TRAITOR. TRAITOR. TRAITOR. HOW CAN YOU HOPE TO SLEEP SOUNDLY, HAVING DONE WHAT YOU HAVE DONE?

"Look," he said to Lydia, "they would have killed me within the hour. There wasn't any possible way of finding you, Mark, Juan, anybody. What sense was there in waiting longer?"

"No sense at all, Tom. You did the smartest thing."

"But was it the *right* thing, Lydia?"

Lynx said, "Father, you had no choice. It was run or die."

He wandered through the ship, making an unending circuit. How soft the walls were, how beautifully upholstered! The lighting was gentle. Restful images flowed and coalesced and transformed themselves on the sloping ceilings. The little garden was a vale of beauty. He had music, fine food, books, cubes. What was it like in the sewers of the underground now?

"We didn't need more martyrs," he told Plato. "The junta was making enough martyrs as it was. We needed leaders. What good is a dead leader?"

"Very wise, my friend. You have made yourself a symbol of heroism, distant, idealized, untouchable, while your colleagues carry on the struggle in your name," Plato said silkily. "And yet you are able to return and serve your people in the future. The service a martyr gives is limited, finite, locked to a single point in time. Eh?"

"I have to disagree," said Ovid. "If a man wants to be a hero, he ought to hold his ground and take what comes. Of course, what sane man wants to be a hero? You did well, friend Voigtland! Give yourself over to feasting and love, and live longer and more happily."

"You're mocking me," he said to Ovid.

"I do not mock. I console. I amuse. I do not mock."

In the night came tinkling sounds, faint bells, crystalline laughter. Figures capered through his brain, demons, jesters, witches, ghouls. He tumbled down into mustiness and decay, into a realm of spiders, where empty husks hung on vast arching webs. THIS IS WHERE THE HEROES GO. Hags embraced him. WELCOME TO VALHALLA. Gnarled midgets offered him horns of mead, and the mead was bitter, leaving a coating of ash on his lips. ALL HAIL. ALL HAIL. ALL HAIL.

"Help me," he said hoarsely to the cubes. "What did I bring you along for, if not to help me?"

"We're trying to help," Hemingway said. "We agree that you did the sensible thing."

"You're saying it to make me happy, You aren't sincere."

"You bastard, call me a liar again and I'll step out of this screen and—"

"Maybe I can put it another way," Juan said craftily. "Tom, you had an *obligation* to save yourself. Saving yourself was the most valuable thing you could have done for the cause. Listen, for all you knew the rest of us had already been wiped out, right?"

"Yes. Yes."

"Then what would you accomplish by staying and being wiped out too? Outside of some phony heroics, what?" Juan shook his head. "A leader in exile is better than a leader in the grave. You can direct the resistance from Rigel, if the rest of us are gone. Do you see the dynamics of it, Tom?"

"I see. I see. You make it sound so reasonable, Juan."

Juan winked. "We always understood each other."

He activated the cube of his father. "What do you say? Should I have stayed or gone?"

"Maybe stay, maybe go. How can I speak for you? Certainly taking the ship was more practical. Staying would have been more dramatic. Tom, Tom, how can I speak for you?"

"Mark?"

"I would have stayed and fought right to the end. Teeth, nails, everything. But that's me. I think maybe you did the right thing, Dad. The way Juan explains it. The right thing for *you*, that is."

Voigtland frowned. "Stop talking in circles. Just tell me this: do you despise me for going?"

"You know I don't," Mark said.

* * * *

The cubes consoled him. He began to sleep more soundly, after a while. He stopped fretting about the morality of his flight. He remembered how to relax.

He talked military tactics with Attila, and was surprised to find a complex human being behind the one-dimensional ferocity. He tried to discuss the nature of tragedy with Shakespeare, but Shakespeare seemed more interested in talking about taverns, politics, and the problems of a playwright's finances. He spoke to Goethe about the second part of Faust, asking if Goethe really felt that the highest kind of redemption came through governing well, and Goethe said, yes, yes, of course. And when Voigtland wearied of matching wits with his cubed great ones, he set them going against one another, Attila and Alexander, Shakespeare and Goethe, Hemingway and Plato, and sat back, listening to such talk as mortal man had never heard. And there were humbler sessions with Juan and his family. He blessed the cubes; he blessed their makers.

"You seem much happier these days," Lydia said.

"All that nasty guilt washed away," said Lynx.

"It was just a matter of looking at the logic of the situation," Juan observed.

Mark said, "And cutting out all the masochism, the self-flagellation."

"Wait a second," said Voigtland. "Let's not hit below the belt, young man."

"But it *was* masochism, Dad. Weren't you wallowing in your guilt? Admit it."

"I suppose I—"

"And looking to us to pull you out," Lynx said. "Which we did."

"Yes. You did."

"And it's all clear to you now, eh?" Juan asked. "Maybe you *thought* you were afraid, thought you were running out, but you were actually performing a service to the republic. Eh?"

Voigtland grinned. "Doing the right thing for the wrong reason."

"Exactly. Exactly."

"The important thing is the contribution you still can make to Bradley's World," his father's voice said. "You're still young. There's time to rebuild what we used to have there."

"Yes. Certainly."

"Instead of dying a futile but heroic death," said Juan.

"On the other hand," Lynx said, "what did Eliot write? *'The last temptation is the greatest treason: To do the right deed for the wrong reason.'*"

Voigtland frowned. "Are you trying to say—"

"And it *is* true," Mark cut in, "that you were planning your escape far in advance. I mean, making the cubes and all, picking out the famous men you wanted to take—"

"As though you had decided that at the first sign of trouble you were going to skip out," said Lynx.

"They've got a point," his father said. "Rational self-protection is one thing, but an excessive concern for your mode of safety in case of emergency is another."

"I don't say you should have stayed and died," Lydia said. "I never would say that. But all the same—"

"Hold on!" Voigtland said. The cubes were turning against him suddenly. "What kind of talk is this?"

Juan said, "And strictly as a pragmatic point, if the people were to find out how far in advance you engineered your way out, and how comfortable you are as you head for exile—"

"You're supposed to help me," Voigtland shouted. "Why are you starting this? What are you trying to do?"

"You know we all love you," said Lydia.

"We hate to see you not thinking clearly, Father," Lynx said.

"Weren't you planning to run out all along?" said Mark.

"Wait! Stop! Wait!"

"Strictly as a matter of—"

Voigtland rushed into the control room and pulled the Juan-cube from the slot.

"We're trying to explain to you, dear—"

He pulled the Lydia-cube, the Mark-cube, the Lynx-cube, the father-cube.

The ship was silent.

He crouched, gasping, sweat-soaked, face rigid, eyes clenched tight shut, waiting for the shouting in his skull to die away.

* * * *

An hour later, when he was calm again, he began setting up his ultrawave call, tapping out the frequency that the underground would probably be using, if any underground existed. The tachyon beam sprang across the void, an all but instantaneous carrier wave, and he heard cracklings, and then a guarded voice saying, "Four Nine Eight Three, we read your signal, do you read me? This is Four Nine Eight Three, come in, come in, who are you?"

"Voigtland," he said. "President Voigtland, calling Juan. Can you get Juan on the line?"

"Give me your numbers, and—"

"What numbers? This is *Voigtland*. I'm I don't know how many billion miles out in space, and I want to talk to Juan. Get me Juan. *Get me Juan.*"

"You wait," the voice said.

Voigtland waited, while the ultrawave spewed energy wantonly into the void. He heard clickings, scrapings, clatterings. "You still there?" the voice said, after a while. "We're patching him in. But be quick. He's busy."

"Well? Who is it?" Juan's voice, beyond doubt.

"Tom here. Tom Voigtland, Juan!"

"It's really you?" Coldly. From a billion parsecs away, from some other universe. "Enjoying your trip, Tom?"

"I had to call. To find out—to find out—how it was going, how everybody is. How Mark—Lydia—you—"

"Mark's dead. Killed the second week, trying to blow up McAllister in a parade."

"Oh. Oh."

"Lydia and Lynx are in prison somewhere. Most of the others are dead. Maybe ten of us left, and they'll get us soon, too. Of course, there's you."

"Yes."

"You bastard," Juan said quietly. "You rotten bastard. All of us getting rounded up and shot, and you get into your ship and fly away!"

"They would have killed me too, Juan. They were coming after me. I only just made it."

"You should have stayed," Juan said.

"No. No. That isn't what you just said to me! You told me I did the right thing, that I'd serve as a symbol of resistance, inspiring everybody from my place of exile, a living symbol of the overthrown government—"

"I said this?"

"You, yes," Voigtland told him. "Your cube, anyway."

"Go to hell," said Juan. "You lunatic bastard."

"Your cube—we discussed it, you explained—"

"Are you crazy, Tom? Listen, those cubes are programmed to tell you whatever you want to hear. Don't you know that? You want to feel like a hero for running away, they tell you you're a hero. It's that simple. How can you sit there and quote what my cube said to you, and make me believe that I said it?"

"But I— You—"

"Have a nice flight, Tom. Give my love to everybody, wherever you're going."

"I couldn't just stay there to be killed. What good would it have been? Help me, Juan! What shall I do now? Help me!"

"I don't give a damn what you do," Juan said. "Ask your cubes for help. So long, Tom."

"Juan—"

"So long, you bastard."

Contact broke.

* * * *

Voigtland sat quietly for a while, pressing his knuckles together. *Listen, those cubes are programmed to tell you whatever you want to hear. Don't you know that? You want to feel like a hero for running away, they tell you you're a hero.* And if you want to feel like a villain? They tell you that too. They meet all needs. They aren't people. They're cubes.

He put Goethe in the slot. "Tell me about martyrdom," he said.

Goethe said, "It has its tempting side. One may be covered with sins, scaly and rough-skinned with them, and in a single fiery moment of self-immolation one wins redemption and absolution, and one's name is forever cherished."

He put Juan in the slot. "Tell me about the symbolic impact of getting killed in the line of duty."

"It can transform a mediocre public official into a magnificent historical figure," Juan said.

He put Mark in the slot. "Which is a better father to have: a live coward or a dead hero?"

"Go down fighting, Dad."

He put Hemingway in the slot. "What would you do if someone called you a rotten bastard?"

"I'd stop to think if he was right or wrong. If he was wrong, I'd give him to the sharks. If he was right, well, maybe the sharks would get fed anyway."

He put Lydia in the slot. Lynx. His father. Alexander. Attila. Shakespeare. Plato. Ovid.

lit In their various ways they were all quite eloquent. They spoke of bravery, self-sacrifice, nobility, redemption.

He picked up the Mark-cube. "You're dead," he said. "Just like your grandfather. There isn't any Mark anymore. What comes out of this cube isn't Mark. It's me, speaking with Mark's voice, talking through Mark's mind. You're just a dummy."

He put the Mark-cube in the ship's converter input, and it tumbled down the slideway to become reaction mass. He put the Lydia-cube in next. Lynx. His father. Alexander. Attila. Shakespeare. Plato. Ovid. Goethe.

He picked up the Juan-cube. He put it in a slot again. "Tell me the truth," he yelled. "What'll happen to me if I go back to Bradley's World?"

"You'll make your way safely to the underground and take charge, Tom. You'll help us throw McAllister out: We can win with you, Tom."

"Crap," Voigtland said. "I'll tell you what'll really happen. I'll be intercepted before I go into my landing orbit. I'll be taken down and put on trial. And then I'll be shot. Right? Right? Tell me the truth, for once. Tell me I'll be shot!"

"You misunderstand the dynamics of the situation, Tom. The impact of your return will be so great that—"

He took the Juan-cube from the slot and put it into the chute that went to the converter.

"Hello?" Voigtland said. "Anyone here?"

The ship was silent.

"I'll miss all that scintillating conversation," he said. "I miss you already. Yes. Yes. But I'm glad you're gone."

He countermanded the ship's navigational instructions and tapped out the program headed RETURN TO POINT OF DEPARTURE. His hands were shaking, just a little, but the message went through. The instruments showed him the change of course as the ship began to turn around. As it began to take him home.

Alone.

POINT OF FOCUS

Originally published in *Astounding Science Fiction*, August 1958.

Federation emissary Holis Bork was a confident man—and, if he felt a twinge of curious uneasiness at his first glimpse of Mellidan VII, it was not because he doubted his own capabilities, or the value of the Federation's name as a civilizing force.

He told himself that it was something subtler and deeper that twinged him, as the warpship spiraled down about the unfederated planet.

Emissary Bork worried about that subliminal reaction through most of the landing period. He sat broodingly with his eyes fixed; the members of his staff gave him a wide berth. It was, he saw, the deference due to a Federation Emissary so obviously deep in creative thinking. The others were clustered at the far end of the observation deck, staring down at the fog-shrouded yellow-green ball that was soon to be the newest addition to the far-flung Federation. Bork listened to them.

Vyn Kumagon was saying, "Look at that place! The atmosphere blankets it like so much soup."

"I wonder what it's like to breathe chlorine?" asked Hu Sdreen. "And to give off carbon tetrachloride instead of $CO2$?"

"To them it's all the same," Kumagon snapped.

Emissary Bork looked away. He had the answer; he knew what was troubling him.

Mellidan VII was *different*. The peoples of the worlds of the Federation, and even the four non-Federated worlds of the Sol system, shared, one seemingly universal characteristic: they breathed oxygen, gave off carbon dioxide. And the Mellidani? A chlorine-carbon tetrachloride cycle which worked well for them—but was strange, *different*. And that difference troubled Federation Emissary Bork on a deep, shadowy, half-grasped plane of thought.

He shook his mind clear and nudged the speaker panel at his wrist. "How long till landing?"

"We enter final orbit in thirty-nine minutes," Control Center told him. "Contact's been made with the Mellidani and they're guiding us in."

Bork leaned back in the comforting webfoam network and twined his twelve tapering fingers calmly together. He was not worried. Despite Mellidan VII's alienness, there would be no problems. In minutes, the landing would be effected—and past experience told him it would be but a matter of time before the Federation had annexed its four hundred eighty-sixth world.

Later, Bork stood by the rear screens, looking down at the planet as the Federation ship whistled downward through the murky green atmosphere. *To civilize is our mission,* he thought. *To offer the benefits—*

It was four years Galactic since a Federation survey ship had first touched down on Mellidan VII. It had been strictly an accidental planetfall; the prelim scouts had thoroughly established that there was little point in bothering to search a chlorine world for oxygen-type life. That was easily understood.

What was not so easily understood was the possibility of a non-oxygen metabolism. Statistics lay against it; the four hundred eighty-five worlds of the Federation all operated on an oxynitrogen atmosphere and a respiration-photosynthesis cycle that endlessly recirculated oxygen and carbon dioxide. The four inhabited worlds of the unfederated system of Sol were similarly constituted. It was a rule to which no exceptions had been found.

But then the scoutship of Dos Nollibar, cruising out of Vronik XII, came tumbling down into the chlorinated soup of Mellidan VIFs atmosphere, three ultrones in its warp-drive fused beyond repair. It took six weeks for a rescue ship to locate and remove the eleven Federation scouts—and by that time, Chief Scout Dos Nollibar and his men had discovered and made contact with the Mellidani.

Standing at the screen watching his ship thunder down into the thick green shroud of the planet, Emissary Bork cast an inward eye back over Nollibar's scout report—a last-minute refresher, as it were.

"*...Inhabitants roughly humanoid in external structure, though probably nearly solid internally. This is subject to later verification when a specimen is available for complete examination.*

"*...Main constituents of atmosphere: hydrogen, chlorine, nitrogen, helium. Smaller quantities of other gases. No oxygen. This mixture is, of course, unbreathable by all forms of Federation life.*

"*...Mean temperature 260 Absolute. Animal life gives off carbon tetrachloride as respiratory waste; this is broken down by plants to chlorine and complex hydrocarbons. Inhabitants consume plants, smaller animal life, drink hydrochloric acid—*

"*...Seat of planetary government apparently located not far from* *our landing-point, unless aliens have deliberately misled, or we have misunderstood. Naturally most of our data is highly tentative in nature, subject to confirmation after this world is enrolled in the Federation and available for further study."*

Which is my job, Bork thought.

For four years, ever since Nollibar had filed his report, Bork had readied himself for the task of bringing Mellidan VII into the Federation. Nollibar had returned with recorded samples of the language, and a few months of phoneme analysis had been sufficient to work out a rough conversion-equation to Federation, good enough for Bork to learn and speak.

There would undoubtedly be a promotion in this for him: to Subgalactic Overchief, perhaps, or Third Warden. Of the ten emissaries whose task it was to bring newly-discovered planets into the Federation, it was he the First Warden had chosen for this job. That was significant, Bork thought: on no other world would the Emissary be forced to forego direct face-to-face contact with the leaders of the species to be absorbed. Here, on the other hand—Bork sensed a presence behind him. He turned.

It was Vyn Kumagon, Adjutant in Charge of Communications. Bork had no way of knowing how long Kumagon had been peering over his shoulder; he resented the intrusion on an emissary's privacy.

And Kumagon's green eyes were faintly slitted—the mark of Gyralin blood somewhere in his heritage. As a pure-bred Vengol of the Federation's First Planet, Bork felt vague contempt for his assistant. "Yes?" he said, mildly but with undertones of scorn.

Kumagon's slitted eyes fixed sharply on the Emissary's. "Sir, the Mellidani have beamed us for some advice."

"Eh?"

"They'd like to know how close to the Terran dome we want to land, sir."

Bork barely repressed a gasp. *"What* Terran dome?"

"They said the Terrans established a base here several months ago. Sir? Are you well? You—"

"Tell them," Bork said heavily, "that we wish to land no closer than five miles from the Terran dome, and no further than ten. Can you translate that into their equivalents?"

"Yes, sir."

"Then transmit it." Bork choked back a strangled cry of rage. Someone, he thought, had blundered in the home office. That Terrans should be allowed to land on a world being groomed for Federation entry—!

Why, it was unthinkable!

The planet was the most forbidding-looking Bork had ever seen, and he had seen a great many. With screens turned to maximal periphery, he could stand in the snout of the ship and look out on Mellidan VII as if he stood outside. It was hardly a pleasant sight.

The land was utterly flat. Long stretches of barren gray-brown soil extended in every direction, sweeping upward into tiny hillocks far toward the horizon. Soil implied the presence of bacteria—anaerobic bacteria, of course. Life had evolved on Mellidan VII despite the total lack of oxygen.

There were seas, too, shimmering shallow pools of carbon tetrachloride that had precipitated out of the atmosphere. Plants grew in these ponds: ugly squishy plants, that looked like hordes of gray bladders strung on thick hairy ropes. They lay flat against the bright surface of the carbon tetrachloride pond, drifting. As Bork watched, a Mellidani appeared, wading knee-deep, gathering the bladders, slinging them over his blocky round shoulders. He was a farmer, no doubt.

At this distance it was difficult to tell much about the alien, except that his body was segmented crustacean-like, humanoid otherwise; his skin looked thick, waxy, leathery. Chief Scout Nollibar had postulated some member of the paraffin series as the chief constituent of Mellidani protoplasm; he was probably right.

Clouds of gaseous chlorine hung thickly overhead, draping the sky with a yellow-green blanket. Somewhere directly above burned the sun Mellidan: a yellow star of some intensity, its heat negated by the planet's distance from it and by the swath of chlorine that was the atmosphere's main component.

One other distinct feature made up the view as Bork saw it. Some eight miles directly westward, the violet-hued arc of a plastic-extrusion habitation dome rose from the bare plain. Bork had seen such domes before—more than forty years before, when he had served as a member of the last mission to Terra.

He had been only a Fifth Attaché then, though soon after he was to begin the rapid climb that would bring him to the rank of Federation Emissary. On that occasion, the emissary had been old Morvil Brek, who had added twelve worlds to the Federation during his distinguished career. Brek had been named to make the fifth attempt to enroll the Sol system.

The mission had been a failure; the Terran government had emphatically rejected any offer to federate, and Emissary Brek then declared the system non-Federated for good, in a bitter little speech which fell short of making its intended effect of altering the Terran decision. The Galactics had departed—and, on the outward trip, Bork had seen the violet domes on the snowswept plains of Sol IX, where the Terrans had established an encampment.

He scowled, now. Terrans on Mellidan VII? *Why? Why?*

"Contact has been made with the Mellidani leaders, sir," Kumagon said gently.

Bork drew his eyes from the Terran dome. It seemed to him he could almost see the Terrans moving about within it, pale-skinned, ten-fingered, almost repellently hairy men with that sly expression always on their faces—Just imagination. He sighed.

"Transfer the line up here," Bork said to his adjutant. "I'll talk to them from my chair."

Bork sprawled in a leisure-loving way into the intricate reticulations of the web foam chair; he nudged a stud at its base and the chair began to quiver gently, massaging him, easing the stress-and-fatigue poisons from his muscles. After a moment, the communicator screen lit up, breaking into the wide-periphery view of the landscape.

Three Mellidani faced him squarely. They were chalk-white and without hair: their eyes were set deep in their round skulls, ringed with massive orbital ridges, veiled from time to time by fast-flickering nictitating membranes, while their mouths—if mouths they were—were but thin lidless slits. Three nostrils formed a squat triangle midway between eyes and mouth, while cupped processes jutting from the sides of the head seemed to equate with ears. Bork was not surprised at this superficial resemblance to the standard humanoid type; there is a certain most efficient pattern of construction for an erect humanoid biped, and virtually all such life adheres to it.

The emissary said, "I greet you in the name of the Federation of Worlds. My name is Holis Bork; my title, Emissary."

The centermost of the aliens moved his lipless mouth; words came forth. The linguistic pattern, too, adhered to norms. "I am Leader this month. My name is unimportant. What does your Federation want with us?

It was the expected quasi-belligerent response. Twenty years of emissary duties had reduced the operation to a series of conditioned reflexes, so far as Bork was concerned. Stimulus A produced Response B, which was dealt with by means of Technique C.

He said, "The Federation is composed of four hundred eighty-five worlds scattered throughout some thirty thousand light-years. Its capital and First Planet is Vengo in the Darkir system; its member peoples live in unmatched unity. Current Federation population is twenty-seven billion people. Membership in the Federation will guarantee you free and equal rights, full representation, and the complete benefits of a Galactic civilization that has been in existence for eleven thousand years."

He paused triumphantly with soundless fanfare. The array of statistics was calculated to arouse a feeling of awe and lead naturally to the next group of response-leads. The Federation's psychometrists had perfected this technique over millennia.

But the Mellidani leader's reaction jarred Bork. The alien said, "Why is it that the Terrans do not belong to the Federation?"

Bork had been ready with the next concept-group; he had already begun to bring forth the second phase of his argument when the impact of the Mellidani's sudden irrelevant question slammed into his nervous system and set the neat circuitry of his mind oscillating wildly.

It was a dizzy moment. But Bork had his nerves under control almost instantly, and a moment later had formulated a new pat reply he hoped would cover the new situation.

"The Terrans," he said, "did not choose to enter the Federation—thereby demonstrating that they lack the wisdom and maturity of a truly Galactic-minded race."

* * * *

It was impossible to tell what emotions were in play behind the alien's almost inflexible features. Bork found himself trembling; he docketed a mental note to have a neural overhaul when he returned to Vengo.

The alien said, "You imply by this that the Federation worlds are superior to the Terran worlds. In what way?"

Again Bork's nerves were jolted. The interview was taking a very unpredictable pattern indeed. *Damn* those Terrans, he thought. And double-damn Security for allowing them to get a foothold here with an emissary on his way!

Sweat dribbled down the emissary's olive-green skin. His military collar was probably drooping by now. He rooted in his mind for some sequence of arguments that would answer the stubborn alien's question, and at length came up with:

"The Federation worlds are superior in that they have complete homogeneity of thought, feeling, and purpose. We have a common ground for intellectual endeavor and for commercial traffic. We share laws, works of art, ways of thinking. The Earth-men have deliberately placed themselves beyond the pale of this communion—cut themselves off from every other civilized world of the galaxy."

"They have not cut themselves off from us. They came here quite willingly and have lived here during three Leaderships."

"They mean to corrupt you," Bork said desperately. "To lead you away from the right path. They are malicious: unable to enter Galactic society themselves through their own antisocial tendencies, they try now to drag an innocent world into the same quagmire, the same—"

Bork stopped suddenly. His hands were shaking; his body was bathed in perspiration. He realized gloomily that for the first time in his career he had no notion whatever of the next line of thought to pursue.

Promotion, glory, past achievements—all down the sink because of failure now, here? He swallowed hard.

"We'll continue our discussions tomorrow," he said hoarsely. "I would not think of keeping you from your daily work."

"Very well. Tomorrow the man at my left will be Leader. Address your words then to him."

In the state he was in, Bork had little further interest in protocol. He broke the contact hastily and sank back in the cradle of webfoam, tense, sweat-drenched.

The pouch of his tunic yielded three green-gold pellets: metabolic compensators. Bork gobbled them hurriedly, and, as his body returned to normal equilibrium, sank back to brood over the ignominious course of the interview.

* * * *

Naturally, Bork thought, the conversation had been monitored and recorded. That meant that Vyn Kumagon and six or seven technicians had been eye-witness to the emissary's fumbling handling of the first interview—and, with the interview already permanently locked into a cellular recorder, there would be many more eavesdroppers, a long chain of them between here and Vengo and the First Warden.

Bork knew he had to redeem himself.

High faith had been placed in him—but who could have anticipated a Terran counter-propaganda force on Mellidani VII? It had shattered his calm.

He would have to rethink his approach.

Undeniably, the Terrans were here. And undeniably they had made overtures of some sort toward the aliens. Of what sort? That was the missing datum. The keystone of all possible speculations was missing—the purpose of the Terrans.

Did they have some strategic use intended for Mellidan VII? That seemed improbable, in view of the world's forbidding nature. No Terran colony could survive here without the protection of a dome. Unless, he thought coldly, they meant to take over the planet and convert it into a new Earth, as they had done with Sol II, Sol IV, and one of the moons of Sol VI. That would mean the death or deportation of the Mellidani, but would the Terrans worry long over that?

Yet—why would they pick an inhabited world for such a project, when there yet remained a dead planet in their own system? Bork forced himself to reject the colonization plan as implausible under any circumstances.

Perhaps Terra had some yet unknown economic need that Mellidan VII met. Perhaps—Bork's head ached. Speculation was not easy for him. After a while he rose and went below to seek sleep.

There was a fixed routine for the assimilation of worlds into the Federation. It was a routine developed over thousands of years—ever since Vengo spread out to absorb its three sister worlds, eleven thousand years Galactic before, and the Federation was born. The routine customarily was successful.

Growth had been slow, at first. Two solar systems the first millennium, yielding five inhabited worlds. Then three systems the second millennium, with four worlds. Eleven worlds the next, seventeen the next—Until four hundred eighty-five worlds had been folded into the protective warmth of the Federation, nineteen during Bork's own lifetime. Only four worlds had ever refused to come in—the four Terran worlds, approached five times without success over the preceding two centuries. And now, Mellidan VII showed signs of recalcitrance. Bork resolved to use the age-old phrases and persuasion techniques until the Mellidani were unable to resist.

Violence, of course was shunned; the Federation had outgrown that millennia ago. But there were other methods.

When the Mellidani trio returned on the following day for their meeting with Bork, the emissary was ready for them, nerves soothed, mind primed and alert. Today, he noticed, the order had indeed been shuffled. The monthly changeover in planetary leadership had taken place.

Bork said, "Yesterday we were discussing the advantages of Federation membership for your world. You suggested that you might be more sympathetic to the Terrans than you are to us. Would you care to tell me just what guarantees the Terrans have made to you?"

"None."

"But—"

"The Terrans have warned us against entering your Federation. They say your promises are false, that you will deceive us and swallow us up in your hugeness."

Bork stiffened. "Did they ask you to sign any sort of treaty with them?"

"No. None whatever."

"Then what have they been doing here since they landed?" Bork demanded, exasperated.

"Taking measurements of our planet, making scientific studies, exploring and learning. They have also been telling us somewhat about your Federation and warning us against you."

"They have no right to poison your minds against us! We came here in good faith to demonstrate to you how it was to your advantage to join the Federation."

"And the Terrans came in good faith to tell us the opposite," returned the alien implacably. Bork had a sudden sense of the unfleshliness of the creature, of its strange hydrocarbon chemistry and its chlorine-breathing lungs. It seemed to him that the stiff white face of the Mellidani was a mask that hid only other masks within.

"Whom should we believe?" the alien asked. "You—or the Terrans?"

Bork moistened tension-parched lips. "The Earthmen clearly lie. We have brought with us films and charts of Galactic progress. The Federation is plainly preferable to the rootless, companionless life the Terrans have chosen. Be reasonable, friends. Should you cut yourself off from the main current of Galactic life by refusing to join the Federation? You're intelligent; I can see that immediately. Why withdraw? If you decline to Federate, it will become impossible for you to have cultural or commercial interchange with any of the Federated worlds. You—"

"Answer this question, please," said the Mellidani abruptly. "Why is this Federation of yours necessary?"

"What?"

"Why can't we have these contacts *without* joining?"

"Why...because—"

Bork gasped like a creature jerked suddenly from its natural element. This sudden nerve-shattering question had thrust itself between his ribs like a keen blade.

He realized he had no answer to the alien's question. No glib catch-phrases rose to his lips. He sputtered inanely, reddened, and finally took recourse to the same tactic of retreat he had employed the day before.

"This is a question that requires further study. I'll take it up with you tomorrow at this time."

The Mellidani faded from the glowing screen. Emissary Bork made contact with Adjutant Kumagon and said, "Get in touch with the Terrans. There has to be an immediate conference with them."

"At once," Kumagon said.

Bork scowled. The adjutant seemed almost pleased. Was that the shadow of a smile flickering on the man's lips?

* * * *

Later that day a hatch near the firing tubes of the Federation ship pivoted open and the shining beetle-like shape of a landcar dropped through, its treads striking the barren Mellidani soil and carrying it swiftly away. Aboard were Emissary Holis Bork and two aides—Fifth Attaché Hu Sdreen and Third Attaché Brul Dirrib.

The landcar sped across the ground, through the shallow pools of precipitated carbon tetrachloride, through the low-hanging thick murk of the sky, and minutes later arrived at the violet-hued Terran habitation dome.

There, a hatch swung open, admitting the car to an air lock. The hatch sealed hissingly; a second lock irised open, and air—oxynitrogen air—bellied in. Several Terrans were waiting as Bork and his aides stepped from the landcar.

Bork felt uneasy in their presence. They were trim, lean, efficient-looking men, all clad more or less alike. One, older than the rest, came forward and lifted his hand in a formal Federation salute, which Bork automatically returned.

"I'm Major General Gambrell," the Terran said, speaking fluent Federation. The second mission to Terra had educated the natives in the Galactic tongue, and they had never forgotten it. "I'm in charge here for the time being," Gambrell said. "Suppose you come on up to my office and we can talk this thing over."

Gambrell led the way up a neat row of low metal houses and entered one several stories high; Bork followed him, signaling for the aides to remain outside. When they were within, Gambrell seated himself behind a battered wooden desk, fished in his pocket, and produced a cigarette pack. He offered it to Bork. "Care to have a smoke?"

"Sorry," the emissary said, repressing his disgust. "We don't indulge."

"Of course. I forgot." Gambrell smiled apologetically. "You don't mind if I smoke, do you?"

Bork shrugged. "Not at all."

Gambrell flicked the igniting capsule at the cigarette's tip, waited a moment, then puffed at the other end. He looked utterly relaxed. Bork was sharply tuned for this meeting; every nerve was tight-strung.

The Earthman said, "All right. Just why have you requested this meeting, Emissary Bork?"

"You know our purpose here on Mellidan VII?" Bork asked.

"Certainly. You're here to enroll the Mellidani in your Federation."

Bork nodded. "Our aim is clear to you, then. But why are *you* here, Major General Gambrell? Why has Earth established this outpost?"

The Earthman ran one hand lightly through the close-cropped thatch of graying hair that covered most of his scalp. Bork thought of the vestigial topknot that was *his* only heritage from the past, and smiled smugly.

After a moment Gambrell said, "We're here to keep Mellidan VII from joining the Federation. Is that clear enough?"

"It is," Bork said tightly. "May I ask what you hope to gain by this deliberate interference? I suppose you plan to use Mellidan VII as some sort of military base, no doubt."

"No."

Bork had gained flexibility during the past few days. He shot an instant rejoinder at the Earthman: "In that case you must have some commercial purpose in mind. What?"

The Earthman shook his head.

"Let me be perfectly honest with you, Emissary Bork. *We don't have any actual use for Mellidan VII.* It's just too alien a world for oxygen-breathers to use without conversion."

Bork frowned. "You have *no use* for Mellidan VII? But...then...that means you came here solely for the purpose of...of—"

"Right. Of keeping it out of the Federation's hands."

The man's arrogance stunned Bork. That Earth should wantonly block a Federating mission for no reason at all—

"This is a very serious matter," Bork said.

"I know. More serious than you yourself think, Emissary Bork. Look here: suppose you tell me why the Federation wants Mellidan VII, now?"

Bork glared at the infuriatingly calm Earthman. "We want it because...because—"

He stopped. The question paralleled the ones the Mellidani leader had asked. It produced the same visceral reaction. These basic questions hit deep, he thought. And there were no ready answers for them.

Gambrell said smoothly, "I see you're in difficulties. Here's an answer for you—*you want it simply because it's there.* Because for eleven thousand years you've Federated every planet you could, swallowed it up in your benevolent arms, thoroughly homogenized its culture into yours and blotted out any minor differences that might have existed. You don't see any reason to stop now. But you don't have any possible use for this world, do you? You can't trade with it, you can't colonize here, you can't turn it into a vacation resort. For the first time in your considerable history you've run up against an inhabited world that's *utterly useless* as Federation stock. But you're trying to Federate it anyway."

"We—"

"Keep quiet," said the Earthman sharply. "Don't try to argue, because you don't know how to argue. Or to think. Vengo's ruled the roost so long you've reduced every cerebral process to a set of conditioned reflexes. And when you strike an exception to a pattern, you just steamroll right on ahead. You find a planet, so you offer it a place in the Federation and proceed to digest it alive. What function does this Federation of yours serve, anyway?"

Bork was on solid ground here. "It serves as a unifying force that holds together the disparate worlds of the galaxy, bringing order out of confusion."

"O.K. I'll buy that statement, even if it does come rolling out of you automatically." The Earthman hunched forward and his eyes fixed coldly on Bork's. "The Federation's so big and complex that it hasn't yet learned that it died three thousand years ago. Its function atrophied, dried up, vanished. *Foosh!* The galaxy is orderly; trade routes are established, patterns of cultural contact built, war forgotten. There's no longer any need for a benevolent tyranny operating out of Vengo that makes sure the whole thing doesn't come apart. But still you go on, bringing the joys of Federation from planet to planet, as if the same chaotic situation prevails now that prevailed in those barbaric days when your warlord ancestors first came down out of Vengo to conquer the universe."

Bork sat very quietly. He was thinking: *the Terran is insane. The things he says have no meaning. The Federation dead? Nonsense!*

"I knew the Earthmen were fools, but I didn't think they were morons as well," the emissary said out loud, lightly. "Anyone can see that the Federation is alive and healthy, and will be for eternity to come."

"Federations don't last that long. They don't even last *half* an eternity. And yours died millennia ago. It's like some great beast whose nervous system is so slow on the trigger it takes hours to realize that it's dead. Well, the Federation will last a couple of thousand years more, on its accumulated momentum. But it's dead now."

Bork rose. "I can't spend any further time on this kind of foolish talking," he said wearily. "I'll have to get back to my base." He fingered the glittering platinum ornaments on his stiff green jacket. "And I don't intend to give up trying to Federate the Mellidani, despite your obstructions."

Gambrell chuckled in an oddly offensive manner. "Keep at it, then. Keep on mouthing clichés and giving them hollow arguments that fall to flinders when you poke at the roots. We've warned the Mellidani. Besides, they can think for themselves, and aren't impressed easily by big words and gilded phrases. They won't be suckers for your routine."

Bork was very quiet for a long moment, staring stonily at the Earthman, trying to see behind those ice-cool gray eyes. At length he said, "Is this all just petty spite on your part? Why are you doing this, Gambrell? If you Terrans don't want to enter the Federation, why don't you keep off by yourselves and stop meddling with our activities?"

"Because the Mellidani represent something unique in the galaxy,"

Gambrell said. "And because *we* see their value, even if you don't. Do you know what would happen if you Federated the Mellidani? Within a century you'd have to exterminate them or expel them from the Federation. They're *alien,* Bork. Totally and absolutely and unchangeably alien. They don't breathe the same kind of atmosphere you do. They don't digest the same foods. Their lungs don't work on the principles yours do. Neither do their brains."

"What does this—"

Gambrell cut him off and continued unstoppably. "They're a cosmic fluke, Bork. They don't conform to the oxygen-carbon pattern of life, and they might very well be the only race in the universe that doesn't. We can't afford to let the Federation come in here and destroy them. And you *will* destroy them, because they're different and the Federation can't abide differences that can't be smoothed out by a little deportation and ideological manipulation and genetic monkeying."

"I wish I could follow this ridiculous line of chatter," Bork snapped savagely. "But I'm afraid I'm wasting your time and mine. Please excuse me."

Sighing, Gambrell said, "You just don't listen to me, do you?"

"I've been listening. What's so important about this *uniqueness* of these people, that must be preserved at all costs?"

Instead of asking, Gambrell crisply said, "Close your right eye, Bork. You're right-handed, aren't you?"

"Yes, but—"

"Close your right eye. There. Suddenly you lose depth perception, notice? Your eyes function stereoscopically; knock out one point of focus and you see things two-dimensionally. Well, we see things two-dimensionally, Bork, all of us. The whole galaxy does. We see things through the eyes of oxygen-breathing carbon entities, and we distort everything to fit that orientation.

"The Mellidani could be our second eye. If we leave them alone, free to look at events and phenomena in their own special alien unique way— they can provide that other point of focus for us. We have to preserve this thing they have; if we let the Federation destroy it by lumping them into the vast all-devouring amoeba of confederate existence, we may never find another race quite so alien, just as we can never regenerate a blinded eye. *That's* why we poisoned their minds against you. That's why we got here first and made sure they would never join the Federation. And they won't."

Angrily, Bork said, "They will! This is ridiculous!"

Gambrell shrugged. "Go ahead, then. Speak ye to the Mellidani, and see how far you get. This isn't an ordinary race you're dealing with. Incidentally, the Mellidani leader has been listening to this whole conversation over a private circuit."

That was the final gesture of contempt. Bork surged to the door, rage clotting his throat, and stalked out of Gambrell's office wordlessly. Federation dead, indeed! Point of focus! The Federation would absorb the Mellidani, no doubt of it. They *would!*

He reached ground-level and found his aides. "Let's get back to the ship," Bork ordered brusquely. "I want to speak to the Mellidani again. The Earthmen haven't won this conflict yet."

They drove through the clinging yellow-green fog to the slim needle that was the Federation ship. As they drove, Bork cast frantically about in his mind for some argument that was new, that was not cliché-riddled and time-worn. And no answers presented themselves.

He felt panic throbbing in his chest. The first dark cracks were starting to appear on the gleaming shield of his self-confidence—and, perhaps, on the greater shield of the Federation's vaunted prestige. The Earth-man's words echoed harshly in his mind. *You'll never get Mellidan VII. The Federation is dead. Point of focus. Alien viewpoint. Necessary. Perspective.*

Then eleven thousand years of Galactic domination reasserted their hold. Bork grew calm; the Earthman's words were air-filled nonsense, without meaning. Mellidan VII was not yet lost. *Not yet.*

We'll show them, he thought fiercely. *We'll show them.* But the old emissary's heart suddenly was not quite sure they would.

POSTMARK GANYMEDE

Originally published in *Amazing Stories*, September 1957.

"I'm washed up," Preston growled bitterly. "They made a postman out of me. Me—a postman!"

He crumpled the assignment memo into a small, hard ball and hurled it at the bristly image of himself in the bar mirror. He hadn't shaved in three days—which was how long it had been since he had been notified of his removal from Space Patrol Service and his transfer to Postal Delivery.

Suddenly, Preston felt a hand on his shoulder. He looked up and saw a man in the trim gray of a Patrolman's uniform.

"What do you want, Dawes?"

"Chief's been looking for you, Preston. It's time for you to get going on your run."

Preston scowled. "Time to go deliver the mail, eh?" He spat. "Don't they have anything better to do with good spacemen than make letter carriers out of them?"

The other man shook his head. "You won't get anywhere grousing about it, Preston. Your papers don't specify which branch you're assigned to, and if they want to make you carry the mail—that's it." His voice became suddenly gentle. "Come on, Pres. One last drink, and then let's go. You don't want to spoil a good record, do you?"

"No," Preston said reflectively. He gulped his drink and stood up. "Okay. I'm ready. Neither snow nor rain shall stay me from my appointed rounds, or however the damned thing goes."

"That's a smart attitude, Preston. Come on—I'll walk you over to Administration."

Savagely, Preston ripped away the hand that the other had put around his shoulders. "I can get there myself. At least give me credit for that!"

"Okay," Dawes said, shrugging. "Well—good luck, Preston."

"Yeah. Thanks. Thanks real lots."

He pushed his way past the man in Space Grays and shouldered past a couple of barflies as he left. He pushed open the door of the bar and stood outside for a moment.

It was near midnight, and the sky over Nome Spaceport was bright with stars. Preston's trained eye picked out Mars, Jupiter, Uranus. There they were—waiting. But he would spend the rest of his days ferrying letters on the Ganymede run.

He sucked in the cold night air of summertime Alaska and squared his shoulders.

* * * *

Two hours later, Preston sat at the controls of a one-man patrol ship just as he had in the old days. Only the control panel was bare where the firing studs for the heavy guns was found in regular patrol ships. And in the cargo hold instead of crates of spare ammo there were three bulging sacks of mail destined for the colony on Ganymede.

Slight difference, Preston thought, as he set up his blasting pattern.

"Okay, Preston," came the voice from the tower. "You've got clearance."

"Cheers," Preston said, and yanked the blast-lever. The ship jolted upward, and for a second he felt a little of the old thrill—until he remembered.

He took the ship out in space, saw the blackness in the viewplate. The radio crackled.

"Come in, Postal Ship. Come in, Postal Ship."

"I'm in. What do you want?"

"We're your convoy," a hard voice said. "Patrol Ship 08756, Lieutenant Mellors, above you. Down at three o'clock, Patrol Ship 10732, Lieutenant Gunderson. We'll take you through the Pirate Belt."

Preston felt his face go hot with shame. Mellors! Gunderson! They would stick two of his old sidekicks on the job of guarding him.

"Please acknowledge," Mellors said.

Preston paused. Then: "Postal Ship 1872, Lieutenant Preston aboard. I acknowledge message."

There was a stunned silence. "*Preston?* Hal Preston?"

"The one and only," Preston said.

"What are you doing on a Postal ship?" Mellors asked.

"Why don't you ask the Chief that? He's the one who yanked me out of the Patrol and put me here."

"Can you beat that?" Gunderson asked incredulously. "Hal Preston, on a Postal ship."

"Yeah. Incredible, isn't it?" Preston asked bitterly. "You can't believe your ears. Well, you better believe it, because here I am."

"Must be some clerical error," Gunderson said.

"Let's change the subject," Preston snapped.

They were silent for a few moments, as the three ships—two armed, one loaded with mail for Ganymede—streaked outward away from Earth. Manipulating his controls with the ease of long experience, Preston guided the ship smoothly toward the gleaming bulk of far-off Jupiter. Even at this distance, he could see five or six bright pips surrounding the huge planet. There was Callisto, and—ah—there was Ganymede.

He made computations, checked his controls, figured orbits. Anything to keep from having to talk to his two ex-Patrolmates or from having to think about the humiliating job he was on. Anything to—

* * * *

"Pirates! Moving up at two o'clock!"

Preston came awake. He picked off the location of the pirate ships—there were two of them, coming up out of the asteroid belt. Small, deadly, compact, they orbited toward him.

He pounded the instrument panel in impotent rage, looking for the guns that weren't there.

"Don't worry, Pres," came Mellors' voice. "We'll take care of them for you."

"Thanks," Preston said bitterly. He watched as the pirate ships approached, longing to trade places with the men in the Patrol ships above and below him.

Suddenly a bright spear of flame lashed out across space and the hull of Gunderson's ship glowed cherry red. "I'm okay," Gunderson reported immediately. "Screens took the charge."

Preston gripped his controls and threw the ship into a plunging dive that dropped it back behind the protection of both Patrol ships. He saw Gunderson and Mellors converge on one of the pirates. Two blue beams licked out, and the pirate ship exploded.

But then the second pirate swooped down in an unexpected dive. "Look out!" Preston yelled helplessly—but it was too late. Beams ripped into the hull of Mellors' ship, and a dark fissure line opened down the side of the ship. Preston smashed his hand against the control panel. Better to die in an honest dogfight than to live this way!

It was one against one, now—Gunderson against the pirate. Preston dropped back again to take advantage of the Patrol ship's protection.

"I'm going to try a diversionary tactic," Gunderson said on untappable tight-beam. "Get ready to cut under and streak for Ganymede with all you got."

"Check."

Preston watched as the tactic got under way. Gunderson's ship traveled in a long, looping spiral that drew the pirate into the upper quadrant of space. His path free, Preston guided his ship under the other two and toward unobstructed freedom. As he looked back, he saw Gunderson steaming for the pirate on a sure collision orbit.

He turned away. The score was two Patrolmen dead, two ships wrecked—but the mails would get through.

Shaking his head, Preston leaned forward over his control board and headed on toward Ganymede.

* * * *

The blue-white, frozen moon hung beneath him. Preston snapped on the radio.

"Ganymede Colony? Come in, please. This is your Postal Ship." The words tasted sour in his mouth.

There was silence for a second. "Come in, Ganymede," Preston repeated impatiently—and then the sound of a distress signal cut across his audio pickup.

It was coming on wide beam from the satellite below—and they had cut out all receiving facilities in an attempt to step up their transmitter. Preston reached for the wide-beam stud, pressed it.

"Okay, I pick up your signal, Ganymede. Come in, now!"

"This is Ganymede," a tense voice said. "We've got trouble down here. Who are you?"

"Mail ship," Preston said. "From Earth. What's going on?"

There was the sound of voices whispering somewhere near the microphone. Finally: "Hello, Mail Ship?"

"Yeah?"

"You're going to have to turn back to Earth, fellow. You can't land here. It's rough on us, missing a mail trip, but—"

Preston said impatiently, "Why can't I land? What the devil's going on down there?"

"We've been invaded," the tired voice said. "The colony's been completely surrounded by iceworms."

"Iceworms?"

"The local native life," the colonist explained. "They're about thirty feet long, a foot wide, and mostly mouth. There's a ring of them about a hundred yards wide surrounding the Dome. They can't get in and we can't get out—and we can't figure out any possible approach for you."

"Pretty," Preston said. "But why didn't the things bother you while you were building your Dome?"

"Apparently they have a very long hibernation-cycle. We've only been here two years, you know. The iceworms must all have been asleep when we came. But they came swarming out of the ice by the hundreds last month."

"How come Earth doesn't know?"

"The antenna for our long-range transmitter was outside the Dome. One of the worms came by and chewed the antenna right off. All we've got left is this short-range thing we're using and it's no good more than ten thousand miles from here. You're the first one who's been this close since it happened."

"I get it." Preston closed his eyes for a second, trying to think things out.

* * * *

The Colony was under blockade by hostile alien life, thereby making it impossible for him to deliver the mail. Okay. If he'd been a regular member of the Postal Service, he'd have given it up as a bad job and gone back to Earth to report the difficulty.

But I'm not going back. I'll be the best damned mailman they've got.

"Give me a landing orbit anyway, Ganymede."

"But you can't come down! How will you leave your ship?"

"Don't worry about that," Preston said calmly.

"We have to worry! We don't dare open the Dome, with those creatures outside. You *can't* come down, Postal Ship."

"You want your mail or don't you?"

The colonist paused. "Well—"

"Okay, then," Preston said. "Shut up and give me landing coordinates!"

There was a pause, and then the figures started coming over. Preston jotted them down on a scratch-pad.

"Okay, I've got them. Now sit tight and wait." He glanced contemptuously at the three mail-pouches behind him, grinned, and started setting up the orbit.

Mailman, am I? I'll show them!

* * * *

He brought the Postal Ship down with all the skill of his years in the Patrol, spiralling in around the big satellite of Jupiter as cautiously and as precisely as if he were zeroing in on a pirate lair in the asteroid belt. In its own way, this was as dangerous, perhaps even more so.

Preston guided the ship into an ever-narrowing orbit, which he stabilized about a hundred miles over the surface of Ganymede. As his ship swung around the moon's poles in its tight orbit, he began to figure some fuel computations.

His scratch-pad began to fill with notations.
Fuel storage—

Escape velocity—

Margin of error—

Safety factor—

Finally he looked up. He had computed exactly how much spare fuel he had, how much he could afford to waste. It was a small figure—too small, perhaps.

He turned to the radio. "Ganymede?"

"Where are you, Postal Ship?"

"I'm in a tight orbit about a hundred miles up," Preston said. "Give me the figures on the circumference of your Dome, Ganymede?"

"Seven miles," the colonist said. "What are you planning to do?"

Preston didn't answer. He broke contact and scribbled some more figures. Seven miles of iceworms, eh? That was too much to handle. He had planned on dropping flaming fuel on them and burning them out, but he couldn't do it that way.

He'd have to try a different tactic.

Down below, he could see the blue-white ammonia ice that was the frozen atmosphere of Ganymede. Shimmering gently amid the whiteness was the transparent yellow of the Dome beneath whose curved walls lived the Ganymede Colony. Even forewarned, Preston shuddered. Surrounding the Dome was a living, writhing belt of giant worms.

"Lovely," he said. "Just lovely."

Getting up, he clambered over the mail sacks and headed toward the rear of the ship, hunting for the auxiliary fuel-tanks.

Working rapidly, he lugged one out and strapped it into an empty gun turret, making sure he could get it loose again when he'd need it.

He wiped away sweat and checked the angle at which the fuel-tank would face the ground when he came down for a landing. Satisfied, he knocked a hole in the side of the fuel-tank.

"Okay, Ganymede," he radioed. "I'm coming down."

He blasted loose from the tight orbit and rocked the ship down on manual. The forbidding surface of Ganymede grew closer and closer.

Now he could see the iceworms plainly.

Hideous, thick creatures, lying coiled in masses around the Dome. Preston checked his spacesuit, making sure it was sealed. The instruments told him he was a bare ten miles above Ganymede now. One more swing around the poles would do it.

He peered out as the Dome came below and once again snapped on the radio.

* * * *

"I'm going to come down and burn a path through those worms of yours. Watch me carefully, and jump to it when you see me land. I want that airlock open, or else."

"But—"

"No buts!"

He was right overhead now. Just one ordinary-type gun would solve the whole problem, he thought. But Postal Ships didn't get guns. They weren't supposed to need them.

He centered the ship as well as he could on the Dome below and threw it into automatic pilot. Jumping from the control panel, he ran back toward the gun turret and slammed shut the plexilite screen. Its outer wall opened and the fuel-tank went tumbling outward and down. He returned to his control-panel seat and looked at the viewscreen. He smiled.

The fuel-tank was lying near the Dome—right in the middle of the nest of iceworms. The fuel was leaking from the puncture.

The iceworms writhed in from all sides.

"Now!" Preston said grimly.

The ship roared down, jets blasting. The fire licked out, heated the ground, melted snow—ignited the fuel-tank! A gigantic flame blazed up, reflected harshly off the snows of Ganymede.

And the mindless iceworms came, marching toward the fire, being consumed, as still others devoured the bodies of the dead and dying.

Preston looked away and concentrated on the business of finding a place to land the ship.

* * * *

The holocaust still raged as he leaped down from the catwalk of the ship, clutching one of the heavy mail sacks, and struggled through the melting snows to the airlock.

He grinned. The airlock was open.

Arms grabbed him, pulled him through. Someone opened his helmet.

"Great job, Postman!"

"There are two more mail sacks," Preston said. "Get men out after them."

The man in charge gestured to two young colonists, who donned spacesuits and dashed through the airlock. Preston watched as they raced to the ship, climbed in, and returned a few moments later with the mail sacks.

"You've got it all," Preston said. "I'm checking out. I'll get word to the Patrol to get here and clean up that mess for you."

"How can we thank you?" the official-looking man asked.

"No need to," Preston said casually. "I had to get that mail down here some way, didn't I?"

He turned away, smiling to himself. Maybe the Chief *had* known what he was doing when he took an experienced Patrol man and dumped him into Postal. Delivering the mail to Ganymede had been more hazardous than fighting off half a dozen space pirates. *I guess I was wrong,* Preston thought. *This is no snap job for old men.*

Preoccupied, he started out through the airlock. The man in charge caught his arm. "Say, we don't even know your name! Here you are a hero, and—"

"Hero?" Preston shrugged. "All I did was deliver the mail. It's all in a day's work, you know. The mail's got to get through!"

PRIME COMMANDMENT

Originally published in *Science Fiction Stories*, January 1958.

If the strangers had come to World on any night but The Night of No Moon, perhaps the tragedy could have been avoided. Even had the strangers come that night, if they had left their ship in a parking orbit and landed on World by dropshaft it might not have happened.

But the strangers arrived on World on The Night of No Moon, and they came by ship—a fine bright vessel a thousand feet long, with burnished gold walls. And because they were a proud and stiff-necked people, and because the people of World were what they were, and because the god of the strangers was not the God of the World, The Night of No Moon was the prelude to a season of blood.

Down at the Ship, the worshipping was under way when the strangers arrived. The ship sat embedded in the side of the hill, exactly where it had first fallen upon World; open in its side was the hatch through which the people of World had come forth.

The bonfire blazed, casting bright shadows on the corroded, time-stained walls of the Ship. The worshipping was under way. Lyle of the Kwitni knelt in a deep genuflection, forehead inches from the warm rich loam of World, muttering in a hoarse monotone the Book of the Ship. At his side stood the priestess Jeen of McCaig, arms flung wide, head thrown back, as she recited the Litany of the Ship in savage bursts of half-chanted song.

"In the beginning there was the ship—"

"Kwitni was the Captain, McCaig the astrogator," came the droning antiphonal response of the congregation, all five hundred of the people of World, crouching in the praying-pit surrounding the Ship.

"And Kwitni and McCaig brought the people through the sky to World—"

"And they looked upon World and found it good," was the response.

"And down through the sky did the people come—"

"Down across the light-years to World."

"Out of the Ship!"

"Out of the Ship!"

On it went, a long and ornate retelling of the early days of World, when Kwitni and McCaig, with the guidance of the Ship, had brought the original eight-and-thirty safely to ground. During the three hundred years the story had grown; six nights a year there was no moon, and the ceremonial retelling took place. And five hundred and thirteen were the numbers of the people on this Night of No Moon when the strangers came.

Jeen of the McCaig was the first to see them, as she stood before the Ship waiting for the ecstasy to sweep over her and for her feet to begin the worship dance. She was young, and this was only her fourth worship; she waited with some impatience for the frenzy to seize her.

Suddenly a blaze of light appeared in the dark moonless sky. Jeen stared. In her twenty years she had never seen fire in the heavens on The Night of No Moon.

And her sharp eyes saw that the fire was coming closer, that something was dropping through the skies toward them. And a shiver ran down her back, and she felt the coolness of the night winds against her lightly clad body. She heard the people stirring uneasily behind her.

Perhaps it was a miracle, she thought. Perhaps the Ship had sent some divine manifestation. Her heart pounded; her flanks glistened with sweat. The worshipping drew near its climax, and Jeen felt the dance-fever come over her, growing more intense as the strange light approached the ground.

She wriggled belly and buttocks sensuously and began the dance, the dance of worship that concluded the ceremony, while from behind her came the pleasure-sounds of the people as they, too, worshipped the Ship in their own ways. For the commandment of the old lawgiver Lorresson had been, *Be happy, my children,* and the people of World expressed their joy while the miracle-light plunged rapidly Worldward.

* * * *

Eleven miles from the Hill of the Ship, the strange light finally touched ground—not a light at all, but a starship, golden-hulled, a thousand feet long and bearing within itself the eight hundred men and women of the Church of the New Resurrection, who had crossed the gulf of light-years in search of a world where they might practice their religion free from interference and without the distraction of the presence of countless billions of the unholy.

The Blessed Myron Brown was the leader of this flock and the captain of their ship, the *New Galilee.* Fifth in direct line from the Blessed Leroy Brown himself, Blessed Myron Brown was majestic of bearing and thunderous of voice, and when his words rang out over the ship phones saying, "Here we may rest here we may live," the eight hundred members of the Church of the New Resurrection rejoiced in their solemn way, and made ready for the landing.

They were not tractable people. The tenets of their Church were two: that the Messiah had come again on Earth, died again, been reborn, and in his resurrection prophesied that the Millennium was at hand—and, secondly, that He had chosen certain people to lead the way in the forthcoming building of New Jerusalem.

And it was through the mouth of Blessed Leroy Brown that He spoke, in the two thousand nine hundred and seventieth year since His first birth, and the Blessed Leroy Brown did name those of Earth who had been chosen for holiness and salvation. Many of the elect declined the designation, some with kindly thanks, some with scorn. The Blessed Leroy Brown died early, the protomartyr of his Church, but his work went on.

And a hundred years passed and the members of his Church were eight hundred in number, proud God-touched men and women who denounced the sinful ways of the world and revealed that judgment was near. There were martyrs, and the way was a painful one for the Blessed. But they persevered, and they raised money (some of their members had been quite wealthy in their days of sin) and when it became clear that Earth was too steeped in infamy for them to abide existence on it any further, they built their ark, the *New Galilee,* and crossed the gulf of night to a new world where they might live in peace and happiness and never know the persecution of the mocking ones.

They were a proud and stubborn people, and they kept the ways of God as they knew them. They dressed in gray, for bright colors were sinful, and they covered their bodies but for face and hands, and when a man knew his wife it was for the production of children alone. They made no graven images and they honored the sabbath, and it was their very great hope that on Beta Andromedae XII they could at last be at peace.

But fifteen minutes after their landing they saw that this was not to be. For, while the women labored to erect camp and the men hunted provisions, the Blessed Enoch Brown, son of the leader Myron, went forth in a helicopter to survey the new planet.

And when he returned from his mission his dour face was deeper than usual with woe, and when he spoke it was in a sepulchral tone.

"The Lord has visited another tribulation upon us, even here in the wilderness."

"What have you seen?" the blessed Myron asked.

"This world is peopled!"

"Impossible! We were given every assurance that this was a virgin world, without colonists, without native life."

"Nevertheless," the Blessed Enoch said bitterly, "There are people here. I have seen them. Naked savages who look like Earthpeople—dancing and prancing by the light of a huge bonfire round the rotting hulk of an abandoned spaceship that lies implanted in a hillside." He scowled. "I flew low over them. Their bodies were virtually bare, and their flesh was oiled, and they leaped wildly and coupled like animals in the open."

For a moment the Blessed Myron Brown stared bleakly at his son, unable to speak. The blood drained from his lean face. When he finally spoke, his voice was thick with anger.

"Even here the Devil pursues us."

"Who can these people be?"

The Blessed Myron shrugged. "It makes little difference. Perhaps they are descendants of a Terran colonial mission—a ship bound for a more distant world, that crashed here and sent no word to Earth." He stared heavenward for a moment, at the dark and moonless sky, and muttered a brief prayer. "Tomorrow," he said, "we will visit these people and speak with them. Now let us build our camp."

* * * *

The morning dawned fresh and clear, the sun rising early and growing warm rapidly, and shortly after morning prayer a picked band of eleven Resurrectionist men made their way through the heavily wooded area that separated their camp from that of the savages. The women of the Church knelt in the clearing and prayed, while the remaining men went about their daily chores.

The Blessed Myron Brown led the party, and with him were his son Enoch and nine others. They strode without speaking through the woods. The Blessed Myron experienced a certain discomfort as the great yellow sun grew higher in the sky and the forest warmed; he was perspiring heavily beneath his thick gray woolen clothes. But this was merely a physical discomfort, and those he could bear with ease.

This other torment, though, that of finding people on this new world—that hurt him. He wanted to see these people with his own eyes, and look upon them.

Near noon the village of the natives came in sight; the Blessed Myron was first to see it. He saw a huddle of crude low huts built around a medium-sized hill, atop which rose the snout of a corroded spaceship that had crashed into the hillside years, perhaps centuries earlier. The Blessed Myron pointed, and they went forward.

And several of the natives advanced from the village to meet them. There was a girl, young and fair, and a man, and all the man wore was a scanty white cloth around his waist, and all the girl wore was the breechcloth and an additional binding around her breasts. The rest of their bodies—lean, tanned—were bare. The Blessed Myron offered a prayer that he would be kept from sin.

The girl stepped forward and said, "I'm the priestess Jeen of the Mc-Caig. This is Lyle of Kwitni, who is in charge. Who are you?"

"You—you speak English?" the Blessed Myron asked.

"We do. Who are you, and what are you doing on World? Where did you come from? What do you want here?"

The girl was openly impudent; and the sight of her sleek thighs made the muscles tighten along the Blessed Myron's jaws. Coldly he said, "We have come here from Earth. We will settle here."

"Earth? Where is that?"

The Blessed Myron smiled knowingly and glanced at his son and at the others. He noticed in some disapproval that Enoch was staring with perhaps too much curiosity at the lithe girl. "Earth is the planet from beyond the sky where you originally came from," he said. "Long ago—before you declined into savagery."

"You came from the place we came from?" The girl frowned. "We are not savages, though."

"You run naked and perform strange ceremonies by night. This is savagery. But all this must change. We will help you regain your stature as Earthmen again; we will show you how to build houses instead of shabby huts. And you must learn to wear clothing again."

"But surely we need no more clothing than this," Jeen said in surprise. She reached out and plucked a section of the Blessed Myron's gray woolen vestments between two of her fingers. "Your clothes are wet with the heat. How can you bear such silly things?"

"Nakedness is sinful," the Blessed Myron thundered.

Suddenly the man Lyle spoke. "Who are you to tell us these things? Why have you come to World?"

"To worship God freely."

The pair of natives exchanged looks. Jeen pointed at the half-buried spaceship that gleamed in the noonday sun. "To worship with us?"

"Of course not! You worship a ship, a piece of metal. You have fallen into decadent ways."

"We worship that which has brought us to World, for it is holy," Jeen snapped hotly. "And you?"

"We, too, worship That which has brought us to the world. But we shall teach you. We—"

The Blessed Myron stopped. He no longer had an audience. Jeen and Lyle had whirled suddenly and both of them sprinted away, back toward the village.

The churchmen waited for more than half an hour. Finally the Blessed Myron said, "They will not come back. They are afraid of us. Let us return to our settlement and decide what is to be done."

They heard laughing and giggling coming from above. The Blessed Myron stared upward.

The trees were thick with the naked people; they had stealthily surrounded them. The Blessed Myron saw the impish face of the girl Jeen.

She called down to him: "Go back to your God and leave us alone, silly men! Leave World by tomorrow morning or we'll kill you!"

Enraged, the Blessed Myron shook his fist at the trees. "You chattering monkeys, we'll make human beings of you again!"

"And make us wear thick ugly clothes and worship a false god? You'd have to kill us first—if you could!"

"Come," the blessed Myron said. "Back to the settlement. We cannot stay here longer."

* * * *

That evening, in the rude church building that had been erected during the day, the elders of the Church of the New Resurrection met in solemn convocation, to discuss the problem of the people of the forest.

"They are obviously descendants of a wrecked colony ship," said the Blessed Myron, "But they make of sin a virtue. They have become as animals. In time they will merely corrupt us to their ways."

The Elder Solomon Kane called for the floor—an ascetic-featured, dour man with the cold, austere mind of a master mathematician or a master theologian. "As I see it, brother, there are three choices facing us: we can return to Earth and apply for a new planet; or we can attempt to convert these people to our ways; or we can destroy them to the last man, woman and child."

The Blessed Dominic Agnello objected: "Return to Earth is impossible. We have not the fuel."

"And," offered the Blessed Myron, "I testily that these creatures are incorrigible and beyond aid. They are none of them among the Blessed. We do not want to inflict slavery upon them, nor can we welcome them into our numbers."

"The alternative," said the Blessed Solomon Kane, "is clearly our only path. We must root them out as if they were a noxious pestilence. How great are their numbers?"

"Three or four hundred. Perhaps as many as five hundred, no more.

PRIME COMMANDMENT | 233

We certainly outnumber them."

"And we have weapons. We can lay them low like weeds in the field."

A light appeared in the eyes of the Blessed Myron Brown. "We shall perform an act of purification. We will blot the heathens from our new world. The slate must be fresh, for here we will build the New Jerusalem."

The Blessed Leonid Markell, a slim mystic with flowing golden hair, smiled gently and said, "We are told, Thou Shalt Not Kill, Brother Myron."

The Blessed Myron whirled on him. "The commandments are given to us, but they need interpretation. Would you say, Thou Shalt Not Kill, as the butcher raises his knife over a cow? Would you say—"

"The doctrine refers only to human life," said the Blessed Leonid softly. "But—"

"I choose to construe it differently," the Blessed Myron said. His voice was deep and commanding, now; it was the voice of the prophet speaking, of the lawgiver. "Here on this world only those who worship God may be considered human. Fleeing from the bitter scorn of our neighbors, we have come here to build a New Jerusalem in this wilderness—and we must remove every obstacle in our way. The Devil has placed these creatures here, to tempt us with their nakedness and laughter and sinful ways."

He stared at the rest of them, and no longer were they his equals round the table, but now merely his disciples, as they had been all the long journey through the stars. "Tomorrow is the sabbath day by our reckoning, and we shall rest. But on the day following we shall go armed to the village of the idolaters, and strike them down. Is that understood by us all?"

"Vengeance is mine, saith the Lord," the Blessed Leonid quoted mildly. But when the time came for the vote, he cast in his lot with the rest, and it was recorded as a unanimous decision. After the day of the Sabbath, the mocking forest-people would be eradicated.

* * * *

But the people of World had laws of their own, and a religion of their own, and they too held a convocation that evening, speaking long and earnestly round the council fire. The priestess Jeen, garbed only in the red paints of death, danced before them, and when Lyle of the Kwitni called for a decision there were no dissenters.

The long night came to an end, and morning broke over World—and the spies returned from the settlement of the strangers, reporting that the strange god still stood in the clearing, and that his followers showed no signs of obeying the command to depart.

"It is death, then," cried the priestess. And she led them in a dance round the ship their God, and the knives were sharpened, and she and Lyle led them through the forest, Lyle carrying one of the swords that had hung in the cabin of the Captain McCaig aboard the Ship, and Jeen the other.

The strangers were sleeping when the five hundred of the people of World burst in on their encampment. They woke, gradually, in confusion, as the forest slayers moved among them, slicing throats. Dozens died before anyone knew what was taking place.

Curiously the strangers made no attempt to defend themselves. Jeen saw the great bearded man, he who had commanded her to wear clothes and who had eyed her body so strangely, and he stood in the midst of his fellows, shouting in a mighty voice, "It is the Sabbath! Lift no weapon on the Sabbath! Pray, brothers, pray!"

And the strangers fell to their knees and prayed, and because they prayed to a false god they died. It was hardly yet noon when the killing was done with, and the eight hundred members of the Church of the New Resurrection lay weltering in blood, every one of them dead.

Jeen the priestess said strangely, "They did not fight back. They let us kill them."

"They said it was the Sabbath," Lyle of the Kwitni remarked. "But of course it was not the Sabbath—the Sabbath is three days hence."

Jeen shrugged. "We are well rid of them, anyway. They would have blasphemed against God."

There was more work to do, yet, after the bodies were carried to the sea. Fifty great trees were felled and stripped of their branches, and the naked trunks were set aside while the men of the tribe climbed the cliff and caused the great ship in which the strangers had come to topple to the ground.

Then a roadway was made of the fifty great logs, and the men and women of the people of World pushed strainingly, and the great ship rolled with a groaning sound down the side of the hill, as the logs tumbled beneath it, and finally it went plunging toward the sea and dropped beneath the waves, sending up a mighty cascade of water.

They were all gone, then, die eight hundred intruders and their false god, the ship. And the people of World returned to their village and wearily danced out the praise of their Ship, their God.

They were not bloodthirsty people, and they would have wished to welcome the eight hundred strange ones into their midst. But the strange ones were blasphemers, and so had to be killed, and their god destroyed.

Jeen was happy, for her faith in God was renewed, and she danced gladly round the pitted and rusting Ship. For her God had been true, and the god of the strangers false, and God's bidding had been done. For it had been written in the Book of the Ship, which old Lorresson the priest recited to the people of World centuries ago in the days of the first McCaig and the first Kwitni, that there were certain commandments by which the people were to live.

And one of these commandments was, Thou Shalt Not Kill, and another was, Remember the Sabbath Day, To Keep It Holy. These the people of World harkened to.

But they were godly people, and the Word was most holy. They had acted in concord with the dictates of Lorresson and McCaig and Kwitni and the Ship itself, their God, when they had slain the intruders and destroyed their ship. For, first of all the commandments they revered, it was written, Thou Shalt Have No Other Gods Before Me.

THE SONGS OF SUMMER

Originally published in *Authentic Science Fiction*, July 1957.

1. Kennon

I was on my way to take part in the Singing, and to claim Corilann's promise. I was crossing the great open field when suddenly the man appeared, the man named Chester Dugan. He seemed to drop out of the sky.

I watched him stagger for a moment or two. I did not know where he had come from so suddenly, or why he was here. He was short—shorter than any of us—fat in an unpleasant way, with wrinkles on his face and an unshaven growth of beard. I was anxious to get on to the Singing, and so I allowed him to fall to the ground and kept moving. But he called to me, in a barbarous and corrupt tongue which I could recognize as our language only with difficulty.

"Hey, you," he called to me. "Give me a hand, will you?"

He seemed to be in difficulties, so I walked over to him and helped him to his feet. He was panting, and appeared almost in a state of shock. Once I saw he was steady on his feet, and seemed to have no further need of me, I began to walk away from him, since I was anxious to get on to the Singing and did not wish to meddle with this man's affairs. Last year was the first time I attended the Singing at Dandrin's, and I enjoyed it very much. It was then that Corilann had promised herself. I was anxious to get on.

But he called to me. "Don't leave me here!" he shouted. "Hey, you can't just walk away like that! Help me!"

I turned and went back. He was dressed strangely, in ugly ill-arranged tight clothes, and he was walking in little circles, trying to adjust his equilibrium. "Where am I?" he asked me.

"Earth, of course," I told him.

"No," he said, harshly. "I don't mean that, idiot. Where, on Earth?"

The concept had no meaning for me. Where, on Earth, indeed? Here, was all I knew: the great plain between my home and Dandrin's, where the Singing is held. I began to feel uneasy. This man seemed badly sick, and I did not know how to handle him. I felt thankful that I was going to the Singing; had I been alone, I never would have been able to deal with him. I realized I was not as self-sufficient as I thought I was.

"I am going to the Singing," I told him. "Are you?"

"I'm not going anywhere till you tell me where I am and how I got here. What's your name?"

"My name is Kennon. You are crossing the great plain on your way to the home of Dandrin, where we are going to have the Singing, for it is summer. Come; I am anxious to get there. Walk with me, if you wish."

I started to walk away a second time, and this time he began to follow me. We walked along silently for a while.

"Answer me, Kennon," he said after a hundred paces or so. "Ten seconds ago I was in New York; now I'm here. How far am I from New York?"

"What is New York?" I asked. At this he showed great signs of anger and impatience, and I began to feel quite worried.

"Where'd you escape from?" he shouted. "You never heard of New York? You never heard of *New York?* New York," he said, "is a city of some eight million people, located on the Atlantic Ocean, on the east coast of the United States of America. Now tell me you haven't heard of that!"

"What is a city?" I asked, very much confused. At this he grew very angry. He threw his arms in the air wildly.

"Let us walk more quickly," I said. I saw now that I was obviously incapable of dealing with this man, and I was anxious to get on to the Singing—where perhaps Dandrin, or the other old ones, would be able to understand him. He continued to ask me questions as we walked, but I'm afraid I was not very helpful.

2. Chester Dugan

I don't know what happened or how; all I know is I got here. There doesn't seem to be any way back, either, but I don't care; I've got a good thing here and I'm going to show these nitwits who's boss.

Last thing I knew, I was getting into a subway. There was an explosion and a blinding flash of light, and before I could see what was happening I blanked out and somehow got here. I landed in a big open field with absolutely nothing around. It took a few minutes to get over the shock. I think I fell down; I'm not sure. It's not like me, but this was something out of the ordinary and I might have lost my balance.

Anyway, I recovered almost immediately and looked around, and saw this kid in loose flowing robes walking quickly across the field not too far away. I yelled to him when I saw he didn't intend to come over to me. He came over and gave me a hand, and then started to walk away again, calm as you please. I had to call him back. He seemed a little reluctant. The bastard.

I tried to get him to tell me where we were, but he played dumb. Didn't know where we were, didn't know where New York was, didn't even know what a city was—or so he said. I would have thought he was crazy, except that I didn't know what had happened to me; for that matter, I might have been the crazy one and not him.

I saw I wasn't making much headway with him, so I gave up. All he would tell me was that he was on his way to the Singing, and the way he said it there was no doubt about the capital S. He said there would be men there who could help me. To this day I don't know how I got here. Even after I spoke and asked around, no one could tell me how I could step into a subway train in 1956 and come out in an open field somewhere around the thirty-fifth century. The crazy bastards have even lost count.

But I'm here, that's all that matters. And whatever went before is down the drain now. Whatever deals I was working on back in 1956 are dead and buried now; this is where I'm stuck, for reasons I don't get, and here's where I'll have to make my pile. All over again—me, Dugan, starting from scratch. But I'll do it. I'm doing it.

* * * *

After this kid Kennon and I had plodded across the fields for a while, I heard the sound of voices. By now it was getting towards nightfall. I forgot to mention that it was getting along towards the end of November back in 1956, but the weather here was nice and summery. There was a pleasant tang of something in the air that I had never noticed in New York's air, or the soup they called air back then.

The sound of the singing grew louder as we approached, but as soon as we got within sight they all stopped immediately.

They were sitting in a big circle, twenty or thirty of them, dressed in light, airy clothing. They all turned to look at me as we got near.

I got the feeling they were all looking into my mind.

The silence lasted a few minutes, and then they began to sing again. A tall, thin kid was leading them, and they were responding to what he sang. They ignored me. I let them continue until I formed a plan; I don't believe in rushing into things without knowing exactly what I'm doing.

I waited till the singing quieted down a bit, and then I yelled "Stop!" I stepped forward into the middle of the ring.

"My name is Dugan," I said, loud, clear, and slow. "Chester Dugan. I don't know how I got here, and I don't know where I am, but I mean to stay here a while. Who's the chief around here?"

They looked at each other in a puzzled fashion and finally an old thin-faced man stepped out of the circle. "My name is Dandrin," he said, in a thin dried little voice. "As the oldest here, I will speak for the people. Where do you come from?"

"That's just it," I said. "I came from New York City, United States of America, Planet Earth, the Universe. Don't any of those things mean anything to you?"

"They are names, of course," Dandrin said. "But I do not know what they are names of. New York City? United States of America? We have no such terms."

"Never heard of New York?" This was the same treatment I had gotten from that dumb kid Kennon, and I didn't like it. "New York is the biggest city in the world, and the United States is the richest country."

I heard hushed mumbles go around the circle. Dandrin smiled.

"I think I see now," he said. "Cities, countries." He looked at me in a strange way. "Tell me," he said. "Just *when* are you from?"

That shook me. "1956," I said. And here, I'll admit, I began to get worried.

"This is the thirty-fifth century," he said calmly. "At least, so we think. We lost count during the Bombing Years. But come, Chester Dugan; we are interrupting the Singing with our talk. Let us go aside and talk, while the others can sing."

* * * *

He led me off to one side and explained things to me. Civilization had broken up during a tremendous atomic war. These people were the survivors, the dregs. There were no cities and not even small towns. People lived in groups of twos and threes here and there, and didn't come together very often. They didn't even *like* to get together, except during the summer. Then they would gather at the home of some old man—usually Dandrin; everyone would meet, and sing for a while, and then go home.

Apparently there were only a few thousand people in all of America. They lived widely scattered, and there was no business, or trade, or culture, or anything else. Just little clumps of people living by themselves, farming a little and singing, and not doing much else. As the old man talked I began to rub my hands together—mentally, of course. All sorts of plans were forming in my head.

He didn't have any idea how I had gotten here, and neither did I; I still don't. I think it just must have been a one-in-a-trillion fluke, a flaw in space or something. I just stepped through at the precise instant and wound up at that open field. But Chester Dugan can't worry about things he doesn't understand. I just accept them.

I saw a big future for myself here, with my knowledge of twentieth century business methods. The first thing, obviously was to reestablish villages. The way they had things arranged now, there really wasn't any civilization. Once I had things started, I could begin reviving other things that these decadent people had lost: money, entertainment, sports, business. Once we got machinery going, we'd be set. We'd start working on a city, and begin expanding. I thanked whoever it was had dropped me here. This was a golden opportunity for me. These people would be putty in my hands.

3. Corilann

It was with Kennon's approval that I did it. Right after the Singing ended for that evening, Dugan came over to me and I could tell from the tone of his conversation that he wanted me for the night. I had already promised myself to Kennon, but Dugan seemed so insistent that I asked Kennon to release me for this one evening, and he did. He didn't mind.

It was strange the way Dugan went about asking me. He never came right out and said anything. I didn't like anything he did that night; and he's ugly.

He kept telling me, "Stay with me, baby; we're going places together." I didn't know what he meant.

The other women were very curious about it the next day. There are so few of us, that it's a novelty to sleep with someone new. They wanted to know how it had been. I told them I enjoyed it.

It was a lie; he was disgusting. But I went back to him the next night, and the one after that, no matter what poor Kennon said. I couldn't help it, despite myself. There was just something about Dugan that drew me. I couldn't help it. But he was disgusting.

4. Dandrin

It was strange to see them standing in neat, ordered, precise rows, they who had never known any order, any rules before, and Dugan was telling them what to do. The dawn of the day before, we had been free and alone, but since then Dugan had come.

He lined everybody up, and, as I sat in the shade and watched, he began explaining his plans. We tried so hard to understand what he meant. I remembered stories I had heard of the old ones, but I had never believed them until I saw Dugan in action.

"I can't understand you people," he shouted at us. "This whole rich world is sitting here waiting for you to walk out and grab it, and you sit around singing instead. Singing! You people are decadent, that's what you are. You need a government—a good, sturdy government—and I'm here to give it to you."

Kennon and some of the others had come to me that morning to find out what was going to happen. I urged them not to do anything, to listen to Dugan and do what he says. That way, I felt, we could eventually learn to understand him and deal with him in the proper manner. I confess that I was curious to see how he would react among us.

I said nothing when he gave orders that no one was to return home after the Singing. We were to stay here, he told us, and build a city. He was going to bring us all the advantages of the twentieth century.

And we listened to him patiently, all but Kennon. It was Kennon who had brought him here, poor young Kennon who had come here for the Singing and for Corilann. And it was Corilann whom Dugan had singled out for his own private property. Kennon had given his approval, the first night, thinking she would come back to him the next day. But she hadn't; she stayed with Dugan.

In a couple of days he had his city all planned and everything apportioned. I think the thought uppermost in everyone's mind was *why:* why does he want us to do these things? Why? We would have to give him time to carry out his plans; provided he did no permanent harm, we would wait and see, and wonder why.

5. Chester Dugan

This Corilann is really stacked. Things were never like this back when! After Dandrin had told me where the unattached women were sitting, I looked them over and picked her. They were all worth a second look, but she was something special. I didn't know at the time that she was promised to Kennon, or I might not have started fooling around with her; I don't want to antagonize these people too much.

I'm afraid Kennon may be down on me a bit. I've taken his girl away, and I don't think he goes for my methods. I'll have to try some psychology on him. Maybe I'll make him my second-in-command.

The city is moving along nicely. There were 120 people at the Singing, and my figures show that fifteen were old people and the rest divided up pretty evenly; everyone is coupled off, and I've arranged the housing to fit the coupling. These people don't have children very often, but I'll fix that; I'll figure out some way of making things better for those with the most children, some sort of incentive. The quicker we build up the population, the better things will be. I understand there's a wild tribe about five hundred miles to the north of here, maybe less (I still don't have any idea where *here* is) who still have some machines and things, and once we're all established I intend to send an expedition out to conquer the wild tribe and bring back the machines.

There's an idea; maybe I'll let Kennon lead the expedition. I'll be giving him a position of responsibility, and at the same time there's a chance he might get knocked off. That kid's going to cause trouble; I wish I hadn't taken his girl.

But it's too late to go back on it. Besides, I need a son, and quickly. If Corilann's baby is a girl, I don't know what I'll do. I can't carry on my dynasty without an heir.

* * * *

There's another kid here that bothers me—Jubilain. He's not like the others; he's very frail and sensitive, and seems to get special treatment. He's the one who leads the Singing. I haven't been able to get him to work on the construction yet, and I don't know if I'm going to be able to.

But otherwise everything is moving smoothly. I'm surprised that old Dandrin doesn't object to what I'm doing. It's long since past the time when the Singing should have broken up, and everyone scattered, but they're all staying right here and working as if I was paying them.

Which I am, in a way. I'm bringing them the benefits of a great lost civilization, which I represent. Chester Dugan, the man from the past. I'm taking a bunch of nomads and turning them into a powerful city. So actually, everyone's profiting—the people, because of what I'm doing for them, and me. Me especially, because here I'm absolute top dog.

I'm worried about Corilann's baby, though. If it's a girl, that means a delay of a year or more before I can have my son, and even then it'll be at least ten years before he's of any use to me. I wonder what would happen if I took a second wife—Jarinne, for example. I watched her while she was stripped down for work yesterday and she looks even better than Corilann. These people don't seem to have any particular beliefs about marriage, anyway, and so I don't know if they'd mind. Then if Corilann had a girl, I might give her back to Kennon.

And that reminds me of another thing: there's no religion here. I'm not much of a Godman myself, but I realize religion's a good thing for keeping the people in line. I'll have to start thinking about getting a priesthood going, as soon as affairs are a little more settled here.

I didn't think it was so much work, organizing a civilization. But once I get it all set up, I can sit back and cool my heels for life. It's a pleasure working with these people. I just can't wait till everything is moving by itself. I've gotten further in two months here than I did in forty years there. It just goes to show: you need a powerful man to keep civilization alive. And Chester Dugan is just the man these people needed.

6. Kennon

Corilann has told me she will have a child by Dugan. This has made me sad, since it might have been my child she would be bearing instead. But I brought Dugan here myself, and so I suppose I am responsible. If I had not come to the Singing, he might have died in the great open field. But now it is too late for such thoughts.

Dugan forbids us to go home, now that the Singing is over. My father is waiting for me at our home, and the hunting must be done before the winter comes, but Dugan forbids us to go home. Dandrin had to explain to us what "forbids" means; I still don't fully understand why or how one person can tell another person what to do. None of us really understands Dugan at all, not even Dandrin, I think. Dandrin is trying hardest to understand him, but Dugan is so completely alien to us that we do not see.

He has made us build what he calls a city—many houses close together. He says the advantage of this is that we may protect each other. But from what? We have no enemies. I have the feeling that Dugan understands us even less than we understand him. And I am anxious to go home for the autumn hunting, now that summer is almost over and the Singing is ended. I had hoped to bring Corilann back with me, but it is my own fault, and I must not be bitter.

Dugan has been very cold towards me. This is surprising, since it was I who brought him to the Singing. I think he is afraid I will try to take Corilann back; in any event, he seems to fear me and show anger towards me.

If only I understood!

7. Kennon

Dugan has certainly gone too far now. For the past week I have been trying to engage him in conversation, to find out what his motives are for doing all the things he is doing. Dandrin should be doing this, but Dandrin seems to have abdicated all responsibility in this matter, and is content to sit idly by, watching all that happens. Dugan does not make him work because he is so old.

I do not understand Dugan at all. Yesterday he told me, "We will rule the world." What does he mean? *Rule?* Does he actually want to tell everyone who lives what he can do and what he cannot do? If all of the people of Dugan's time were like this, it is small wonder they destroyed everything. What if two people told the same man to do different things? What if they told each other to do things? My head reels at the thought of Dugan's world. People living together in masses, and telling each other what to do; it seems insane. I long to be back with my father for the hunting. I had hoped to bring him a daughter as well, but it seems this is not to be.

Dugan has offered me Jarinne as my wife. Jarinne says she has been with Dugan, and that Corilann knows. Dandrin warns me not to accept Jarinne because it will anger Dugan. But if it will anger Dugan, why did he offer her to me? And—now it occurs to me—by what right does he offer me another person?

Jarinne is a fine woman. She could make me forget Corilann.

And then Dugan told me that soon there will be an expedition to the north; we will take weapons and conquer the wild men. Dugan has heard of the machines of the wild men, and he says he needs them for our city. I told him that I had to leave immediately to help my father with the hunting, that I have stayed here long enough. Others are saying the same thing: this summer the Singing has lasted too long.

* * * *

Today I tried to leave. I gathered my friends and told them I was anxious to go home, and I asked Jarinne to come with me. She accepted, though she reminded me that she had been with Dugan. I told her I might be able to forget that. She said she knew it wouldn't matter to me if it had been anyone else (of course not; why should it?) but that I might object because it had been Dugan. I said good-bye to Corilann, who now is swollen with Dugan's child; she cried a little.

And then I started to leave. I did not talk to Dandrin, for I was afraid he would persuade me not to go. I opened the gate that Dugan has just put up, and started to leave.

Suddenly Dugan appeared. "Where do you think you're going?" he asked, in his hard, cold rasp of a voice. "Pulling out?"

"I have told you," I said quietly, "it is time to help my father with the hunting. I cannot stay in your city any longer." I moved past him and Jarinne followed. But he ran around in front of me.

"No one leaves here, understand?" He waved his closed hand in front of me. "We can't build a city if you take off when you want to."

"But I must go," I said. "You have detained me here long enough." I started to walk on, and suddenly he hit me with his closed hand and knocked me down.

I went sprawling over the ground, and I felt blood on my face from where he had hurt my nose. People all around were watching. I got up slowly. I am bigger and much stronger than Dugan, but it had never occurred to me that one person might hit another person. But this is one of the many things that has come to our world.

I was not so unhappy for myself; pain soon ceases. But Jubilain the Singer was watching when he hit me, and such sights should be kept from Singers. They are not like the rest of us. I am afraid Jubilain has been seriously disturbed by the sight.

After he had knocked me down, Dugan walked away. I got up and went back inside the gate. I do not want to leave now. I must talk to Dandrin. Something must be done.

8. Jubilain

Summer to autumn to every old everyone, sing winter to quiet to baby fall down. My head head hurts. My my hurts head. Bloody was Kennon.

Kennon was bloody and Dugan was angry and summer to autumn to.

Jubilain is very sad. My head hurts. Dugan hit Kennon in the face. With his hand, his hand hand hand rolled up in a ball Dugan hit Kennon. Outside the gates. Consider the gates. Consider.

They have spoiled the song. How can I sing when Dugan hits Kennon? My head hurts. Sing summer to autumn, sing every old everyone. It is good that the summer is ending, for the songs are over. How can I sing? Bloody was Kennon.

Jubilain's head hurts. It did not hurt before did not hurt. I could sing before. Summer to autumn to every old everyone. Corilann's belly is big with Dugan, and Jubilain's head hurts. Will there be more Dugans?

And more Kennons. No more Jubilains. No more songs. The songs of summer are silent and slippery. My head hurts. Hurts hurts hurts. I can sing no more. Nononononono

9. Dandrin

This is tragic. I am an old fool.

I have been sitting in the shade, like the dried old man I am, while Dugan has destroyed us. Today he struck a man—Kennon. Kennon, whom he has mistreated from the start. Poor Kennon. Dugan has brought strife to us, now, along with his city and his gates.

But that is not the worst of it. Jubilain watched the whole thing, and we have lost our Singer. Jubilain simply was unable to assimilate the incident. A Singer's mind is not like our minds; it is a delicate, sensitive instrument. But it cannot comprehend violence. Our Singer has gone mad; there will be no more songs.

We must destroy Dugan. It is sad that we must come to his level and talk of destroying, but it is so. Now he is going to bring us warfare, and that is a gift we do not need. The fierce men of the north will prove strong adversaries for a people that has not fought for a thousand years. Why could we not have been left to ourselves? We were happy and peaceful people, and now we must talk of destroying.

I know the way to do it, too. If only my mind is strong enough, if only it has not dried in the sun during the years, I can lead the way. If I can link with Kennon, and Kennon with Jarinne, and Jarinne with Corilann, and Corilann with—

If we can link, we can do it. Dugan must go. And this is the best way; this way we can dispose of him and still remain human beings.

I am an old fool. But perhaps this dried old brain still is good for something. If I can link with Kennon—

10. Chester Dugan

All resistance has crumbled now. I'm set up for life—Chester Dugan, ruler of the world. It's not much of a world, true enough, but what the hell. It's mine.

It's amazing how all the grumbling has stopped. Even Kennon has given in—in fact, he's become my most valuable man, since that time I had to belt him. It was too bad, I guess, to ruin such a nice nose, but I couldn't have him walking off that way.

He's going to lead the expedition to the north tomorrow, and he's leaving Jarinne here. That's good. Corilann is busy with her baby, and I think I need a little variety anyway. Good-looking kid Corilann had; takes after his old man. It's amazing how everything is working out.

I hope to get electricity going soon, but I'm not too sure. The stream here is kind of weak, and maybe we'll have to throw up a dam first. In fact, I'm sure of it. I'll speak to Kennon about it before he leaves.

This business of rebuilding a civilization from scratch has its rewards. God, am I lean! I've lost all that roll of fat I was carrying around. I suppose part of the reason is that there's no beer here, yet—but I'll get to that soon enough. Everything in due time. First, I want to see what Kennon brings back from the north. I hope he doesn't ruin anything by ripping it out. Wouldn't it be nice to find a hydraulic press or a generator or stuff like that? And with my luck, we probably will.

Maybe we'll do without religion a little while longer. I spoke to Dandrin about it, but he didn't seem to go for the idea of being priest. I might just take over that job myself, once things get straightened out. I'd like to work out some sort of heating system before the winter gets here. I've figured out that we're somewhere in New Jersey or Pennsylvania, and it'll get pretty cold here unless things have changed. (Could the barbarian city to the north be New York? Sounds reasonable.)

It's funny the way everyone lies down and says yes when I tell them to do something. These people have no guts, that's their trouble. One good thing about civilization—you have to have guts to last. I'll put guts in these people, all right. I'll probably be remembered for centuries and centuries. Maybe they'll think of me as a sort of messiah in the far future when everything's blurred? Why not? I came to them out of the clouds, didn't I? From heaven.

Messiah Dugan! Lawsy-me, if they could only see me now!

I still can't get over the way everything is moving. It's almost like a dream. By next spring we'll have a respectable little city here, practically overnight. And we can hold a super-special Singing next summer and snaffle in the folk from all around.

Too bad about that kid Jubilain, by the way; he's really gone off his nut. But I always thought he was a little way there anyway. Maybe I'll teach them some of the old songs myself. It'll help to make me popular here. Although, come to think of it, I'm pretty popular now. They're all smiling at me all the time.

11.

"Kennon? Kennon? Hear me?"

"I hear you, Dandrin. I'll get Jarinne."

"Here I am. Corilann?"

"Here, Jarinne. And pulling hard. Let's try to get Onnar."

"Pull hard!"

"Onnar in." "And Jekkaman." "Hello, Dandrin."

"Hello."

"All here?"

"One hundred twenty."

"Tight now." "We're right tight."

"Let's get started then. All together."

"Hello? Hello, Dugan. Listen to us, Dugan. Listen to us. Listen to us. Hold on tight! Listen to us, Dugan."

"Open up all the way, now."

"Are you listening, Dugan?"

* * * *

12. Dandrin plus Kennon plus Jarinne plus Corilann plus n

I think we'll be able to hold together indefinitely, and so it can be said that the coming of Dugan was an incredible stroke of luck for us. This new blending is infinitely better than trying to make contact over thousands of miles!

Certainly we'll have to maintain this *gestalt* (useful word; I found it in Dugan's mind when I entered) until after Dugan's death. He's peacefully dreaming now, dreaming of who knows what conquests and battles and expansions, and I don't think he'll come out of it. He may live on in his dream for years, and I'll have to hold together and sustain the illusion until he dies. I hope we're making him happy at last. He seems to have been a very unhappy man.

And just after I joined together, it occurred to me that we'd better stay this way indefinitely, just in case any more Dugans get thrown at us from the past. (Could it have been part of a Design? I wonder.) They must all have been like that back then. It's a fine thing that bomb was dropped.

We'll keep Dugan's city, of course. He did make some positive contributions to us—me. His biggest contribution was me; I never would have formed otherwise. I would have been scattered—Kennon on his farm, Dandrin here, Corilann there. I would have maintained some sort of contact among us, the way I always did even before Dugan came, but nothing like this! Nothing at all.

There's the question of what to do with Dugan's child. Kennon, Corilann, and Jarinne are all raising him. We don't need families now that we have me. I think we'll let Dugan's child in with us for a while; if he shows any signs of being like his father, we can always put him to sleep and let him share his father's dream.

I wonder what Dugan is thinking of. Now all his projects will be carried out; his city will grow and cover the world; we will fight and kill and plunder, and he will be measurelessly happy—though all these things take place only within the boundaries of his fertile brain. We will never understand him. But I am happy that all these things will happen only within Dugan's mind so long as I am together and can maintain the illusion for him.

Our next project is to reclaim Jubilain. I am sad that he cannot be with us yet, for how rare and beautiful I would be if I had a Singer in me! That would surely be the most wonderful of blendings. But that will come. Patiently I will unravel the strands of Jubilain's tangled mind, patiently I will bring the Singer back to us.

For in a few months it will be summer again, and time for the Singing. It will be different this year, for we will have been together in me all winter, and so the Singing will not be as unusual an event as it has been, when we have come to each other covered with a winter's strangeness. But this year I will be with us, and we will be I; and the songs of summer will be trebly beautiful in Dugan's city, while Dugan sleeps through the night and the day, for day and night on night and day.

SPACEROGUE

Originally published in *Infinity Science Fiction*, November, 1958.

Chapter One

They were selling a proteus in the public auction place at Borlaam when the stranger wandered by. The stranger's name was Barr Herndon, and he was a tall man with a proud, lonely face. It was not the face he had been born with, though his own had been equally proud, equally lonely.

He shouldered his way through the crowd. It was a warm and muggy day, and a number of idling passersby had stopped to watch the auction. The auctioneer was an Agozlid, squat and bull-voiced, and he held the squirming proteus at arm's length, squeezing it to make it perform.

"Observe, ladies and gentlemen—observe the shapes, the multitude of strange and exciting forms!"

The proteus now had the shape of an eight-limbed star, blue-green at its core, fiery red in each limb. Under the auctioneer's merciless prodding it began to change slowly as its molecules lost their hold on one another and sought a new conformation.

A snake, a tree, a hooded deathworm—

The Agozlid grinned triumphantly at the crowd, baring fifty inch-long yellow teeth. "What am I bid?" he demanded in the guttural Borlaamese language. "Who wants this creature from another sun's world?"

"Five stellors," said a bright-painted Borlaamese noblewoman down front.

"Five stellors! Ridiculous, milady. Who'll begin with fifty? A hundred?"

Barr Herndon squinted for a better view. He had seen proteus lifeforms before and knew something of them. They were strange, tormented creatures, living in agony from the moment they left their native world. Their flesh flowed endlessly from shape to shape, and each change was like the wrenching apart of limbs by the rack.

"Fifty stellors," chuckled a member of the court of Seigneur Krellig, absolute ruler of the vast world of Borlaam. "Fifty for the proteus."

"Who'll say seventy-five?" pleaded the Agozlid. "I brought this being here at the cost of three lives, slaves worth more than a hundred between them. Will you make me take a loss? Surely five thousand stellors—"

"Seventy-five," said a voice.

"Eighty," came an immediate response.

"One hundred," said the noblewoman in the front row.

The Agozlid's toothy face became mellow as the bidding rose spontaneously. The proteus wriggled, attempted to escape, altered itself wildly and pathetically. Herndon's lips compressed tightly. He knew something himself of what suffering meant.

"Two hundred," he said.

"A new voice!" crowed the auctioneer. "A voice from the back row! Five hundred, did you say?"

"Two hundred," Herndon repeated coldly.

"Two fifty," said a nearby noble promptly.

"And twenty-five more," a hitherto-silent circus proprietor said.

Herndon scowled. Now that he had entered into the situation, he was—as always—fully committed to it. He would not let the others get the proteus.

"Four hundred," he said.

For an instant there was silence in the auction ring, silence enough for the mocking cry of a low-swooping sea bird to be clearly audible. Then a quiet voice from the front said, "Four fifty."

"Five hundred," Herndon said.

"Five fifty."

Herndon did not immediately reply, and the Agozlid auctioneer craned his stubby neck, looking around for the next bidder. "I've heard five-fifty," he said crooningly. "That's good, but not good enough."

"Six hundred," Herndon said.

"Six twenty-five."

Herndon fought a savage impulse to draw his needier and gun down his bidding opponent. Instead he tightened his jaws and said, "Six-fifty."

The proteus squirmed and became a pain-smitten pseudo-cat on the auction stand. The crowd giggled in delight.

"Six-seventy-five," came the voice.

It had become a two-man contest now, with the others merely hanging on for the sport of it, waiting to see which one would weaken first. Herndon eyed his opponent: He was a courtier, a swarthy red-bearded man with blazing eyes and a double row of jewels around his doublet. He looked immeasurably wealthy. There was no hope of outbidding him.

"Seven hundred stellors," Herndon said. He glanced around hurriedly, found a small boy standing nearby, and called him over.

"Seven twenty-five," said the noble.

Herndon, whispered, "You see that man down front—the one who just spoke? Run down there and tell him his lady has sent for him and wants him at once."

He handed the boy a golden five-stellor piece. The boy stared at it popeyed a moment, grinned, and slid through the onlookers toward the front of the ring.

"Nine hundred," Herndon said.

It was considerably more than a proteus might be expected to bring at auction and possibly more than even the wealthy noble cared to spend. But Herndon was aware there was no way out for the noble except retreat, and he was giving him that avenue.

"Nine hundred is bid," the auctioneer said. "Lord Moaris, will you bid more?"

"I would," Moaris grunted. "But I am summoned and must leave." He looked blankly angry, but he did not question the boy's message. Herndon noted that down for possible future use. It had been a lucky guess, but Lord Moaris of the Seigneur's court came running when his lady bid him do so.

"Nine hundred is bid," the auctioneer repeated. "Do I hear more? Nine hundred for this fine proteus—who'll make it an even thousand?"

There was no one. Seconds ticked by, and no voice spoke. Herndon waited tensely at the edge of the crowd as the auctioneer chanted, "At nine hundred once, at nine hundred for two, at nine hundred ultimate—

"Yours for nine hundred, friend. Come forward with your cash. And I urge you all to return in ten minutes when we'll be offering some wonderful pink-hued maidens from Villidon." His hands described a feminine shape in the air with wonderfully obscene gusto.

Herndon came forward. The crowd had begun to dissipate, and the inner ring was deserted as he approached the auctioneer. The proteus had taken on a froglike shape and sat huddled in on itself like a statue of gelatin.

Herndon eyed the foul-smelling Agozlid and said, "I'm the one who bought the proteus. Who gets my money?"

"I do," croaked the auctioneer. "Nine hundred stellors gold, plus thirty stellors fee, and the beast's yours."

Herndon touched the money plate at his belt, and a coil of hundred-stellor links came popping forth. He counted off nine of them, broke the link, and laid them on the desk before the Agozlid. Then he drew six five-stellor pieces from his pocket and casually dropped them on the desk.

"Let's have your name for the registry," said the auctioneer after counting out the money and testing it with a soliscope.

"Barr Herndon."

"Home world?"

Herndon paused a moment. "Borlaam."

The Agozlid looked up. "You don't seem much like a Borlaamese to me. Pure-bred?"

"Does it matter to you? I am. I'm from the River Country of Zonnigog, and my money's good."

Painstakingly the Agozlid inscribed his name in the registry. Then he glanced up insolently and said, "Very well, Barr Herndon of Zonnigog. You now own a proteus. You'll be pleased to know that it's already indoctrinated and enslaved."

"This pleases me very much," said Herndon flatly.

The Agozlid handed Herndon a bright planchet of burnished copper with a nine-digit number inscribed on it. "This is the code key. In case you lose your slave, take this to Borlaam Central and they'll trace it for you." He took from his pocket a tiny projector and slid it across the desk. "And here's your resonator. It's tuned to a mesh network installed in the proteus on the submolecular level—it can't change to affect it. You don't like the way the beast behaves, just twitch the resonator. It's essential for proper discipline of slaves."

Herndon accepted the resonator. He said, "The proteus probably knows enough of pain without this instrument. But I'll take it."

The auctioneer seized the proteus and scooped it down from the auction stand, dropping it next to Herndon. "Here you are, friend. All yours now."

The marketplace had cleared somewhat; a crowd had gathered at the opposite end where some sort of jewel auction was going on, but as Herndon looked around, he saw he had a clear path over the cobbled square to the quay beyond.

He walked a few steps away from the auctioneer's booth. The auctioneer was getting ready for the next segment of his sale, and Herndon caught a glimpse of three frightened-looking naked Villidon girls behind the curtain being readied for display.

He stared seaward. Two hundred yards away was the quay, rimmed by the low sea wall, and beyond it was the bright green expanse of the Shining Ocean. For an instant his eyes roved beyond the ocean, to the far continent of Zonnigog where he had been born. Then he looked at the terrified little proteus, halfway through yet another change of shape.

Nine hundred and thirty-five stellors altogether for this proteus. Herndon scowled bitterly. It was a tremendous sum of money, far more than he could easily have afforded to throw away in one morning—particularly his first day back on Borlaam after his sojourn on the out-planets.

But there had been no help for it. He had allowed himself to be drawn into a situation, and he refused to back off halfway. Not anymore, he said to himself, thinking of the burned and gutted Zonnigog village plundered by the gay looters of Seigneur Krellig's army.

"Walk toward the sea wall," he ordered the proteus.

A half-formed mouth said blurredly, "M-master?"

"You understand me, don't you? Then walk toward the sea wall. Keep going and don't turn around."

He waited. The proteus formed feet and moved off in an uncertain shuffle over the well-worn cobbles. Nine hundred thirty-five stellors, he thought bitterly.

He drew his needler.

The proteus continued walking through the marketplace and toward the sea. Someone yelled, "Hey, that thing's going to fall in! We better stop it!"

"I own it," Herndon called coolly. "Keep away from it if you value your own lives."

He received several puzzled glances, but no one moved. The proteus had almost reached the edge of the sea wall now and paused indecisively. Not even the lowest of lifeforms will welcome its own self-destruction no matter what surcease from pain can be attained thereby.

"Mount the wall," Herndon called to it.

Blindly, the proteus obeyed. Herndon's finger caressed the firing knob of the needler. He watched the proteus atop the low wall staring down into the murky harbor water and counted to three.

On the third count he fired. The slim needle projectile sped brightly across the marketplace and buried itself in the back of the proteus' body. Death must have been instantaneous; the needle contained a nerve poison that was effective on all known forms of life.

Caught midway between changes, the creature stood frozen on the wall an instant, then toppled forward into the water. Herndon nodded and holstered his weapon. He saw people's heads nodding. He heard a murmured comment: "Just paid almost a thousand for it, and first thing he does is shoot it."

It had been a costly morning. Herndon turned as if to walk on, but he found his way blocked by a small wrinkle-faced man who had come out of the jewelry-auction crowd across the way.

"My name is Bollar Benjin," the little prune of a man said. His voice was a harsh croak. His body seemed withered and skimpy. He wore a tight gray tunic of shabby appearance. "I saw what you just did."

"What of it? It's not illegal to dispose of slaves in public," Herndon said.

"Only a special kind of man would do it, though," said Bollar Benjin. "A cruel man—or a foolhardy one. Which are you?"

"Both," Herndon said. "And now if you'll let me pass—"

"Just one moment." The croaking voice suddenly acquired the snap of a whip. "Talk to me a moment. If you can spare a thousand stellors to buy a slave you kill the next moment, you can spare me a few words."

"What do you want with me?"

"Your services," Benjin said. "I can use a man like you. Are you free and unbonded?"

Herndon thought of the thousand stellors—almost half his wealth—that he had thrown away just now. He thought of the Seigneur Krellig, whom he hated and whom he had vowed so implacably to kill. And he thought of the wrinkled man before him.

"I am unbonded," he said, "but my price is high. What do you want, and what can you offer?"

Benjin smiled obliquely and dipped into a hidden pocket of his tunic. When he drew forth his hand, it was bright with glittering jewels.

"I deal in these," he said. "I can pay well."

The jewels vanished into the pocket again. "If you're interested," Benjin said, "come with me."

Herndon nodded. "I'm interested."

Chapter Two

Herndon had been gone from Borlaam for a year before this day. A year before—the seventeenth of the reign of the Seigneur Krellig—a band of looters had roared through his home village in Zonnigog, destroying and killing. It had been a high score for the Herndon family—his father and mother killed in the first sally, his young brother stolen as a slave, his sister raped and ultimately put to death.

The village had been burned. And only Barr Herndon had escaped, taking with him twenty thousand stellors of his family's fortune and killing eight of the Seigneur's best men before departing.

He had left the system, gone to the nineteen-world complex of Meld, and on Meld XVII he had bought himself a new face that did not bear the telltale features of the Zonnigog aristocracy. Gone were the sharp, almost razorlike cheekbones, the pale skin, the wide-set black eyes, the nose jutting from the forehead.

For eight thousand stellors the surgeons of Meld had taken these things away and given him a new face: broad where the other had been high, tan-skinned, narrow-eyed, with a majestic hook of a nose quite unlike any of Zonnigog. He had come back wearing the guise of a spacerogue, a freebooter, an unemployed mercenary willing to sign oil to the highest bidder.

The Meldian surgeons had changed his face, but they had not changed his heart. Herndon nurtured the desire for revenge against Krellig—Krellig the implacable, Krellig the invincible, who cowered behind the great stone walls of his fortress for fear of the people's hatred.

Herndon could be patient. But he swore death to Krellig, someday and somehow.

He stood now in a narrow street in the Avenue of Bronze, high in the winding complex of streets that formed the Ancient Quarter of the City of Borlaam, capital of the world of the same name. He had crossed the city silently, not bothering to speak to his gnomelike companion Benjin, brooding only on his inner thoughts and hatred.

Benjin indicated a black metal doorway to their left. "We go in here," he said. He touched his full hand to the metal of the door, and it jerked upward and out of sight. He stepped through.

Herndon followed, and it was as if a great hand had appeared and wrapped itself about him. He struggled for a moment against the stasis field.

"Damn you, Benjin, unwrap me!"

The stasis field held; calmly the little man bustled about Herndon, removing his needier, his four-chambered blaster, and the ceremonial sword at his side.

"Are you weaponless?" Benjin asked. "Yes; you must be. The field subsides."

Herndon scowled. "You might have warned me. When do I get my weapons back?"

"Later," Benjin said. "Restrain your temper and come within."

He was led to an inner room where three men and a woman sat around a wooden table. He eyed the four-some curiously. The men comprised an odd mixture: One had the unmistakable stamp of noble birth on his face, while the other two had the coarseness of clay. As for the woman, she was hardly worth a second look: Slovenly, big-breasted, and raw-faced, she was undoubtedly the mistress of one or more of the others.

Herndon stepped toward them.

Benjin said, "This is Barr Herndon, free spacerogue. I met him at the market. He had just bought a proteus at auction for nearly a thousand stellors. I watched him order the creature toward the sea wall and put a needle in its back."

"If he's that free with his money," remarked the noble-seeming one in a rich bass voice, "what need does he have of our employ?"

"Tell us why you killed your slave," Benjin said.

Herndon smiled grimly. "It pleased me to do so."

One of the leather-jerkined commoners shrugged and said, "These spacerogues don't act like normal men. Benjin, I'm not in favor of hiring him."

"We need him," the withered man retorted. To Herndon he said, "Was your act an advertisement, perhaps? To demonstrate your willingness to kill and your indifference to the moral codes of humanity?"

"Yes," Herndon lied. It would only hurt his own cause to explain that he had bought and then killed the proteus only to save it from a century-long life of endless agony. "It pleased me to kill the creature. And it served to draw your attention to me."

Benjin smiled and said, "Good. Let me explain who we are, then. First, names: This is Heitman Oversk, younger brother of the Lord Moaris."

Herndon stared at the noble. A second son—ah, yes. A familiar pattern. Second sons, propertyless but bearing within themselves the spark of nobility, frequently deviated into shadowy paths. "I had the pleasure of outbidding your brother this morning," he said.

"Outbidding Moaris? Impossible!"

Herndon shrugged. "His lady beckoned him in the middle of the auction, and he left. Otherwise the proteus would have been his, and I'd have nine hundred stellors more in my pocket right now."

"These two," Benjin said, indicating the commoners, "are named Dorgel and Razumod. They have full voice in our organization; we know no social distinctions. And this—" gesturing to the girl—"is Marya. She belongs to Dorgel, who does not object to making short-term loans."

Herndon said, *"I* object. But state your business with me, Benjin."

The dried little man said, "Fetch a sample, Razumod."

The burly commoner rose from his seat and moved into a dark corner of the poorly lit room; he fumbled at a drawer for a moment, then returned with a gem that sparkled brightly even through his fisted fingers. He tossed it down on the table where it gleamed coldly. Herndon noticed that neither Heitman Oversk nor Dorgel let their glance linger on the jewel more than a second, and he likewise turned his head aside.

"Pick it up," Benjin said.

The jewel was ice-cold. Herndon held it lightly and waited.

"Go ahead," Benjin urged. "Study it. Examine its depths. It's a lovely piece, believe me."

Hesitantly Herndon opened his cupped palm and stared at the gem. It was broad-faceted, with a luminous inner light and—he gasped—a face within the stone. A woman's face, languorous, beckoning, seeming to call to him as from the depths of the sea—

Sweat burst out all over him. With an effort he wrenched his gaze from the stone and cocked his arm; a moment later he had hurled the gem with all his force into the farthest corner of the room. He whirled, glared at Benjin, and leaped for him.

"Cheat! Betrayer!"

His hands sought Benjin's throat, but the little man jumped lithely back, and Dorgel and Razumod interposed themselves hastily between them. Herndon stared at Razumod's sweaty bulk a moment and gave ground, quivering with tension.

"You might have warned me," he said.

Benjin smiled apologetically. "It would have ruined the test. We must have strong men in our organization. Oversk, what do you think?"

"He threw down the stone," Heitman Oversk said heavily. "It's a good sign. I think I like him."

"Razumod?"

The commoner gave an assenting grunt, as did Dorgel. Herndon tapped the table and said, "So you're dealing in starstones? And you gave me one without warning? What if I'd succumbed?"

"We would have sold you the stone and let you leave," Benjin said.

"What sort of work would you have me do?"

Heitman Oversk said, "Our trade is to bring starstones in from the Rim worlds where they are mined and sell them to those who can afford our price. The price, incidentally, is fifty thousand stellors. We pay eight thousand for them and are responsible for shipping them ourselves. We need a supervisor to control the flow of starstones from our source world to Borlaam. We can handle the rest at this end."

"It pays well," Benjin added. "Your wage would be five thousand stellors per month, plus a full voice in the organization."

Herndon considered. The starstone trade was the most vicious in the galaxy; the hypnotic gems rapidly became compulsive, and within a year after being exposed to one constantly, a man lost his mind and became a drooling idiot, able only to contemplate the kaleidoscopic wonders locked within his stone.

The way to addiction was easy. Only a strong man could voluntarily rip his eyes from a starstone, once he had glimpsed it. Herndon had proved himself strong. The sort of man who could slay a newly purchased slave could look up from a starstone.

He said, "What are the terms?"

"Full bonding," Benjin said. "Including surgical implantation of a safety device."

"I don't like that."

"We all wear them," Oversk said. "Even myself."

"If all of you wear them," Herndon said, "to whom are you responsible?"

"There is joint control. I handle the out-world contacts; Oversk, here, locates prospective patrons. Dorgel and Razumod are expediters who deal in collection problems and protection. We control each other."

"But there must be somebody who has the master control for the safety devices," Herndon protested. "Who is that?"

"It rotates from month to month. I hold them this month," Benjin said. "Next month it is Oversk's turn."

Herndon paced agitatedly up and down in the darkened room. It was a tempting offer; five thousand a month could allow him to live on high scales. And Oversk was the brother of Lord Moaris, who was known to be the Seigneur's confidante.

And Lord Moaris' lady controlled Lord Moaris. Herndon saw a pattern taking shape, one that would ultimately put the Seigneur Krellig within his reach.

But he did not care to have his body invaded by safety devices. He knew how those worked; if he were to cheat the organization, betray it, attempt to leave it without due cause, whoever operated the master control could reduce him to a groveling pain-racked slave instantly. The safety device could only be removed by the surgeon who had installed it.

It meant accepting the yoke of this group of starstone smugglers. But there was a higher purpose in mind for Herndon.

"I conditionally accept," he said. "Tell me specifically what my duties will be."

Benjin said, "A consignment of starstones has been mined for us on our source world and is soon to be shipped. We want you to travel to that world and accompany the shipment through space to Borlaam. We lose much by way of thievery on each shipment—and there is no way of insuring starstones against loss."

"We know who, our thief is," Oversk said. "You would be responsible for finding him in the act and killing him."

"I'm not a murderer," Herndon said quietly.

"You wear the garb of a spacerogue. That doesn't speak of a very high moral caliber," Oversk said.

"Besides, no one mentions murder," said Benjin. "Merely execution. Yes: execution."

Herndon locked his hands together before him and said, "I want two months' salary in advance. I want to see evidence that all of you are wearing neuronic mesh under your skins before I let the surgeon touch me."

"Agreed," Benjin said after a questioning glance around the room.

"Furthermore, I want as an outright gift the sum of nine hundred thirty golden stellors, which I spent this morning to attract the attention of a potential employer."

It was a lie, but there was cause for it. It made sense to establish a dominating relationship with these people as soon as possible. Then later concessions on their part would come easier.

"Agreed," Benjin said again, more reluctantly.

"In that case," Herndon said, "I consider myself in your employ. I'm ready to leave tonight. As soon as the conditions I state have been fulfilled to my complete satisfaction, I will submit my body to the hands of your surgeon."

Chapter Three

He bound himself over to the surgeon later that afternoon after money to the amount of ten thousand, nine hundred and thirty golden stellors had been deposited to his name in the Royal Borlaam Bank in Galaxy Square and after he had seen the neuronic mesh that was embedded in the bodies of Benjin, Oversk, Dorgel, and Razumod. Greater assurance of good faith than this he could not demand; he would have to risk the rest.

The surgeon's quarters were farther along the Avenue of Bronze, in a dilapidated old house that had no doubt been built in Third Empire days. The surgeon himself was a wiry fellow with a puckered ray slash across one cheek and a foreshortened left leg. A retired pirate-vessel medic, Herndon realized. No one else would perform such an operation unquestioningly. He hoped the man had skill.

The operation itself took an hour, during which time Herndon was under total anesthesia. He woke to find the copper operating dome lifting off him. He felt no different, even though he knew a network of metal had been blasted into his body on the submolecular level.

"Well? Is it finished?"

"It is," the surgeon said.

Herndon glanced at Benjin. The little man held a glinting metal object on his palm. "This is the control, Herndon. Let me demonstrate."

His hand closed, and instantaneously Herndon felt a bright bolt of pain shiver through the calf of his leg. A twitch of Benjin's finger and an arrow of red heat lanced Herndon's shoulder. Another twitch and a clammy hand seemed to squeeze his heart.

"Enough!" Herndon shouted. He realized he had signed away his liberty forever, if Benjin chose to exert control. But it did not matter to him. He had actually signed away his liberty the day he had vowed to watch the death of Seigneur Krellig.

Benjin reached into his tunic pocket and drew forth a little leather portfolio. "Your passport and other traveling necessities," he explained.

"I have my own passport," Herndon said.

Benjin shook his head. "This is a better one. It comes with a visa to Vyapore." To the surgeon he said, "How soon can he travel?"

"Tonight, if necessary."

"Good. Herndon, you'll leave tonight."

The ship was the *Lord Nathiir*, a magnificent superliner bound on a thousand-light-year cruise to the Rim stars. Benjin had arranged for Herndon to travel outward on a luxury liner without cost as part of the entourage of Lord and Lady Moaris. Oversk had obtained the job for him—second steward to the noble couple, who were vacationing on the Rim pleasure planet of Molleccogg. Herndon had not objected when he learned that he was to travel in the company of Lord—and especially Lady—Moaris.

The ship was the greatest of the Borlaam luxury fleet. Even on Deck C, in his steward's quarters, Herndon rated a full-grav room with synthik drapery and built-in chromichron; he had never lived so well even at his parents' home, and they had been among the first people of Zonnigog at one time.

His duties called for him to pay court upon the nobles each evening so that they might seem more resplendent in comparison with the other aristocrats traveling aboard. The Moarises had brought the largest entourage with them, over a hundred people, including valets, stewards, cooks, and paid sycophants.

Alone in his room during the hour of blastoff, Herndon studied his papers. A visa to Vyapore. *So that* was where the starstones came from—! Vyapore, the jungle planet of the Rim where civilization barely had a toehold. No wonder the starstone trade was so difficult to control.

When the ship was safely aloft and the stasis generators had caused the translation into nullspace, Herndon dressed in the formal black and red court garments of Lord Moaris' entourage. Then, making his way up the broad companionway, he headed for the Grand Ballroom where Lord Moaris and his lady were holding court for the first night of the voyage outward.

The ballroom was festooned with ropes of living light. A dancing bear from Albireo XII cavorted clumsily near the entrance as Herndon entered. Borlaamese in uniforms identical to his own stood watch at the door and nodded to him when he identified himself as Second Steward.

He stood for a moment alone at the threshold of the ballroom watching the glittering display. The *Lord Nathiir* was the playground of the wealthy, and a goodly number of Borlaam's wealthiest were here, vying with the ranking nobles, the Moarises, for splendor.

Herndon felt a twinge of bitterness. His people were from beyond the sea, but by rank and preference he belonged in the bright lights of the ballroom, not standing here in the garment of a steward. He moved forward.

The noble couple sat on raised thrones at the far end, presiding over a dancing area in which the grav had been turned down; the dancers drifted gracefully, like figures out of fable, feet touching the ground only at intervals.

Herndon recognized Lord Moaris from the auction. A dour, short, thick-bodied individual he was, resplendent in his court robes, with a fierce little beard stained bright red after the current fashion. He sat stiffly upright on his throne, gripping the armrests of the carved chair as if he were afraid of floating off toward the ceiling. In the air before him shimmered the barely perceptible haze of a neutralizer field designed to protect him from the shots of a possible assassin.

By his side sat his Lady, supremely self-possessed and lovely. Herndon was astonished by her youth. No doubt the nobles had means of restoring lost freshness to a woman's face, but there was no way of recreating the youthful bloom so convincingly. The Lady Moaris could not have been more than twenty-three or twenty-five.

Her husband was several decades older. It was small wonder that he guarded her so jealously.

She smiled in sweet content at the scene before her. Herndon, too, smiled—at her beauty and at the use to which he hoped to put it. Her skin was soft pink; a wench of the bath Herndon had met below decks had told him she bathed in the cream of the ying apple twice daily. Her eyes were wide-set and clear, her nose finely made, her lips two red arching curves. She wore a dress studded with emeralds; it flowed from her like light. It was open at the throat, revealing a firm bosom and strong shoulders. She clutched a diamond-crusted scepter in one small hand.

Herndon looked around, found a lady of the court who was unoccupied at the moment, and asked her to dance. They danced silently, gliding in and out of the grav field; Herndon might have found it a pleasant experience, but he was not primarily in search of pleasant experiences now. He was concerned only with attracting the attention of the Lady Moaris.

He was successful. It took time, but he was by far the biggest and most conspicuous man of the court assembled there, and it was customary for Lord and Lady to leave their thrones, mingle with their courtiers, even dance with them. Herndon danced with lady after lady until finally he found himself face to face with the Lady Moaris.

"Will you dance with me?" she asked. Her voice was like liquid gossamer.

Herndon lowered himself in a courtly bow. "I would consider it the greatest of honors, milady."

They danced. She was easy to hold; he sensed her warmness near him, and he saw something in her eyes—a distant pinched look of pain, perhaps—that told him all was not well between Lord and Lady.

She said, "I don't recognize you. What's your name?"

"Barr Herndon, milady. Of Zonnigog."

"Zonnigog, indeed! And why have you crossed ten thousand miles of ocean to our city?"

Herndon smiled and gracefully dipped her through a whirling series of pirouettes. "To seek fame and fortune, milady. Zonnigog is well and good to live in, but the place to become known is the City of Borlaam. For this reason I petitioned the Heitman Oversk to have me added to the retinue of the Lord Moaris."

"You know Oversk, then? Well?"

"Not at all well. I served him a while; then I asked to move on."

"And so you go, climbing up and over your former masters until you scramble up the shoulders of the Lord Moaris to the feet of the Seigneur. Is that the plan?"

She smiled disarmingly, drawing any possible malice from the words she had uttered. Herndon nodded, saying in all sincerity, "I confess this is my aim. Forgive me, though, for saying that there are reasons that might cause me to remain in the service of the Lord Moaris longer than I had originally intended."

A flush crossed her face. She understood. In a half-whisper she said, "You are impertinent. I suppose it comes with good looks and a strong body."

"Thank you, milady."

"I wasn't complimenting you," she said as the dance came to an end and the musicians subsided. "I was criticizing. But what does it matter? Thank you for the dance."

"May I have the pleasure of milady's company once again soon?" Herndon asked.

"You may—but not too soon." She chuckled. "The Lord Moaris is highly possessive. He resents it when I dance twice the same evening with one member of the court."

Sadness darkened Herndon's face a moment. "Very well, then. But I will go to Viewplate A and stare at the stars a while. If the Lady seeks a companion, she will find one there."

She stared at him and flurried away without replying. But Herndon felt a glow of satisfaction. The pieces were dropping into place.

Viewplate A, on the uppermost deck of the vast liner, was reserved for the first-class passengers and the members of their retinues. It was an enormous room shrouded at all times in darkness, at one end of which a viewscreen opened out onto the glory of the heavens. In nullspace, a hyperbolic section of space was visible at all times, the stars in weird out-of-focus colors forming a breathtaking display. Geometry went awry. A blazing panorama illuminated the room.

The first-class viewing room was also known to be a trysting place. There, under cover of darkness, ladies might meet and make love to cooks, lords to scullery maids. An enterprising rogue with a nolight camera might make a fortune taking a quick shot of such a room and blackmailing his noble victims. But scanners at the door prevented such devices from entering.

Herndon stood staring at the fiery gold and green of the closest stars a while, his back to the door, until he heard a feminine voice whisper to him.

"Barr Herndon?"

He turned. In the darkness it was difficult to tell who spoke; he saw a girl about the height of the Lady Moaris, but in the dimness of the illumination of the plate he could see it was not the Lady. This girl's hair was dull red; the Lady's was golden. And he could see the pale whiteness of this girl's breasts; the Lady's garment, while revealing, had been somewhat more modest.

This was a lady of the court, then, perhaps enamored of Herndon, perhaps sent by the Lady Moaris as a test or as a messenger.

Herndon said, "I am here. What do you want?"

"I bring a message from—a noble lady," came the answering whisper.

Smiling in the darkness, Herndon said. "What does your mistress have to say to me?"

"It cannot be spoken. Hold me in a close embrace as if we were lovers, and I will give you what you need."

Shrugging, Herndon clasped the go-between in his arms with feigned passion. Their lips met; their bodies pressed tight. Herndon felt the girl's hand searching for his and slipping something cool, metallic into it. Her lips left his, traveled to his ear, and murmured:

"This is her key. Be there in half an hour."

They broke apart. Herndon nodded farewell to her and returned his attention to the glories of the viewplate. He did not glance at the object in his hand, but merely stored it in his pocket.

He counted out fifteen minutes in his mind, then left the viewing room and emerged on the main deck. The ball was still in progress, but he learned from a guard on duty that the Lord and Lady Moaris had already left for sleep and that the festivities were soon to end.

Herndon slipped into a washroom and examined the key, for a key it was. It was a radionic opener, and imprinted on it was the number 1160.

His throat felt suddenly dry. The Lady Moaris was inviting him to her room for the night—or was this a trap, and would Moaris and his court be waiting for him to gun him down and provide themselves with some amusement? It was not beyond these nobles to arrange such a thing.

But still—he remembered the clearness of her eyes and the beauty of her face. He could not believe she would be party to such a scheme.

He waited out the remaining fifteen minutes. Then, moving cautiously along the plush corridors, he found his way to Room 1160.

He listened a moment. Silence from within. His heart pounded frantically, irking him; this was his first major test, possibly the gateway to all his hopes, and it irritated him that he felt anxiety.

He touched the tip of the radionic opener to the door. The substance of the door blurred as the energy barricade that composed it was temporarily dissolved. Herndon stepped through quickly. Behind him the door returned to a state of solidity.

The light of the room was dim. The Lady Moaris awaited him, wearing a gauzy dressing gown. She smiled tensely at him; she seemed ill at ease.

"You came, then."

"Would I do otherwise?"

"I—wasn't sure. I'm not in the habit of doing things like this."

Herndon repressed a cynical smile. Such innocence was touching but highly improbable. He said nothing, and she went on: "I was caught by your face—something harsh and terrible about it struck me. I had to send for you to know you better."

Ironically Herndon said, "I feel honored. I hadn't expected such an invitation."

"You won't—think it's cheap of me, will you?" she said plaintively. It was hardly the thing Herndon expected from the lips of the noble Lady Moaris. But as he stared at her slim body revealed beneath the filmy robe, he understood that she might not be so noble after all once the gaudy pretense was stripped away. He saw her as perhaps she truly was: a young girl of great loveliness married to a domineering nobleman who valued her only for her use in public display. It might explain this bedchamber summons to a Second Steward.

He took her hand. "This is the height of my ambitions, milady. Beyond this room, where can I go?"

But it was empty flattery he spoke. He darkened the room illumination exultantly. *With your conquest, Lady Moaris*, he thought, *do I begin the conquest of the Seigneur Krellig!*

Chapter Four

The voyage to Molleccogg lasted a week, absolute time aboard ship. After their night together, Herndon had occasion to see the Lady Moaris only twice more, and on both occasions she averted her eyes from him, regarding him as if he were not there.

It was understandable. But Herndon held a promise from her that she would see him again in three months' time when she returned to Borlaam; and she had further promised that she would use her influence with her husband to have Herndon invited to the court of Seigneur.

The *Lord Nathiir* emerged from nullspace without difficulty and was snared by the landing field of Molleccogg Spacefield. Through the viewing screen on his own deck, Herndon saw the colorful splendor of the pleasure planet on which they were about to land growing larger now that they were in the final spiral.

But he did not intend to remain long on the world of Molleccogg.

He found the Chief Steward and applied for a leave of absence from Lord Moaris' service without pay.

"But you've just joined us," the Steward protested. "And now you want to leave?"

"Only for a while," Herndon said. "I'll be back on Borlaam before any of you are. I have business to attend to on another world in the Rim area, and then I promise to return to Borlaam at my own expense to rejoin the retinue of the Lord Moaris."

The Chief Steward grumbled and complained, but he could not find anything particularly objectionable in Herndon's intentions, and so finally he reluctantly granted the spacerogue permission to leave Lord Moaris' service temporarily. Herndon packed his court costume and clad himself in his old spacerogue garb; when the great liner ultimately put down in Danzibool Harbor on Molleccogg, Herndon was packed and ready, and he slipped off ship and into the thronged confusion of the terminal.

Bollar Benjin and Heitman Oversk had instructed him most carefully on what he was to do now. He pushed his way past a file of vile-smelling lily-faced green Nnobonn and searched for a ticket seller's window. He found one eventually and produced the prepaid travel vouchers Benjin had given him.

"I want a one-way passage to Vyapore," he said to the flat-featured, triple-eyed Guzmanno clerk who stared out from back of the wicker screen.

"You need a visa to get to Vyapore," the clerk said. "These visas are issued at infrequent intervals to certified personages. I don't see how you—"

"I have a visa," Herndon snapped, and produced it. The clerk blinked—one-two-three, in sequence—and his pale rose face flushed deep cerise.

"So you do," he remarked at length. "It seems to be in order. Passage will cost you eleven hundred sixty-five stellors of the realm."

"I'll take a third-class ship," Herndon said. "I have a paid voucher for such a voyage."

He handed it across. The clerk studied it for a long moment, then said: "You have planned this very well. I accept the voucher. Here."

Herndon found himself holding one paid passage to Vyapore aboard the freight ship *Zalasar*.

The *Zalasar* turned out to be very little like the *Lord Nathiir*. It was an old-fashioned unitube ship that rattled when it blasted off, shivered when it translated to nullspace, and quivered all the week-long journey from Molleccogg to Vyapore. It was indeed a third-class ship. Its cargo was hardware: seventy-five thousand dry-strainers, eighty thousand pressors, sixty thousand multiple fuse screens, guarded by a supercargo team of eight taciturn Ludvuri. Herndon was the only human aboard. Humans did not often get visas to Vyapore.

They reached Vyapore seven days and a half after setting out from Molleccogg. Ground temperature as they disembarked was well over a hundred. Humidity was overpowering. Herndon knew about Vyapore: It held perhaps five hundred humans, one spaceport, infinite varieties of deadly local life, and several thousand nonhumans of all descriptions, some of them hiding, some of them doing business, some of them searching for starstones.

Herndon had been well briefed. He knew who his contact was, and he set about meeting him.

There was only one settled city on Vyapore, and because it was the only one, it was nameless. Herndon found a room in a cheap boardinghouse run by a swine-eared Dombruun and washed the sweat from his face with the unpleasantly acrid water of the tap.

Then he went downstairs into the bright noonday heat. The stench of rotting vegetation drifted in from the surrounding jungle on a faint breeze. Herndon said at the desk, "I'm looking for a Vonnimooro named Mardlin. Is he around?"

"Over there," said the proprietor, pointing.

Mardlin the Vonnimooro was a small, weasely-like creature with the protuberant snout, untrustworthy yellow eyes, and pebbly brown-purple fur of his people. He looked up when Herndon approached. When he spoke, it was in lingua spacia with a whistling, almost obscene inflection.

"You looking for me?"

"It depends," Herndon said. "Are you Mardlin?"

The jackal-like creature nodded. Herndon lowered himself to a nearby seat and said in a quiet voice, "Bollar Benjin sent me to meet you. Here are my credentials."

He tossed a milky-white clouded cube on the table between them. Mardlin snatched it up hastily in his leathery claws and nudged the activator. An image of Bollar Benjin appeared in the cloudy depths, and a soft voice said, "Benjin speaking. The bearer of this card is known to me, and I trust him fully in all matters. You are to do the same. He will accompany you to Borlaam with the consignment of goods."

The voice died away, and the image of Benjin vanished. The jackal scowled. He muttered, "If Benjin sent a man to convey his goods, why must I go?"

Herndon shrugged. "He wants both of us to make the trip, it seems. What do you care? You're getting paid, aren't you?"

"And so are you," snapped Mardlin. "It isn't like Benjin to pay two men to do the same job. And I don't like you, Rogue."

"Mutual," Herndon responded heartily. He stood up. "My orders say I'm to take the freighter *Dawnlight* back to Borlaam tomorrow evening. I'll meet you here one hour before to examine the merchandise."

He made one other stop that day. It was a visit with Brennt, a jewel monger of Vyapore who served as the funnel between the native starstone miners and Benjin's courier, Mardlin.

Herndon gave his identifying cube to Brennt and said, once he had satisfactorily proved himself, "I'd like to check your books on the last consignment."

Brennt glanced up sharply. "We keep no books on starstones, idiot. What do you want to know?"

Herndon frowned. "We suspect our courier of diverting some of our stones to his own pocket. We have no way of checking up on him since we can't ask for vouchers of any kind in starstone traffic."

The Vyaporan shrugged. "All couriers steal."

"Starstones cost us eight thousand stellors apiece," Herndon said. "We can't afford to lose any of them at that price. Tell me how many are being sent in the current shipment."

"I don't remember," Brennt said.

Scowling, Herndon said, "You and Mardlin are probably in league. We have to take his word for what he brings us—but always three or four of the stones are defective. We believe he buys, say, forty stones from you, pays the three hundred twenty thousand stellors over to you from the account we provide, and then takes three or four from the batch and replaces them with identical but defective stones worth a hundred stellors or so apiece. The profit to him is better than twenty thousand stellors a voyage.

"Or else," Herndon went on, "you deliberately sell him defective stones at eight thousand stellors. But Mardlin's no fool, and neither are we."

"What do you want to know?" the Vyaporan asked.

"How many functional starstones are included in the current consignment?"

Sweat poured from Brennt's face. "Thirty-nine," he said after a long pause.

"And did you also supply Mardlin with some blanks to substitute for any of these thirty-nine?"

"N-no," Brennt said.

"Very good," said Herndon. He smiled. "I'm sorry to have seemed so overbearing, but we had to find out this information. Will you accept my apologies and shake?"

He held out his hand. Brennt eyed it uncertainly, then took it. With a quick inward twitch Herndon jabbed a needle into the base of the other's thumb. The quick-acting truth drug took only seconds to operate.

"Now," Herndon said, "the preliminaries are over. You understand the details of our earlier conversation. Tell me, now, how many starstones is Mardlin paying you for?"

Brennt's fleshless lips curled angrily, but he was defenseless against the drug. "Thirty-nine," he said.

"At what total cost?"

"Three hundred twelve thousand stellors."

Herndon nodded. "How many of those thirty-nine are actually functional starstones?"

"Thirty-five," Brennt said reluctantly.

"The other four are duds?"

"Yes."

"A sweet little racket. Did you supply Mardlin with the duds?"

"Yes. At two hundred stellors each."

"And what happens to the genuine stones that we pay for but that never arrive on Borlaam?"

Brennt's eyes rolled despairingly. "Mardlin—Mardlin sells them to someone else and pockets the money. I get five hundred stellors per stone for keeping quiet."

"You've kept very quiet today," Herndon said. "Thanks very much for the information, Brennt. I really should kill you—but you're much too valuable to us for that. We'll let you live, but we're changing the terms of our agreement. From now on we pay you only for actual functioning starstones, not for an entire consignment. Do you like that setup?"

"No," Brennt said.

"At least you speak truthfully now. But you're stuck with it. Mardlin is no longer courier, by the way. We can't afford a man of his tastes in our organization. I don't advise you try to make any deals with his successor, whoever he is."

He turned and walked out of the shop.

Herndon knew that Brennt would probably notify Mardlin that the game was up immediately so the Vonnimooro could attempt to get away. Herndon was not particularly worried about Mardlin's escaping since he had a weapon that would work on the jackal-creature at any distance whatever.

But he had sworn an oath to safeguard the combine's interests, and Herndon was a man of his oath. Mardlin was in possession of thirty-nine starstones for which the combine had paid. He did not want the Vonnimooro to take those with him.

He legged it across town hurriedly to the house where the courier lived while at the Vyapore end of his route. It took him fifteen minutes from Brennt's to Mardlin's—more than enough time for a warning.

Mardlin's room was on the second story. Herndon drew his weapon from his pocket and knocked.

"Mardlin?"

There was no answer. Herndon said, "I know you're in there, jackal. The game's all over. You might as well open the door and let me in."

A needle came whistling through the door and embedded itself against the opposite wall after missing Herndon's head by inches. Herndon stepped out of range and glanced down at the object in his hand.

It was the master control for the neuronic network installed in Mardlin's body. It was quite carefully gradated; shifting the main switch to *six* would leave the Vonnimooro in no condition to fire a gun. Thoughtfully Herndon nudged the indicator up through the degrees of pain to *six* and left it there.

He heard a thud within.

Putting his shoulder to the door, he cracked it open with one quick heave. He stepped inside. Mardlin lay sprawled in the middle of the floor writhing in pain. Near him, but beyond his reach, lay the needier he had dropped.

A suitcase sat open and half-filled on the bed. He had evidently intended an immediate getaway.

"*Shut ... that ... thing ... off ...*" Mardlin muttered through pain-twisted lips.

"First some information," Herndon said cheerfully. "I just had a talk with Brennt. He says you've been doing some highly improper things with our starstones. Is this true?"

Mardlin quivered on the floor but said nothing. Herndon raised the control a quarter of a notch, intensifying the pain but not yet bringing it to the killing range.

"Is this true?" he repeated.

"Yes—yes! Damn you, shut it off."

"At the time you had the network installed in your body, it was with the understanding that you'd be loyal to the combine and so it would never need to be used. But you took advantage of circumstances and cheated us. Where's the current consignment of stones?"

"... suitcase lining," Mardlin muttered.

"Good," Herndon said. He scooped up the needier, pocketed it, and shut off the master control switch. The pain subsided in the Vonnimooro's body, and he lay slumped, exhausted, too battered to rise.

Efficiently Herndon ripped away the suitcase lining and found the packet of starstones. He opened it. They were wrapped in shielding tissue that protected any accidental viewer. He counted through them; there were thirty-nine, as Brennt had said.

"Are any of these defective?" he asked.

Mardlin looked up from the floor with eyes yellow with pain and hatred. "Look through them and see."

Instead of answering, Herndon shifted the control switch past *six* again. Mardlin doubled up, clutching his head with clawlike hands. "Yes! Yes! Six defectives!"

"Which means you sold six good ones for forty-eight thousand stellors, less the three thousand you kicked back to Brennt to keep quiet. So there should be forty-five thousand stellors here that you owe us. Where are they?"

"Dresser drawer ... top ..."

Herndon found the money neatly stacked. A second time he shut off the control device, and Mardlin relaxed.

"Okay," Herndon said. "I have the cash and the stones. But there must be thousands of stellors that you've previously stolen from us."

"You can have that, too! Only don't turn that thing on again, please!"

Shrugging, Herndon said, "There isn't time for me to hunt down the other money you stole from us. But we can ensure against your doing it again."

He fulfilled the final part of Benjin's instructions by turning the control switch to *ten*, the limit of sentient endurance. Every molecule of Mardlin's wiry body felt unbearable pain; he screamed and danced on the floor, but only for a moment. Nerve cells unable to handle the overload of pain stimuli short-circuited. In seconds his brain was paralyzed. In less than a minute he was dead, though his tortured limbs still quivered with convulsive postmortuary jerks.

Herndon shut the device off. He had done his job. He felt neither revulsion nor glee.

He gathered up jewels and money and walked out.

Chapter Five

A month later he arrived on Borlaam via the freighter *Dawnlight* as scheduled and passed through customs without difficulty despite the fact that he was concealing more than three hundred thousand stellors' worth of proscribed starstones on his person.

His first stop was the Avenue of Bronze where he sought out Benjin and the Heitman Oversk.

He explained crisply and briefly his activities since leaving Borlaam, neglecting to mention the matter of the shipboard romance with the Lady Moaris. While he spoke, both Benjin and Oversk stared eagerly at him, and when he told of intimidating Brennt and killing the treacherous Mardlin, they beamed.

Herndon drew the packet of starstones from his cloak and laid them on the wooden table. "There," he said. "The starstones. There were some defectives, as you know, and I've brought back cash for them." He added forty-five thousand stellors to the pile.

Benjin quickly caught up the money and the stones and said, "You've done well, Herndon. Better than we expected. It was a lucky day when you killed that proteus."

"Will you have more work for me?"

Oversk said, "Of course. You'll take Mardlin's place as the courier. Didn't you realize that?"

Herndon had realized it, but it did not please him. He wanted to remain on Borlaam, now that he had made himself known to the Lady Moaris. He wanted to begin his climb toward Krellig. And if he were to shuttle between Vyapore and Borlaam, the all-important advantage he had attained would be lost.

But the Lady Moaris would not be back on Borlaam for nearly two months. He could make one more round trip for the combine without seriously endangering his position. After that he would have to find some means of leaving their service. Of course, if they preferred to keep him on, they could compel him, but—

"When do I make the next trip?" he asked.

Benjin shrugged lazily. "Tomorrow, next week, next month—who knows? We have plenty of stones on hand. There is no hurry for the next trip. You can take a vacation now while we sell these."

"No," Herndon said. "I want to leave immediately." Oversk frowned at him. "Is there some reason for the urgency?"

"I don't want to stay on Borlaam just now," Herndon said. "There's no need for me to explain further. It pleases me to make another trip to Vyapore."

"He's eager," Benjin said. "It's a good sign."

"Mardlin was eager at first, too," Oversk remarked balefully.

Herndon was out of his seat and at the nobleman's throat in an instant. His needler grazed the skin of Oversk's Adam's apple.

"If you intended by that comparison to imply—"

Benjin tugged at Herndon's arm. "Sit down, Rogue, and relax. The Heitman is tired tonight, and the words slipped out. We trust you. Put the needler away."

Reluctantly Herndon lowered the weapon. Oversk, white-faced despite his tan, fingered his throat where Herndon's weapon had touched it but said nothing. Herndon regretted his hasty action and decided not to demand an apology. Oversk still could be useful to him.

"A spacerogue's word is his bond," Herndon said. "I don't intend to cheat you. When can I leave?"

"Tomorrow, if you wish," Benjin said. "We'll cable Brennt to have another shipment ready for you."

This time he traveled to Vyapore aboard a transport freighter since there were no free tours with noblemen to be had at this season. He reached the jungle world a little less than a month later. Brennt had thirty-two jewels waiting for him. Thirty-two glittering little starstones, each in its protective sheath, each longing to rob some man's mind away with its beckoning dreams.

Herndon gathered them up and arranged a transfer of funds to the amount of two hundred fifty-six thousand stellors. Brennt eyed him bitterly throughout the whole transaction, but it was obvious that the Vyaporan was in fear for his life, and would not dare attempt duplicity. No word was said of Mardlin or his fate.

Bearing his precious burden, Herndon returned to Borlaam aboard a second-class liner out of Diirhav, a neighboring world of some considerable population. It was expensive, but he could not wait for the next freight ship. By the time he returned to Borlaam, the Lady Moaris would have been back several weeks. He had promised the Steward he would rejoin Moaris' service, and it was a promise he intended to keep.

It had become winter when he reached Borlaam again with his jewels. The daily sleet rains sliced across the cities and the plains, showering them with billions of icy knifelike particles. People huddled together, waiting for the wintry cold to end.

Herndon made his way through streets clogged with snow that glistened blue-white in the light of the glinting winter moon and delivered his gems to Oversk in the Avenue of Bronze. Benjin, he learned, would be back shortly; he was engaged in an important transaction.

Herndon warmed himself by the heat wall and accepted cup after cup of Oversk's costly Thrucian blue wine to ease his inner chill. The commoner Dorgel entered after a while, followed by Marya and Razumod, and together they examined the new shipment of starstones Herndon had brought back, storing them with the rest of their stock.

At length Benjin entered. The little man was almost numb with cold, but his voice was warm as he said, "The deal is settled, Oversk! Oh—Herndon—you're back, I see. Was it a good trip?"

"Excellent," Herndon said.

Oversk remarked, "You saw the Secretary of State, I suppose. Not Krellig himself."

"Naturally. Would Krellig let someone like me into his presence?"

Herndon's ears rose at the mention of his enemy's name. He said, "What's this about the Seigneur?"

"A little deal," Benjin chortled. "I've been doing some very delicate negotiating while you were away. And I signed the contract today."

"*What* contract?" Herndon demanded.

"We have a royal patron now, it seems. The Seigneur Krellig has gone into the starstone business himself. Not in competition with us, though. He's bought a controlling interest in us."

Herndon felt as if his vital organs had been transmuted to lead. In a congealed voice he said, "And what are the terms of this agreement?"

"Simple. Krellig realized the starstone trade, though illegal, was unstoppable. Rather than alter the legislation and legalize the trade, which would be morally undesirable and which would also tend to lower the price of the gems, he asked the Lord Moaris to place him in contact with some group of smugglers who would work for the Crown. Moaris, naturally, suggested his brother. Oversk preferred to let me handle the negotiations, and for the past month I've been meeting secretly with Krellig's Secretary of State to work out a deal."

"The terms of which are?"

"Krellig guarantees us immunity from prosecution and at the same time promises to crack down heavily on our competition. He pledges us a starstone monopoly, in other words, and so we'll be able to lower our price to Brennt and jack up the selling price to whatever the traffic will bear. In return for this we turn over eight percent of our gross profits to the Seigneur and agree to supply him with six starstones annually, at cost, for the Seigneur to use as gifts to his enemies. Naturally we also transfer our fealties from the combine to the Seigneur himself. He holds our controls to assure loyal service."

Herndon sat as if stunned. His hands felt chilled; coldness rippled through his body. Loyalty to Krellig? His enemy, the person he had sworn to destroy?

The conflict seared through his mind and body. How could he fulfill his earlier vow, now that this diametrically opposed one was in effect? Transfer of fealty was a common thing. By the terms of Benjin's agreement, Herndon now was a sworn vassal of the Seigneur.

If he killed Krellig, that would violate his bond. If he served the Seigneur in all faith, he would break trust with himself and leave home and parents unavenged. It was an impossible dilemma. He quivered with the strain of resolving it.

"The Spacerogue doesn't look happy about the deal," oversk commented. "Or are you sick, Herndon?"

"I'm all right," Herndon said stonily. "It's the cold outside, that's all. Chills a man."

Fealty to Krellig! Behind his back they had sold themselves and him to the man he hated most. Herndon's ethical code was based entirely on the concept of loyalty and unswerving obedience, of the sacred nature of an oath. But now he found himself bound to two mutually exclusive oaths. He was caught between them, racked and drawn apart; the only escape from the torment was death.

He stood up. "Excuse me," he said. "I have an appointment elsewhere in the city. You can reach me at my usual address if you need me for anything."

It took him the better part of a day to get to see the Chief Steward of Moaris Keep and explain to him that he had been unavoidably detained in the far worlds, that he fully intended to re-enter the Moaris service and perform his duties loyally and faithfully. After quite some wrangling he was reinstated as one of the Second Stewards and given functions to carry out in the daily life of the sprawling residence that was Moaris Keep.

Several days passed before he caught as much as a glimpse of the Lady Moaris. That did not surprise him; the Keep covered fifteen acres of Borlaam City, and Lord and Lady occupied private quarters on the uppermost level, the rest of the huge place being devoted to libraries, ballrooms, art galleries, and other housings for the Moaris treasures, all of these rooms requiring a daily cleaning by the household staff.

He saw her finally as he was passing through the fifth-level hallway in search of the ramp that would take him to his next task, cataloguing the paintings of the sixth-level gallery: He heard a rustle of crinoline first, and then she proceeded down the hall, flanked on each side by copper-colored Toppidan giants and in front and back by glistening-gowned ladies in waiting.

The Lady Moaris herself wore sheer garments that limned the shapely lines of her body. Her face was sad; it seemed to Herndon, as he saw her from afar, that she was under some considerable strain.

He stepped to one side to let the procession go past; but she saw him and glanced quickly to the side at which he stood. Her eyes widened in surprise as she recognized him. He did not dare a smile. He waited until she had moved on, but inwardly he gloated. It was not difficult to read the expression in her eyes.

Later that day a blind Agozlid servant came up to him and silently handed him a sealed note. Herndon pocketed it, waiting until he was alone in a corridor that was safe from the Lord Moaris' spy rays. He knew it was safe; the spy ray in that corridor had been defective, and he himself had removed it that morning, meaning to replace it later in the day.

He broke the seal. The note said simply: *I have waited a month for you. Come to me tonight; M. is to spend the night at the Seigneur's palace. Karla will admit you.*

The photonically sensitized ink faded from sight in a moment; the paper was blank. Smiling, he thrust it in a disposal hatch.

He quietly made his way toward the eleventh-level chamber of the Lady Moaris when the Keep had darkened for the night. Her lady in waiting Karla, the bronze-haired one who had served as go-between aboard the *Lord Nathiir*, was on duty. Now she wore night robes of translucent silk; a test of his fidelity, no doubt. Herndon carefully kept his eyes from her body and said, "I am expected."

"Yes. Come with me."

It seemed to him that the look in her eyes was a strange one: desire, jealousy, hatred, perhaps? But she turned and led him within, down corridors lit only with a faint night glow. She nudged an opener; a door before him flickered and was momentarily nullified. He stepped through, and it returned to the solid state behind him.

The Lady Moaris was waiting.

She wore only the filmiest of gowns, and the longing was evident in her eyes. Herndon said, "Is this safe?"

"It is. Moaris is away at Krellig's." Her lip curled in a bitter scowl.

"He spends half his nights there toying with the Seigneur's cast-off women. The room is sealed against spy rays. There's no way he can find out you've been here."

"And the girl—Karla? You trust her?"

"As much as I can trust anyone." Her arms sought his shoulders. "My rogue," she murmured, "why did you leave us at Molleccogg?"

"Business of my own, milady."

"I missed you. Molleccogg was a bore without you."

Herndon smiled gravely. "Believe me, I didn't choose to. But I had sworn to carry out duty elsewhere."

She pulled him urgently to her. Herndon felt pity for this lovely noblewoman, first in rank among the ladies of the court, condemned to seek lovers among the stewards and grooms.

"Anything I have is yours," she promised him. "Ask for anything! Anything!"

"There is one prize you might secure for me," Herndon said grimly.

"Name it. The cost doesn't matter."

"There is no cost," Herndon said. "I simply seek an invitation to the court of the Seigneur. You can secure this through your husband. Will you do it for me?"

"Of course," she whispered. She clung to him hungrily. "I'll speak to Moaris—tomorrow."

Chapter Six

At the end of the week Herndon visited the Avenue of Bronze and learned from Bollar Benjin that sales of the starstones proceeded well, that the arrangement under royal patronage was a happy one, and that they would soon be relieved of most of their stock. It would, therefore, be necessary for him to make another trip to Vyapore during the next several weeks. He agreed, but requested an advance of two months' salary.

"I don't see why not," Benjin agreed. "You're a valuable man, and we have the money to spare."

He handed over a draft for ten thousand stellors. Herndon thanked him gravely, promised to contact him when it was time for him to make the journey to Vyapore, and left.

That night he departed for Meld XVII where he sought out the surgeon who had altered his features after his flight from sacked Zonnigog. He requested certain internal modifications. The surgeon was reluctant, saying the operation was a risky one, very difficult, and entailed a fifty percent chance of total failure, but Herndon was stubborn.

It cost him twenty-five thousand stellors, nearly all the money he had, but he considered the investment a worthy one. He returned to Borlaam the next day. A week had elapsed since his departure.

He presented himself at Moaris Keep, resumed his duties, and once again spent the night with the Lady Moaris. She told him that she had wangled a promise from her husband and that he was soon to be invited to court. Moaris had not questioned her motives, and she said the invitation was a certainty.

Some days later a message was delivered to Barr Herndon of Zonnigog. It was in the hand of the private secretary to Moaris, and it said that the Lord Moaris had chosen to exert his patronage in favor of Barr Herndon and that Herndon would be expected to pay his respects to the Seigneur Krellig.

The invitation from the Seigneur came later in the day, borne by a resplendent Toppidan footman, commanding him to present himself at the court reception the following evening on pain of displeasing the Seigneur. Herndon exulted. Now he had attained the pinnacle of Borlaamese success; he was to be allowed into the presence of the sovereign. This was the culmination of all his planning.

He dressed in the court robes that he had purchased weeks before for just such an event—robes that had cost him more than a thousand stellors, sumptuous with inlaid precious gems and rare metals. He visited a tonsorial parlor and had an artificial beard affixed in the fashion of many courtiers who disliked growing beards but who desired to wear them at ceremonial state functions. He was bathed and combed, perfumed, and otherwise prepared for his debut at court. He also made certain that the surgical modifications performed on him by the Meldian doctor would be effective when the time came.

The shadows of evening dropped. The moons of Borlaam rose, dancing brightly across the sky. The evening fireworks display cast brilliant light through the winter sky, signifying that this was the birth month of Borlaam's Seigneur.

Herndon sent for the carriage he had hired. It arrived, a magnificent four-tube model bright with gilt paint, and he left his shabby dwelling place. The carriage soared into the night sky; twelve minutes later it descended in the courtyard of the Grand Palace of Borlaam, that monstrous heap of masonry that glowered down at the capital city from the impregnable vantage point of the Hill of Fire.

Floodlights illuminated the Grand Palace. Another man might have been stirred by the imposing sight; Herndon merely felt an upwelling of anger. Once his family had lived in a palace, too—not of this size, to be sure, for the people of Zonnigog were modest and unpretentious in their desires. But it had been a palace all the same until the armies of Krellig razed it.

He dismounted from his carriage and presented his invitation to the haughty Seigneurial guards on duty. They admitted him after checking to see that he carried no concealed weapons, and he was conducted to an antechamber in which he found the Lord Moaris.

"So you're Herndon," Moaris said speculatively. He squinted and tugged at his beard.

Herndon compelled himself to kneel. "I thank you for the honor your Grace bestows upon me this night."

"You needn't thank me," Moaris grunted. "My wife asked for your name to be put on my invitation list. But I suppose you know all that. You look familiar, Herndon. Where have I seen you before?"

Presumably Moaris knew that Herndon had been employed in his own service. But he merely said, "I once had the honor of bidding against you for a captive proteus in the slave market, milord."

A flicker of recognition crossed Moaris's seamed face, and he smiled coldly. "I seem to remember," he said.

A gong sounded.

"We mustn't keep the Seigneur waiting," said Moaris. "Come."

Together they went forward to the Grand Chamber of the Seigneur of Borlaam.

Moaris entered first, as befitted his rank, and took his place to the left of the monarch, who sat on a raised throne decked with violet and gold. Herndon knew protocol; he knelt immediately.

"Rise," the Seigneur commanded. His voice was a dry whisper, feathery-sounding, barely audible and yet commanding all the same. Herndon rose and stared levelly at Krellig.

The monarch was a tiny man, dried and fleshless; he seemed almost to be a humpback. Two beady, terrifying eyes glittered from a wrinkled, world-weary face. Krellig's lips were thin and bloodless, his nose a savage slash, his chin wedge-shaped.

Herndon let his eyes rove. The hall was huge, as he had expected; vast pillars supported the ceiling, and rows of courtiers flanked the walls. There were women, dozens of them: the Seigneur's mistresses, no doubt.

In the middle of the hall hung suspended something that looked to be a giant cage completely cloaked in thick draperies of red velvet. Some pet of the Seigneur's probably lurked within: a vicious pet, Herndon theorized, possibly a Villidonian gyrfalcon with honed talons.

"Welcome to the court," the Seigneur murmured.

"You are the guest of my friend Moaris, eh?"

"I am, sire," Herndon said. In the quietness of the hall his voice echoed cracklingly.

"Moaris is to provide us all with some amusement this evening," remarked the monarch. The little man chuckled in anticipatory glee. "We are very grateful to your sponsor, the Lord Moaris, for the pleasure he is to bring to us this night."

Herndon frowned. He wondered obscurely whether he was to be the source of amusement. He stood his ground unafraid; before the evening had ended, he himself would be amused at the expense of the others.

"Raise the curtain," Krellig commanded.

Instantly two Toppidan slaves emerged from the corners of the throne room and jerked simultaneously on heavy cords that controlled the curtain over the cage. Slowly the thick folds of velvet lifted, revealing, as Herndon had suspected, a cage.

There was a girl in the cage.

She hung suspended by her wrists from a bar mounted at the roof of the cage. She was naked; the bar revolved, turning her like an animal trussed to a spit. Herndon froze, not daring to move, staring in sudden astonishment at the slim, bare body dangling there.

It was a body he knew well.

The girl in the cage was the Lady Moaris.

Seigneur Krellig smiled benignly; he murmured in a gentle voice, "Moaris, the show is yours, and the audience awaits. Don't keep us waiting."

Moaris slowly moved toward the center of the ballroom floor. The marble under his feet was brightly polished and reflected him; his boots thundered as he walked.

He turned, facing Krellig, and said in a calm, controlled tone, "Ladies and gentlemen of the Seigneur's court, I beg leave to transact a little of my domestic business before your eyes. The lady in the cage, as most of you, I believe, are aware, is my wife."

A ripple of hastily hushed comment was emitted by the men and women of the court. Moaris gestured, and a spotlight flashed upward, illuminating the woman in the cage.

Herndon saw that her wrists were cruelly pinioned and that the blue veins stood out in sharp relief against her pale arms. She swung in a small circle as the bar above her turned in its endless rotation. Beads of sweat trickled down her back and stomach, and the harsh, sobbing intake of her breath was audible in the silence.

Moaris said casually, "My wife has been unfaithful to me. A trusted servant informed me of this not long ago: she has cheated me several times with no less a personage than an obscure member of our household, a groom or a lackey or some other person. When I questioned her, she did not deny this accusation. The Seigneur"—Moaris bowed in a throneward direction—"has granted me permission to chastise her here, to provide me with greater satisfaction and you with a moment of amusement."

Herndon did not move. He watched as Moaris drew from his sash a glittering little heat gun. Calmly the nobleman adjusted the aperture to minimum. He gestured; a side of the cage slid upward, giving him free target.

He lifted the heat gun.

Flick!

A bright tongue of flame licked out, and the girl in the cage uttered a little moan as a pencil-thin line was seared across her flanks.

Flick!

Again the beam played across her body. Flick! Again. Lines of pain were traced across her breasts, her throat, her knees, her back. She revolved helplessly as Moaris amused himself, carving line after line along her body with the heat ray. It was only with an effort that Herndon held still. The members of the court chuckled as the Lady Moaris writhed and danced in an effort to escape the inexorable lash of the beam.

Moaris was an expert. He sketched patterns on her body, always taking care that the heat never penetrated below the upper surface of the flesh. It was a form of torture that might endure for hours, until the blood bubbled in her veins and she died.

Herndon realized the Seigneur was peering at him. "Do you find this courtly amusement to your taste, Herndon?" Krellig asked.

"Not quite, sire." A hum of surprise rose that such a newcomer to the court should dare to contradict the Seigneur. "I would prefer a quicker death for the lady."

"And rob us of our sport?" Krellig asked.

"I would indeed do that," said Herndon. Suddenly he thrust open his jeweled cloak; the Seigneur cowered back as if he expected a weapon to come forth, but Herndon merely touched a plate in his chest, activating the device that the Meldian had implanted in his body. The neuronic mesh functioned in reverse; gathering a charge of deadly force, it sent the bolt surging along Herndon's hand. A bright arc of fire leaped from Herndon's pointing finger and surrounded the girl in the cage.

"Barr!" she screamed, breaking her silence at last, and died.

Again Herndon discharged the neuronic force, and Moaris, his hands singed, dropped his heat gun.

"Allow me to introduce myself," Herndon said as Krellig stared white-faced at him and the nobles of the court huddled together in fright. "I am Barr Herndon, son of the First Earl of Zonnigog. Somewhat over a year ago a courtier's jest roused you to lay waste to your fief of Zonnigog and put my family to the sword. I have not forgotten that day."

"Seize him!" Krellig shrieked.

"Anyone who touches me will be blasted with the fire," Herndon said. "Any weapon directed at me will recoil upon its owner. Hold your peace and let me finish.

"I am also Barr Herndon, Second Steward to Lord Moaris, and the lover of the woman who died before you. It must comfort you, Moaris, to know that the man who cuckolded you was no mere groom but a noble of Zonnigog.

"I am also," Herndon went on in the dead silence, "Barr Herndon the spacerogue, driven to take up a mercenary's trade by the destruction of my household. In that capacity I became a smuggler of starstones, and"—he bowed—"through an ironic twist, found myself owing a debt of fealty to none other than you, Seigneur.

"I hereby revoke that oath of fealty, Krellig—and for the crime of breaking an oath to my monarch, I sentence myself to death. But also, Krellig, I order a sentence of death upon your head for the wanton attack upon my homeland. And you, Moaris—for your cruel and barbaric treatment of this woman whom you never loved, you must die, too.

"And all of you—you onlookers and sycophants, you courtiers and parasites, you, too, must die. And you, the court clowns, the dancing bears and captive lifeforms of far worlds, I will kill you, too, as once I killed a slave proteus—not out of hatred but simply to spare you from further torment."

He paused. The hall was terribly silent; then someone to the right of the throne shouted, "He's crazy! Let's get out of here!"

He dashed for the great doors, which had been closed. Herndon let him get within ten feet of safety, then blasted him down with a discharge of life force. The mechanism within his body recharged itself, drawing its power from the hatred within him and discharging through his fingertips.

Herndon smiled at Lord Moaris, pale now. He said, "I'll be more generous to you than you to your Lady. A quick death for you."

He hurled a bolt of force at the nobleman. Moaris recoiled, but there was no hiding possible; he stood bathed in light for a moment, and then the charred husk dropped to the ground.

A second bolt raked the crowd of courtiers. A third Herndon aimed at the throne; the costly hangings of the throne area caught first, and Krellig half-rose before the bolt of force caught him and hurled him back dead.

Herndon stood alone in the middle of the floor. His quest was at its end; he had achieved his vengeance. All but the last: on himself, for having broken the oath he had involuntarily sworn to the Seigneur.

Life held no further meaning for him. It was odious to consider returning to a spacerogue's career, and only death offered absolution from his oaths.

He directed a blazing beam of force at one of the great pillars that supported the throne room's ceiling. It blackened, then buckled. He blasted apart another of the pillars, and the third.

The roof groaned; after hundreds of years the tons of masonry were suddenly without support. Herndon waited, then smiled in triumph as the ceiling hurtled down at him.

THERE WAS AN OLD WOMAN

Originally published in *Infinity Science Fiction*, November 1958.

Since I was raised from earliest infancy to undertake the historian's calling, and since it is now certain that I shall never claim that profession as my own, it seems fitting that I perform my first and last act as a historian.

I shall write the history of that strange and unique woman, the mother of my thirty brothers and myself, Miss Donna Mitchell.

She was a person of extraordinary strength and vision, our mother. I remember her vividly, seeing her with all her sons gathered round her in our secluded Wisconsin farmhouse on the first night of summer, after we had returned to her from every part of the country for our summer's vacation. One-and-thirty strapping sons, each one of us six feet one inch tall, with a shock of unruly yellow hair and keen, clear blue eyes, each one of us healthy, strong, well nourished, each one of us twenty-one years and fourteen days old—one-and-thirty identical brothers.

Oh, there were differences between us, but only we and she could perceive them. To outsiders, we were identical; which was why, to outsiders, we took care never to appear together in groups. We ourselves knew the differences, for we had lived with them so long.

I knew my brother Leonard's cheekmole—the right cheek it was, setting him off from Jonas, whose left cheek was marked with a flyspeck. I knew the faint tilt of Peter's chin, the slight oversharpness of Dewey's nose, the florid tint of Donald's skin. I recognized Paul by his pendulous earlobes, Charles by his squint, Noel by the puckering of his lower lip. David had a blue-stubbled face, Mark flaring nostrils, Claude thick brows.

Yes, there were differences. We rarely confused one with another. It was second nature for me to distinguish Edward from Albert, George from Philip, Frederick from Stephen. And Mother never confused us.

She was a regal woman, nearly six feet in height, who even in middle age had retained straightness of posture and majesty of bearing. Her eyes, like ours, were blue; her hair, she told us, had once been golden like ours. Her voice was a deep, mellow contralto; rich, firm, commanding, the voice of a strong woman. She had been professor of biochemistry at some Eastern university (she never told us which one, hating its name so) and we all knew by heart the story of her bitter life and of our own strange birth.

"I had a theory," she would say. "It wasn't an orthodox theory, and it made people angry to think about it, so of course they threw me out. But I didn't care. In many ways that was the most fortunate day of my life."

"Tell us about it, Mother," Philip would invariably ask. He was destined to be a playwright; he enjoyed the repetition of the story whenever we were together.

She said:

"I had a theory. I believed that environment controlled personality, that given the same set of healthy genes any number of different adults could be shaped from the raw material. I had a plan for testing it—but when I told them, they discharged me. Luckily, I had married a wealthy if superficial-minded executive, who had suffered a fatal coronary attack the year before. I was independently wealthy, thanks to him, and free to pursue independent research, thanks to my university discharge. So I came to Wisconsin and began my great project."

We knew the rest of the story by heart, as a sort of litany.

We knew how she had bought a huge, rambling farm in the flat green country of central Wisconsin, a farm far from prying eyes. Then, how on a hot summer afternoon she had gone forth to the farm land nearby, and found a field hand, tall and brawny, and to his great surprise seduced him in the field where he worked.

And then the story of that single miraculous zygote, which our mother had extracted from her body and carefully nurtured in special nutrient tanks, irradiating it and freezing it and irritating it and dosing it with hormones until, exasperated, it subdivided into thirty-two, each one of which developed independently into a complete embryo.

Embryo grew into foetus, and foetus into child, in Mother's ingenious artificial wombs. One of the thirty-two died before birth of accidental narcosis; the remainder survived, thirty-one identical males sprung from the same egg, to become us.

With the formidable energy that typified her, Mother singlehandedly nursed thirty-one baby boys; we thrived, we grew. And then the most crucial stage of the experiment began. We were differentiated at the age of eighteen months, each given his own room, his own particular toys, his own special books later on. Each of us was slated for a different profession. It was the ultimate proof of her theory. Genetically identical, physically identical except for the minor changes time had worked on our individual bodies, we would nevertheless seek out different fields of employment.

She worked out the assignments at random, she said. Philip was to be a playwright, Noel a novelist, Donald a doctor. Astronomy was Allan's goal, Barry's, biology, Albert's the stage. George was to be a concert pianist, Claude a composer, Leonard a member of the bar, Dewey a dentist. Mark was to be an athlete; David, a diplomat. Journalism waited for Jonas, poetry for Peter, painting for Paul.

Edward would become an engineer, Saul a soldier, Charles a statesman; Stephen would go to sea. Martin was aimed for chemistry, Raymond for physics, James for high finance. Ronald would be a librarian, Robert a bookkeeper, John a priest, Douglas a teacher. Anthony was to be a literary critic, William an architect, Frederick an airplane pilot. For Richard was reserved a life of crime; as for myself, Harold, I was to devote my energies to the study and writing of history.

This was my mother's plan. Let me tell of my own childhood and adolescence, to illustrate its workings.

* * * *

My first recollections are of books. I had a room on the second floor of our big house. Martin's room was to my left, and in later years I would regret it, for the air was always heavy with the stink of his chemical experiments. To my right was Noel, whose precocious typewriter sometimes pounded all night as he worked on his endless first novel.

But those manifestations came later. I remember waking one morning to find that during the night a bookcase had been placed in my room, and in it a single book—Hendrik Willem van Loon's *The Story of Mankind*. I was four, almost five, then; thanks to Mother's intensive training we were all capable readers by that age, and I puzzled over the big type, learning of the exploits of Charlemagne and Richard the Lionhearted and staring at the squiggly scratches that were van Loon's illustrations.

Other books followed, in years to come. H. G. Wells's *Outline of History*, which fascinated and repelled me at the same time. Toynbee, in the Somervell abridgement, and later, when I had entered adolescence, the complete and unabridged edition. Churchill, and his flowing periods and ringing prose. Sandburg's poetic and massive life of Lincoln; Wedgwood on the Thirty Years' War; Will Durant, in six or seven blocklike volumes.

I read these books, and where I did not understand I read on anyway, knowing I would come back to that page in some year to come and bring new understanding to it. Mother helped, and guided, and chivvied. A sense of the panorama of man's vast achievement sprang up in me. To join the roll of mankind's chroniclers seemed the only possible end for my existence.

Each summer from my fourteenth to my seventeenth, I traveled—alone, of course, since Mother wanted to build self-reliance in us. I visited the great historical places of the United States: Washington, DC, Mount Vernon, Williamsburg, Bull Run, Gettysburg. A sense of the past rose in me.

Those summers were my only opportunities for contact with strangers, since during the year and especially during the long snowbound winters we stayed on the farm, a tight family unit. We never went to public school; obviously, it was impossible to enroll us, en masse, without arousing the curiosity my mother wished to avoid.

Instead, she tutored us privately, giving us care and attention that no professional teacher could possibly have supplied. And we grew older, diverging towards our professions like branching limbs of a tree.

As a future historian, of course, I took it upon myself to observe the changes in my own society, which was bounded by the acreage of our farm. I made notes on the progress of my brothers, keeping my notebooks well hidden, and also on the changes time was working on Mother. She stood up surprisingly well, considering the astonishing burden she had taken upon herself. Formidable was the best word to use in describing her.

We grew into adolescence. By this time Martin had an imposing chemical laboratory in his room; Leonard harangued us all on legal fine points, and Anthony pored over Proust and Kafka, delivering startling critical interpretations. Our house was a beehive of industry constantly, and I don't remember being bored for more than three consecutive seconds, at any time. There were always distractions: Claude and George jostling for room on the piano bench while they played Claude's four-hand sonata, Mark hurling a baseball through a front window, Peter declaiming a sequence of shocking sonnets during our communal dinner.

We fought, of course, since we were healthy individualists with sound bodies. Mother encouraged it; Saturday afternoon was wrestling time, and we pitted our growing strengths against one another.

Mother was always the dominant figure, striding tall and erect around the farm, calling to us in her familiar boom, assigning us chores, meeting with us privately. Somehow she had the knack of making each of us think we were the favorite child, the one in whose future she was most deeply interested of all. It was false, of course; though once Jonas unkindly asserted that Barry must be her real favorite, because he, like her, was a biologist.

I doubted it. I had learned much about people through my constant reading, and I knew that Mother was something extraordinary—a fanatic, if you like, or merely a woman driven by an inner demon, but still and all a person of overwhelming intellectual drive and conviction, whose will to know the truth had led her to undertake this fantastic experiment in biology and human breeding.

I knew that no woman of that sort could stoop to petty favoritism. Mother was unique. Perhaps, had she been born a man, she would have changed the entire course of human development.

When we were seventeen, she called us all together round the big table in the common room of our rambling home. She waited, needing to clear her throat only once in order to cut the hum of conversation.

"Sons," she said, and the echo rang through the entire first floor of the house. "Sons, the time has come for you to leave the farm."

We were stunned, even those of us who were expecting it. But she explained, and we understood, and we did not quarrel.

One could not become a doctor or a chemist or a novelist or even a historian in a total vacuum. One had to enter the world. And one needed certain professional qualifications.

We were going to college.

Not all of us, of course. Robert was to be a bookkeeper; he would go to business school. Mark had developed, through years of practice, into a superb right-handed pitcher, and he was to go to Milwaukee for a major-league tryout. Claude and George, aspiring composer and aspiring pianist, would attend an Eastern conservatory together, posing as twins.

The rest of us were to attend colleges, and those who were to go on to professions such as medicine or chemistry would plan to attend professional schools afterwards. Mother believed a college education was essential, even to a poet or a painter or a novelist.

Only one of us was not sent to any accredited institution. He was Richard, who was to be our criminal. Already he had made several sallies into the surrounding towns and cities, returning a few days or a few weeks later with money or jewels and with a guilty grin on his face. He was simply to be turned loose into the school of Life, and Mother warned him never to get caught.

As for me, I was sent to Princeton and enrolled as a liberal-arts student. Since, like my brothers, I was privately educated, I had no diplomas or similar records to show them, and they had to give me an equivalency examination in their place. Evidently I did quite well, for I was immediately accepted. I wired Mother, who sent a check for $3,000 to cover my first year's tuition and expenses.

I enrolled as a history major; among my first-year courses were Medieval English Constitutional History and the Survey of Western Historical Currents; naturally, my marks were the highest in the class in both cases. I worked diligently and even with a sort of frenzied fury. My other courses, in the sciences or in the arts, I devoted no more nor no less time to than was necessary, but history was my ruling passion.

At least, through my first two semesters of college.

June came, and final exams, and then I returned to Wisconsin, where Mother was waiting. It was 21 June when I returned; since not all colleges end their spring semester simultaneously, some of my brothers had been home for more than a week, others had not yet arrived. Richard had sent word that he was in Los Angeles, and would be with us after the first of July. Mark had signed a baseball contract and was pitching for a team in New Mexico, and he, too, would not be with us.

The summer passed rapidly.

We spent it as we had in the old days before college, sharing our individual specialities, talking, meeting regularly and privately with Mother to discuss the goals that still lay ahead. Except for Claude and George, we had scattered in different directions, no two of us at the same school.

I returned to Princeton that fall for my sophomore year. It passed, and I made the homeward journey again, and in the fall traveled once more eastward. The junior year went by likewise.

And I began to detect signs of a curious change in my inward self. It was a change I did not dare mention to Mother on those July days when I met with her in her room near the library. I did not tell my brothers, either. I kept my knowledge to myself, brooding over it, wondering why it was that this thing should happen to me, why I should be singled out.

For I was discovering that the study of history bored me utterly and completely.

The spirit of rebellion grew in me during my final year in college. My marks had been excellent; I had achieved Phi Beta Kappa and several graduate schools were interested in having me continue my studies with them. But I had been speaking to a few chosen friends (none of whom knew my bizarre family background, of course) and my values had been slowly shifting.

I realized that I had mined history as deeply as I ever cared to. Waking and sleeping, for more than fifteen years, I had pondered Waterloo and Bunker Hill, considered the personalities of Cromwell and James II, held imaginary conversations with Jefferson and Augustus Caesar and Charles Martel. And I was bored with it.

It began to become evident to others, eventually. One day during my final semester a friend asked me, "Is there something worrying you, Harry?"

I shook my head quickly—too quickly. "No," I said. "Why? Do I look worried?"

"You look worse than worried. You look obsessed."

We laughed about it, and finally we went down to the student center and had a few beers, and before long my tongue had loosened a little.

I said, "There *is* something worrying me. And you know what it is? I'm afraid I won't live up to the standards my family set for me."

Guffaws greeted me. "Come off it, Harry! Phi Beta in your junior year, top class standing, a brilliant career in history ahead of you—what do they want from you, blood?"

I chuckled and gulped my beer and mumbled something innocuous, but inside I was curdling.

Everything I was, I owed to Mother. She made me what I am. But I was played out as a student of history; I was the family failure, the goat, the rotten egg. Raymond still wrestled gleefully with nuclear physics, with Heisenberg and Schrödinger and the others. Mark gloried in his fast ball and his slider and his curve. Paul daubed canvas merrily in his Greenwich Village flat near NYU, and even Robert seemed to take delight in keeping books.

Only I had failed. History had become repugnant to me. I was in rebellion against it. I would disappoint my mother, become the butt of my brothers' scorn, and live in despair, hating the profession of historian and fitted by training for nothing else.

I was graduated from Princeton summa cum laude, a few days after my twenty-first birthday. I wired Mother that I was on my way home, and bought train tickets.

It was a long and grueling journey to Wisconsin. I spent my time thinking, trying to choose between the unpleasant alternatives that faced me.

I could attempt duplicity, telling my mother I was still studying history, while actually preparing myself for some more attractive profession—the law, perhaps.

I could confess to her at once my failure of purpose, ask her forgiveness for disappointing her and flawing her grand scheme, and try to begin afresh in another field.

Or I could forge ahead with history, compelling myself grimly to take an interest, cramping and paining myself so that my mother's design would be complete.

None of them seemed desirable paths to take. I brooded over it, and was weary and apprehensive by the time I arrived at our farm.

The first of my brothers I saw was Mark. He sat on the front porch of the big house, reading a book which I recognized at once and with some surprise as Volume I of Churchill. He looked up at me and smiled feebly.

I frowned. "I didn't expect to find *you* here, Mark. According to the local sports pages the Braves are playing on the Coast this week. How come you're not with them?"

His voice was a low murmur. "Because they gave me my release," he said.

"What?"

He nodded. "I'm washed up at twenty-one. They made me a free agent; that means I can hook up with any team that wants me."

"And you're just taking a little rest before offering yourself around?"

He shook his head. "I'm through. Kaput. Harry, I just can't stand baseball. It's a silly, stupid game. You know how many times I had to stand out there in baggy knickers and throw a bit of horsehide at some jerk with a club in his paws? A hundred, hundred-fifty times a game, every four days. For what? What the hell does it all mean? Why should I bother?"

There was a strange gleam in his eyes. I said, "Have you told Mother?"

"I don't dare! She thinks I'm on leave or something. Harry, how can I tell her—"

"I know." Briefly, I told him of my own disenchantment with history. We were mutually delighted to learn that we were not alone in our affliction. I picked up my suitcases, scrambled up the steps, and went inside.

Dewey was cleaning up the common room as I passed through. He nodded hello glumly. I said, "How's the tooth trade?"

He whirled and glared at me viciously.

"Something wrong?" I asked.

"I've been accepted by four dental schools, Harry."

"Is that any cause for misery?"

He let the broom drop, walked over to me, and whispered, "I'll murder you if you tell Mother this. But the thought of spending my life poking around in foul-smelling oral cavities sickens me. Sickens."

"But I thought—"

"Yeah. You thought. You've got it soft; you just need to dig books out of the library and rearrange what they say and call it new research. I have to drill and clean and fill and plug and—" He stopped. "Harry, I'll kill you if you breathe a word of this. I don't want Mother to know that I didn't come out the way she wanted."

I repeated what I had said to Mark—and told him about Mark, for good measure. Then I made my way upstairs to my old room. I felt a burden lifting from me; I was not alone. At least two of my brothers felt the same way. I wondered how many more were at last rebelling against the disciplines of a lifetime.

Poor Mother, I thought! Poor Mother!

Our first family council of the summer was held that night. Stephen and Saul were the last to arrive, Stephen resplendent in his Annapolis garb, Saul crisp looking and stiff-backed from West Point. Mother had worked hard to wangle appointments for those two.

We sat around the big table and chatted. The first phase of our lives, Mother told us, had ended. Now, our preliminary educations were complete, and we would undertake the final step towards our professions—those of us who had not already entered them.

Mother looked radiant that evening, tall, energetic, her white hair cropped mannishly short, as she sat about the table with her thirty-one strapping sons. I envied and pitied her: envied her for the sweet serenity of her life, which had proceeded so inexorably and without swerving towards the goal of her experiment, and pitied her for the disillusioning that awaited her.

For Mark and Dewey and I were not the only failures in the crop.

I had made discreet inquiries during the day. I learned that Anthony found literary criticism to be a fraud and a sham, that Paul knew clearly he had no talent as a painter (and, also, that very few of his contemporaries did either), that Robert bitterly resented a career of bookkeeping, that piano playing hurt George's fingers, that Claude had had difficulty with his composing because he was tone deaf, that the journalistic grind was too strenuous for Jonas, that John longed to quit the seminarial life because he had no calling, that Albert hated the uncertain Bohemianism of an actor's life—

We circulated, all of us raising for the first time the question that had sprouted in our minds during the past several years. I made the astonishing discovery that not one of Donna Mitchell's sons cared for the career that had been chosen for him.

The experiment had been a resounding flop.

Late that evening, after Mother had gone to bed, we remained together, discussing our predicament. How could we tell her? How could we destroy her life's work? And yet, how could we compel ourselves to lives of unending drudgery?

Robert wanted to study engineering; Barry, to write. I realized I cared much more for law than for history, while Leonard longed to exchange law for the physical sciences. James, our banker-manque, much preferred politics. And so it went, with Richard (who claimed five robberies, a rape, and innumerable picked pockets) pouring out his desire to settle down and live within the law as an honest farmer.

It was pathetic.

Summing up the problem in his neat forensic way, Leonard said,

"Here's our dilemma: Do we all keep quiet about this and ruin our lives, or do we speak up and ruin Mother's experiment?"

"I think we ought to continue as is, for the time being," Saul said. "Perhaps Mother will die in the next year or two. We can start over then."

"Perhaps she *doesn't* die?" Edward wanted to know. "She's tough as nails. She may last another twenty or thirty or even forty years."

"And we're past twenty-one already," remarked Raymond. "If we hang on too long at what we're doing, it'll be too late to change. You can't start studying for a new profession when you're thirty-five."

"Maybe we'll get to *like* what we're doing by then," suggested David hopefully. "Diplomatic service isn't as bad as all that, and I'd say—"

"What about me?" Paul yelped. "I can't paint and I know I can't paint. I've got nothing but starvation ahead of me unless I wise up and get into business in a hurry. You want me to keep messing up good white canvas the rest of my life?"

"It won't work," said Barry in a doleful voice. "We'll have to tell her."

Douglas shook his head. "We can't do that. You know just what she'll do. She'll bring down the umpteen volumes of notes she's made on this experiment, and ask us if we're going to let it all come to naught."

"He's right," Albert said. "I can picture the scene now. The big organ-pipe voice blasting us for our lack of faith, the accusations of ingratitude—"

"Ingratitude?" William shouted. "She twisted us and pushed us and molded us without asking our permission. Hell, she *created* us with her laboratory tricks. But that didn't give her the right to make zombies out of us."

"Still," Martin said, "we can't just go to her and tell her that it's all over. The shock would kill her.

"Well?" Richard asked in the silence that followed. "What's wrong with that?"

For a moment, no one spoke. The house was quiet; we heard footsteps descending the stairs. We froze.

Mother appeared, an imperial figure even in her old housecoat. "You boys are kicking up too much of a racket down here," she boomed. "I know you're glad to see each other again after a year, but I need my sleep."

She turned and strode upstairs again. We heard her bedroom door slam shut. For an instant we were all ten-year-olds again, diligently studying our books for fear of Mother's displeasure.

I moistened my lips. "Well?" I asked. "I call for a vote on Richard's suggestion."

Martin, as a chemist, prepared the drink, using Donald's medical advice as his guide. Saul, Stephen, and Raymond dug a grave, in the woods at the back of our property. Douglas and Mark built the coffin.

Richard, ending his criminal career with a murder to which we were all accessories before the fact, carried the fatal beverage upstairs to Mother the next morning, and persuaded her to sip it. One sip was all that was necessary; Martin had done his work well.

Leonard offered us a legal opinion: It was justifiable homicide. We placed the body in its coffin and carried it out across the fields. Richard, Peter, Jonas and Charles were her pallbearers; the others of us followed in their path.

We lowered the body into the ground and John said a few words over her. Then, slowly, we closed over the grave and replaced the sod, and began the walk back to the house.

"She died happy," Anthony said. "She never suspected the size of her failure." It was her epitaph.

As our banker, James supervised the division of her assets, which were considerable, into thirty-one equal parts. Noel composed a short figment of prose which we agreed summed up our sentiments.

We left the farm that night, scattering in every direction, anxious to begin life. All that went before was a dream from which we now awakened. We agreed to meet at the farm each year, on the anniversary of her death, in memory of the woman who had so painstakingly divided a zygote into thirty-two viable cells, and who had spent a score of years conducting an experiment based on a theory that had proved to be utterly false.

We felt no regret, no qualm. We had done what needed to be done, and on that last day some of us had finally functioned in the professions for which Mother had intended us.

I, too. My first and last work of history will be this, an account of Mother and her experiment, which records the beginning and the end of her work. And now it is complete.

THE WOMAN YOU WANTED

Originally published in *Future Science Fiction*, April 1958.

The offices of the Interstellar Survey Commission were on Greek Street, just off Soho Square. The day that Bradmire decided to sign up for a Commission post was a warm, almost muggy one—unusual for London in late August—and he felt strangely clammy as he left his Bayswater flat and waited opposite Hyde Park for the Number Seventeen bus.

He thought of all he was giving up. Not much, was it, really? A handful of friends, all of them at loose ends much like himself. Books—well, he could take some with him.

Music—that, too. No more concerts at dear shabby old Royal Festival Hall, but he could take musicdisks with him on the trip. The Commission were *very* good to the young men who signed up. The eight-year tour of duty was worth fifteen thousand quid, tax-free; that was good pay, all things considered, and the work was fascinating.

A lot better than living in an archaic London flat and scribbling poetry. A lot better than spending afternoons in the British Museum and evenings writing critical essays for ephemeral little magazines. Bradmire was slowly coming to the realization that the London literary life was not for him. In the Cambridge days, it had been fine to look forward to London—but now he was here, and it was merely hollow and irritating to him.

So he would go to space. He would become a planet-rover and record data as a minion of the Survey Commission, and perhaps when he returned he would write a best-seller and live in peace and plenty in some Cornwall town.

They would make a fuss over him as he signed the contract. Others had told him how it was. They gave you a fistful of pound notes and told you to go out and enjoy yourself for a week; they clucked over you as they found out what you would want by way of comforts on the trip; and they psych-tested you for your android companion—

Who would be the woman of his dreams. The tests were infallible; they always gave you the woman you wanted, synthetic of course, to aid you in stability-maintenance during the long trip. Bradmire was slightly doubtful about making love to an android, but one of his more decadent friends had already tried it and said it was almost like the real thing—and after a while, no doubt, you wouldn't be able to tell the difference.

He wondered. There was a grim, almost fatalistic smile on his face as he spied the Number Seventeen bus topping the rise in the hill. Low-slung, a humming teardrop, it came toward him and stopped as he waved his hand at it. He clambered aboard.

"Wardour Street," he told the robot-conductor.

"Sixpence," said the blank-faced metal being.

Bradmire dropped one of the shiny little copper coins into the slot, entered the passenger section of the bus, and tumbled into his seat. The bus sped along down Bayswater Road toward Marble Arch, and thence into the archaic hodgepodge that was London's West End.

He examined his money. Two copper sixpences, one of the old silver kind; a florin; a pair of pennies, and a bright gold guinea. Twenty-four shillings and eightpence, of which one of the pennies—the battered old large-size Charles III piece—was his good-luck coin, and therefore unspendable. It wasn't very much cash at all. And there wouldn't be any money forthcoming from the publishers for at least a week, by which time he would be very hungry indeed.

His back was to the wall. He had no choice but to sign up.

Let Marian and John and Kenneth and the others chide him for selling out, he thought doggedly. Let them. He was tired of bohemianism—and with all of the universe waiting to be explored, it was hopelessly provincial to remain in London.

He got off the bus at Wardour and walked east along Oxford Street, turning south and taking a twisting route through Dean onto Greek Street. The Commission building was one of the new ones, tall and gleaming, fronted with glossy plastic, that had been erected in Soho in the last decade; the architect had inscribed a glittering gold "2129" on the facade for the benefit of future historians.

Bradmire fingered the card in his pocket. It bore the name of Sir Adrian Laurence, Recruiting Chairman, Suite 1100. He moistened his lips nervously.

The double doors swung open at his approach. A robot waited inside, seven feet tall and mirror-bright. Bradmire felt unutterably shabby. He straightened his tattered frock coat and said, "Suite 1100, please."

Of course, the robot's expression did not change, but it seemed to Bradmire that it had smiled condescendingly as it said, in suave Oxford tones, "Naturally, sir. The grav tube on your left."

"T-thank you," Bradmire stammered. He had never been sure whether robots were entitled to politeness.

He stepped into the grav tube and drifted upward to the eleventh floor; there he was deposited in a shining corridor. A vast door loomed above, with an immense 1100 inscribed on it. Bradmire went forward.

The door rolled back when he was within a foot of it, and he found himself confronted by a blonde receptionist of quite unnerving proportions. He wondered whether she, too, were an android.

"May I help you?" she asked sweetly.

"I'm—looking for Sir Adrian Laurence," he blurted. "I want to sign up. I mean…"

"I understand," she said, and it seemed to Bradmire that she did. "Come this way, please?"

She led him down a brightly-lit foyer. He followed, studying her construction avidly, and deciding that if she were a sample of Commission androids he wouldn't object to getting one.

"May I have your name, please?" she asked as they reached a broad oak door.

"Bradmire. David H. K. Bradmire."

She inclined her head toward a minute speaker-grid set into the rich oak and said, "Mr. David Bradmire to see you, Sir Adrian."

The door opened. Bradmire stared at a man of his own height, fiftyish, with a baronet's yellow wig and a strikingly modern blue-and-red dress suit. "Won't you come in, Mr. Bradmire?"

The office was furnished in the best of taste. Bradmire took a seat in a quivering web hammock facing Sir Adrian's desk and said, "You know why I'm here, of course. I want to sign up for a Commission post."

"Excellent! Drink?"

Bradmire accepted a cognac and a cigar as if he were fully accustomed to such luxuries before noon every day. He leaned back comfortably. He felt fully at ease, now, with no lingering doubts.

"What is your profession, Mr. Bradmire?"

Bradmire grinned. "I'm a poet and essayist, Sir Adrian. Came down from Cambridge in '29. Average income, 2129-2132, three hundred fifty pounds per annum. So I'm throwing in the towel."

Sir Adrian's face darkened. "You know that's not really so, of course. You aren't giving up your ambitions. You're merely—shall we say—*postponing* them until you're more mature. How old are you?"

"Twenty-six."

"Ah. You'll return from the stars at age thirty-four, still a young man in today's world. You'll be wealthy—fifteen thousand pounds, plus accrued interest. You'll have a vast store of experience; you'll have seen dozens of bizarre alien worlds, gone places and done things few of your poetic contemporaries have done. And you'll have the comforting knowledge that you have done something valuable for society. Then you'll be able to create, David! You'll have something to say to humanity—and humanity will listen, and reward you!"

Bradmire admitted to himself that Sir Adrian made it sound remarkably attractive—desirable, in fact. Not at all the hopeless last-resort gesture he had seen it as. He felt adrenalin surging through his body.

He said, "I'm roughly familiar with the terms, but would you run through them again...?"

"Of course." Sir Adrian knotted his hands together, smiling. "You sign on for an eight-year term, of which the first three months is spent in preliminary instruction. We supply you with a small two-person scoutship which is equipped with an automatic course computer. There'll be nothing for you to do but wander from star to star and beam reports to us on planetary systems, possible life forms, and so forth. We need thousands of men to do this work, which is why the terms are so attractive.

"Your pay is fifteen thousand pounds, placed on deposit for you at Lloyd's and collectible on the day of your return. It's tax-free. You'll also be supplied with whatever books, musicdisks, or other recreational equipment you desire." He paused. "And also, our laboratories will furnish you with a female android companion who will be as close to your desired specifications as modern science can manage."

"It has to be an android, sir? I mean, I couldn't take any human girl I happened to know..."

Theoretically, you could, of course. But the requirement is that she must come within .0001 of your subconscious specifications, and we find in practical application that such women are *extremely* rare. But the manufactured synthetics are—ah—highly desirable, and fully human in all but their origin."

"Suppose I—don't want any companion. What if I want to go it alone?"

"Impossible, I'm afraid. Our ships are expensive, and we can't take the risk of losing any. Solitaries are inherently unstable. The sort of man we want is mentally alert, gregarious, well-balanced, and—ahem—normally heterosexual. It's been our experience that other types don't provide satisfactory performances."

Bradmire chuckled. "I don't know how well-balanced I am, but I can testify to the heterosexual part."

"I hope so. If you accede to our terms, we can test you in a matter of seconds to judge your suitability. Another drink?"

"Don't mind if I do," Bradmire said.

* * * *

Three hours later, and quite some miles away, Bradmire finished what he had to say with, "...so I signed up." It was early in the afternoon; he sat in The Kenya, one of London's cozy old espresso-houses, in South Kensington near Exhibition Road. He sipped his cappuccino and smiled at the little group of friends around the table.

"And they gave you fifty pounds expense money?" John Ryson asked incredulously. He was a slim, pale lad, down from Cambridge like Bradmire, who had been working intermittently on an immense narrative poem for the past four years. "Fifty pounds just to throw away in a week?"

"You saw the notes," Bradmire said. "Ten crisp little green fivers. Ten pretty little portraits of Queen Diane." He scooped three gold guinea coins from his pockets and stacked them on the table. They represented change from his first purchase, a box of cigars for his friends. He tapped the gleaming profile of Henry X and grinned in cheerful commerciality. "I hope you'll pardon this rather vulgar display on my part, chums. But it's been years since I last had three of these little things all at the same time, and I feel like crowing about it."

"Fifteen thousand when you get back," Bert Selfridge muttered. He was thirty-two, going prematurely gray, with a sharp little beard. He taught Remedial Grammar at University College. "A fortune! And for what? Chasing around from star to star, looking for little green men."

"Jealous, Burt? Why don't you sign up, then? Surely what I'll be doing is just as valuable to humanity as teaching the rudiments of our language to a bunch of rebellious would-be chemists and engineers."

"Aren't you giving up too much, though?" Ryson wanted to know. "Eight solid years..."

"But there's no reason why I can't write during that time. And I'll have no room and board problems, and no yammering landladies or squalling back-alley tomcats. And the company of my perfect woman."

"Perfection can get tiresome," Selfridge said half to his beard.

"Have you tried it?" Bradmire retorted.

"When are you leaving, David?" asked Marian Hawkes.

Bradmire glanced across the table at her. She was a quiet girl with a deep, soft, easy-to-listen to voice—but she rarely spoke. She was either terribly shy or terribly arrogant, Bradmire had decided earlier; either way, the effect was the same.

"At the end of this week," he said. "I passed the first battery of psychological tests this afternoon. All they do is strap a funny hat on your head and throw a switch, and *bzzz!* A meter ticks, and you're either in or out. I was okayed."

"What are the qualifications?" Marian asked.

"Not very much," Bradmire told her. "Good health, sound mental outlook, general stability. And heterosexuality."

"They didn't have to test you for that," Tyson said. "We could have given them affidavits for you."

Bradmire chuckled. He had always had a reputation as a ladies' man—and, as is usually true in such cases, the reputation was far in excess of actuality, through little fault of his own. "They insisted on doing it their way." He smiled. "In two days I go back to—ah—get fitted for my android light-o'love. At the end of the week, it's off to indoctrination camp in Scotland for three months, and then into the great beyond. Eight years from now I return, rich, muscular, space-bronzed."

"And we can come to you for loans," Selfridge said. "You won't forget your poor old arty friends."

"Not if they're still arty and hungry," Bradmire said. "But I suspect I won't find any of you here when I get back. You'll all have taken the same route I did."

"All except Marian," said Ryson. "She isn't eligible? Or is she?"

Bradmire shook his head, grinning. "Women aren't wanted for this job. Men only—with a plastoprotein girlfriend built to specs."

He rose and glanced at his watch. The time was 1400.

"Gentlemen—and lady—I'm tired of drinking coffee, and no doubt so are you. I move we adjourn next door to the George and Dragon. We've got an hour till closing time—and the drinks are on me!"

* * * *

He woke with quite a head the next morning, but he had invested half-a-crown in some anti-hangover tablets; and after he popped one of the little green lozenges back of his tongue he felt much better about things. He depolarized his window and stared out. The sun—*imagine it,* he thought, *the sun shining in London!*—poured through the opening. The streets were damp, though; it had been raining. He wondered whether they would ever manage to get London's weather under control, the way they had done in—say, New York. Probably not. But it would be nice to come home, eight years hence, to a London in which the damnable rain fell on a neat predictable schedule that could be published in advance each day in the *Times*.

He donned his clothes and fumbled through his pockets for his cash. He found four crumpled five-pound notes and a handful of guinea pieces and small change—all that was left out of his fifty quid expense-money. He realized he had spent as much last night as he had in the whole last month, practically.

* * * *

Books littered the room, and some new musicdisks, and a few empty wine-bottles. He saw that at some time during the previous day he had acquired a new cravat—*whatever for,* he wondered, *where I'm going?*—and that he had stained his clothes with what might have been spilled champagne.

Well, the Commission had intended him to have a good time, and he had certainly succeeded. He had scattered the shillings like a new Maecenas; and though he scarcely remembered what had happened, he imagined it must have been a grand night for all. John had been there, and Art, and Kenneth, and Marian Hawkes, and that other little slip of a girl with the improbable figure, and two or three others. The word had gone round London that Bradmire had had a windfall, and all his friends had gathered round to join in the fun.

He remembered arguing Yeats versus Synge bitterly with a verse playwright named Buxton; he remembered swilling barley wine with a blubbery Celtic bard from Glasgow—or was it Dublin? And he remembered kissing someone under a table; Marian Hawkes, maybe, or else that girl Joanne. Well, it didn't matter which one, or why. Come the end of the week, nothing much of his past life would matter at all.

He picked up a book, neat and bright in its jacket. A poetry anthology, thick and costly; he'd coveted it a long while, and now it was his—just for putting his name on a paper that promised away his next eight years. Someone had spilled a little champagne on the book, too. That was too bad, but in a way he liked the idea of having some tangible souvenir of last night's celebration.

The phone rang. He snatched it off the hook before it had rung twice, and said, "Bradmire here."

"David, this is Sir Adrian Laurence. Of the Survey Commission, you know."

"I haven't forgotten, sir."

"Good. I trust you've been enjoying yourself since yesterday morning?"

"Very much so," Bradmire said, grinning. "It's a long time since I've had fifty quid all in one lump."

"Poverty's a thing of the past as far as you're concerned, son. But I wanted to remind you: you have an appointment with us tomorrow at noon. To select your companion, you remember."

"I haven't forgotten *that* either," Bradmire said. "Do I report at your office?"

"That won't be necessary. Room 707's the place to go. I'll be waiting for you there."

* * **

It *had* been Marian Hawkes he had kissed, and not the other girl, after all.

He found that out that evening, when the group assembled in a pub near Clerkenwell Road and Hatton Garden, and then wandered westward toward the Bloomsbury flat of publisher's assistant Kenneth Prior. By that time there were seven or eight in the group, and Bradmire—who was happily down to two guineas by this time—found himself walking along Theobalds Road with Marian.

"Do you still think Yeats' plays were all that good?" she asked. "Or was it just the barley wine that got you so enthusiastic?"

"What's that? Oh—yes." He chuckled wryly. "I guess I *did* get a little too passionate and lose some of my critical objectivity. But I hardly remember most of the things I did last night."

There was a sly tone in her voice as she said, "I wonder just how much of last night you've forgotten."

He smiled. They turned up into Great Russell Street, and he started walking a little faster so they could catch up with the rest of the group. He found himself liking this soft-spoken girl, and he knew that was dangerous; in four days he'd be departing, and this was no time to start any emotional relationships. Especially not after having ignored the girl for the year he had known her.

But somehow he found himself hoping that his synthetic android would be rather like Marian Hawkes—tall, willowy, well built, with a soft deep voice and a sly sense of humor. He wouldn't mind spending eight years in a two-man spaceship with someone like that.

In fact, he found himself kissing her again that night. Some time after that, he argued Yeats versus Synge again, and landed a sound punch in Buxton's well-padded belly when words grew too hot. Sometime after that he had wandered across the city, not alone, into Victoria Embankment, and tossed a guinea piece into the Thames under the shadow of Scotland Yard. After that, he recalled crossing Waterloo Bridge and wandering round the slums of Southwark, and then doubling back over Westminster Bridge, watching the sun rise while walking by the Serpentine, and getting home to his flat just before 0700.

He slept three hours, waking at ten, and dressed and breakfasted. He surveyed his holdings and found that last night left him with the sum of seven and ninepence. Well, no matter, he thought; Sir Adrian had said he could have more expense money if he ran through the first fifty pounds.

He took the underground tube at Lancaster Gate, and got off at Tottenham Court Road. Precisely at noon, red eyed and weary but keenly anticipating what was to come, he presented himself at Room 707 in the

Survey Commission building.

It looked like a very ordinary office. There was an attractive receptionist back of the desk, and a framed solido of King Henry on the wall. Sir Adrian was waiting for him, along with a smiling little man with disconcerting green eyes and a white smock.

Sir Adrian introduced him as Dr. Hammersmith, the Commission's Chief of Testing. Hammersmith stared at him with coolly-appraising eyes, as if giving him an on-the-spot psych-testing. Then he said, in clipped Scots tones, "Very good. Will you come this way please, Mr. Bradmire?"

He was led on into an inner office that was dark; Hammersmith nudged a stud and subtle electroluminescents fluttered into life, revealing a truly startling quantity of ponderous apparatus. It seemed to Bradmire that one entire wall of the big office was devoted to a monstrous pile of frightening gearwork: massive tubes and coils and strangely-throbbing lights, dials and meters, electromagnets and unidentifiable mechanisms.

"Is that thing—for me?" he asked in a hushed voice.

Hammersmith smiled. "It does look a little imposing, doesn't it? Yes, that's our psych-tester."

He gestured toward a desk in the back of the office and said, "Would you sit there, please?"

Bradmire did so—and noticed that it was no desk, but rather an additional machine covered with dials and indicators. He lowered himself with some trepidation into the chair riveted to the floor in front of it, observing that a formidable array of devices seemed to be installed right behind him.

He grinned feebly. "What's going to happen?"

Sir Adrian said, "We're going to let you choose a mate. The Singestault Selector makes our job a good deal easier and quicker."

"What do you mean? How do you go about designing androids?"

Hammersmith said, "We keep fifty or sixty basic androids on hand in the building at all times. We're going to march them through this office while you analyze them with the Selector, and we'll pick out the one who most approximates your ideal. Usually it's possible to find one that has an index of correlation of, say, 77%. We earmark her for you and send the others back to storage. Then, by using the data the Selector has received from you, we make psychical and physical alterations in her until her Selector score is 99.999%. Then she's yours—the woman you wanted."

Bradmire felt strangely unnerved by Hammersmith's bland confidence. "Suppose," he said in a hoarse voice, "suppose there isn't any android in stock who correlates better than fifty percent. What then?"

Hammersmith shrugged, "Then we design one from scratch for you. But this takes much longer; it's far easier to begin with a standard model and custom-shape her. Sometimes we come quite close."

"A boy in here last week," Sir Adrian said, "found an android who was within 95% of his ideal. All we had to do was add an inch of bosom and give her a tape on famous cricket stars and she was perfect for him. Of course, it's rarely that simple. Shall we begin?"

"I—I guess so," Bradmire said. His fingertips felt cold; he felt irrationally tense. "We might as well get started."

Hammersmith lowered a sort of crown over his head—a recording instrument, some kind of electroencephalograph. There were other detectors attached to his wrists and ankles. He felt as if he were being prepared for execution, not for finding a perfect mate.

"Keep your hands on these buttons," Hammersmith said. "They'll register changes in skin temperature. We'll also be picking up pulse alterations, adrenalin counts, and eighty or ninety other things. It's foolproof."

He stepped back and threw a master lever. Bradmire heard a humming sound as all the complex machinery around him came to life. The needle on the Singestault Selector's main gauge fluttered momentarily and dropped back to zero.

In front of him and overhead a battery of lights flashed on, creating a hazy sort of field—with a woman's silhouette in the middle of the field. Quite a handsome silhouette too, Bradmire thought.

A door opened. A girl stepped out and began to walk with measured steps toward the silhouette.

She was tall and dark of complexion, and she wore a skin-tight two-piece outfit that hid absolutely nothing of her long, curved legs and high bosom. Her hair was cropped short; her nose was a bit too long, and there was something faintly haughty about her eyes. She looked human, all too human, and Bradmire would not have objected to having her.

She passed through the silhouette. She was a bit too tall and a trifle too narrow in the hips. Bradmire glanced at the detector. It was registering only 58%. A long way from his ideal, evidently.

But the Commission had plenty of other girls, it seemed. Narrow-hips passed on through the field and out of the room, and already another was advancing—short, buxom, with a liquidly undulating way of walking. Bradmire had never cared much for short girls. This one rang up 32% on the gauge, and passed on.

There was a wide and varied assortment. Short ones, tall ones, blondes, brunettes, some with hair of no color he had ever seen. Some who came through the field brazenly nude, others prudishly concealed.

Haughty ones, shy ones, farmgirl-type ones. Girls in evening gowns and girls in spacesuits and girls in nothing at all.

Dozens of them must have gone by. Sweat dribbled down Bradmire's face, and the apparatus strapped to him felt oppressively heavy. He had lost all count and had no idea which had scored what. An icy, regal-looking one had tallied the low score, 11%, and a slim long-haired brunette in tight rubberoid halter and tights had recorded 69%, the high so far. Bradmire wondered how long it would go on, and whether he would find anyone who outscored the 69-percenter. As far as he was concerned, the brunette would do, in a pinch.

A new girl was coming out; they moved in endless series. This one was a tall blonde, clad in rubberoid from neck to ankles—revealing thereby both a sense of modesty and a startlingly good figure. Her eyes were wide and clear, her smile elfin.

Bradmire felt an inward tingle. He looked down at the Selector. The needle was oscillating wildly and coming to rest someplace above the 98% level.

He looked back at the platform, at the girl. She was standing in the Selector field, and the silhouette framed her almost perfectly.

And something else was quite surprising. She was a perfect double for Marian Hawkes.

"Hold everything," Bradmire said loudly. "This looks like the one. The Selector says she's almost perfect—and I agree!"

The lights went on suddenly. Bradmire blinked and looked around. Sir Adrian and Hammersmith were paying no attention to him; a white-smocked technician had burst into the office.

He was shouting, "Dr. Hammersmith, there's been a mistake! A human girl got in the android lineup by mistake! We were checking the potentials, and one of the last ones nearly blew out our board!"

So that explains it, Bradmire thought. It isn't Marian's double at all. It's Marian. But how—and what—and why…?

Confusion seemed to be ruling in the testing laboratory. The android girls had all re-entered, and were milling about in alarm. Hammersmith was swearing. Above everything else, Bradmire heard Sir Adrian's commanding voice: "How could something like that happen?"

The hapless technician shrugged. "She just slipped through, that's all. But it's easy enough to find out who it is. We just look for the one who has a navel, and that's our girl."

"Very well," Sir Adrian thundered. "Bradmire, I'm sorry about all this. We'll have to check."

"But look here, sir—I hit better than 99% on that last girl. She's obviously the one I want."

"Hmm." Sir Adrian and Hammersmith examined the selector gauge. "Most unusual, eh? Which girl was the one who got this score, Bradmire?"

"That one, sir."

He pointed to Marian, who stood gravely in the midst of the android girls, trying her best to look like one of them.

Hammersmith removed the paraphernalia that bound Bradmire, and he crossed the room to her.

"All right, the rest of you!" Sir Adrian snapped. "Let's see your stomachs. And there's trouble waiting for the one who isn't a laboratory product!"

At Marian's side, Bradmire whispered, "How the deuce did you get into that lineup?"

She smiled. "Last night you gave me ten guineas for a bottle of champagne. I put it to a better use and bribed one of the technicians to let me in."

"But how did you know the machine would pick you?"

"It didn't take a machine, silly. Everyone knew it but you, all along. This was my last chance, wasn't it?"

Bradmire grinned at her and turned around. The android girls had formed into a line again, only now fifty bare and navelless feminine stomachs were revealed. It was a somewhat dazzling sight.

"Odd," Sir Adrian said. "They all seem to be synthetics, all right. But the detector-board said—ah. There's one other." He looked at Marian. "Kindly unzip, young lady."

Bradmire stepped forward and said, "I don't think that will be necessary, Sir Adrian."

"What?"

"She may or may not be an android; I'm not sure myself; But the Selector plainly says she's the woman I wanted. I don't think we need to continue this session any further."

"But if there's been a violation..."

"Does it matter, if she's human?" Bradmire said. "The thing that counts is the compatibility index. And that's pretty close to perfect."

And I should have seen that a long time ago, he thought.

Sir Adrian looked puzzled; but then, he began to laugh. "I begin to understand. Very well; the Selector tells the truth—and we'll overlook any irregularities in the procedure. Dr. Hammersmith, the session's over. And if you two will follow me to my office, we'll assign you to Indoctrination for Survey work."

As they left, Bradmire whispered to the girl, "You are Marian Hawkes, aren't you? Not just a clever android imitation? I mean..."

She giggled deliciously. "The only way to find that out is to look for my navel, isn't it?"

He reached for her belt. She slapped his wrist gently. "Not here, silly. Later. We'll have plenty of time for things like that on the way to Betelgeuse."

VALLEY BEYOND TIME

Originally published in *Science Fiction Adventures*, December, 1957.

Chapter One

The Valley, Sam Thornhill thought, had never looked lovelier. Drifting milky clouds hung over the two towering bare purple fangs of rock that bordered the Valley on either side and closed it off at the rear. Both suns were in the sky, the sprawling pale red one and the more distant, more intense blue; their beams mingled, casting a violet haze over tree and shrub and on the fast-flowing waters of the river that led to the barrier.

It was late in the forenoon, and all was well. Thornhill, a slim, compactly made figure in satinfab doublet and tunic, dark blue with orange trim, felt deep content. He watched the girl and the man come toward him up the winding path from the stream, wondering who they were and what they wanted with him.

The girl, at least, was attractive. She was dark of complexion and just short of Thornhill's own height; she wore a snug rayon blouse and a yellow knee-length lustrol sheath. Her bare shoulders were wide and sun-darkened.

The man was small, well set, hardly an inch over five feet tall. He was nearly bald; a maze of wrinkles furrowed his domed forehead. His eyes caught Thornhill's attention immediately. They were very bright, quick eyes that darted here and there in rapid glittering motions—the eyes of a predatory animal, of a lizard perhaps ready to pounce.

In the distance Thornhill caught sight of others, not all of them human. A globular Spican was visible near the stream's edge. Then Thornhill frowned for the first time; who were they, and what business had they in his Valley?

"Hello," the girl said. "My name's Marga Fallis. This is La Floquet. You just get here?"

She glanced toward the man named La Floquet and said quietly, "He hasn't come out of it yet, obviously. He must be brand-new."

"He'll wake up soon," La Floquet said. His voice was dark and sharp.

"What are you two muttering?" Thornhill demanded angrily. "How did you get here?"

"The same way you did," the girl said, "and the sooner you admit that to yourself—"

Hotly, Thornhill said, "I've always been here, damn you! This is the Valley! I've spent my whole life here! And I've never seen either of you before. Any of you. You just appeared out of nowhere, you and this little rooster and those others down by the river, and I—" He stopped, feeling a sudden wrenching shaft of doubt.

Of course I've always lived here, he told himself.

He began to quiver. He leaped abruptly forward, seeing in the smiling little man with the wisp of russet hair around his ears the enemy that had cast him forth from Eden. "Damn you, it was fine till *you* got here! You had to spoil it! I'll pay you back, though."

Thornhill sprang at the little man viciously, thinking to knock him to the ground. But to his astonishment he was the one to recoil; La Floquet remained unbudged, still smiling, still glinting birdlike at him. Thornhill sucked in a deep breath and drove forward at La Floquet a second time. This time he was efficiently caught and held; he wriggled, but though La Floquet was a good twenty years older and a foot shorter, there was surprising strength in his wiry body. Sweat burst out on Thornhill. Finally he gave ground and dropped back.

"Fighting is foolish," La Floquet said tranquilly. "It accomplishes nothing. What's your name?"

"Sam Thornhill."

"Now, attend to me. What were you doing in the moment before you first knew you were in the Valley?"

"I've always been in the Valley," Thornhill said stubbornly.

"Think," said the girl. "Look back. There was a time before you came to the Valley."

Thornhill turned away, looking upward at the mighty mountain peaks that hemmed them in, at the fast-flowing stream that wound between them and out toward the Barrier. A grazing beast wandered on the up reach of the foothill, nibbling the sharp-toothed grass. Had there ever been a someplace else, Thornhill wondered?

No. There had always been the Valley, and here he had lived alone and at peace until that final deceptive moment of tranquility, followed by this strange unwanted invasion.

"It usually takes several hours for the effect to wear off," the girl said. "Then you'll remember ... the way we remember. Think. You're from Earth, aren't you?"

"Earth?" Thornhill repeated dimly.

"Green hills, spreading cities, oceans, spaceliners. Earth. No?"

"Observe the heavy tan," La Floquet pointed out. "He's from Earth, but he hasn't lived there for a while. How about Vengamon?"

"Vengamon," Thornhill declared, not questioningly this time. The strange syllables seemed to have meaning: a swollen yellow sun, broad plains, a growing city of colonists, a flourishing ore trade. "I know the word," he said.

"Was that the planet where you lived?" the girl prodded. "Vengamon?"

"I think—" Thornhill began hesitantly. His knees felt weak. A neat pattern of life was breaking down and cascading away from him, sloughing off as if it had never been at all.

It had *never been*.

"I lived on Vengamon," he said.

"Good!" La Floquet cried. "The first fact has been elicited! Now to think where you were the very moment before you came here. A spaceship, perhaps? Traveling between worlds? Think, Thornhill."

He thought. The effort was mind-wracking, but he deliberately blotted out the memories of his life in the Valley and searched backward until—

"I was a passenger on the liner *Royal Mother Helene*, bound into Vengamon from the neighboring world of Jurinalle I ... had been on holiday. I was returning to my—my plantation? No, not plantation. Mine. I own mining land on Vengamon. That's it, yes—mining land." The light of the double suns became oppressively warm; he felt dizzy. "I remember now: The trip was an uneventful one; I was bored and dozed off a few minutes. Then I recall sensing that I was outside the ship, somehow—and—blank. Next thing, I was here in the Valley."

"The standard pattern," La Floquet said. He gestured to the others down near the stream. "There are eight of us in all, including you. I arrived first—yesterday, I call it, though actually there's been no night. The girl came after me. Then three others. You're the third one to come today."

Thornhill blinked. "We're just being picked out of nowhere and dumped here? How is it possible?"

La Floquet shrugged. "You will be asking that question more than once before you've left the Valley. Come. Let's meet the others."

The small man turned with an imperious gesture and retraced his steps down the path; the girl followed, and Thornhill fell in line behind her. He realized he had been standing on a ledge overlooking the river, one of the foothills of the two great mountains that formed the Valley's boundaries.

The air was warm, with a faint breeze stirring through it. He felt younger than his thirty-seven years, certainly; more alive, more perceptive. He caught the fragrance of the golden blossoms that lined the riverbed and saw the light sparkle of the double sunlight scattered by the water's spray.

He thought of glancing at his watch. The hands read 14:23. That was interesting enough. The day hand said 7 July 2671. It was still the same day, then. On 7 July 2671 he had left Jurinalle for Vengamon, and he had lunched at 11:40. That meant he had probably dozed off about noon—and unless something were wrong with his watch, only two hours had passed since then. Two hours. And yet—the memories still said, though they were fading fast now—he had spent an entire life in this Valley, unmarred by intruders until a few moments before.

"This is Sam Thornhill," La Floquet suddenly said. "He's our newest arrival. He's out of Vengamon."

Thornhill eyed the others curiously. There were five of them, three human, one humanoid, one nonhumanoid. The nonhumanoid, globular in its yellow-green phase just now but seeming ready to shift to its melancholy brownish-red guise, was a being of Spica. Tiny clawed feet peeked out from under the great melonlike body; dark grapes atop stalks studied Thornhill with unfathomable alien curiosity.

The humanoid, Thornhill saw, hailed from one of the worlds of Regulus. He was keen-eyed, pale orange in color. The heavy flap of flesh swinging from his throat was the chief external alien characteristic of the being. Thornhill had met his kind before.

Of the remaining three, one was a woman, small, plain-looking, dressed in drab gray cloth garments. There were two men: a spidery spindle-shanked sort with mild scholarly eyes and an apologetic smile and a powerfully built man of thirty or so, shirtless, scowling impatiently.

"As you can see, it's quite a crew," La Floquet remarked to Thornhill. "Vellers, did you have any luck down by the barrier?"

The big man shook his head. "I followed the main stream as far as I dared. But you get beyond that grassy bend down there and come smack against that barrier, like a wall you can't see planted in the water." His accent was broad and heavy; he was obviously of Earth, Thornhill thought, and not from one of the colony worlds.

La Floquet frowned. "Did you try swimming underneath? No, of course you didn't. Eh?"

Vellers' scowl grew darker. "There wasn't any percentage in it, Floquet. I dove ten—fifteen feet, and the barrier was still like glass—smooth and clean to the touch, y'know, but strong. I didn't aim to go any lower."

"All right," La Floquet said sharply. "It doesn't matter. Few of us could swim that deep, anyway." He glanced at Thornhill. "You see that this lovely Valley is likely to become our home for life, don't you?"

"There's no way out?"

The small man pointed to the gleaming radiance of the barrier, which rose in a high curving arc from the water and formed a triangular wedge closing off the lower end of the Valley. "You see that thing down there. We don't know what's at the other end, but we'd have to climb twenty thousand feet of mountain to find out. There's no way out of here."

"Do we *want* to get out?" asked the thin man in a shallow, petulant voice. "I was almost dead when I came here, La Floquet. Now I'm alive again. I don't know if I'm so anxious to leave here."

La Floquet whirled. His eyes flashed angrily as he said, "Mr. McKay, I'm delighted to hear of your recovery. But life still waits for me outside this place, lovely as the Valley is. I don't intend to rot away in here forever—not La Floquet!"

McKay shook his head slowly. "I wish there were some way of stopping you from looking for a way out. I'll die in a week if I go out of the Valley. If you escape, La Floquet, you'll be my murderer!"

"I just don't understand," Thornhill said in confusion. "If La Floquet finds a way out, what's it to you, McKay? Why don't you just stay here?"

McKay smiled unhappily. "I guess you haven't told him, then," he said to La Floquet.

"No. I didn't have a chance." La Floquet turned to Thornhill. "What this dried-up man of books is saying is that the Watcher has warned us that if one of us leaves the Valley, all the others must go."

"The Watcher?" Thornhill repeated.

"It was he who brought you here. You'll see him again. Occasionally he talks to us and tells us things. This morning he told us this: that our fates are bound together."

"And I ask you not to keep searching for the way out," McKay said dolefully. "My life depends on staying in the Valley!"

"And mine on getting out!" La Floquet blazed. He lunged forward and sent McKay sprawling to the ground in one furious gesture of contempt.

McKay turned even paler and clutched at his chest as he landed. "My heart! You shouldn't—"

Thornhill moved forward and assisted McKay to his feet. The tall, stoop-shouldered man looked dazed and shaken, but unhurt. He drew himself together and said quietly, "Two days ago a blow like that would have killed me. And now—you see?" he asked, appealing to Thornhill. "The Valley has strange properties. I don't want to leave. And he—he's condemning me to die!"

"Don't worry so over it," La Floquet said lightly. "You may get your wish. You may spend all your days here among the poppies."

Thornhill turned and looked up the mountainside toward the top. The mountain peak loomed, snow-flecked, shrouded by clinging frosty clouds; the climb would be a giant's task. And how would they know until they had climbed it whether merely another impassable barrier lay beyond the mountain's crest?

"We seem to be stuck here for a while," Thornhill said. "But it could be worse. This looks like a pleasant place to live."

"It is," La Floquet said. "If you like pleasant places. They bore me. But come: Tell us something of yourself. Half an hour ago you had no past; has it come back to you yet?"

Thornhill nodded slowly. "I was born on Earth. Studied to be a mining engineer. I did fairly well at it, and when they opened up Vengamon, I moved out there and bought a chunk of land while the prices were low. It turned out to be a good buy. I opened a mine four years ago. I'm not married. I'm a wealthy man, as wealth is figured on Vengamon. And that's the whole story, except that I was returning home from a vacation when I was snatched off my spaceship and deposited here."

He took a deep breath, drawing the warm, moist air into his lungs. For the moment he sided with McKay; he was in no hurry to leave the Valley. But he could see that La Floquet, that energetic, driving little man, was bound to have his way. If there was any path leading out of the Valley, La Floquet would find it.

His eyes came to rest on Marga Fallis. The girl was handsome, no doubt about it. Yes, he could stay here a while longer under these double suns, breathing deep and living free from responsibility for the first time in his life. But they were supposed to be bound together: Once one left the Valley, all would. And La Floquet was determined to leave.

A shadow dimmed the purple light.

"What's that?" Thornhill said. "An eclipse?"

"The Watcher," McKay said softly. "He's back. And it wouldn't surprise me if he's brought the ninth member of our little band."

Thornhill stared as a soft blackness descended over the land, the suns still visible behind it but only as tiny dots of far-off radiance. It was as if a fluffy dark cloak had enfolded them. But it was more than a cloak—much more. He sensed a *presence* among them, watchful, curious, as eager for their welfare as a brooding hen. The alien darkness wrapped itself over the entire Valley.

This is the last of your company, said a soundless voice that seemed to echo from the mountain walls. The sky began to brighten. Suddenly as it had come, the darkness was gone, and Thornhill once again felt alone.

"The Watcher had little to say this time," McKay commented as the light returned.

"Look!" Marga cried.

Thornhill followed the direction of her pointing arm and looked upward toward the ledge on which he had first become aware of the Valley around him.

A tiny figure was wandering in confused circles up there. At this distance it was impossible to tell much about the newcomer. Thornhill became chilled. The shadow of the Watcher had come and gone, leaving behind yet another captive for the Valley.

Chapter Two

Thornhill narrowed his eyes as he looked toward the ledge. "We ought to go get him," he said.

La Floquet shook his head. "We have time. It takes an hour or two for the newcomers to lose that strange illusion of being alone here; you remember what it's like."

"I do," Thornhill agreed. "It's as if you've lived all your life in paradise … until gradually it wears off and you see others around you—as I saw you and Marga coming up the path toward me." He walked a few paces away from them and lowered himself to a moss-covered boulder. A small, wiry, catlike creature with wide cupped ears emerged from behind it and rubbed up against him; he fondled it idly as if it were his pet.

La Floquet shaded his eyes from the sunlight. "Can you see what he's like, that one up there?"

"No, not at this distance," Thornhill said.

"Too bad you can't. You'd be interested. We've added another alien to our gallery, I fear."

Thornhill leaned forward anxiously. "From where?"

"Aldebaran," La Floquet said.

Thornhill winced. The humanoid aliens of Aldebaran were the coldest of races, fierce, savage beings who hid festering evil behind masks of outward urbanity. Some of the out-worlds referred to the Aldebaranians as devils, and they were not so far wrong. To have one here, a devil in paradise, so to speak—

"What are we going to do?" Thornhill asked.

La Floquet shrugged. "The Watcher has put the creature here, and the Watcher has his own purposes. We'll simply have to accept what comes."

Thornhill rose and paced urgently up and down. The silent, small, mousy woman and McKay had drawn off to one side; the Spican was peering at his own plump image in the swirling waters, and the Regulan, not interested in the proceedings, stared aloofly toward the leftward mountain. The girl Marga and La Floquet remained near Thornhill.

"All right," Thornhill said finally. "Give the Aldebaranian some time to come to his senses. Meanwhile, let's forget about him and worry about ourselves. La Floquet, what do you know about this Valley?"

The small man smiled blandly. "Not very much. I know we're on a world with Earth-norm gravity and a double sun system. How many red-and-blue double suns do you know of, Thornhill?"

He shrugged. "I'm no astronomer."

"I am ... was ..." Marga said. "There are hundreds of such systems. We could be anywhere in the galaxy."

"Can't you tell from the constellations at night?" Thornhill asked.

"There *are* no constellations," La Floquet said sadly. "The damnable part is that there's always at least one of the suns in the sky. This planet has no night. We see no stars. But our location is unimportant." The fiery little man chuckled. "McKay will triumph. We'll never leave the Valley. How could we contact anyone, even if we were to cross the mountains? We cannot."

A sudden crackle of thunder caught Thornhill's attention. A great rolling boom reverberated from the sides of the mountains, dying away slowly.

"Listen," he said.

"A storm," said La Floquet. "Outside the confines of our barrier. The same happened yesterday at this time. It storms ... but not in here. We live in an enchanted Valley where the sun always shines and life is gentle." A bitter grimace twisted his thin, bloodless lips. "Gentle!"

"Get used to it," Thornhill said. "We may be here a long time."

His watch read 16:42 when they finally went up the hill to get the Aldebaranian. In the two hours he had seen a shift in the configuration of the suns—the red had receded, the blue grown more intense—but it was obvious that there would be no night, that light would enter the Valley around the clock. In time he would grow used to that. He was adaptable.

Nine people, plucked from as many different worlds and cast within the space of twenty-four hours into this timeless valley beyond the storms, where there was no darkness. Of the nine, six were human, three were alien. Of the six, four were men, two were women.

Thornhill wondered about his companions. He knew so little about them yet. Vellers, the strong man, was from Earth; Thornhill knew nothing more of him. McKay and the mousy woman were ciphers. Thornhill cared little about them. Neither the Regulan nor the Spican had uttered a word yet—if they could speak the Terran tongues at all. As for Marga, she was an astronomer and was lovely, but he knew nothing else. La Floquet was an interesting one—a little dynamo, shrewd and energetic but close-mouthed about his own past.

There they were. Nine pastless people. The present was as much of a mystery to them as the future.

By the time they reached the mountain ledge, Thornhill and La Floquet and the girl, the Aldebaranian had seen them and was glaring coldly at them. The storm had subsided in the land outside the Valley, and once again white clouds drifted in over the barrier.

Like all his race the Aldebaranian, a man of medium height and amiable appearance, was well fleshed, with pouches of fat swelling beneath his chin and under his ears. He was gray of skin and dark of eye, with gleaming little hooked incisors that glinted terrifyingly when he smiled. He had extra joints in his limbs as well.

"At last some others join me," the alien remarked in flawless Terran Standard as they approached. "I knew life could hardly go on here as it had."

"You're mistaken," La Floquet said. "It's a delusion common to new arrivals. You haven't lived here all your life, you know. Not really."

The Aldebaranian smiled. "This surprises me. But explain, if you will."

La Floquet explained. In a frighteningly short space of time the alien had grasped the essential nature of the Valley and his position in it. Thornhill watched coldly; the speed with which the Aldebaranian cast off delusion and accepted reality was disturbing.

They returned to the group at the river's edge. By now Thornhill was beginning to feel hungry; he had been in the Valley more than four hours. "What do we do about food?" he asked.

La Floquet said, "It falls from the skies three times a day. Manna, you know. The Watcher takes fine care of us. You got here around the time of the afternoon fall, but you were up there in your haze while we ate. It's almost time for the third fall of the day now."

The red sun had faded considerably now, and a haunted blue twilight reigned. Thornhill knew enough about solar mechanics to be aware that the big red sun was nearly dead; its feeble bulk gave little light. Fierce radiation came from the blue sun, but distance afforded protection. How this unlikely pair had come together was a matter for conjecture—some star capture in eons past, no doubt.

White flakes drifted slowly downward. As they came, Thornhill saw the Spican hoist its bulk hastily from the ground, saw the Regulan running eagerly toward the drifting flakes. McKay stirred; Vellers, the big man, tugged himself to his feet. Only Thornhill and the Aldebaranian looked at all doubtful.

"Suppertime," La Floquet said cheerfully. He punctuated the statement by snapping a gob of the floating substance from the air with a quick, sharp gesture and cramming it into his mouth.

The others, Thornhill saw, were likewise catching the food before it touched ground. The animals of the Valley were appearing—the fat, lazy-looking ruminants, the whippetlike dogs, the catlike creatures—and busily were devouring the manna from the ground.

Thornhill shrugged and shagged a mass as it hung before him in the air. After a tentative sniff he hesitantly swallowed a mouthful.

It was like chewing cloud stuff—except that this cloud had a tangy, wine-like taste; his stomach felt soothed almost immediately. He wondered how such unsubstantial stuff could possibly be nourishing. Then he stopped wondering and helped himself to a second portion, then a third.

The fall stopped finally, and by then Thornhill was sated. He lay outstretched on the ground, legs thrust out, head propped up against a boulder.

Opposite him was McKay. The thin, pale man was smiling. "I haven't eaten this way in years," he said. "Haven't had much of an appetite. But now—"

"Where are you from?" Thornhill asked, interrupting.

"Earth, originally. Then to Mars when my heart began acting up. They thought the low gravity would help me, and of course it did. I'm a professor of medieval Terran history. That is, I *was*—I was on a medical leave until—until I came here." He smiled complacently. "I feel reborn here, you know? If only I had some books—"

"Shut up," growled Vellers. "You'd stay here forever, wouldn't you, now?"

The big man lay near the water's edge staring moodily out over the river.

"Of course I would," snapped McKay testily. "And Miss Hardin, too, I'd wager."

"If we could leave the two of you here together, I'm sure you'd be very happy," came the voice of La Floquet. "But we can't do that. Either all of us stay, or all of us get out of here."

The argument appeared likely to last all night. Thornhill looked away. The three aliens seemed to be as far from each other as possible, the Spican lying in a horizontal position looking like a great inflated balloon that had somehow come to rest, the little Regulan brooding in the distance and fingering its heavy dewlap, the Aldebaranian sitting quietly to one side listening to every word, smiling like a pudgy Buddha.

Thornhill rose. He bent over Marga Fallis and said, "Would you care to take a walk with me."

She hesitated just a moment. "I'd love to," she said.

They stood at the edge of the water watching the swift stream, watching golden fish flutter past with solemnly gaping mouths. After a while they walked on upstream, back toward the rise in the ground that led to the hills, which in turn rose into the two mighty peaks.

Thornhill said, "That La Floquet. He's a funny one, isn't he? Like a little gamecock, always jumping around and ready for a fight."

"He's very dynamic," Marga agreed quietly.

"You and he were the first ones here, weren't you? It must have been strange, just the two of you in this little Eden, until the third one showed up." Thornhill wondered why he was probing after these things. Jealousy, perhaps? Not *perhaps*. Certainly.

"We really had very little time alone together. McKay came right after me, and then the Spican. The Watcher was very busy collecting."

"*Collecting,*" Thornhill repeated. "That's all we are. Just specimens collected and put here in this Valley like little lizards in a terrarium. And this Watcher—some strange alien being, I guess." He looked up at the starless sky, still bright with day. "There's no telling what's in the stars. Five hundred years of space travel, and we haven't seen it all."

Marga smiled. She took his hand, and they walked on farther into the low-lying shrubbery, saying nothing. Thornhill finally broke the silence.

"You said you were an astronomer, Marga?"

"Not really." Her voice was low for a woman's and well modulated; he liked it. "I'm attached to the Bellatrix VII observatory, but strictly as an assistant. I've got a degree in astronomy, of course. But I'm just sort of hired help in the observatory."

"Is that where you were when—when—"

"Yes," she said. "I was in the main dome taking some plates out of the camera. I remember it was a very delicate business. A minute or two before it happened, someone called me on the main phone downstairs, and they wanted to transfer the call up to me. I told them it would have to wait; I couldn't be bothered until I'd finished with my plates. And then everything blanked out, and I guess my plates don't matter now. I wish I'd taken that call, though."

"Someone important?"

"Oh—no. Nothing like that."

Somehow Thornhill felt relieved. "What about La Floquet?" he asked. "Who is he?"

"He's sort of a big-game hunter," she said. "I met him once before when he led a party to Bellatrix VII. Imagine the odds on any two people in the universe meeting twice! He didn't recognize me, of course, but I remembered him. He's not easy to forget."

"He *is* sort of picturesque," Thornhill said.

"And you? You said you owned a mine on Vengamon."

"I do. I'm actually quite a dull person," said Thornhill. "This is the first interesting thing that's ever happened to me." He grinned wryly. "The fates caught up with me with a vengeance, though. I guess I'll never see Vengamon again now. Unless La Floquet can get us out of here, and I don't think he can."

"Does it matter? Will it pain you never to go back to Vengamon?"

"I doubt it," Thornhill said. "I can't see any urgent reason for wanting to go back. And you, and your observatory?"

"I can forget my observatory soon enough," she said.

Somehow he moved closer to her; he wished it were a little darker, perhaps even that the Watcher would choose this instant to arrive and afford a shield of privacy for him for a moment. He felt her warmth against him.

"Don't," she murmured suddenly. "Someone's coming."

She pulled away from him. Scowling, Thornhill turned and saw the stubby figure of La Floquet clambering toward them.

"I do hope I'm not interrupting any tender scenes," the little man said quietly.

"You might have been," Thornhill admitted. "But the damage is done. What's happened to bring you after us? The charm of our company?"

"Not exactly. There's trouble down below. Vellers and McKay had a fight."

"Over leaving the Valley?"

"Of course." La Floquet looked strangely disturbed. "Vellers hit him a little too hard, though. He killed him."

Marga gasped. "McKay's dead?"

"Very. I don't know what we ought to do with Vellers. I wanted you two in on it."

Hastily Thornhill and Marga followed La Floquet down the side of the hill toward the little group clumped on the beach. Even at a distance Thornhill could see the towering figure of Vellers staring down at his feet where the crumpled body of McKay lay.

They were still a hundred feet away when McKay rose suddenly to his feet and hurled himself on Vellers in a wild headlong assault.

Chapter Three

Thornhill froze an instant and grasped La Floquet's cold wrist.

"I thought you told me he was dead?"

"He *was*," La Floquet insisted. "I've seen dead men before. I know the face, the eyes, the slackness of the lips—Thornhill, this is impossible!"

They ran toward the beach. Vellers had been thrown back by the fury of the resurrected McKay's attack; he went tumbling over, with McKay groping for his throat in blind murderousness.

But Vellers' strength prevailed. As Thornhill approached, the big man plucked McKay off him with one huge hand, held him squirming in the air an instant, and rising to his feet, hurled McKay down against a beach boulder with sickening impact. Vellers staggered back, muttering hoarsely to himself.

Thornhill stared down. A gash had opened along the side of McKay's head; blood oozed through the sparse graying hair, matting it. McKay's eyes, half-open, were glazed and sightless; his mouth hung agape, tongue lolling. The skin of his face was gray.

Kneeling, Thornhill touched his hand to McKay's wrist, then to the older man's lips. After a moment he looked up. "This time he's really dead," he said.

La Floquet was peering grimly at him. "Get out of the way!" he snapped suddenly, and to Thornhill's surprise he found himself being roughly grabbed by the shoulder and flung aside by the wiry game hunter.

Quickly La Floquet flung himself down on McKay's body, straddling it with his knees pressing against the limp arms, hands grasping the slender shoulders. The beach was very silent; La Floquet's rough, irregular breathing was the only sound. The little man seemed poised, tensed for a physical encounter.

The gash on McKay's scalp began to heal.

Thornhill watched as the parted flesh closed over; the bruised skin lost its angry discoloration. Within moments only the darkening stain of blood on McKay's forehead gave any indication that there had been a wound.

Then McKay's slitted eyelids closed and immediately reopened, showing bright, flashing eyes that rolled wildly. Color returned to the dead man's face. Like a riding whip suddenly turned by conjury into a serpent, McKay began to thrash frantically. But La Floquet was prepared. His muscles corded momentarily as he exerted pressure; McKay writhed but could not rise. Behind him Thornhill heard Vellers mumbling a prayer over and over again while the mousy Miss Hardin provided a counterpoint of harsh sobs; even the Regulan uttered a brief comment in his guttural, consonant-studded language.

Sweat beaded La Floquet's face, but he prevented McKay from repeating his previous wild charge. Perhaps a minute passed; then McKay relaxed visibly.

La Floquet remained cautiously astride him. "McKay? McKay, do you hear me? This is La Floquet."

"I hear you. You can get off me now; I'm all right."

La Floquet gestured to Thornhill and Vellers. "Stand near him. Be ready to grab him if he runs wild again." He eyed McKay suspiciously for a moment, then rolled to one side and jumped to his feet.

McKay remained on the ground a moment longer. Finally he hoisted himself to a kneeling position, and shaking his head as if to clear it, stood erect. He took a few hesitant, uncertain steps. Then he turned, staring squarely at the three men, and in a quiet voice said, "Tell me what happened to me."

"You and Vellers quarreled," La Floquet said. "He—knocked you unconscious. When you came to, something must have snapped inside you—you went after Vellers like a madman. He knocked you out a second time. You just regained consciousness."

"No!" Thornhill half-shouted in a voice he hardly recognized as his own. "Tell him the truth, La Floquet! We can't gain anything by pretending it didn't happen."

"What truth?" McKay asked curiously.

Thornhill paused an instant. "McKay, you were dead. At least once. Probably twice, unless La Floquet was mistaken the first time. I examined you the second time—after Vellers bashed you against that rock. I'd swear you were dead. Feel the side of your head ... where it was split open when Vellers threw you down."

McKay put a quivering hand to his head, drew it away bloody, and stared down at the rock near his foot. The rock was bloodstained, also.

"I see blood, but I don't feel any pain."

"Of course not," Thornhill said. "The wound healed almost instantaneously. And you were revived. *You came back to life, McKay!*"

McKay turned to La Floquet. "Is this thing true, what Thornhill's telling me? You were trying to hide it?"

La Floquet nodded.

A slow, strange smile appeared on McKay's pale, angular face. "It's the Valley, then! I was dead—and I rose from the dead! Vellers—La Floquet—you fools! Don't you see that we live forever here in this Valley that you're so anxious to leave? I died twice ... and it was like being asleep. Dark, and I remember nothing. You're sure I was dead, Thornhill?"

"I'd swear to it."

"But of course you, La Floquet—you'd try to hide this from me, wouldn't you? Well, do you still want to leave here? We can live forever in the Valley, La Floquet!"

The small man spat angrily. "Why bother? Why live here like vegetables, eternally, never to move beyond those mountains, never to see what's on the other side of the stream? I'd rather have a dozen unfettered years than ten thousand in this prison, McKay!" He scowled.

"You had to tell him," La Floquet said accusingly to Thornhill.

"What difference does it make?" Thornhill asked. "We'd have had a repetition sooner or later. We couldn't hide it from anyone." He glanced up at the arching mountains. "So the Watcher has ways of keeping us alive? No suicide, no murder ... and no way out."

"There *is* a way out," La Floquet said stubbornly. "Over the mountain pass. I'm sure of it. Vellers and I may go to take a look at it tomorrow. Won't we, Vellers?"

The big man shrugged. "It's fine with me."

"You don't want to stay here forever, do you, Vellers?" La Floquet went on. "What good is immortality if it's the immortality of prisoners for life? We'll look at the mountain tomorrow, Vellers."

Thornhill detected a strange note in La Floquet's voice, a curiously strained facial expression, as if he were pleading with Vellers to support him, as if he were somehow afraid to approach the mountain alone. The idea of La Floquet's being afraid of anything or anyone seemed hard to accept, but Thornhill had that definite impression.

He looked at Vellers, then at La Floquet. "We ought to discuss this a little further, I think. There are nine of us, La Floquet. McKay and Miss Hardin definitely want to remain in the Valley; Miss Fallis and I are uncertain, but in any event we'd like to stay here a while longer. That's four against two among the humans. As for the aliens—"

"I'll vote with La Floquet," said the Aldebaranian quietly. "Important business waits for me outside."

Troublemaker, Thornhill thought. "Four against three, then, with the Spican and the Regulan unheard from. And I guess they'll stay unheard from since we can't speak their languages."

"I can speak Regulan," volunteered the Aldebaranian. Without waiting for further discussion, he wheeled to face the grave dewlapped being and exchanged four or five short, crisp sentences with him. Turning again, he said, "Our friend votes to leave. This ties the score, I believe."

"Just a second," Thornhill said hotly. "How do we know that's what he said? Suppose—"

The mask of affability slipped from the alien's face. "Suppose *what?*" he asked coldly. "If you intend to put a shadow on my honor, Thornhill—" He left the sentence unfinished.

"It would be pretty pointless dueling here," Thornhill said, "unless your honor satisfies easily. You couldn't very well kill me for long. Perhaps a temporary death might soothe you, but let's let it drop. I'll take your interpreting job in good faith. We're four apiece for staying or trying to break out."

La Floquet said, "It was good of you to take this little vote, Thornhill. But it's not a voting matter. We're individuals, not a corporate entity, and I choose not to remain here so long as I can make the attempt to escape." The little man spun on his heel and stalked away from the group.

"There ought to be some way of stopping him," said McKay thickly. "If he escapes—"

Thornhill shook his head. "It's not as easy as all that. How's he going to get off the planet, even if he does pass the mountains?"

"You don't understand," McKay said. "The Watcher simply said if one of us *leaves the Valley*, all must go. And if La Floquet succeeds, it's death for me."

"Perhaps we're dead already," Marga suggested, breaking her long silence. "Suppose each of us—you in your spaceliner, me in my observatory—died at the same moment and came here. What if—"

The sky darkened in the now-familiar manner that signaled the approach of the Watcher.

"Ask him," Thornhill said. "He'll tell you all about it."

The black cloud descended.

You are not dead, came the voiceless answer to the unspoken question. *Though some of you will die if the barrier be passed.*

Again Thornhill felt chilled by the presence of the formless being. "Who are you?" he shouted. "What do you want with us?"

I am the Watcher.

"And what do you want with us?" Thornhill repeated.

I am the Watcher, came the inflexible answer. Fibrils of the cloud began to trickle away in many directions; within moments the sky was clear. Thornhill slumped back against a rock and looked at Marga.

"He comes and he goes, feeds us, keeps us from killing ourselves or each other. It's like a zoo, Marga! And we're the chief exhibits!"

La Floquet and Vellers came stumping toward them. "Are you satisfied with the answers to your questions?" La Floquet demanded. "Do you still want to spend the rest of your days here?"

Thornhill smiled. "Go ahead, La Floquet. Go climb the mountain. I'm changing my vote. It's five-three in favor of leaving."

"I thought you were with me," said McKay.

Thornhill ignored him. "Go on, La Floquet. You and Vellers climb that mountain. Get out of the Valley—if you can."

"Come with us," La Floquet said.

"Ah, no—I'd rather stay here. But I won't object if you go."

Fleetingly, La Floquet cast a glance at the giant tooth that blocked the Valley's exit, and it seemed to Thornhill that a shadow of fear passed over the little man's face. But La Floquet clamped his jaws tight and through locked lips said, "Vellers, are you with me?"

The big man shrugged amiably. "It can't hurt to take a look, I figure."

"Let's go, then," La Floquet said firmly. He threw one black, infuriated glance at Thornhill and struck out for the path leading to the mountain approach.

When he was out of earshot, Marga said, "Sam, why'd you do that?"

"I wanted to see how he'd react. I saw it."

McKay tugged at his arm fretfully. "I'll die if we leave the Valley! Don't you see that, Mr. Thornhill?"

Sighing, Thornhill said, "I see it. But don't worry too much about La Floquet. He'll be back before long."

Slowly the hours passed, and the red sun slipped below the horizon, leaving only the distant blue sun to provide warmth. Thornhill's wristwatch told him it was past ten in the evening—nearly twelve hours since the time he had boarded the spaceliner on Jurinalle, more than four hours since his anticipated arrival time in the main city of Vengamon. They would have searched in vain for him by now and would be wondering how a man could vanish so thoroughly from a spaceship in hyperdrive.

The little group sat together at the river's edge. The Spican had shifted fully into his brownish-red phase and sat silently like some owl heralding the death of the universe. The other two aliens kept mainly to themselves as well. There was little to be said.

McKay huddled himself into a knob-kneed pile of limbs and stared up at the mountain as if hoping to see some sign of La Floquet and Vellers. Thornhill understood the expression on his face; McKay knew clearly that if La Floquet succeeded in leaving the Valley's confines, he would pay the price of his double resurrection in the same instant. McKay looked like a man seated below a thread-hung sword.

Thornhill himself stared silently at the mountain, wondering where the two men were now, how far they would get before La Floquet's cowardice forced them to turn back. He had no doubt now that La Floquet dreaded the mountain—otherwise he would have made the attempt long before instead of merely threatening it. Now he had been goaded into it by Thornhill, but would he be successful? Probably not; a brave man with one deep-lying fear often never conquered that fear. In a way

Thornhill pitied little La Floquet; the gamecock would be forced to come back in humiliation, though he might delay that moment as long as he possibly could.

"You seem troubled," Marga said.

"Troubled? No, just thinking."

"About what?"

"About Vengamon, and my mine there ... and how the vultures have probably already started to go after my estate."

"You don't miss Vengamon, do you?" she said.

He smiled and shook his head. "Not yet. That mine was my whole life, you know. I took little vacations now and then, but I thought only of the mine and my supervisors and how lazy they were, and the price of ore in the interstellar markets. Until now. It must be some strange property of this Valley, but for the first time the mine seems terribly remote, as if it had always belonged to someone else. Or as if *it* had owned *me* and I'm free at last."

"I know something of how you feel," Marga said. "I lived in the observatory day and night. There were always so many pictures to be taken, so many books to read, so much to do—I couldn't bear the thought of missing a day or even of stopping my work to answer the phone. But there are no stars here, and I hardly miss them."

He took her hand lightly in his. "I wonder, though—If La Floquet succeeds, if we ever do get out of this Valley and back into our ordinary lives, will we be any different? Or will I go back to double-entry bookkeeping and you to stellar luminosities?"

"We won't know until we get back," she said. *"If* we get back. But look over there."

Thornhill looked. McKay and Miss Hardin were deep in a serious conversation, and McKay had shyly taken her hand. "Love comes at last to Professor of Medieval History McKay." Thornhill grinned. "And to Miss Something-or-Other Hardin, whoever she is."

The Regulan was asleep; the Aldebaranian stared broodingly at his feet, drawing pictures in the sand. The bloated sphere that was the Spican was absorbed in its own alien thoughts. The Valley was very quiet.

"I used to pity creatures in the zoos," Thornhill said. "But it's not such a bad life after all."

"So far. We don't know what the Watcher has in store for us."

A mist rolled down from the mountain peak, drifting in over the Valley. At first Thornhill thought the Watcher had returned for another visit with his captives; he saw, though, that it was merely a thin mountain mist dropping over them. It was faintly cold, and he drew Marga tighter against him.

He thought back over thirty-seven years as the mist rolled in. He had come through those thirty-seven years well enough, trim, athletic, with quick reflexes and a quicker mind. But not until this day—it was hard to believe this was still his first day in the Valley—had he fully realized life held other things besides mining and earning money.

It had taken the Valley to teach him that; would he remember the lesson if he ever returned to civilization? Might it not be better to stay here, with Marga, in eternal youth?

He frowned. Eternal youth, yes ... but at the cost of his free will. He was nothing but a prisoner here, if a pampered one.

Suddenly he did not know what to think.

Marga's hand tightened against his. "Did you hear something? Footsteps, I think. It must be La Floquet and Vellers coming back from the mountain."

"They couldn't make it," Thornhill said, not knowing whether to feel relief or acute disappointment. He heard the sound of voices—and two figures, one small and wiry, one tall and broad, advanced toward them through the thickening mist. He turned to face them.

Chapter Four

Despite the dim illumination of twilight and the effects of the fog Thornhill had no difficulty reading the expression on La Floquet's face. It was not pleasant. The little man was angry both with himself and with Thornhill, and naked hatred was visible in his sharp features.

"Well?" Thornhill asked casually. "No go?"

"We got several thousand feet before this damned fog closed in around us. It was almost as if the Watcher sent it on purpose. We had to turn back."

"And was there any sign of a pass leading out of the Valley?"

La Floquet shrugged. "Who knows? We couldn't as much as see each other! But I'll find it. I'll go back tomorrow when both suns are in the sky—and I'll find a way out!"

"You devil," came McKay's thin, dry voice. "Won't you ever give up?"

"Not while I can still walk!" La Floquet shouted defiantly. But there was a note of mock bravado in his voice. Thornhill wondered just what had really happened up there on the mountain path.

He was not kept long in ignorance. La Floquet stalked angrily away, adopting a pose of injured arrogance, leaving Vellers standing near Thornhill. The big man looked after him and shook his head.

"The liar!"

"What's that?" Thornhill asked, half-surprised.

"There was no fog on the mountain," Vellers muttered bitterly. "He found the fog when we came back down, and he took it as an excuse. The little bullfrog makes much noise, but it's hollow."

Thornhill said earnestly, "Tell me, what happened up there? If there wasn't any fog, why'd you turn back?"

"We got no more than a thousand feet up," Vellers said. "He had been leading. But then he dropped back and got very pale. He said he couldn't go on any farther."

"Why? Was he afraid of the height?"

"I don't think so," Vellers said. "I think he was afraid of getting to the top and seeing what's there. Maybe he knows there isn't any way out. Maybe he's afraid to face it. I don't know. But he made me follow him back down."

Suddenly Vellers grunted heavily, and Thornhill saw that La Floquet had come up quietly behind the big man and jabbed him sharply in the small of the back. Vellers turned. It took time for a man six feet seven to turn.

"Fool!" La Floquet barked. "Who told you these lies? Why this fairy tale, Vellers?"

"Lies? Fairy tale? Get your hands off me, La Floquet. You know damn well you funked out up there. Don't try to fast-talk your way out now."

A muscle tightened convulsively in the corner of La Floquet's slit of a mouth. His eyes flashed; he stared at Vellers as if he were some beast escaped from a cage. Suddenly La Floquet's fists flicked out, and Vellers stepped back, crying out in pain. He swung wildly at the smaller man, but La Floquet was untouchable, humming in under Vellers' guard to plant a stinging punch on the slablike jaw, darting back out again as the powerful Vellers tried to land a decisive blow. La Floquet fought like a fox at bay.

Thornhill moved uneasily forward, not wanting to get in the way of Vellers' massive fists as the giant tried vainly to hit La Floquet. Catching the eye of the Aldebaranian, Thornhill acted. He seized Vellers' arm and tugged it back while the alien similarly blocked off La Floquet.

"Enough!" Thornhill snapped. "It doesn't matter which one of you's lying. Fighting's foolish—you told me that yourself earlier today, La Floquet."

Vellers dropped back sullenly, keeping one eye on La Floquet. The small man smiled. "Honor must be defended, Thornhill, Vellers was spreading lies about me."

"A coward and a liar, too," Vellers said darkly.

"Quiet, both of you," Thornhill told them. "Look up there!"

He pointed.

A gathering cloud hung low over them. The Watcher was drawing near—had been, unnoticed, all during the raging quarrel. Thornhill looked up, waiting, trying to discern some living form within the amorphous blackness that descended on them. It was impossible. He saw only spreading clouds of night hiding the dim sunlight.

He felt the ground rocking gently, quivering in a barely perceptible manner. What now, he wondered, peering at the enfolding darkness. A sound like a faroff musical chord echoed in his ears—a subsonic vibration, perhaps, making him giddy, soothing him, calming him the way gentle stroking might soothe a cat.

Peace among you, my pets, the voiceless voice said softly, almost crooningly. *You quarrel too much. Let there be peace....*

The subsonic note washed up over him, bathed him, cleansed him of hatred and anger. He stood there smiling, not knowing why he smiled, feeling only peace and calmness.

The cloud began to lift; the Watcher was departing. The unheard note diminished in intensity, and the motion of the ground subsided. The Valley was at rest, in perfect harmony. The last faint murmur of the note died away.

For a long while no one spoke. Thornhill looked around, seeing an uncharacteristic blandness loosen the tight set of La Floquet's jaws, seeing Vellers' heavy-featured, angry face begin to smile. He himself felt no desire to quarrel with anyone.

But deep in his mind the words of the Watcher echoed and thrust at him: *Peace among you, my pets.*

Pets.

Not even specimens in a zoo, Thornhill thought with increasing bitterness as the tranquility induced by the subsonic began to leave him. Pets. Pampered pets.

He realized he was trembling. It had seemed so attractive, this life in the Valley. He tried to cry out, to shout his rage at the bare purple mountains that hemmed them in, but the subsonic had done its work well. He could not even vocalize his anger.

Thornhill looked away, trying to drive the Watcher's soothing words from his mind.

In the days that followed they began to grow younger. McKay, the oldest, was the first to show any effects of the rejuvenation. It was on the fourth day in the Valley—days being measured, for lack of other means, by the risings of the red sun. The nine of them had settled into a semblance of a normal way of life by that time. Since the time when the Watcher had found it necessary to calm them, there had been no outbreaks of bitterness among them; instead, each went about his daily life quietly, almost sullenly, under the numbing burden of the knowledge of their status as *pets*.

They found they had little need for sleep or food; the manna sufficed to nourish them, and as for sleep, that could be had in brief cat naps when the occasion demanded. They spent much of their time telling each other of their past lives, hiking through the Valley, swimming in the river. Thornhill was beginning to get terribly bored with this kind of existence.

McKay had been staring into the swiftly running current when he first noticed it. He emitted a short, sharp cry; Thornhill, thinking something was wrong, ran hurriedly toward him.

"What happened?"

McKay hardly seemed in difficulties. He was staring intently at his reflection in the water. "What color is my hair, Sam?"

"Why, gray—and—and a little touch of brown!" McKay nodded. "Exactly. I haven't had brown in my hair in twenty years!"

By this time most of the others had gathered. McKay indicated his hair and said, "I'm growing younger. I feel it all over. And look—look at La Floquet's scalp!"

In surprise the little man clapped one hand to the top of his skull—and drew the hand away again, thunderstruck. "I'm growing hair again," he said softly, fingering the gentle fuzz that had appeared on his tanned, sun-freckled scalp. There was a curious look of incredulity on his wrinkled brown face. "That's impossible!"

"It's also impossible for a man to rise from the dead," Thornhill pointed out. "The Watcher is taking very good care of us."

He looked at all of them—at McKay and La Floquet, at Vellers, at Marga, at Lona Hardin, at the aliens. Yes, they had all changed. They looked healthier, younger, more vigorous.

He had felt the change in himself from the start. The Valley, he thought. Was this the Watcher's doing or simply some marvelous property of the area?

Suppose the latter, he thought. Suppose through some charm of the Valley they were growing ever younger.

Would it stop? Would the process level off?

Or, he wondered, had the Watcher brought them all here solely for the interesting spectacle of observing nine adult beings retrogressing rapidly into childhood?

That "night"—they called the time when the red sun left the sky "night" even though there was no darkness—Thornhill learned three significant things.

He learned he loved Marga Fallis, and she him.

He learned that their love could have no possible consummation within the Valley.

And he learned that La Floquet, whatever had happened to him on the mountain peak, had not yet forgotten how to fight.

Thornhill had asked Marga to walk with him into the secluded wooded area high on the mountain path where they could have some privacy. She seemed oddly reluctant to accept, which surprised and dismayed him, for at all other times since the beginning she had gladly accepted any offers of his company. He urged her again, and finally she agreed.

They walked silently for a while. Gentle-eyed cat creatures peered at them from behind shrubs, and the air was moist and warm. Peaceful white clouds drifted high above them.

Thornhill said, "Why didn't you want to come with me, Marga?"

"I'd rather not talk about it," she said.

He shied a stone into the underbrush. "Four days, and you're keeping secrets from me already?" He started to chuckle; then, seeing her expression, he cut short his laughter. "What's wrong?"

"Is there any reason why I *shouldn't* keep secrets from you?" she asked. "I mean, is there some sort of agreement between us?"

He hesitated. "Of course not. But I thought—"

She smiled, reassuring him. "I thought, too. But I might as well be frank. This afternoon La Floquet asked me to be his woman."

Stunned, Thornhill stammered, "He—why—"

"He figures he's penned in here for life," Marga said. "And he's not interested in Lona. That leaves me, it seems. La Floquet doesn't like to go without women for long."

Thornhill moistened his lips but said nothing.

Marga went on. "He told me point-blank I wasn't to go into the hills with you anymore. That if I did, he'd make trouble. He wasn't going to take no for an answer, he told me."

"And what answer did you give—if I can ask?"

She smiled warmly; blue highlights danced in her dark eyes as she said, "Well—I'm here, aren't I? Isn't that a good enough answer to him?"

Relief swept over Thornhill like an unchecked tide. He had known of La Floquet's rivalry from the start, but this was the first time the little man had ever made any open overtures toward Marga. And if those overtures had been refused—

"La Floquet's interesting," she said as they stopped to enter a sheltered, sweet-smelling bower of thickly entwined shrubs. They had discovered it the night before. "But I wouldn't want to be number four hundred eighty-six on his string. He's a galaxy roamer; I've never fallen for that type. And I feel certain he'd never have been interested in me except as something to amuse him while he was penned up in this Valley."

She was very close to him, and in the bower not even the light of the blue star shone very brightly. *I love her*, he thought suddenly to himself, and an instant later he found his voice saying out loud, "I love you, Marga. Maybe it took a miracle to put us both in this Valley, but ..."

"I know what you mean. And I love you, too. I told La Floquet that."

He felt an irrational surge of triumph. "What did he say?"

"Not much. He said he'd kill you if he could find some way to do it in the Valley. But I think that'll wear off soon."

His arm slipped around hers. They spoke wordlessly with one another for several moments.

It was then that Thornhill discovered that sex was impossible in the Valley. He felt no desire, no tingling of need, *nothing*.

Absolutely nothing. He enjoyed her nearness, but neither needed nor could take anything more.

"It's part of the Valley," he whispered. "Our entire metabolic systems have been changed. We don't sleep more than an hour a day, we hardly eat (unless you call that fluff food), our wounds heal, the dead rise—and now this. It's as if the Valley casts a spell that short-circuits all biological processes."

"And there's nothing we can do?"

"Nothing," he said tightly. "We're pets. Growing ever younger and helpless against the Watcher's whims."

He stared silently into the darkness, listening to her quiet sobbing. How long can we go on living this way, he wondered. How long?

We have to get out of this Valley, he thought. *Somehow*.

But will we remember one another once we do? Or will it all fade away like a child's dream of fairyland?

He clung tightly to her, cursing his own weakness even though he knew it was hardly his fault. There was nothing they could say to one another.

But the silence was abruptly broken.

A deep, dry voice said, "I know you're in there. Come on out, Thornhill. And bring the girl with you."

Thornhill quickly rose to a sitting position. "It's La Floquet!" he whispered.

"What are you going to do? Can he find us in here?"

"I'm sure of it. I'm going to have to go out there and see what he wants."

"Be careful, Sam!"

"He can't hurt me. This is the Valley, remember?" He grinned at her and clambered to his feet, stooping as he passed through the clustered underbrush. He blinked as he made the transition from darkness to pale light.

"Come on out of there, Thornhill!" La Floquet repeated. "I'll give you another minute, and then I'm coming in!"

"Don't fret," Thornhill called. "I'm on my way out."

He battled past two clinging, enwrapped vines and stepped into the open. "Well, what do you want?" he demanded impatiently.

La Floquet smiled coldly. There was little doubt of what he wanted. His small eyes were bright with anger, and there was murder in his grin. Held tight in one lean, corded hand was a long, triangular sliver of rock whose jagged edge had been painstakingly abraded until it was knife-sharp. The little man waited in a half-crouch, like a tiger or a panther impatient to spring on its prey.

Chapter Five

They circled tentatively around each other, the big man and the small one. La Floquet seemed to have reached a murderous pitch of intensity; muscles quivered in his jaws as he glared at Thornhill.

"Put that knife down," Thornhill said. "Have you blown your stack, La Floquet? You can't kill a man in the Valley. It won't work."

"Perhaps I can't kill a man. Still, I can wound him."

"What have I ever done to you?"

"You came to the Valley. I could have handled the others, but you—! You were the one who taunted me into climbing the mountain. You were the one who took Marga."

"I didn't take anyone. You didn't see me twisting her arm. She picked me over you, and for that I'm genuinely sorry."

"You'll be more than sorry, Thornhill!"

Thornhill forced a grin. This little kill dance had gone on too long as it was. He sensed Marga not far behind him watching in horror.

"Why you murderous little paranoid, give me that piece of stone before you slash yourself up!" He took a quick step forward, reaching for La Floquet's wrist. The little man's eyes blazed dangerously. He pirouetted backward, snapping a curse at Thornhill in some alien language, and drove the knife downward with a low, cry of triumph.

Thornhill swerved, but the jagged blade ripped into his arm three inches above the elbow, biting into the soft flesh on the inside of his biceps, and La Floquet sliced quickly downward, cutting a bloody trail for nearly eight inches. Thornhill felt a sudden sharp burst of pain down to the middle of his forearm, and a warm flow of blood gushed past his wrist into the palm of his hand. He heard Marga's sharp gasp.

Then he moved forward, ignoring the pain, and caught La Floquet's arm just as the smaller man was lifting it for a second slash. Thornhill twisted; something snapped in La Floquet's arm, and the little man gave forth a brief moan of pain. The knife dropped from suddenly uncontrollable fingers and landed slightly on an angle, its tip resting on a pebble. Thornhill planted his foot on the dagger and leaned down heavily, shattering it.

Each of them now had only limited use of his right hand. La Floquet charged back toward Thornhill like someone possessed, head down as if to butt, but at the last moment swerved upward, driving his good hand into Thornhill's jaw. Thornhill rocked backward, pivoted around, smashed down at La Floquet, and heard teeth splinter. He wondered when the Watcher would show up to end the fight—and whether these wounds would heal.

La Floquet's harsh breathing was the only sound audible. He was shaking his head, clearing it, readying himself for a new assault. Thornhill tried to blank out the searing pain of the gash in his arm.

He stepped forward and hit La Floquet quickly, spinning him half around; bringing his slashed right hand up, Thornhill drove it into La Floquet's middle. A wall of rocklike muscle stunned his fist. But the breath had been knocked from La Floquet; he weaved uncertainly, gray-faced, wobbly-legged. Thornhill hit him again, and he toppled.

La Floquet crumpled into an awkward heap on the ground and stayed there. Thornhill glanced at his own arm. The cut was deep and wide, though it seemed to have missed any major veins and arteries; blood welled brightly from it, but without the familiar arterial spurt.

There was a curious fascination in watching his own blood flow. He saw Marga's pale, frightened face beyond the dim haze that surrounded him; he realized he had lost more blood than he thought, perhaps was about to lose consciousness as well. La Floquet still slumbered. There was no sign of the Watcher.

"Sam—"

"Pretty little nick, isn't it?" He laughed. His face felt warm.

"We ought to bind that some way. Infection—"

"No. There's no need of that. I'll be all right. This is the Valley."

He felt an intense itching in the wounded arm; barely did he fight back the desire to claw at the gash with his fingernails.

"It's—it's healing!" Marga said.

Thornhill nodded. The wound was beginning to close.

First the blood ceased flowing as ruptured veins closed their gaping sides and once again began to circulate the blood. The raw edges of the wound strained toward each other, puckering, reaching for one another, finally clasping. A bridge of flesh formed over the gaping slit in his arm. The itching was impossibly intense.

But in a few moments more it was over; a long livid scar remained, nothing more. Experimentally he touched the new flesh; it was warm, yielding, real.

La Floquet was stirring. His right forearm had been bent at an awkward angle; now it straightened out. The little man sat up groggily. Thornhill tensed in case further attack was coming, but there was very little fight left in La Floquet.

"The Watcher has made the necessary repairs," Thornhill said. "We're whole again except for a scar here and there. Get up, you idiot."

He hoisted La Floquet to his feet.

"This is the first time anyone has bested me in a fight," La Floquet said bitterly. His eyes had lost much of their eager brightness; he seemed demolished by his defeat. "And you were unarmed, and I had a knife."

"Forget that," Thornhill said.

"How can I? This filthy Valley—from which there is no escape, not even suicide—and I am not to have a woman. Thornhill, you're just a businessman. You don't know what it's like to set codes of behavior for yourself and then not be able to live by them." La Floquet shook his head sadly. "There are many in the galaxy who would rejoice to see the way this Valley has humiliated me. And there is not even suicide here! But I'll leave you with your woman."

He turned and began to walk away, a small, almost pathetic figure now, the fighting cock with his comb shorn and his tail feathers plucked. Thornhill contrasted him with the ebullient little figure he had first seen coming toward him up the mountain path, and it was a sad contrast indeed. He slouched now, shoulders sloping in defeat.

"Hold it, La Floquet!"

"You have beaten me—and before a woman. What more do you want with me, Thornhill?"

"How badly do you want to get out of this Valley?" Thornhill asked bluntly.

"What—"

"Badly enough to climb that mountain again?"

La Floquet's face, pale already, turned almost ghostly beneath his tan. In an unsteady voice he said, "I ask you not to taunt me, Thornhill."

"I'm not. I don't give a damn what phobia it is that drove you back from the mountain that night. I think that mountains can be climbed. But not by one or two men. If we *all* went up there—or most of us—"

La Floquet smiled wanly. "You would go, too? And Marga?"

VALLEY BEYOND TIME | 335

"If it means out, yes. We might have to leave McKay and Lona Hardin behind, but there'd still he seven of us. Possibly there's a city outside the Valley; we might be able to send word and be rescued."

Frowning, La Floquet said, "Why the sudden change of heart, Thornhill? I thought you liked it here ... you and Miss Fallis both, that is. I thought *I* was the only one willing to climb that peak."

Thornhill glanced at Marga and traded secret smiles with her. "I'll decline to answer that, La Floquet. But I'll tell you this: The quicker I'm outside the influence of the Valley, the happier I'll be!"

When they had reached the foot of the hill and called everyone together, Thornhill stepped forward. Sixteen eyes were on him—counting the two stalked objects of the Spican as eyes.

He said, "La Floquet and I have just had a little discussion up in the hill. We've reached a few conclusions I want to put forth to the group at large.

"I submit that it's necessary for the well-being of all of us to make an immediate attempt at getting out of the Valley. Otherwise, we're condemned to a slow death of the most horrible kind—gradual loss of our faculties."

McKay broke in, saying, "Now you've shifted sides again, Thornhill! I thought maybe—"

"I haven't been on any side," he responded quickly. "It's simply that I've begun thinking. Look: We were all brought here within a two-day span, snatched out of our lives no matter where we were, dumped down in a seemingly impassable Valley by some unimaginably alien creature. Item: We're watched constantly, tended and fed. Item: Our wounds heal almost instantly. Item: We're growing younger. McKay, you yourself were the first to notice that.

"Okay, now. There's a mountain up there, and quite probably there's a way out of the Valley. La Floquet tried to get there, but he and Vellers couldn't make it; two men can't climb a twenty-thousand-foot peak alone without provisions, without help. But if we all go—"

McKay shook his head. "I'm happy here, Thornhill. You and La Floquet are jeopardizing that happiness."

"No," La Floquet interjected. "Can't you see that we're just house pets here? That we're the subjects of a rather interesting experiment, nothing more? And that if this rejuvenation keeps up, we may all be babies in a matter of weeks or months?"

"I don't care," McKay said stubbornly. "I'll die if I leave the Valley—my heart can't take much more. Now you tell me I'll die if I stay. But at least I'll pass backward through manhood before I go—and I can't have those years again outside."

"All right," Thornhill said. "Ultimately it's a matter of whether we all stay here so McKay can enjoy his youth again, or whether we try to leave. La Floquet, Marga, and I are going to make an attempt to cross the mountain. Those of you who want to join us can. Those of you who'd rather spend the rest of their days in the Valley can stay behind and wish us bad luck. Is that clear?"

Seven of them left the following "morning," right after the breakfast-time manna fall. McKay stayed behind with little Lona Hardin. There was a brief, awkward moment of farewell-saying. Thornhill noticed how the lines were leaving McKay's face, how the old scholar's hair had darkened, his body broadened. In a way he could see McKay's point of view, but there was no way he could accept it.

Lona Hardin, too, was younger looking, and perhaps for the first time in her life she was making an attempt to disguise her plainness. Well, Thornhill thought, these two might find happiness of a sort in the Valley, but it was the mindless happiness of a puppet, and he wanted none of it for himself.

"I don't know what to say," McKay declared as the party set out. "I'd wish you good luck—if I could."

Thornhill grinned. "Maybe we'll be seeing you two again. I hope not, though."

Thornhill led the way up the mountain's side; Marga walked with him, La Floquet and Vellers a few paces behind, the three aliens trailing behind them. The Spican, Thornhill was sure, had only the barest notion of what was taking place; the Aldebaranian had explained things fairly thoroughly to the grave Regulan. One factor seemed common: All of them were determined to leave the Valley.

The morning was warm and pleasant; clouds hid the peak of the mountain. The ascent, Thornhill thought, would be strenuous but not impossible—provided the miraculous field of the Valley continued to protect them when they passed the timberline and provided the Watcher did not interfere with the exodus.

There was no interference. Thornhill felt almost a sensation of regret at leaving the Valley and in the same moment realized this might be some deceptive trick of the Watcher's, and he cast all sentiment from his heart.

By midmorning they had reached a considerable height, a thousand feet or more above the Valley. Looking down, Thornhill could barely see the brightness of the river winding through the flat basin that was the Valley, and there was no sign of McKay far below.

The mountain sloped gently upward toward the timberline. The real struggle would begin later, perhaps, on the bare rock face, where the air might not be so balmy as it was here, the wind not quite as gentle.

When Thornhill's watch said noon, he called a halt and they unpacked the manna—wrapped in broad, coarse, velvet-textured leaves of the thick-trunked trees of the Valley—they had saved from the morning fall. The manna tasted dry and stale, almost like straw, with just the merest vestige of its former attractive flavor. But as Thornhill had guessed, there was no noontime manna fall here on the mountain slope, and so the party forced the dry stuff down their throats, not knowing when they would have fresh food again.

After a short rest Thornhill ordered them up. They had gone no more than a thousand feet when an echoing cry drifted up from below:

"Wait! Wait, Thornhill!"

He turned. "You hear something?" he asked Marga.

"That was McKay's voice," La Floquet said.

"Let's wait for him," Thornhill ordered.

Ten minutes passed, and then McKay came into view, running upward in a springy long-legged stride, Lona Hardin a few paces behind him. He caught up with the party and paused a moment, catching his breath.

"I decided to come along," he said finally. "You're right, Thornhill! We have to leave the Valley."

"And he figures his heart's better already," Lona Hardin said. "So if he leaves the Valley now, maybe he'll be a healthier man again."

Thornhill smiled. "It took a long time to convince you, didn't it?" He shaded his eyes and stared upward. "We have a long way to go. We'd better not waste any more time."

Chapter Six

Twenty thousand feet is less than four miles. A man should be able to walk four miles in an hour or two. But not four miles *up*.

They rested frequently, though there was no night and they had no need to sleep. They moved on inch by inch, advancing perhaps five hundred feet over the steadily more treacherous slope, then crawling along the mountain face a hundred feet to find the next point of ascent. It was slow, difficult work, and the mountain spired yet higher above them until it seemed they would never attain the summit.

The air, surprisingly, remained warm, though not oppressively so; the wind picked up as they climbed. The mountain was utterly bare of life; the gentle animals of the Valley ventured no higher than the timberline, and that was far below. The party of nine scrambled up over rock falls and past sheets of stone.

Thornhill felt himself tiring, but he knew the Valley's strange regenerative force was at work, carrying off the fatigue poisons as soon as they built up in his muscles, easing him, giving him the strength to go on. Hour after hour they forced their way up the mountainside.

Occasionally he would glance back to see La Floquet's pale, fear-tautened face. The little man was terrified of the height, but he was driving gamely on. The aliens straggled behind; Vellers marched mechanically, saying little, obviously tolerant of the weaker mortals to whose pace he was compelled to adjust his own.

As for Marga, she uttered no complaint. That pleased Thornhill more than anything.

They were a good thousand feet from the summit when Thornhill called a halt.

He glanced back at them—at the oddly unweary, unlined faces. *How we've grown young!* he thought suddenly. *McKay looks like a man in his late forties; I must seem like a boy. And we're all fresh as daisies, as if this were just a jolly hike.*

"We're near the top," he said. "Let's finish off whatever of the manna we've got. The downhill part of this won't be so bad."

He looked up. The mountain tapered to a fine crest, and through there a pass leading down to the other side was visible. "La Floquet, you've got the best eyes of any of us. You see any sign of a barrier up ahead?"

The little man squinted and shook his head. "All's clear so far as I can see. We go up, then down, and we're home free."

Thornhill nodded. "The last thousand feet, then. Let's go!"

The wind was whipping hard against them as they pushed on through the dense snow that cloaked the mountain's highest point. Up here some of the charm of the Valley seemed to be gone, as if the cold winds barreling in from the outlands beyond the crest could in some way negate the gentle warmth they experienced in the Valley. Both suns were high in the sky, the red and the blue, the blue visible as a hard blotch of radiance penetrating the soft, diffuse rays of the red.

Thornhill was tiring rapidly, but the crest was in sight. Just a few more feet and they'd stand on it—

Just up over this overhang—

The summit itself was a small plateau, perhaps a hundred feet long. Thornhill was the first to pull himself up over the rock projection and stand on the peak; he reached back, helped Marga up, and within minutes the other seven had joined them.

The Valley was a distant spot of green far below; the air was clear and clean, and from here they could plainly see the winding river heading down valley to the yellow-green radiance of the barrier.

Thornhill turned. "Look down there," he said in a quiet voice.

"It's a world of deserts!" La Floquet exclaimed.

The view from the summit revealed much of the land beyond the Valley, and it seemed the Valley was but an oasis in the midst of utter desertion. For mile after gray mile, barren land stretched before them, an endless plain of rock and sand rolling on drearily to the farthest horizon.

Beyond, this. Behind, the Valley.

Thornhill looked around. "We've reached the top. You see what's ahead. Do we go on?"

"Do we have any choice?" McKay asked. "We're practically out of the Watcher's hands now. Down there perhaps we have freedom. Behind us—"

"We go on," La Floquet said firmly.

"Down the back slope, then," said Thornhill. "It won't be easy. There's the path over there. Suppose we—"

The sudden chill he felt was not altogether due to the whistling wind. The sky suddenly darkened; a cloak of night settled around them.

Of course, Thornhill thought dully. *I should have foreseen this.*

"The Watcher's coming!" Lona Hardin screamed as the darkness, obscuring both the bleakness ahead and the Valley behind, closed around them.

Thornhill thought, *It was part of the game. To let us climb the mountain, to watch us squirm and struggle, and then to hurl us back into the Valley at the last moment as we stand on the border.*

Wings of night nestled around them. He felt the coldness that signified the alien presence, and the soft voice said, *Would you leave, my pets? Don't I give you the best of care? Why this ingratitude?*

"Let's keep going," Thornhill muttered. "Maybe it can't stop us. Maybe we can escape it yet."

"Which way do we go?" Marga asked. "I can't see anything. Suppose we go over the edge?"

Come, crooned the Watcher, *come back to the Valley. You have played your little game. I have enjoyed your struggles, and I'm proud of the battle you fought. But the time has come to return to the warmth and the love you may find in the Valley below—*

"Thornhill!" cried La Floquet suddenly, hoarsely. "I have it! Come help me!"

The Watcher's voice died away abruptly; the black cloud swirled wildly. Thornhill whirled, peering through the darkness for some sign of La Floquet—

And found the little man on the ground, wrestling with—something. In the darkness, it was hard to tell—

"It's the Watcher!" La Floquet grunted. He rolled over, and Thornhill saw a small snakelike being writhing under La Floquet's grip, a bright-scaled serpent the size of a monkey.

"Here in the middle of the cloud—*here's* the creature that held us here!" La Floquet cried. Suddenly, before Thornhill could move, the Aldebaranian came bounding forward, thrusting beyond Thornhill and Marga, and flung himself down on the strugglers. Thornhill heard a guttural bellow; the darkness closed in on the trio, and it was impossible to see what was happening.

He heard La Floquet's cry: "Get ... this devil ... off me! He's helping the Watcher!"

Thornhill moved forward. He reached into the struggling mass, felt the blubbery flesh of the Aldebaranian, and dug his fingers in hard. He wrenched; the Aldebaranian came away. Hooked claws raked Thornhill's face. He cursed; you could never tell what an Aldebaranian was likely to do at any time. Perhaps the creature had been in league with the Watcher all along.

He dodged a blow, landed a solid one in the alien's plump belly, and crashed his other fist upward into the creature's jaw. The Aldebaranian rocked backward. Vellers appeared abruptly from nowhere and seized the being.

"No!" Thornhill yelled, seeing what Vellers intended. But it was too late. The giant held the Aldebaranian contemptuously dangling in the air, then swung him upward and outward. A high ear-piercing shriek resounded. Thornhill shuddered. It takes a long time to fall twenty thousand feet.

He glanced back now at La Floquet and saw the small man struggling to stand up, arms still entwined about the serpentlike being. Thornhill saw a metalmesh helmet on the alien's head. The means by which they'd been controlled, perhaps.

La Floquet took three staggering steps. "Get the helmet off him!" he cried thickly. "I've seen these before. They are out of the Andromeda sector ... telepaths, teleports ... deadly creatures. The helmet's his focus point."

Thornhill grasped for it as the pair careened by; he missed, catching instead a glimpse of the Watcher's devilish, hate-filled eyes. The Watcher had fallen into the hands of his own pets—and was not enjoying it.

"I can't see you!" Thornhill shouted. "I can't get the helmet!"

"If he gets free, we're finished," came La Floquet's voice. "He's using all his energy to fight me off ... but all he needs to do is turn on the subsonics—"

The darkness cleared again. Thornhill gasped. La Floquet, still clutching the alien, was tottering on the edge of the mountain peak, groping for the helmet in vain. One of the little man's feet was virtually standing on air. He staggered wildly. Thornhill rushed toward them, grasped the icy metal of the helmet, and ripped it away.

In that moment both La Floquet and the Watcher vanished from sight. Thornhill brought himself up short and peered downward, hearing nothing, seeing nothing—

There was just one scream ... not from La Floquet's throat but from the alien's. Then all was silent. Thornhill glanced at the helmet in his hands, thinking of La Floquet, and in a sudden impulsive gesture hurled the little metal headpiece into the abyss after them.

He turned, catching one last glimpse of Marga, Vellers, McKay, Lona Hardin, the Regulan, and the Spican. Then, before he could speak, mountain peak and darkness and indeed the entire world shimmered and heaved dizzyingly about them, and he could see nothing and no one.

He was in the main passenger cabin of the Federation Spaceliner *Royal Mother Helene* bound for Vengamon out of Jurinalle. He was lying back in the comfortable pressurized cabin, the gray nothingness of hyperspace outside forming a sharp contrast to the radiant walls of the cabin, which glowed in soft yellow luminescence.

Thornhill opened his eyes slowly. He glanced at his watch: *12:13, 7 July 2671*. He had dozed off about 11:40 after a good lunch. They were due in at Port Vengamon later that day, and he would have to tend to mine business immediately. There was no telling how badly they had fouled things up in the time he had been vacationing on Jurinalle.

He blinked. Of a sudden, strange images flashed into his eyes—a valley somewhere on a barren, desolate planet beyond the edge of the galaxy. A mountain peak, and a strange alien being, and a brave little man falling to the death he dreaded, and a girl—

It couldn't have been a dream, he told himself. *No.*

Not a dream. It was just that the Watcher yanked us out of space-time for his little experiment, and when I destroyed the helmet, we re-entered the continuum at the instant we had left it.

A cold sweat burst out suddenly all over his body. *That means*, he thought, *that La Floquet's not dead. And Marga—Marga—*

Thornhill sprang from his gravity couch, ignoring the sign that urged him to PLEASE REMAIN IN YOUR COUCH WHILE SHIP IS UNDERGOING SPIN, and rushed down the aisle toward the steward. He gripped the man by the shoulder, spun him around.

"Yes, Mr. Thornhill? Is anything wrong? You could have signaled me, and—"

"Never mind that. I want to make a subradio call to Bellatrix VII."

"We'll be landing on Vengamon in a couple of hours, sir. Is it so urgent?"

"Yes."

The steward shrugged. "You know, of course, that shipboard subradio calls may take some time to put through, and that they're terribly expensive—"

"Damn the expense, man! Will you put through my call or won't you?"

"Of course, Mr. Thornhill. To whom?"

He paused and said carefully, "To Miss Marga Fallis, in some observatory on Bellatrix VII." He peeled a bill from his wallet and added, "Here. There'll be another one for you if the call's put through in the next half an hour. I'll wait."

The summons finally came. "Mr. Thornhill, your call's ready. Would you come to Communications Deck, please?"

They showed him to a small, dimly lit cubicle. There could be no vision on an interstellar subradio call, of course, just voice transmission. But that would be enough. "Go ahead, Bellatrix-*Helene*. The call is ready," an operator said.

Thornhill wet his lips. "Marga? This is Sam—Sam Thornhill!"

"Oh!" He could picture her face now. "It—it wasn't a dream, then. I was so afraid it was!"

"When I threw the helmet off the mountain, the Watcher's hold was broken. Did you return to the exact moment you had left?"

"Yes," she said. "Back in the observatory, with my camera plates and everything. And there was a call for me, and at first I was angry and wouldn't answer it the way I always won't answer, and then I thought a minute and had a wild idea and changed my mind—and I'm glad I did, darling!"

"It seems almost like a dream, doesn't it? The Valley, I mean. And La Floquet, and all the others. But it wasn't any dream," Thornhill said. "We were really there. And I meant the things I said to you."

The operator's voice cut in sharply: *"Standard call time has elapsed, sir. There will be an additional charge of ten credits for each further fifteen-second period of your conversation."*

"That's quite all right, Operator," Thornhill said. "Just give me the bill at the end. Marga, are you still there?"

"Of course, darling."

"When can I see you?"

"I'll come to Vengamon tomorrow. It'll take a day or so to wind things up here at the observatory. Is there an observatory on Vengamon?"

"I'll build you one," Thornhill promised. "And perhaps for our honeymoon we can go looking for the Valley."

"I don't think we'll ever find it," she said. "But we'd better hang up now. Otherwise you'll become a pauper talking to me."

He stared at the dead phone a long moment after they broke contact, thinking of what Marga looked like, and La Floquet, and all the others. Above all, Marga.

It wasn't a dream, he told himself. He thought of the shadow-haunted Valley where night never fell and men grew younger, and of a tall girl with dark flashing eyes who waited for him now half a galaxy away.

With quivering fingers he undid the sleeve of his tunic and looked down at the long, livid scar that ran almost the length of his right arm, almost to the wrist. Somewhere in the universe now was a little man named La Floquet who had inflicted that wound and died and returned to his point of departure, who now was probably wondering if it had all ever happened. Thornhill smiled, forgiving La Floquet for the ragged scar inscribed on his arm, and headed up the companionway to the passenger cabin, impatient now to see Vengamon once more.

WE KNOW WHO WE ARE

Originally published in *Amazing Stories*, July 1970.

"We know who we are and what we want to be," say the people of Shining City whenever they feel particularly uncertain about things. Shining City is at least a thousand years old. It may be even older, but who can be sure? It stands in the middle of a plain of purple sand that stretches from the Lake of No Return to the River Without Fish. It has room for perhaps six hundred thousand people. The recent population of Shining City has been perhaps six hundred people. They know who they are. They know what they want to be.

Things got trickier for them after the girl who was wearing clothes came walking in out of the desert.

Skagg was the first one to see her. He knew immediately that there was something unusual about her, and not just that she was wearing clothes. Anybody who ever goes out walking in the desert puts clothes on, because the heat is fierce—there being no Cool Machine out there—and the sun would roast you fast if you didn't have some kind of covering, and the sand would blow against you and pick the meat from your bones. But the unusual thing about the girl was her face. It wasn't a familiar one. Everybody in Shining City knew everybody else, and Skagg didn't know this girl at all, so she had to be a stranger, and strangers just didn't exist.

She was more than a child but less than a woman, and her body was slender and her hair was dark, and she walked the way a man would walk, with her arms swinging and her knees coming high and her legs kicking outward. When Skagg saw her he felt afraid, and he had never been afraid of a woman before.

"Hello," she said. "I speak Language. Do you?"

Her voice was deep and husky, like the wind on a winter day pushing itself between two of the city's towers. Her accent was odd, and the words came out as if she were holding her tongue in the wrong part of her mouth. But he understood her.

He said, "I speak Language, and I understand what you say. But who are you?"

"Fa Sol La," she sang.

"Is that your name?"

"That is my name. And yours?"

"Skagg."

"Do all the people in this city have names like Skagg?"

"I am the only Skagg," said Skagg. "Where do you come from?"

She pointed eastward. "From a place beside the River Without Fish. Is this Shining City?"

"Yes," Skagg said.

"Then I am where I want to be." She unslung the pack that she was carrying over one shoulder and set it down, and then she removed her robe, so that she was as naked as he was. Her skin was very pale, and there was practically no flesh on her. Her breasts were tiny and her buttocks were flat. From where he stood, Skagg could easily have mistaken her for a boy. She picked up the pack again. "Will you take me into your city?" she asked.

They were on the outskirts, in the region of the Empty Buildings. Skagg sometimes went there when he felt that his mind was too full. Tall tapering towers sprouted here. Some were sagging and others had lost their outer trim. Repair Machines no longer functioned in this part of the city.

"Where do you want to go?" he asked.

"To the place where the Knowing Machine is," said Fa Sol La.

Frowning, he said, "How do you know about the Machine?"

"Everyone in the world knows about the Knowing Machine. I want to see it. I walked all the way from the River Without Fish to see the Knowing Machine. You'll take me there, won't you, Skagg?"

He shrugged. "If you want. But you won't be able to get close to it. You'll see. You've wasted your time."

They began to walk toward the center of the city.

She moved with such a swinging stride that he had to work hard to keep up with her. Several times she came close to him, so that her hip or thigh brushed his skin, and Skagg felt himself trembling at the strangeness of her. They were silent a long while. The morning sun began to go down and the afternoon sun started to rise, and the double light, blending, cast deceptive shadows and made her body look fuller than it was. Near the Mirror Walls a Drink Machine came up to them and refreshed them. She put her head inside it and gulped as if she had been dry for months, and then she let the fluid run out over her slim body. Not far on a Riding Machine found them and offered to transport them to the center. Skagg gestured to her to get in, but she waved a no at him.

"It's still a great distance," he said.

"I'd rather walk. I've walked this far, and I'll walk to the end. I can see things better."

Skagg sent the machine away. They went on walking. The morning sun disappeared and now only the green light of afternoon illuminated Shining City.

She said, "Do you have a woman, Skagg?"

"I don't understand."

"Do you have a woman, I said."

"I heard the words. But how does one *have* a woman? What does it mean?"

"To live with. To sleep with. To share pleasure with. To have children with."

"We live by ourselves," he said. "There's so much room here, why crowd together? We sleep sometimes with others, yes. We share pleasure with everyone. Children rarely come."

"You have no regular mates here, then?"

"I have trouble understanding. Tell me how it is in your city."

"In my city," she said, "a man and a woman live together and do all things together. They need no one else. Sometimes, they realize they do not belong together and then they split up and seek others, but often they have each other for a lifetime."

"This sounds quite strange," said Skagg.

"We call it love," said Fa Sol La.

"We have love here. All of us love all of us. We do things differently, I suppose. Does any man in your city have you, then?"

"No. Not any more. I had a man, but he was too simple for me. And I left and walked to Shining City."

She frightened him even more, now.

They had started to enter the inhabited part of the city. Behind them were the long stately avenues and massive residential structures of the dead part; ahead lay the core, with its throbbing machines and eating centers and bright lights.

"Are you happy here?" Fa Sol La asked as they stepped between a Cleansing Machine's pillars and were bathed in blue mist.

"We know who we are," Skagg said, "and what we want to be. Yes, I think we're happy."

"I think you may be wrong," she said, and laughed, and pressed her body tight up against him a moment, and sprinted ahead of him like something wild.

A Police Machine rose from the pavement and blocked her way. It shot out silvery filaments that hovered around her, ready to clamp close if she made a hostile move. She stood still. Skagg ran up and said, "It's all right. She's new to the city. Scan her and accept her."

The machine bathed both of them in an amber glow and went away.

"What are you afraid of here?" Fa Sol La asked.

"Animals sometimes come in from the desert. We have to be careful. Did it scare you?"

"It puzzled me," she said.

Others were nearing them now. Skagg saw Glorr, Derk, Prewger, and Simit; and more were coming. They crowded around the girl, none daring to touch her but everyone staring hard.

"This is Fa Sol La," said Skagg. "I discovered her. She comes from a city at the River Without Fish and walked across the desert to visit us."

"What is your city called?" Derk demanded.

"River City," she said.

"How many people live there?" asked Prewger.

"I don't know. Many but not *very* many."

"How old are you?" Simit blurted.

"Five no-suns," she said.

"Did you come alone?" Glorr said.

"Alone."

"Why did you come here?" Prewger asked.

She said, "To see the Knowing Machine," and they moved as if she had proclaimed herself to be the goddess of death.

"The Knowing Machine is dangerous," said Prewger.

"No one may get close to it," said Simit.

"We fear it," said Glorr.

"It will kill you," said Derk.

Fa Sol La said, "Where is the Knowing Machine?"

They backed away from her. Derk summoned a Soothing Machine and had a drink from it. Prewger stepped into a Shelter Machine. Simit went among the others who had gathered, whispering her answers to them. Glorr turned his face away and bowed his head.

"Why are you so afraid?" she asked.

Skagg said, "When the city was built, the builders used the Knowing Machine to make themselves like gods. And the gods killed them. They came out of the machine full of hate, and took weapons against one another, until only a few were left. And those who remained said that no one ever again would enter the Machine."

"How long ago was that?"

"How should I know?" said Skagg.

"Show me the machine."

He hesitated. He spoke a few faltering syllables of refusal.

She pressed herself close against him and rubbed her body against his. She put her teeth lightly on the lobe of his ear. She ran her fingers along the strong muscles of his back.

"Show me the machine," she said. "I love you, Skagg. Can you refuse me the machine?"

He quivered. Her strangeness attracted him powerfully. He was eight no-suns old, and he knew every woman in Shining City all too well, and though he feared this girl he also was irresistibly drawn to her.

"Come," he whispered.

They walked down sleek boulevards and glowing skyways, crossed brooks and ponds and pools, passed spiky statues and dancing beacons. It was a handsome city, the finest in the world, and Fa Sol La trilled and sighed at every beautiful thing in it.

"They say that those who live here never go anywhere else," she said. "Now I begin to understand why. Have you ever been to another city, Skagg?"

"Never."

"But you go outside sometimes?"

"To walk in the desert, yes. Most of the others never even do that."

"But outside—there are so many cities, Skagg, so many different kinds of people! A dozen cities, a whole world! Don't you ever want to see them?"

"We like it here. We know what we want."

"It's lovely here. But it isn't right for you to stay in one place forever. It isn't *human*. How would people ever have come to this world in the first place, if our ancestors had done as you folk do?"

"I don't concern myself with that. Shining City cares for us, and we prefer not to go out. Obviously most others stay close to their cities too, since you are the first visitor I can remember."

"Shining City is too remote from other cities," Fa Sol La said. "Many dream of coming here, but few dare, and fewer succeed. But we travel everywhere else. I have been in seven cities besides my own, Skagg."

The idea of that disturbed him intensely.

She went on, "Traveling opens the mind. It teaches you things about yourself that you never realized."

"We know who we are," he said.

"You only think you do."

He glared at her, turned, pointed. "This is the Knowing Machine," he said, glad to shift subjects.

They stood in the center of the great cobbled plaza before the machine. Two hundred strides to the east rose the glossy black column, flanked by the protective columns of shimmering white metal. The door-opening was faintly visible. Around the brow of the column the colors

WE KNOW WHO WE ARE | 349

flickered and leaped, making the range of the spectrum as they had done for at least a thousand years.

"Where do I go in?" she asked.

"No one goes in."

"I'm going in. I want you to come in with me, Skagg."

He laughed. "Those who enter die."

"No. No. The machine teaches love. It opens you to the universe. It awakens your mind. We have books about it. We *know*."

"The machine kills."

"It's a lie, Skagg, made up by people whose souls were full of hate. They didn't want anyone to experience the goodness that the machine brings. It isn't the first time that men have prohibited goodness out of the fear of love."

Skagg smiled. "I have a fear of death, girl, not of love. Go into the machine, if you like. I'll wait here."

Fury and contempt sparkled in her eyes. Without another word she strode across the plaza. He watched, admiring the trimness of her body, the ripple of her muscles. He did not believe she would enter the machine. She passed the Zone of Respect and the Zone of Obeisance and the Zone of Contemplation, and went into the Zone of Approach, and did not halt there, but entered the Zone of Peril, and as she walked on into the Zone of Impiety he cursed and started to run after her, shouting for her to halt.

Now she was on the gleaming steps. Now she was ascending. Now she had her hand on the sliding door.

"Wait!" he screamed. "No! I love you!"

"Come in with me, then."

"It will kill us!"

"Then farewell," she said, and went into the Knowing Machine.

Skagg collapsed on the rough red cobblestones of the Zone of Approach and lay there sobbing, face down, clutching at the stones with his fingers, remembering how vulnerable and fragile she had looked, and yet how strong and sturdy she was, remembering her small breasts and lean thighs, and remembering too the strangeness about her that he loved. Why had she chosen to kill herself this way?

After a long while he stood up and started to leave. Night had come and the first moons were out. The taste of loss was bitter in mouth.

"Skagg?" she called.

She was on the steps of the Knowing Machine. She ran toward him, seemingly floating, and her face was flushed and her eyes were radiant.

"You lived?" he muttered. "You came out?"

"They've been lying, Skagg. The machine doesn't kill. It's there to help. It was marvelous, Skagg."

"What happened?"

"Voices speak to you, and tell you what to do. And you put a metal thing on your head, and fire shoots through your brain, and you *see*, Skagg, you see everything for the first time."

"Everything? What everything?"

"Life. Love. Stars. The connections that hold people together. It's all there. Ecstasy. It feels like having a whole planet making love to you. You see the patterns of life, and when you come out you want everybody else to see them too, so they don't have to walk around crippled and cut off all the time. I just tried a little bit. You can take it mild, strong, any level you like. And when you take it, you begin to understand. You're in tune at last. You receive signals from the universe. It opens you, Skagg. Oh, come inside with me, won't you? I want to go in and take it stronger. And I want you to share it with me."

He eluded her grasping hand. "I'm afraid."

'Don't be. I went in. I came out."

"It's forbidden."

"Because it's good, Skagg. People have always been forbidding other people to have anything this good. And once you've had it, you'll know why. You'll see the kind of power that hate and bitterness have— and you'll know how to soar to the sky and escape that power."

She tugged at him. He moved back.

"I can't go in," he said.

"Are you that afraid of dying?"

"They tell us that the machine makes people monstrous."

"Am I a monster?"

"They tell us that there are certain things we must never know."

"Anybody who says that is the true monster, Skagg."

"Perhaps. Perhaps. But I can't. Look—they're all watching us. You see them, here in the shadows? Everybody in Shining City is here! How could I go in? How could I do something so filthy when all of them—"

"I feel so sorry for you," she said softly. "To be afraid of love—to pull back from knowledge—"

"I can't help myself."

Gently she said, "Skagg, I'm going back in, and this time I'm going to ask for the most they can give. If there's any love in your soul, come in after me. I'll wait in there for you. And afterward we'll go off together— we'll visit every city in the world together—"

He shook his head.

She came close to him. He jumped away, as if afraid she would seize him and haul him into the machine, but she went to him and kissed him, a light brushing of lips on lips, and then she turned and went back into the machine.

He did not follow, but he did not leave.

The moons crossed in the sky, and the rain-sphere passed over the city, and the birds of night followed it, and a Riding Machine came to him and offered to take him to his home, and the red light of the morning sun began to streak the sky, and still the door of the Knowing Machine did not open, and still Fa Sol La stayed within. Skagg was alone in the plaza now.

"I'll wait in there for you," she had said.

The others, his friends, his neighbors, had gone home to sleep. He was alone. At sunrise he went forward into the Zone of Peril and stayed there awhile, and after an hour he entered the Zone of Impiety, and as the full morning heat descended he found himself going up the steps quite calmly and opening the door of the Knowing Machine.

"Welcome to Therapeutic Center Seven," a deep voice said from above, speaking in Language but using an accent even less familiar than the girl's. "Please move to your left for elementary sensory expansion treatment. You will find helmets on the wall. Place a helmet snugly on your head and—"

"Where's the girl?" he asked.

The voice continued to instruct him. Skagg ignored it, and went to his right, along a corridor that curved to circle the column. He found her just around the bend. She wore a helmet and her eyes were open, but she leaned frozen against the wall, strangely pale, strangely still. He put his ear between her breasts and heard nothing. He touched her skin and it seemed already to be growing cold. She did not close her eyes when his fingertip neared them.

There was on her face an expression of such joy that he could hardly bear to look at it.

The voice said, "In the early stages of therapy, a low level of stimulation is recommended. Therefore we request that you do not attempt to draw a greater degree of intensification than you are able at this stage to—"

Skagg took the helmet from her head. He lifted her in his arms and found that she weighed almost nothing. Carefully he set her down. Then, taking another helmet from the rack, he held it with both hands for a long time, listening to the instructions and hearing once more the girl's talk of ecstasy and soaring, and comparing all that he saw here to the things that everyone always had said about the Knowing Machine. After a while he put the helmet back in the rack without using it, and picked up the girl again, and carried her body out of the machine.

As he went down the steps, he saw that the others had gathered again and were gaping at him.

"You were in the machine?" Simit asked.

"I was in the machine," said Skagg.

"It killed her but not you?" Derk wanted to know.

"She used it. I didn't. First she used it a little, and then she used it too much, and the second time it killed her." Skagg kept walking as he spoke. They followed him.

"It is death simply to go inside the machine," Prewger said.

"This is wrong," said Skagg. "You can enter safely. Death comes only from using the machine. From using it wrongly."

"She was a fool," said Glorr. "She was punished."

"Maybe so," Skagg said. "But the machine gives us love. The machine gives us goodness."

He put the girl on the ground and summoned a Service Machine. Skagg gave it the girl's pack, asking that it be outfitted with a Water Machine and a Food Machine and a Shelter Machine. The Service Machine went away and came back a short while later. After inspecting the pack, Skagg strapped it over his shoulder. Then he picked up the girl again and began to walk.

"Where are you going with her?" Glorr asked.

"Out of the city. I will find a place for her body to rest in the desert."

"When you return, will you go into the Knowing Machine again?" Simit asked.

"I won't return for a long time," said Skagg. "I have some traveling to do. First to River City, and then to other places, maybe. And then, when I've found my courage, when I know who I really am and what I really want to be, I'll come back here and go into the machine and use it as it was meant to be used. And nothing will ever be the same in Shining City again."

He walked more quickly away from them, out toward the Empty Buildings, toward the plain of purple sand. He wondered how long it would take him to reach that other city beside the River Without Fish, and whether he would meet anyone like Fa Sol La when he got there.

His friends stood watching him until he was out of sight.

"He has become a madman," said Prewger.

"A dangerous madman," Glorr said.

"Would you do such a thing?" Simit asked.

"Do you mean, go into the machine, or go to another city?" said Derk.

"Either one."

"Of course not," said Derk.

"Of course not," said Glorr as well. "I know who I am. I know what I want to be."

"Yes," Simit said, shuddering. "Why should we do such things? We know who we are."

"We know what we want to be," said Prewger.

Made in the USA
San Bernardino, CA
09 August 2018